A Sentimental Traitor

A Sentimental Traitor

MICHAEL DOBBS

**SIMON &
SCHUSTER**

London · New York · Sydney · Toronto · New Delhi

A CBS COMPANY

First published in Great Britain by Simon & Schuster UK Ltd, 2012
A CBS COMPANY

1 3 5 7 9 10 8 6 4 2

Simon & Schuster UK Ltd
1st Floor
222 Gray's Inn Road
London
WC1X 8HB

www.simonandschuster.co.uk

Simon & Schuster Australia, Sydney
Simon & Schuster India, New Delhi

A CIP catalogue record for this book is available
from the British Library

ISBN HB 978-0-85720-367-0
ISBN TPB 978-0-85720-368-7
ISBN Ebook 978-0-85720-369-4

Typeset by M Rules
Printed and bound by CPI Group (UK) Ltd, Croydon, CR0 4YY

Dedicated to the memory of
Warwick Hele.
Teacher and Gentleman.

CHAPTER ONE

Five days before Christmas.

They were young, innocent, excited, pumped high on an overload of Cola and fries. They were also vulnerable and entirely undeserving of great misfortune. Kids – thirty-seven of them and none older than fifteen, wrapped in brightly coloured ski jackets and scarves against the December cold, their arms laden with the plunder they had snatched from the stalls of the Christmas Fair during their day trip to Brussels. These were the children of the US diplomatic community in London: pampered, privileged, and now headed home.

One of them, Cartagena, named after the town of her conception, was crying, wiping tears from her cherry cheeks and still complaining about the tumble she'd taken on the outdoor ice rink, but no one appeared to be taking much notice so she gave up. Even at the age of eight she was wise enough to realize she had already lost the sympathy vote and wouldn't have any tears left to impress her parents if she kept this up. Soon she had put aside her dramatic hobble and was skipping along with the rest of the crowd as they made their way to the departure gate. An ancient Tiger Moth biplane in the colours of the Swedish air force was suspended from the rafters high above their heads. Cartagena looked up, incredulous. Did they really used to fly that stuff?

It was a scheduled flight, departing on time, not always what was expected at this time of year, but in any event it wouldn't have mattered very much to the outcome. The men of evil intent who were waiting for it were already in position.

It had been a makeshift affair, organized at the last minute. The three men had hired the boat the previous day at IJmuiden on the Dutch coast, an Aquabell thirty-three-footer, a fishing boat with its cabin up front, substantial deck aft, and three-hundred-horsepower diesels that could get it out of trouble in the push of a throttle. It had been hired with few words and only the most cursory inspection of the three men's paperwork. As soon as they got on board it was clear to the owner they knew how to handle it, and any lingering doubts he might have entertained were buried beneath the substantial wad of euros they produced, although the strange box-object in its canvas shroud that was lugged on board had nothing to do with fishing. Most likely a drugs run, he reckoned, or perhaps people smuggling, dropping Middle Eastern filth off on some deserted stretch of East Anglia. He couldn't care less, not at almost double his usual rate and in a bundle of cash that was already forming a bulge in his pocket. If the British couldn't keep an eye on their own coastline, why the hell should he lose sleep? He scratched his crotch and hurried off to the nearest bar.

Now the three men waited anxiously, the boat turning into the swell of the North Sea, keeping station beneath the flight path. On another night and in a less chaotic world they would have taken more time, employed more sophisticated equipment to track the plane, but they had to make do with an iPhone loaded with a Plane Finder app. Yet it was a remarkable tool. Press a button and tiny red icons began creeping across a map with the details and destinations of almost every commercial flight in the air including their call signs, flight paths, positions, heights, speeds. Everything in real time, and all a terrorist in a hurry would need. As they waited, they unwrapped their cargo from its polystyrene shroud, checking and rechecking every part of the gear they had brought on board. They had spent wisely. The shoulder-held surface-to-air missile they had acquired was the latest Russian model, an SA-24 Grinch, one of the best in the business, its sophistication so simple that operating it was easy enough even for ragheads: one as a spotter, the other the shooter. And as they waited, on their tiny iPhone screen the red marker of Speedbird 235 began its crawl across the map towards them.

The Airbus was climbing, its twin CFM engines burning eighty-three litres of fuel a minute through the crystal air of the winter night. Soon they were crossing the coast slightly to the south of Ostende, and even as they passed into the dark embrace of the North Sea, the pilots could see the gentle glow of the English coast more than sixty miles away. The flight would be short, a little over the hour, cruising at twenty-two thousand feet before descending and flying almost directly west along the Thames estuary and across London to Heathrow.

'God's light,' the captain whispered as the lights of the English coast began to emerge on the horizon, like a thousand candles being waved in greeting. On a night like this a man could gaze all the way to Heaven. Karl was a family man, four teenage girls, and crammed into the aft hold was a bulging bag full of presents he'd grabbed in a frantic half-hour through the crew duty-free at Brussels. Every year as they grew older the struggle to find something they appreciated got more difficult, but he didn't complain. All too soon they would be gone. Damn.

It was the last flight of the day. The milk run. There were one hundred and eight passengers on board, two pilots and five hosties, making a total of one hundred and fifteen on the manifest. The hosties – cabin crew – were moving down the aisle serving the boxes of antiseptic sandwiches and snacks that passed as in-flight refreshment. The napkins had dreary motifs of holly printed on them, the sole concession the PC brigade at corporate headquarters had made to the festive season, so the hosties had retaliated and were wearing reindeer horns with flashing red lights on the tips.

'Time to make an idiot of myself,' the captain muttered as he rose from his seat and pulled a Santa Claus hat over his head.

'But, Karl, you do it so brilliantly,' Bryan, his first officer, replied.

'Just make sure you don't crash the bloody thing while I'm gone.'

'Haven't done that in almost months,' Bryan said, smiling.

The captain disappeared, but only for a few minutes. Not much scope for distraction on a short flight. By the time he returned, the first officer was already talking to air traffic control and confirming the details of their course adjustment and descent, twisting the control knobs to set the coordinates into the flight computer. 'Speed: two-two-zero, flight level: one-five-zero,' he was repeating.

'Glad you managed to keep us in the sky this time,' the captain muttered, draping his hat over the clothes hook behind him. As he slipped back into his seat, from the corner of his eye he saw the hat fall forlornly to the floor. He sighed. His wife kept telling him he was getting too old to fly, but too old to play Santa Claus? He thought about retrieving it, but decided it could wait. He would tidy up later if Abi, the senior attendant, didn't find it first. She was always complaining about his untidiness. He fastened his harness. 'I have control,' he declared, reasserting his authority. Yet no sooner had the words been acknowledged by his colleague when from somewhere behind they heard a crash – no, a series of crashes, an extended, evil noise, like the gates of Hell swinging open. In the same heartbeat the master alarm began to chime out a warning, and the Airbus started to bounce around the sky like a sweet wrapper caught in an updraught.

From their vantage point fifteen thousand feet below, the three attackers gazed on, in glorious anticipation, which slowly froze to disbelief. The spotter had acquired the target, through night-vision goggles bought on the Internet. The skies in this part of the world were lonely at night and Speedbird 235 stood out starkly against the clutter of distant stars. The Grinch was a one-shot throwaway system, almost kid's stuff; all the shooter had to do was clip on the power unit, press a button, and they were set. As he tracked the aircraft through the eyepiece he engaged it with a half-trigger, then another gentle squeeze. Nothing more. The missile did the rest. The eruption of sound and light battered the two men's wits. By the time they had recovered and the fug of smoke had disappeared, the missile was already at a great distance, its trail a distinctive spiral through the night sky as it went in pursuit, constantly adjusting its attitude to stay locked on to the heat signature of the engines. They watched it closing in. They saw it strike. They even witnessed the sharp flare of impact. Then Speedbird 235 carried on.

No explosion. No ripping of the wing away from its mounting. No tattered fuselage tumbling from the sky. Above them, the strobe lights of the Airbus were still flashing from the wingtips. A malfunction, a dud perhaps, always a risk when these things were bought on the black market, or was it because the missile was at the very limit of its effective range, and even beyond? The plane continued on its path through the night. They had failed, catastrophically, and in their line of business there was always a price to be paid for failure. For a few minutes they argued, screamed, hurled curses at each other, threatened to drag each other's mothers from the whorehouse, frantically interrogated the screen of their iPhone and stretched their necks until they could no longer see the lights of the aircraft as it flew on, and on. In despair, the phone was hurled overboard, as far as it could be thrown. Then they hit the throttle and sped back into the darkness.

Back in the cockpit, there was no sense of panic. An engine had gone, that was the obvious answer, and they had practised for that any number of times on the simulator at Cranebank. Anyway, the ECAM aircraft monitoring system was telling them all they needed to know.

'Eng Fail. Eng One Fail,' the screen reported.

The captain reached forward to switch off the distracting howl of the master alarm. 'I have control. Read ECAM,' he instructed the first officer, his voice formal, unflustered. ECAM was a brilliant device, designed not only to tell them what the trouble was but how to fix it. In an equally formal tone the first officer began calling out the instructions from the screen when, without warning, the instructions changed.

'HYD Green Reservoir Low Level.'

Bugger. One of the three hydraulic systems had gone down. Thank God the designers of this wonderful beast had built in three such systems – Green, Yellow and Blue – so they still had two left. Failsafe. Hell, this bird could fly on just one, no great problem, it had happened to most experienced pilots one time or another. But it was time to let others know of their little difficulty.

'Speedbird 235, Speedbird 235,' the captain spoke into his radio. 'Mayday. Mayday. Mayday. Engine failure.'

The voice of an air traffic controller responded immediately. 'Acknowledged, Speedbird 235. Let me know your intentions.'

Intentions? They would carry on, of course. No drama. The Green hydraulics were the primary system and controlled things like the steering of the nose wheel, the landing gear, the main braking system, lots of other things, too, but there were plenty of backups. The landing gear could be dropped manually, there was emergency braking available on Yellow. And ECAM was giving them the safety procedure, something they'd practised a hundred times on the simulators. Isolate the engine, pull back to idle, master switch off, activate the fire system that cut off the supply of fuel and air to the engine in case of a leak. Losing an engine and one set of hydraulics wasn't much of a problem, but you didn't want this sort of thing spreading. The Airbus flew on, her path straight and true.

They were still concentrating on the ECAM instructions

when Abi appeared at the flight-deck door. They buzzed her through. She was frowning, twisting the antlers nervously in her hands.

'Guys, stop screwing around. Please?'

'We have an engine down, Abi.'

'I know that! Bits of it are falling off the back of the airplane. The kids don't know whether to scream or take photos. What should I tell them?'

The captain slipped into his formal briefing, reporting the engine and hydraulic failure to her, stating his intention to continue on to Heathrow, giving his estimate of timing. They were barely seventy miles from touchdown; they'd be on the ground in little more than a quarter of an hour. 'It'll be a normal landing, I think, Abi, but because of the hydraulics our steering's stuffed, so we won't be able to get off the runway. There'll be a lot of vehicles to greet us and plenty of flashing blue lights. Totally normal for this sort of thing. No evacuation, no slides, we'll just stop on the runway instead of taxiing to the gate. Understood?'

Abi repeated his instructions back to him in confirmation. 'Tell me you've done this sort of thing before, Karl?' she added when she had finished the routine.

'Don't worry, Abi, several times. You OK with this?'

'It'll give me something to talk about in the nail bar. Men drivers.'

'Tell the other girls I'll be buying drinks when we get down.'

'To celebrate the fact you can land a plane with only a few bits falling off?'

'Christmas. I was thinking Christmas. This is my last trip.'

'Make sure it's not ours, too,' she replied, defiant. Dear Abi, she could give as good as she got. 'And for Heaven's sake, tidy up this cabin,' she added, bending to pick up the fallen Santa hat. She tried to hang it back on its hook, but the hook was broken, flapping from its fixture. Perhaps the bang had been more severe than they'd thought. She folded it neatly and put it in her pocket.

'Time for me to talk to the passengers,' the captain said. 'Tell them they're in luck, going to get an early landing.' He paused. 'And if you see anything more going on back there' – he meant falling off – 'let me know. Secure the cabin, Abi, prepare for immediate landing. See you on the ground.'

'Good luck, you guys.' She placed a hand on the captain's shoulder. He squeezed it tenderly, and for a fraction longer than was necessary. Then she disappeared back into the plane.

'How many times you really done this before?' the first officer asked, trying to sound nonchalant as the flight-deck door closed behind her.

'Hundreds of times,' his colleague replied. 'In the simulator.'

'And they told me *I* was a jerk.'

'No point in putting the wind up her. You know how

emotional these hosties get, but this is nothing we can't handle.'

'Tell me, Karl, you and Abi ever had a thing going?' the first officer asked nonchalantly, his eyes still fixed on ECAM. 'I always thought . . .'

Silence. The captain concentrated on his controls.

'Hell, I would,' the first officer added.

The captain sighed. 'Just concentrate on your job and give me the readings, jerk.'

In front of them, the lights of the Thames estuary were burning bright and already the pilots could see the dark snake of the river that would lead them home.

Then ECAM started pinging again. For a single heartbeat the first officer thought it was a repeat of the earlier information, but it wasn't going to be that easy.

'Shit, we've lost Yellow,' he spat.

The second hydraulic system was losing pressure. That was the moment when they both knew they were in trouble – not desperate trouble, but deepening. It meant they had no brakes, no flaps, the landing would be very fast and there was an excellent chance they'd run right out of tarmac. The emergency services wouldn't be there as spectators any longer.

'You know, Karl, I'm hoping this is a sim.'

'I'll rip the balls off someone if it is.'

'On the other hand . . .'

'Nothing we haven't done before. On the sim.'

'Yeah, I almost got down in one piece last time I tried it.'

The banter was heavy, but they knew they now faced a serious task – and some tough decisions.

'So where are we going to put her down?' the first officer asked.

'You tell me. Is Stansted an option?'

If they diverted north, it would mean they'd avoid flying over central London.

'I don't think so,' the first officer replied, flicking rapidly through the plates of his airfield handbook. 'Runway Zero Four there is only three thousand and fifty-nine metres,' he read out loud. 'We'll need more than that.'

'So Heathrow it is.'

'Heathrow Two Seven Right is three thousand nine hundred metres. That should do it.'

'It will bloody well have to.'

The Airbus was now becoming difficult to control, the pilot's sidestick refusing to cooperate. Every time it was shifted or turned, the plane decided to do something else, its own thing. It was like trying to command a wayward cat. They flew on through the night, but with much less certainty.

The two men weren't frightened, they had their training to fall back on. Anyway, there was too much for them to do, no time for thought or fear. There was air traffic control to inform, Abi to brief once more – this would be an emergency landing, the passengers would have to be set in the brace position, not an easy task with so many kids on board. But they could still make it on one engine and one hydraulic system.

They were flying over the mouth of the estuary. Ten thousand feet, two hundred and twenty knots, two hundred and fifty miles an hour. Only ten minutes to landing. Ahead of them they could see the lights of the Dome and Kings Cross station, and beyond that the towers of the Parliament building and the stacks of Battersea Power Station. Everything was set out before them, dressed in its finery, London getting ready to celebrate Christmas.

Abi answered the summons to the cockpit. She listened quietly and very intently as the captain gave her the fresh briefing, repeating it back to him to show she had understood.

'Soon home, love,' the captain concluded, trying to reassure her.

But it wasn't destined to be that simple.

The missile hadn't exploded, yet the damage it inflicted had been catastrophic. The missile had hit the front part of the engine, sending shards of searing-hot metal into the hydraulic bay that lay just behind the wing. The missile itself had broken up and part of that, too, had bounced off the engine and been hurled into the bay, where it had made a direct hit on the first hydraulic reservoir. These were about the size of industrial pressure cookers, and Green had been destroyed immediately. Meanwhile the turbine discs in the rear of the crippled engine – that part of the engine where the energy was concentrated – had begun to spin out of control, speeding up until they shattered and flew apart. It was a fragment of one of these discs that had punctured the second reservoir. Green was dead, Yellow was dying.

The Blue System had survived intact, at first, but even though the hoses feeding it were made of stainless steel, in the intense slipstream that was ripping through the damaged fuselage, one of these had been bent and forced up against a fragment of missile casing that had lodged in the bay. As the plane flew on, the hose was pounded ceaselessly, remorselessly, against the razor-sharp shard of metal, until it, too, failed.

They were down to five thousand feet. Not much more than six minutes to Heathrow. They knew they weren't going to make it.

No discussion, no time for that, and nothing in the manual for this, it was all instinct, an instantaneous throw of the dice.

'I'm going for the river,' the captain said.

'Better that than another Lockerbie.'

'I agree. Particularly when we're doing the flying.'

The captain had to make a choice; he might still be left with some fragment of control before the last of the hydraulic fluid pissed away in the night air. Better the river than a crowded city centre, the scars on the landscape that had been left on Lockerbie. So, close the remaining thrust lever, shut down the final engine, trim the aircraft, try to glide her down. Damn it, that pilot had done it a couple of years back, the one who'd ditched in the Hudson, got everyone off alive when his engines had failed. But he'd still had hydraulics.

'Shall I get Abi?' Bryan asked.

'Don't see the point. No need to terrify the kids.'

'Just us, then.'

'Yes, just the two of us.'

Ahead of them, the Thames wound its way between the flare path of the riverbanks, twisting so sharply at points that on the ground it often deceived the eye, but from the cockpit they could see it all, laid out in spectacular and terrifying detail. They would have to get down before the bridges came into play. Hit one of those and … But the stretch leading up to Tower Bridge seemed about right. The captain lined her up, one last touch on the sidestick, and then all control was gone. They were gliding, their path set, for better or much worse. In the cockpit, without the engines, it seemed unnaturally quiet, except for a persistent banging that was coming from somewhere behind. He pushed home the ditching button that sealed off the cabin, gave them a chance of floating.

'Should I go through the emergency ditching procedures?' the first officer asked, holding the manual open, struggling to read in the dim emergency lighting.

'I seem to remember it talks about making sure the galleys are turned off, useful stuff like that.'

Slowly, the first officer's shoulders sagged, like an abandoned tent. He closed the book and put it aside.

'London, this is Speedbird Mayday. I've lost all

hydraulics and I'm trying to get into the river by Tower Bridge.'

Only the slightest hesitation before: 'Er, Speedbird Mayday. Say again?'

'Repeat, ditching near Tower Bridge. No hydraulics. We have one-one-five – repeat one-one-five – souls on board. That includes a whole playschool of kids.'

'Speedbird Mayday, your message acknowledged. Emergency services will be informed.' The controller's voice had begun strong and matter of fact, but suddenly it ran out of breath. He had to clear his throat before he added: 'Good luck.'

The captain found nothing to say in reply. He leaned down, cancelled the radio. The cockpit fell silent.

In the passenger compartment there was a surprising lack of panic. They'd been told they were only a few minutes from the airport and the change in the noise of the remaining engine wasn't unusual as a plane prepared to land. Abi had done her job well. Yet she was too good to fool herself. Now she was strapped in her own seat, by the forward bulkhead beside another member of the cabin crew. She bowed her head in silent prayer and was struggling not to show her fear when through her tear-blurred eyes she saw a small girl appear in front of her. It was Cartagena. She was holding a glass-eyed teddy bear with a drooping, much-sucked ear.

'We told them we're all going to be OK, didn't we, Edward?' she lisped, interrogating the bear. She gazed up at Abi, her grey eyes filled with earnest. 'My daddy told me he would never let anything happen to me.'

'And who is your daddy, darling?' Abi stammered, struggling desperately to hold back the tears.

'He's the ambassador.'

'Would you and Edward Bear like to come and sit here on my lap?' Abi asked. It defied every regulation, but there was no time to get the child back in her own seat. Anyway, there was no point.

Gratefully, Cartagena climbed into her arms as the other hostie looked on in horror, understanding all too well what this must mean.

'You want to tell me about Edward Bear?' Abi asked. 'Does he have brothers and sisters?'

So Cartagena began to spell out Edward's complicated family history while Abi, her arms wrapped protectively around the little girl, her face buried in the child's hair, thanked God for the distraction.

Back in the cockpit, the two pilots stared ahead of them at the dark water that was now fast approaching. They were almost down to the height of the buildings scattered around Canary Wharf. The captain did a little mental arithmetic. They'd hit at around two hundred and twenty knots, and not quite level, around two degrees. Not a lot, but enough to spear the nose into the water and flip the plane on its back. That's if they didn't hit anything first. He'd once talked about these things with an old-timer, a retired test pilot who'd told him how it worked. You never drown, it seems. The plane hits the water and stops, but you don't. Your head is fired forward and snaps your neck; either that or it shakes your brain to jelly.

'Bryan, something I need to tell you.'

'Yes?' The first officer was startled from his thoughts, tearing his eyes away from the approaching water and the bridge beyond.

'You were right.'

'About what?'

'Me and Abi.'

The two men turned to face each other. Slowly, as though it were made of lead, the captain extended his hand. His first officer took it. Then, once more, they stared out at what lay ahead, and said not another word.

The captain had chosen a section of the river called the Pool of London. This was the old mercantile centre, the site of the once-great port of the capital city and deep enough for a World War Two destroyer and even small liners. It was also playing host to a Polish tall ship, its masts towering more than a hundred feet above its wooden decks as it waited for passage through Tower Bridge later that night to begin a Christmas goodwill visit. The wingtip of the Airbus brushed the tallest of the masts, causing the plane to yaw. The aircraft was no longer level, the port wing hit the water first, tearing away from the fuselage, which then cartwheeled twice. As the chaos of the crash subsided, only the tail was clearly distinguishable, sticking out defiantly above the river, surrounded by floating debris and a small oil fire.

Even after the waters had ceased their raging and settled to nothing more than a dark tidal ripple, there was no sign of anyone on board. They were all dead.

Lake Taupo, New Zealand

Benjamin Usher, the British Prime Minister, a face fashioned for caricature. As a boy he had taken a tumble down the slope of a Cumbrian fell near his home, which had left him with a squashed nose, ragged ear and a scar high on his cheek. The passage of later years had given him wrinkles that left him looking rather like a bulldog. Resilient. Determined. Even a little stubborn. He was going to need all those qualities in the coming weeks; he had an election to fight, and no Prime Minister takes such moments for granted, even when eight points ahead in the polls, as he was. He had never forgotten the words of one of his predecessors, Harold Macmillan, who had been asked to define what worried him most. 'Events, dear boy, events,' he had replied.

At the moment Speedbird 235 hit the water a short distance downriver from the Houses of Parliament, Usher was tucked far away from his problems, or so he thought, in a luxury resort beside Lake Taupo on New Zealand's north island, where he was attending the biennial meeting of Commonwealth heads of government. It had been a fruitful three days, swapping ideas and intimacies with leaders from vigorous economies like India, Canada, and

Australia; countries that had escaped the economic permafrost that seemed to have settled on Europe and its currency, and now the deliberations were almost at an end, time to wrap things up and head home for Christmas. It was early morning on Lake Taupo, and the Prime Minister was enjoying his breakfast, sitting on the verandah of his lodge soaking up birdsong, when a nervous steward spilled orange juice over the Prime Minister's immaculately laundered shirt. Only a few drops, but sufficient to drench the steward in embarrassment. Clumsy bugger. Yet Usher was an old hand, knew there would be a photographer's lens pointing at him from behind some bush or across the lake, so instead of succumbing to an instinctive scowl he burst into laughter, making sure that the steward and the wide world beyond realized he couldn't care less. It was to prove an unfortunate image, in the circumstances.

He first heard of the tragedy on the Thames while he was changing into a fresh shirt – only the sketchiest details, no one knew yet the scale of the disaster or the death toll, or even that there was a death toll, but it was not something that could be ignored. He immediately asked for an earlier flight home, but was told there was none. In any event there were still important details needing to be wrapped up at the conference, so with some misgivings he stayed on those few extra hours. Another misfortune.

The contrasting images of the wreckage and that smile were played side by side. The Prime Minister's refusal to walk out of the conference led to questions about his sense of priorities. And even before he had arrived back in London, two days after the tragedy, the media had already made up their collective mind about this act of callousness, Usher's failure to capture the sombre spirit of the moment, and on that point they were not for turning, no matter what the Downing Street press spokesman offered in explanation. Grossly unfair, of course, a despicable distortion, but such, in the end, is the fate of all prime ministers.

Makhachkala, inside the Russian Federation

There were other casualties. Even before the waters had time to settle above the fuselage of Speedbird 235, a small group of wind-scuffed portable cabins standing on a rocky outcrop overlooking the shore of the Caspian Sea were set ablaze. The spot was a little to the north of the dreary Russian city of Makhachkala, and the cabins were completely destroyed. The fire raised little local interest and was immediately attributed to unknown delinquents before it was filed away as being solved. The authorities had far more important things to attract their attention; the province of Chechnya was only down the road with its population of insurgents and suicide bombers, while the entire Caspian was a sea of troubles.

It was the world's largest inland sea, or lake, and beneath it lay an ocean of oil and gas worth trillions of dollars. That made the region even more unstable. The

21

countries that clustered around the Caspian shore – Russia, Iran, Azerbaijan, Kazakhstan and Turkmenistan – were without exception led by posses of adventurers and political bandits whose loathing was mutual. It was a region of irredeemable conflict, yet its peoples were never going to be left to fight it out amongst themselves, for there were too many others who were desperate to claim a share of the riches. There were plans to lay rival pipelines across the floor of the Caspian, which ensured that the neighbours fought amongst themselves ever more bitterly, arguing about where the pipelines should cross, and who should control them. And while they fought, the waters of the Caspian became more muddied, the sturgeon swam ever closer to extinction, and the Russians and Iranians ferried in warships to back up their rival claims. It was a desperate, bloody place, and nobody gave a damn about a Portakabin or two.

Mayfair, London

Even though he was only three miles away from the catastrophe beside Tower Bridge, Harry Jones heard nothing. He was in his mews house, his head bowed in concentration as he pored over the final draft of his election manifesto. He wasn't enjoying it, never did. As a former soldier he knew that wars always carried their share of casualties, and what was politics, except for war without the ethical bits? Careers in Westminster were never more than a headline away from disaster, and one day they would get him, too. People glibly assumed Harry was better protected than most Members of Parliament – he was independently and almost indecently wealthy, had a thumping parliamentary majority and every year received a personalized Christmas card from the Queen, yet he took none of this for granted. So he sat in his darkened study, with light cast from a solitary desk lamp, working and reworking every word.

'Harry, you going to be long?'

He looked up. Jemma was leaning against the doorjamb, yawning. A wisp of thick marmalade hair tumbled across her forehead and she was clad in nothing but a towel. Even in silhouette the effect was exceptionally distracting, the sort of woman men found difficult in describing without using their hands.

'Five minutes, Jem,' he said, returning to his typescript.

'Make them short minutes,' she suggested, dropping her towel before turning back to the bedroom.

He rewrote a couple of lines, marking corrections with his Parker Duofold, then reread the whole thing once more, but it was late, his brain too tired, he couldn't catch the subtleties or the pace. Part of him, the obsessive part, said it needed another few minutes, one last look, his career depended on it, but instead he screwed the cap back firmly onto his pen and put it to one side. It was Christmas, dammit, time to follow his star, or at least the trail of light that led towards the bedroom.

Avenue de Cortenbergh, Brussels

The lights were still blazing on the fifth floor of the anonymous office building, a block down from the Park du Cinquantenaire. That was unusual. This was the European Quarter, the heart of government, where officials administered an empire that stretched from the Black Sea to the Atlantic and up as far as the Arctic Circle, although many of them had fled Brussels and already returned to their homes for Christmas. In any event, the business of running the Union of Europe was meant to be regular and methodical, it wasn't supposed to be in need of unexpected late nights.

Even more surprisingly, the lights were coming from EATA – the European Anti-Terrorist Agency. Not that EATA was like the CIA or MI6, or those thugs at the FSB in Moscow; it was a relative infant in the intelligence game, no teeth, no claws, no spies wandering abroad with poison-tipped umbrellas or exploding toothpaste. The remit of EATA was simple, its task was to gather information about matters of public security and put it in a form that their busy bosses could digest. Other intelligence agencies joked that most of the job consisted of pasting up press cuttings and could better be done by circulating *The Week* magazine or the *Wall Street Journal*, but European bureaucracy never willingly took a short cut. Or worked a late night.

Midnight struck, the avenue grew silent except for the

passing of an occasional street-cleaning truck. The park was deserted, its trees bowing their bare branches, the birds asleep. Yet still the lights in EATA burned. That could mean but one of two possibilities. Either the cleaners had been very careless. Or something was going very badly wrong.

CHAPTER TWO

All politics is image, and throughout his career Ben Usher had tried to build the appearance of a Man with the Common Touch. That's why he and his entourage had flown back home on a scheduled flight, which made communication difficult, and in business class, which made sleep well-nigh impossible. When eventually he touched down at Heathrow he was tired and knew he had already lost control of events. Not a good place to be.

His car was waiting at the foot of the aircraft stairs to whisk him away, avoiding the media melee that was waiting for him. Usher wasn't hiding, merely finding the space to collect his thoughts; he knew there would be an even larger pack of hounds waiting for him at Downing Street, and he was old enough to remember the fate of Jim Callaghan, another Prime Minister who had returned from sunnier shores during troubled times. Callaghan hadn't dodged the Heathrow pack but had spoken to them, very briefly but unguardedly. 'Crisis? What Crisis?' the headlines reported him as saying. In truth he'd never uttered those words, they hadn't even passed through his mind, yet that hadn't stopped them being engraved on his tombstone a few months later. A Prime Minister couldn't be too careful, not with en election in the offing.

On the road back in to central London, a Stars & Stripes dangled limply beside a Union Jack from an overpass. As they came closer to the centre, there were more, from lamp posts, in windows, stretched across barriers. Usher telephoned ahead to make sure that the Downing Street flag was flying, and at half mast.

When he arrived he walked directly to the Cabinet Room, which was crowded. He was quickly brought up to date with developments – there weren't any of substance, apart from the bodies, which were still being washed up on mudflats and shorelines downstream. The wreckage was being recovered, the Air Accident Investigation Board already at its work, the flight recorders already being decoded in their laboratories. In the meantime few facts, only theories, and none of them explained how he could deal with the families' grief. A message to say that the American ambassador had called, twice. A shower, a change of clothes, a careful selection of a sombre tie.

There was no one else on the stairs as he walked slowly back down from the top-floor apartment. He had this feeling of being entirely alone. He struggled to find some words he might use, a phrase or two that might help bring a traumatized country together. Put him back in control. Something that came from within. But he was tired from the flight and he felt empty.

He was still juggling phrases in his mind, dropping them, when he reached the black-and-white marble-tiled hallway. He could hear the buzz of impatience from the crowd beyond the steel door. He was making one last check of his tie when he found his political secretary at his elbow. A young man, always eager to please, sometimes too much so.

'The American Embassy on the phone again.'

'The ambassador?'

'No. His wife.'

'Save me from this ...' Usher muttered, trying to turn away.

'Wants a quick word. Just one. Needs it, she says. Now. She's hanging on.'

The ambassador's wife was a delightful woman, a Virginian, big blue eyes, late thirties, just a little flirty in the way diplomatic wives are encouraged to be, who played her part to the full but who had never wanted more than to be a softball and cookie-baking mom. Yet now ... Now Usher felt himself go solid inside. Like a machine. He'd talk to her later, knew he wouldn't be able to keep it together if he did it now. Already the polls were showing he was being blamed, not for the accident but for his poor choice in being elsewhere, in the sun while little children suffered, and he knew he could afford no more slips. So no distractions, not even for her. He shook his head. The young man backed off, a look of disappointment creeping into his eye. And once more, Usher was on his own.

He had been rushing, trying to cram too much in, and was sweating a little when at last he emerged from the front door of Number Ten to face the massed ranks of microphones, camera lenses and television lights, every one of them pointed at him.

'Christ, it's cold,' he muttered to himself as for the first time in days he felt the bite of the British winter. He wondered if that's what it had been like for King Charles. 1649. A freezing January day, so it was written, when he'd stepped out from the Banqueting Hall just a little way along Whitehall and onto his scaffold. The King had worn two shirts in order to stop him shivering, in case the crowd mistook it for fear. At this moment, Usher felt very close to the King.

Somehow the years of experience kicked in, and he found the words. Not the precise and carefully crafted phrases that had been prepared for him but thoughts that came from within, that's what mattered now, some sincere-sounding reflection that might do justice to the fact that there had been no survivors, not a single one. He spoke of sorrow, of unfairness, of pain spread wide and tragedy shared. About children who had carried the futures of their families with them, of others who had been hoping for nothing more than to share the special spirit of Christmas with those they loved, of pilots who had done their duty with courage and huge skill, and had avoided an even greater calamity.

'I can't pretend to imagine what's going through your

hearts right now,' he said, speaking directly into a camera lens, trying to reach a conclusion. 'If it were my own ...' There was an unmistakable catch in his voice; there was no need to finish the thought. 'Perhaps all I can do right now is my duty. And that, it seems to me, is to make one promise above all else to those families – British, American, Belgian, French, the others, too – those of you who have lost loved ones and will find Christmas such a desperately painful time this year. To you, I promise you this.'

Flashbulbs blazed away, the television lights shone into his eyes, he couldn't see a thing. He spoke very slowly.

'We will find out what went wrong.'

It wasn't much of a commitment, not if anyone stopped to analyse it, nothing more than what would happen as a matter of course, but it was necessary that he should say it. There had already been so much speculation about poor design and inadequate maintenance, even a bird strike, a flock of Canadian geese that might have been ingested into the engine and blown the front off. Just a few more days, then they would know for certain. Give those who were suffering some sort of reassurance, and perhaps they would stop blaming him. Pity's sake, it wasn't his fault, yet still he felt responsible and that sense of guilt drove him on.

'I vow to you all,' he said, his voice swelling with passion. 'We will discover what happened. And who was responsible.'

No! It was supposed to be *what* was responsible, not *who*. But it was too late, a slip of the tongue, a frozen thought. It had been said. Only a couple of words, but already more than enough. *It was someone's fault! Someone was to blame!*

And the media weren't going to stop until they had that someone and had dragged him out into the cold, just like poor King Charlie.

—⁂—

Despite the season, Patricia Vaine sat at an outside table on the Place de Luxembourg in Brussels, her coffee neglected, her cigarette turning to ash, shivering in her overcoat despite the glow of the overhead heater, staring into nothing.

Vaine was English by birth, European by employment. A sound Catholic education at St Mary's in Ascot and a rather more adventurous few years spent stretching her mind and occasionally her legs at Oxford, had taken her on a rapidly rising track through the labyrinth of the British Foreign & Commonwealth Office, but she'd always suspected she would never be allowed to make it to the top. Partly it was her Catholicism – the Blairs had made being a 'left footer' unfashionable – but perhaps more so because she was intellectual, better than most, and there were times when she couldn't resist the temptation to show it. She was forty-six, had blue eyes accentuated by a well-boned face and carefully built blonde hair, and if her hairdresser was aware of the first signs of grey, he hid it so well that few realized she wasn't, and never had been, entirely the genuine article. For a middle-aged woman she had the ability to cross and uncross her legs to the distraction of most men, an asset she had found more effective in Brussels than ever she had in stuffy London. Intellect and ankles; she used both as weapons.

Distraction formed a large part of her remit; indeed, it was possible to spend a long time walking through the corridors of the European capital without ever finding out what she did there, and even if one did stumble across a clue, most men usually got confused by the seductive combination of perfume and tobacco, or the ridiculous notion that a woman couldn't do 'that sort of job'. From behind the inconspicuous but carefully monitored security of the building on Avenue de Cortenbergh, Patricia Vaine headed up EATA. Her operation rarely appeared on organizational charts, and even then only as a footnote, as a subsidiary of Europe's External Action Service. Yet in truth, as the European Union's fledgling intelligence service, EATA was potentially one of the most influential centres of power in Brussels.

It wasn't supposed to happen, no national government had agreed to it, but neither had anyone objected. It was inevitable that something like EATA would come into being. The European Union had all the other trappings – a flag, an anthem, a president, a seriously screwed-up currency and a foreign policy of sorts. And, inevitably, ambition. They needed their own intelligence operation, a full hand of cards, and Vaine had set about delivering it. EATA was housed in a modest office block a short walk from the park, and lacked any sign of the usual extravagance that accompanied most European buildings like the Commission offices at the Berlaymont, and least of all the imperial splendours of the Parliament itself. The only clues that gave away EATA's home were the air-tight security pods through which staff and visitors alike had to pass, and the guards, who were all armed. This was Patricia Vaine's kingdom, and she had shown herself to be remarkably inventive, like an alchemist of old creating gold from nothing – although that was an easier trick in Brussels than most capitals.

That was another thing, money was never a problem, even though EATA wasn't supposed to exist and couldn't be identified in any budget. It had been twenty years since the EU had last had its accounts signed off by its auditors and everyone was in on the game – Irish farmers, who got subsidies for flocks of sheep that didn't exist, as well as Spanish fishermen who were paid to throw fish back into the sea. It was inevitable that Greek farmers would join in the fun. They were given millions for growing tobacco, even while the EU spent still more millions trying to persuade people to give up smoking. 'There's no accounting for ideals,' as one Commissioner had blithely explained. And if in its early days EATA couldn't hope to match the resources of its national rivals, there was nothing to stop information liaison officers wining and dining every political hack, opinion former and press man in the business. Why pay for information when you could rent it by the meal?

And, as EATA's ambitions grew and its demands inevitably became more complex, they could always out-source, hire in a bit of muscle or experience, lean on friends. It was through one of Vaine's contacts in this world of dusty mirrors that she had first picked up reports about a notorious Islamist gun-for-hire who had been spotted scurrying through northern Europe. There was talk of a deal being done in some dark place, whispers about a sur-face-to-air missile. Dirty, delightful stuff. It seemed to Vaine to be a solid lead, and since it was *her* lead she'd decided to cook it a little longer, follow it a little further to see where it might take her. It seemed like an excellent idea at the time; after all, she needed a few prize scalps to establish EATA's credibility. Dear God, she'd had no idea that it was all so imminent, or the intended target a plane full of kids.

Which left her with this huge bladder-bursting problem that made her head ache and her coffee go cold. If she were to reveal now what she had known but hadn't understood and had kept hidden for too long, she would be shown no mercy. Her organization would be ripped apart. Rivals would say she was more guilty than the terrorists them-selves. It would bring an end to her career, to EATA, to all her dreams. And where was the benefit in that?

She couldn't speak out, yet she knew she couldn't simply leave the matter. Pity's sake, she wasn't a monster. Despite the glow from the gas heater above her head, her hands began to tremble with cold, and the long trail of cigarette ash dropped helplessly to the floor.

Concentrate, damn you, don't drown in cheap emotion! But what to do? She had to rise above it, remember there was a bigger game being played here. The European Union needed time to take more solid shape, there were bound to be growing pains, weren't there? She believed passionately in that dream, of Europe, as one, united, renewed. That's why she had come here. And there was always a price to be paid for dreams.

She'd sat outside the coffee shop so long that the light was beginning to fade. A sparrow hopped onto the table, watching carefully, cheekily, bobbing its head several times before darting forward to grab the crumbs of biscuit that lay in the saucer and fluttering away with its evening meal. But she saw nothing, except what was playing in her mind. Only when the cigarette had burned so low that it scorched her fingers did she come back to reality. And reality, she had always believed, was what you made it. She took one final lungful of tobacco before pulling out her phone and scrolling through her list of contacts.

'Hamish, this is Patricia Vaine,' she said when at last a man's voice answered. 'I need to see you. This evening.'

Her fingernails tapped impatiently on the glass tabletop as she soaked up the man's protest.

'No, Hamish, I'm afraid you're going to have to disappoint your wife and be a little late for that dinner, no matter whom she's invited.' Whom, never who; she was always careful to use the correct pronoun, even when it seemed a little clumsy. 'Why? My dear Hamish, because you're a journalist. And you're just about to get a story. Rather a big one. Perhaps the biggest of your dull and undistinguished career.'

—∾—

'Mr Jones?'

The bar steward raised an eyebrow. Harry looked at his watch, inspected his empty glass with a frown, as though it were a museum exhibit, then nodded. He'd intended to wait until his friend arrived, but 'Sloppy' was late and Harry's spirits low.

He'd spent much of the afternoon on the banks of the Thames, watching the recovery of the wreckage. The river wasn't particularly deep at this point but the hours of daylight were short, the navy divers could work only at low tide and the visibility was zero. Often they had to use their fingertips to work out what they had encountered, and there were still bodies unaccounted for. It made for slow progress. Aviation fuel was leaking and the tide swirled the pollution back and forth.

They recovered the flight data and cockpit voice recorders first, from the tail section that was still sticking grotesquely from the water. Then it was the failed engine, dredged from the dark mud, and after that the tail itself, its colours made more brilliant and grotesque by the beams of a thousand spotlights as it was grappled by a floating crane onto one of the barges moored alongside, and slowly brought towards a low-loader lorry from the Joint Air

36

Recovery and Transport Squadron. As it was hoisted onto the flatbed it swung to and fro, and seemed to take for ever to be manoeuvred into place and made secure. Whenever it twisted, even a little, a stream of dark, filthy water gushed out, spattering around, like blood.

As a matter of course it was treated as a crime scene, but the police didn't bother trying to restrict those tens of thousands who came to watch. Tower Bridge was closed, as was St Katherine's Dock alongside, and for their own safety the air space above was denied to news helicopters, but for the rest the river provided the most popular, yet sombre stage in town. The crowds were so thick in places that those at the back couldn't see; they waited their turn. There were tears, many prayers both silent and spoken, particularly when motor launches of the river police drew alongside, and bodies were brought up from the darkness. The police tried to provide some sort of screen, for dignity, but there were television cameras on every roof and balcony, at every angle. The world saw everything. The salvage workers paused, a hush of grief and respect fell along the riverbanks, and all that could be heard was the timeless lapping of the Thames.

The cockpit section had broken in two. As they began lifting the main fragment, it reminded everyone of the iconic image of the Lockerbie disaster, and when it suddenly twisted in its cradle the crowd began to scream, as though at any moment they might see the body of the pilot still strapped in his seat, waving like Ahab lashed to the whale's back. They needn't have worried; the captain's body still hadn't been found.

Harry walked to his next appointment, needing the bite of the air to cut through his melancholy. Four miles, which even at his pace took him over an hour. His destination was the Special Forces Club, located in a modest Edwardian terrace behind Harrods. Its origins, as the name implied, was to provide a watering hole for those who had served in any of the clandestine forces, as Harry had in the Special Air Service, and although in recent years the club's financial plight had forced it to loosen its membership requirements, it still retained its air of mystery. From the outside the building was as anonymous as any of the other buildings in the street, apart from the nest of CCTV cameras above the door, while inside the receptionist was always welcoming and quietly observant. A small notice requested members and guests to leave their 'cloaks and daggers' in the downstairs hallway, while the modest but elegant staircase was lined with a double row of photographs, portraits, mostly black and white, of men and women who had served and often died heroically in their country's service. Small legends beneath each portrait related their tales and kept the memories fresh. When Harry had made it up to the first-floor bar he had ordered a bottle of champagne, trying to revive some of the Christmas spirit, and waited for his friend, but he had almost finished the second glass by the time he saw his arrival on one of the CCTV screens behind the bar. He watched as Jimmy Sopwith-Dane, known as 'Sloppy' to his many friends, paused on the pavement, took a deep breath of winter air, then hauled himself up the few steps to the front door, using the railings for support.

Harry flinched. Dark memories spat at him. He and Sloppy had been fellow officers in the Life Guards serving in Northern Ireland during the bad days, colleagues who became close friends – too close, perhaps, because, one rain-pissing day in the hills of Armagh, Sloppy had taken a bullet meant for Harry. It had busted his knee so badly he'd been invalided out of the Army. Not that it had broken his spirit, for Sopwith-Dane was the sort who could charm a smile from a stone. People trusted him, warmed to his humour, and only the dullest failed to see the depth of talent and single-mindedness that lay behind the foppish facade. After he'd been kicked out of the Army he'd migrated to the City, where he now ran a private and very discreet wealth management service, just a few clients but with more than thirty million pounds of their money to play with. In fact, Harry had been his first client, had to be, Harry owed him, and perhaps owed him more than ever now, because it had become clear in recent months that Sloppy's knee was breaking down. Made him just a tad unreliable with his timing. The smile that had been so free and wild seemed to have grown stiff, as though battling constant pain, but there was never a word of complaint, which made Harry feel worse.

'See you started without me, as usual,' Sloppy greeted as

he came into the bar, waving, exposing a large measure of pink cuff and regimental cufflinks.

'Testing it was up to your usual standard.'

Without prompting, the steward poured another glass but Sloppy waved it away. 'Need something a little stronger than that. Large Bushmills. On the rocks.' He laughed, trying to turn it into a joke, but the furrows around his eyes ran deep. He levered himself stiffly onto the bar stool beside Harry.

'You suffering?'

'Not much,' he lied. 'But I'm thinking of swapping it for a new one.'

'The knee?'

'You know me, no half measures. The whole sodding leg.' He swallowed the whiskey in one gulp and pushed the glass back across the counter for another. Harry sat silent, struggling to find words. He knew his friend wasn't exaggerating, he could see it in the red-rimmed eyes and the flecks of grey that had suddenly crept into the hair.

'Not to worry, you old tart,' Sloppy reassured. 'Off just above the knee, they reckon' – he made a sawing gesture with his hand – 'and I'll be running marathons. Better than ever. Bouncing along like a bloody rabbit on one of those carbon-fibre blade thingies. Cost you a fortune in sponsor-ship.' He began to laugh.

'So stop whingeing and have another drink.'

But already Sloppy was downing his second glass. They relaxed quickly, almost too quickly, the alcohol smoothing away some of the new creases in Sloppy's face. In the end they didn't bother with the dining room but spread themselves on a sofa, while the steward brought them more drink and plates of food.

'She frowning in disapproval, d'you think?' Sloppy asked, squinting at the portrait of the club's formidable patron, the Princess Royal, which hung on the far wall.

'Just disappointed she can't join us, I expect.'

'Or is it a smile? She has a lovely smile, you know. Never thought I'd ever lust after the Colonel of the Regiment. Any regiment, come to that. What do you say, Harry, you think I need counselling?'

'Probably just another drink.'

Private banter that betrayed not a hint of disrespect. They'd both put their lives on the line in the name of her mother, the Queen, and carried the scars like a crow carries its feathers. Yet they were in drink, which was often the case when they were together, and this evening they both had cause. But Sloppy, in particular, drank to forget.

'I could get wrecked just watching you,' Harry laughed as another whiskey disappeared down Sloppy.

'Brilliant idea. But not before we remember our little bit of business. You know I only love you for your money.' He dug inside his jacket pocket and pulled out an envelope containing three sheets of carefully folded paper. He pushed aside the wreckage of their meal that lay scattered across the low table in front and smoothed the creases from the sheets.

Money. Never a problem for Harry, not since his

businessman father had died with nothing but his socks on in the arms of a much younger woman, and left him a fortune that was large enough to have been seen by many as indelicate and some of which was almost certainly illicit. Harry had suddenly been catapulted from a life where he'd paid his own way through university by working night shifts at McDonald's, to one in which he couldn't be bought, bribed or bullied. He'd never forgotten his years of youthful poverty, didn't take his financial comfort for granted, but he was happy to let Sloppy handle the details. It did them both a favour.

'Need three signatures,' Sloppy instructed. 'Use your own pen. You can afford it.'

'More bloody paper?' Harry complained casually, rubbing his eyes.

'You suggested we throw more of your money into the hands of those mercenary little bastards who run the economies in the Far East, remember?'

'You said they were all sweat shops.'

'I lied. You know I lie. Why dig up my old lies?' Sloppy protested theatrically.

'Get on with it,' Harry said, leaning forward and trying to focus.

'Right. The client is always right, even when he's a small-minded prick like your good self.'

'Tell me, do you abuse all your clients?'

'Of course. Please don't feel picked out for special treatment.'

Harry chuckled and waved his hand for yet more alcohol.

'Right, concentrate,' Sloppy continued. 'I'm delighted to tell you that Nissan, the Bank of China and Matsushita Electric turn out to be highly respectable. Not sweat shops at all, quite dreary, in fact. But the way the currencies are going they'll probably make you a small fortune and me a much larger one in all the commission I'm going to skim. So before you and I drink the entire portfolio, we're going to throw some of your money around the derivatives field and hedge some of the currency expectations so that—'

But already Harry was waving his hands in surrender. 'I don't mind you kicking me to death, but boring me to death's not part of the deal,' he laughed, reaching for his Duofold.

'But I haven't even got to the small print,' Sloppy protested.

Harry's relationship with Sloppy was one of the most solid and reassuring parts of his life, not simply because of the income it produced but the friendship it reinforced. These were men who had trusted each other with their lives, and always would. So he signed. Three times.

It would be months before he realized he'd just lost two million pounds. And that it was only the start.

—∾—

Sloppy hobbled down the street. He'd ducked out of sharing a taxi with Harry, made up some excuse; he needed to be alone. The pain was blinding him. It followed him every step, of every day, and had done for years. He found what he was looking for, a late-night pharmacy. He wandered past the shelves, picked up a toothbrush he didn't want, presented it to the pharmacist at the till, and while she was ringing it up asked for two packets of non-prescription painkillers.

'I'm afraid I can only let you have the one,' she said, apologetically. 'Have you taken these before, sir?'

'No.'

'It's just that they contain codeine and can be addictive. They're for a maximum of three days. Is that OK?'

'Sure.'

'Please read the instructions on the label carefully.' She dropped them into his bag along with the toothbrush.

'Of course. Thanks.' Silly bitch. How many times had he heard this prim little lecture? If only they'd done their job properly in the first place maybe he wouldn't be staggering around London, his guts being ripped out with every step. He took the bag, snatched at it, clutched it perhaps too tight, trying to throttle it, and walked out, biting his lip.

He wasn't quite sure where he was, he'd lost his bearings in the dark. He found himself leaning on a lamp post, taking a deep breath; he grabbed for the painkillers, ripping off the cardboard cover in his haste.

He popped two pills from their plastic coffins and threw them in his mouth, but it was parched, lined with sand, and he almost choked as he struggled to swallow. When at last he looked up he saw he was facing the battered gloss-black door of a pub. God was looking out for him, after all. He pushed his way through the door, dragging his foot behind him. It caught on the step and he almost stumbled, but no one looked up. Just another Christmas drunk. Silently he cursed their ignorance and ingratitude. He ordered a large whiskey, on the rocks, found a corner seat away from the other drinkers, and found the pills once again and popped out another four. He swallowed them in one mouthful, washed down with whiskey.

The torn packet stared up at him from the sticky varnish of the tabletop, preaching.

For short term use only. Swallow 1 or 2 tablets every 4 to 6 hours. WARNING: Do not exceed the stated dose. Do not take more than 6 tablets in 24 hours.

Six? He was doing sixty of these a day. The entire packet would be gone by breakfast. In fact, they'd be his breakfast.

He glanced around furtively, but no one was watching. No one gave a damn. Why, he was nothing more than yet another City dick in his expensive cashmere overcoat quietly popping a couple of pills, and who didn't pop pills nowadays, for pain or pleasure? But with Sloppy it was always pain. Had been for years. The military surgeons could do extraordinary things, sometimes impossible things, but not miracles. The bullet that had smashed into his knee had shattered, scattering splinters of metal and bone, and some were still there, stuck inside, still trying to kill him, causing infection, tiny sinuses of pus and agony that had eaten away at the main nerve system to his foot and lower leg so that he couldn't feel much of anything but pain, which meant he kept injuring himself, which caused even more pain, and now it had got to the point of so much pain that before long they would have to chop his leg off like a leper. Don't worry, they had smiled, we'll give you the latest Ferrari version. Well, fuck them.

And fuck Harry, too. He loved the man, but why should he still be paying for him after all these years? He was going to lose his leg yet nothing seemed to muddy the course for Harry Jones, MP, Privy Councillor, George Cross, Military Cross, millionaire, lots of other bits, too. And all because Sloppy had taken that bullet for him. Harry owed him, they both knew it; why, wasn't it the guilt that kept Harry knocking on his door, giving his business to a cripple?

And that's why Sloppy was in so much trouble. From doing his best for Harry. It was for Harry and his other clients that he'd jumped on board a hedge fund that had been rolling like an express train barely a year ago, with everybody kicking each other's arses to get a seat. Now it was a train wreck, run out of track, total wipeout. And suddenly he was down a couple of million. Nothing Sloppy couldn't manage, but he'd had a mauling and needed a break. Short-term funds that would keep the monthly statements looking fat. Until he could sort it all out.

Which is precisely what the paperwork in his pocket

would do. Smooth things over, just a few months, until the other investments came through and he'd be able to lose it all in the wash up. Sharing, just like they'd always done. Jones and Jimmy. He'd taken the bullet, now Harry would take a bit of a kicking. Only difference was, Harry would never know it.

CHAPTER THREE

Christmas got cancelled. No one made it official, but its spirit drained away with the dark water that seeped from every fragment of recovered wreckage. Every evening, as the light faded and night took hold, a crowd began to gather on the plaza of Trafalgar Square. Candles were placed around the rims of the fountains, drawing thousands, silent in their grief. Mourning was something their grandparents had hidden behind closed curtains, yet now they poured forth, clutching their own candles, like a meadow of brilliant daisies in a soft breeze. Then the singing began, hymns and folk songs, and the national anthems, forlornly. A shrine of flowers began to spread around the base of Nelson's Column, while high above, through a blustery scattering of snow, the admiral seemed to be searching the skies for sight of the lost children.

More candles. A memorial service was held at St Paul's Cathedral, attended by many of the parents of the lost children and a congregation that overflowed down the steps before the west doors. The Bishop of London gave a sermon that talked of lights extinguished and sorrows which found homes and multiplied in the darkness. Then he tried to rekindle hope by telling of life reborn at Christmastime, which he pronounced Christi-mastime, like some medieval monk, yet it was a hope too far, beyond even his considerable rhetorical powers.

The Queen's Christmas message had already been recorded. Now it had to be hurriedly rewritten, a new script prepared. She decided she would deliver it live, something she hadn't done since the death of Diana. Flags flew at half mast across the capital, even the Royal Standard above the Palace, although protocol suggested it should only be flown in that manner upon a royal death. The formalities were pushed aside; they seemed inadequate and irrelevant when so many coffins were involved.

The Vice President of the United States flew from Washington on a military transport to collect the coffins, forty-one of them: all the children and four other American citizens who had been on board Speedbird 235. Each coffin was covered in a flag, and laid out with military precision, immaculate and endless rows of death that filled the hold of the C5-Galaxy.

And after the sorrow and shock came anger. As two nations wept, the demand for answers grew more insistent, far outstripping the ability of the authorities to satisfy them. An engine had gone down, the hydraulics ripped apart, but that was already clear from the radio traffic between the cockpit and Air Traffic Control. The pilot was a hero, putting his stricken craft down with extraordinary skill on a spot where the only collateral damage was a tall ship's mast, but what else had happened wasn't yet clear. It was ironic that after the third day, his was the only body that had still not been recovered. The other bodies were taken to local hospitals where autopsies were conducted under the supervision of pathologists who specialized in aviation accidents.

The pieces of wreckage were taken to the headquarters of the Air Accident Investigation Branch, set in secluded woods beside Farnborough airfield, south-west of London. Police had blocked off the long access road that ran from the public highway to the office block and hangars that hid the AAIB's very private work from prying eyes. A large area beside the hangars was fenced off, but even the fencing couldn't completely conceal the litter of shattered airframes and fragments of helicopter that filled it to overflowing, evidence of its most recent work. Three large shipping containers stood in one corner, the streaks of rust running down their sides testament to the fact that they had been there for many years. They held the most sensitive parts of the wreckage from the Lockerbie bomb. The last useful grains of forensic evidence had long since been squeezed and scraped from the scraps, but no one had yet had the political courage to allow them to be destroyed, so they festered, like bad memories.

One of the hangars had been hurriedly cleared, and as the fragments of Speedbird 235 began to arrive on the back of the low-loaders they were laid out in sequence, like the pieces of a jigsaw. Even before the pieces had been unloaded the structural inspectors, systems analysts, flight recorder engineers and other teams of specialists started to pore over the remnants as they began the meticulous task of trying to determine how, and why, the aircraft had been torn apart. There was a problem, of course. Cuts. Like all government departments the AAIB was under pressure, less money, discarded personnel, their strength whittled away. And it was Christmas. Yet for this, and for so many dead, they did what budgets would not allow. The recorders arrived immersed in a tank of river water to guard against corrosion that would start once they were exposed to the air. They were lifted gently, almost with reverence, and placed in ovens to be baked at eighty degrees Centigrade, painstakingly drying them out. The process took almost two days. Only then could the harrowing information they contained be extracted and analysed.

During the crash the engines had been ripped off, the belly of the aircraft hideously punctured, bulkheads ripped apart, the fuselage broken. All was gathered, washed down, set out, and examined. The inspectors were experts, they knew how to fly many different types of aircraft and did so on a regular basis for commercial airlines in order to keep themselves up to speed. They also knew how every seal, nut, switch, hatch, lamp, circuit board and piece of Velcro was supposed to be assembled. Just as a forensic pathologist takes apart the bodies of the victims to confirm how they had died, so these men did much the same, except they worked in the opposite direction, piecing the body back together once more.

Their first break came on the second night, when the recorders had been dried out and their examination could begin. The cockpit voice recorder was harrowing. The cabin had four microphones, open regardless of the connection with Air Traffic Control, picking up every word, making it possible to triangulate the origin of every sound. That's why they were able to tell it had been the first officer, Bryan, who had screamed so pathetically in the millisecond before the recording went dead. The power had been cut off. An inevitable consequence when your cockpit smashes into a river at a hundred and fifty miles an hour.

It was on the same evening that an inspector watched a flat-bed bringing in the cowling from the failed engine. It had been ripped away and floated downriver, and had taken some time to be recovered. Even while the truck was reversing in order to unload, the inspector was up beside the cowling, taking a closer look. He had seen something that startled him, a hole punched through the outside of the skin that had created a characteristic petal effect of torn metal on the inside.

He had the cowling unloaded onto a trolley that he then pushed to the corner of the hangar where the engines were being inspected. The failed engine was a tangle of fuel pipes, debris and crumpled titanium blades that at first seemed not to make much sense, even to the specialists who had arrived from the engine manufacturers, but when the pierced skin of the cowling was matched up against it, suddenly one mystery faded away, to be replaced by another. The evidence was before him, before them all, yet not one of them was willing to believe.

He was twisting his head, stretching his neck, trying to get a new perspective on the damage when he heard his name. A colleague who had been investigating the hydraulics compartment was calling. His voice sounded excited, and perhaps a little afraid, repeating the inspector's name with increasing urgency.

'Mike! For God's sake, Mike! Get over here.'

The hydraulics bay was also the compartment where the undercarriage was retracted during flight. As Mike stepped around a scrap of fuselage skin that had yet to find its proper place, he found the other man bent over the twin wheel assembly. He was biting on his knuckle.

'What is it?' Mike asked, but he got no answer. The other man was lost for words, except for one single sharp obscenity that rushed forth on a gasp of air.

When Mike joined him, and saw what he was looking at, he did the same. Embedded in the thick Dunlop tyre was a shard of aluminium that was covered in dull-green paint. Most of the immense fuselage of Speedbird 235 was constructed from aluminium, but not an inch of it was painted this colour.

It was a missile fin.

—⚬—

They planned to go out for dinner. The Wolseley, her favourite, with its elegant Twenties' atmosphere. As Harry sat propped up on the bed he watched her step from the shower, her pointed toe searching like a ballerina for the towel spread across the floor. Water was still dribbling down her body as she lifted her arms carelessly to tie up her damp hair. She looked stunning. Yet Harry was troubled.

Jemma Laing was a primary school teacher whom he'd met at a charity function. Glorious red hair, a little on the short side, with the soft, pale complexion so characteristic of Scots women whose skin seem to have been washed clean of any blemish by a thousand years of soft breezes and rain. She and Harry had been going out for nearly four months and he knew she was growing tired of stopping over, living out of an overnight bag. The time had come for her to make a deeper mark on his life and he couldn't find a single reason to object, to prevent her from claiming some cupboard space, beginning the process of manoeuvring alongside him, except . . .

He'd been married twice before. His first wife, Julia, had filled his life in a manner that made him question and revalue everything around him, with the sum always greater than what had gone before. She'd begun gathering together all those loose parts of his young character and tying them neatly together when she had died, killed in a skiing accident for which Harry would for ever blame himself. She'd been pregnant, too. Perhaps that was why he had punished himself second time around with Melanie, a

54

woman who loved to turn men's heads, couldn't stop, even after she and Harry had got married. He thought she was somewhere in Cheshire now, married to an older man who made cheese. A lot of cheese, for she had expensive tastes. Since Mel, many women had passed through Harry's life. Some he had loved, but none had been able to keep up with him. His fault. Until Jemma. She had been careful not to make demands, even to hint that he should slow down, but he had begun to acknowledge that perhaps it was time he did. And with Christmas just a couple of days away, maybe it was time to ask her to hang around a little longer, empty the overnight bag.

'You still planning on going to your parents for Christmas?' he asked, hoping the question sounded casual as she towelled her hair dry. She flicked it back over her head.

'They're expecting me.'

She was an Edinburgh girl, with eyes that reminded him of sun on the firth. She was early thirties, ten years younger than Harry and all grown up, but it was an outcome her parents seemed ill-inclined to share. They were Church of Scotland, small lives lived out in a pebble-dash terrace in the suburb of Livingstone. There would be no room there for Harry, except in her bed, which they wouldn't allow, not at Christmas or at any other time unless they were married. London ways had never proved popular in Livingstone, not with neighbours peering from behind every curtain.

'I'd like you to come, Harry.' She bit her lip, afraid she sounded too serious. 'It would be the sofa in the downstairs room, and the floorboards creak.' She laughed, trying to make light of it.

'Not with you?'

'No. Anyway, I still sleep in my old metal-framed bed. The springs complain like a shutter in a storm. Not your style.'

'No,' he sighed, as she wrapped the towel around herself.

She stared at him, searching. 'I don't have to go. I could stay here. In London.'

There it was. They both knew what it meant. Christmas together, here, in Harry's home. Cupboard space. He liked this woman, knew he wanted more of her, accepted that she had a right to ask and to be taken seriously.

He looked away, broke her gaze. 'Better not let your parents down, if you've promised.'

A cloud passed across her eyes, the sun gone. 'No, you're probably right. Silly of me.'

'We're still on for New Year's?'

'If that's what you want.'

'Of course.'

A dullness had crept into her voice; he'd hurt her, couldn't help it. He was scared, couldn't afford to get this wrong again, hurt her even more, and himself most of all. Yet even as he argued with himself he heard Julia's voice – 'You're a total tosser, Jones!' And he knew she was right.

'Let me get dressed, will you?' Jemma said softly. 'A girl needs a little privacy.'

One moment wanting to share their lives, the next demanding privacy. He wanted to say something, to apologize, put things right, but already she had turned her back. He rolled off the bed and went downstairs to drown in another whisky.

—⁓—

Had it been any other day than Christmas Eve, the matter might have been handled so much more skilfully, but chaos chooses its own moment. The country was already closing down for the long festive break. The dull-green fragment of aluminium was being tested by forensic experts and even though it was too early for any confirmation that it was from a missile, it was enough for the men from the AAIB to put a call in to the private office of the Secretary of State for Transport, under whose auspices they fell. Yet she was already weaving her way down the slopes of Verbier, her office on skeleton staff, and nobody returned the call.

It was left to the *Telegraph* to break the news. It took the rest of the media only hours to follow.

'*Was It A Bomb?*' the front page screamed, above an image of the aircraft tail sticking from the water that had become iconic. And already the government was being dragged behind events.

The report quoted 'usually reliable intelligence sources',

which nevertheless remained unnamed, saying that a new terrorist cell was reported to be operating in northern Europe. It was believed to be Islamist, and although its precise origins were as yet unclear its objective was to 'punish the Western democracies for persistent interference in the affairs of the Muslim world' by finding and destroying a substantial target, preferably American. 'Intelligence officers are speculating that the target might have been Speedbird 235 and the 115 passengers on board.' There followed a lengthy history of Middle Eastern terrorism stretching from Carlos the Jackal to Yasser Arafat, Palestinian groups to the Taliban, al-Megrahi and al-Qaeda that covered more than forty bloody years. 'Memories of the Lockerbie bomb still burn deeply into the psyche of the anti-terrorist forces of Britain and the United States. Could this be yet another example of their failure?' the *Telegraph* asked.

It was perilously thin stuff, a theory hanging from a thread, yet that had never stood in the way of a good headline and within hours the story had been picked up by the rest of the media and was swimming in a sea of speculation. This time when the telephone rang and Ben Usher answered, it wasn't either the American ambassador or his wife, but the President himself. The two men hadn't always got on; a relationship that was supposed to be 'special' and had more recently been described as 'essential' was now openly referred to as 'stretched', and became more so as the American leader described how unsettling such news was 'at a time when Americans should be home celebrating peace and love with their families'. The man had never been known to leave a cliché under-rehearsed.

'Mr President, there is not a single shred of evidence in my possession to substantiate these reports,' Usher replied. He was standing in the window of his study at Chequers, the Prime Minister's country retreat, watching a family of crows tussle on the lawn while his wife was downstairs putting the final touches to the Christmas tree. Was there no escape?

'So it's untrue?' the President persisted.

'Totally. So far as we know.'

'So far as you know?'

'I'm not God,' Usher protested.

'But we play God, you and I, that's our job. If it's not true, you should give those imposters of the press one hell of a kicking.'

'I don't control the media any more than you do,' Usher all but spat.

'I've got a million of the miserable bastards screaming at me trying to nail down this story. It's your story, Ben. If it's not going to fly, kill it. Kill it dead. Before it really rips the ass out of Christmas.'

So, later that dreary and grey afternoon, a denial was issued. The Downing Street press spokesman confirmed it. There was no suggestion of a bomb. The denial had the benefit of being the truth, but as the world was soon to discover, it wasn't the whole truth. And Ben Usher, a man whose only crime was to get his timings wrong through no fault of his own, was about to be destroyed.

—∞—

Patricia Vaine sat by her fire, stroking the cat in her lap, listening to the spitting of beech logs. She was sipping a glass of something that was cold and white but was too preoccupied to identify it immediately. From the kitchen came the sounds of her husband rattling the pans and plates that would soon produce their Christmas lunch. Turkey – Felix was conventional, in some things, at least.

She had first met Felix at Oxford. They had both been auditioning for the university drama society. He had made little impression either on her or on the casting directors, but their paths had crossed by chance many years later in an antiques shop near Sloane Square. She had wandered in searching for a battered mirror and found him staring back at her. He'd had a serious bike accident that had left him with a frozen spine; he moved stiffly, turned his head from his hips, looked out from the corners of his eyes, which gave him a leering aspect, but Felix and Patricia proved to be a complement of opposites. He was urbane, she was intense, he was a cook while she was always in a hurry, he saw the colour of life while she counted the casualties, and since neither had much desire for children their desperately orthodox sex life didn't seem to present a problem.

When they had married she'd kept her maiden name,

not using his surname of Wilton; it gave her an additional measure of independence that she treasured, and often proved useful in her working world of middle-aged men. How much she would come to welcome the distance that different names and lifestyles carried was brought home three years after their wedding, when she discovered he was bisexual. The evenings when she thought he was out visiting art galleries were instead spent on a poorly lit path near Holland Park, a habit he could no longer cover up when a youth who called himself Wayne appeared at their doorstep and demanded money. Patricia had answered the door, listened to his tale, then told him that her husband was too busy in the kitchen to be interrupted, but if Wayne were still standing on her step in thirty seconds, she would go to the kitchen, return with a ceramic blade and cut his balls off herself. It had had the desired effect, Wayne had vanished back into the darker recesses of the night. Patricia, educated by nuns, was the sort of woman through whom the milk of sexual tolerance flowed in only inter-mittent streaks, so that evening she had moved her husband's clothes into the spare room, and thereafter they never slept together or mentioned a word about their sep-arate sex lives.

Yet, in the game of spies that was so often fuelled by suspicion, Felix remained her rock. She could talk to him like no other and his advice, although instinctive rather than informed, was sound, often saving her from her own impulsiveness. And she led her own double life, spending her working week in Brussels while returning to London or their country cottage in the folds of Salisbury Plain most weekends. He never asked what she got up to, which was why she felt so comfortable about sharing – some things, at least.

'What is it?' she asked as he reappeared, wrapped in an apron, bending his back with care to top up her glass.

'Pouilly Fuissé, a big one. Someone from the European Parliament sent it to you in return for a favour. You remember?'

She shook her head distractedly; she did so many favours. 'I wonder what the Prime Minister will be having?'

'Not your favourite man, is he?' Felix said.

'I'm told he starts off his day with a full English, and Marmite spread thick on white toast.'

'Not just the backbone of a Little Englander but the belly, too.'

'Wretched halfwit,' she muttered. She ran her finger around the rim of her glass, it let out a siren's wail; the cat, a Norwegian Forest breed called Freya, stirred in complaint, while Felix perched on the arm of a chair, sensing she wanted to talk.

'He's in a spot of bother,' she mused.

'Serves him right.'

'Could get worse.'

'Which he would also deserve.'

'The question is, Felix, should I make sure of it?'

He paused, considered, his lips pursed. 'Why should you interfere?'

Slowly she raised her eyes from the fire. 'I already have.'

'Why?'

'Why?' She stirred, as though feeling a draught. With abrupt fingers she shoved the cat off her lap; it stalked away, its tail raised in complaint. 'Because,' she said, returning to her theme, 'he's in the way.'

Her husband placed his glass to one side and knelt down awkwardly by the fire. He grabbed a poker, raked the embers, then picked up another log. 'You have to keep feeding a fire, you know, once it's started. Mustn't let it go out.' He dropped the log onto its bed of glowing ash. Vivid red and amber sparks chased each other up the chimney.

—⚏—

Hamish Hague, the *Telegraph*'s Brussels correspondent, had also come home to Britain for Christmas. He was a dour and rotund Scot whose head was flat on top and broad at the chin, as though it had been moulded with a bucket, with wiry grey hair like waves breaking on a shore. He had never been seen dressed in anything other than an ancient and shapeless tweed suit that carried with it the aroma of sweet pipe tobacco, and he walked with the gait of a penguin. He was known as McDeath by wine-swillers throughout Fleet Street, one of the old-timers who sat in the *Telegraph*'s vast open-plan news room and tapped away with two fingers on his keyboard as though he was poking out an alligator's eyes. Now his cheeks were more than usually flushed. He'd been looking forward to a relaxed time out on the moors of Perthshire massacring partridge, but instead found himself upstairs in the overheated office of his editor with the door firmly closed. Montague Strauss was many years younger than his man from Brussels. His dark hair had receded in his twenties, leaving his head looking like a light bulb, and his eyes were too close and bulbous, as though his brain was being pinched. The task given to him by his proprietors was to bring the newspaper up alongside a new generation of readers, but he was experienced enough to recognize there were times, like now, when even he was out of his depth.

'What you're saying, Hamish, is we got it wrong. That it wasn't a bomb.'

'No, what I'm saying is that *you* got it wrong, Monty,' Hamish replied, his soft Lowland accent and steady eyes suggesting that he was not a man to rush to his judgements. 'What I wrote about was a cell of terrorists. You decided it had to be a bomb.'

'You didn't mention a bloody missile.'

'I didn't know about a bloody missile. Which is why I didn't write about it. Or a bomb.'

'So how sure are you of this?' Strauss waved his hand at the screen, where for the last half hour he'd been staring at Hague's latest copy.

He got nothing in reply but a stare of rebuke.

'We'll look bloody fools if—'

'We won't.'

'You going to tell me who your source is?' The fact that he asked rather than demanded made it clear he recognized just how sensitive this was. It also implied that he trusted Hamish.

'Maybe. Out on the moors. Not in here, not with all these glass walls.' Hague knew newspaper offices leaked like sieves. 'There's a night train, if you're interested.'

'Some other time,' the editor snapped. He'd never been nearer a bloodied partridge than a dining table in Hampstead. He also knew the older man was winding him up. Still, he deserved it. He had overplayed the bomb bit. He needed to get this one right.

'You are saying that the plane was shot down by a missile.'

'That's what I've written.'

'Russian,' the editor said, chewing his cheek.

'An SA-24 Igla-S 9K338 portable air-defence missile system. But you can call it a Grinch,' Hamish added doggedly. He knew when to play pedantic. It confused the hell out of whizz-kids who never did much more than scrape the surface of things.

'Photos? Diagrams? The technical shit?'

'All downloadable from Wikipedia.'

Strauss put his feet up on his desk and gazed out of the window, which had one of the meanest views in Westminster. Everything was grey; it was raining. He scratched distractedly at his crotch. 'OK, Hamish, so why should we expect readers to believe this missile theory when two days ago we told them it was a bomb?'

'Because it's not a theory. Because this time you're not going to allow anyone to muck around with my copy behind my back. And because there's more.'

More? Strauss stopped scratching. He twisted around so violently his chair threatened to tip. He was about to shout and thunder that no matter how long Hague had been on the bloody books he wasn't going to screw with him, but then came a flash of understanding, a moment in a younger man's life that would mark the rest of his career as an editor, and possibly pick him out as a great one. He sensed he had to back off, let this cautious old Scotsman play him for a pike, that it didn't matter, so long as he delivered. 'OK. This is your story, Hamish. What have you got?'

'The biggest bit of all.'

'What, bigger than a sodding missile?'

'The terror cell. The guys who fired it.'

'You know . . .?'

The Scot had eyes the colour of autumn hazel; they held the other man, not rushing, not striking too quickly, wanting to make sure he was firmly and inextricably hooked. 'Not the identity, not yet. Just the nationality.' Then he whispered one word. 'Egyptian.'

—✺—

Humiliations, like buses, tend to arrive in quantity.

'I know it's Christmas. I've got my entire family waiting

for me by the fire but I haven't even made it out of my dressing gown. And do you know why? Because you can't track down a single bloody soul who knows a single bloody thing about the story that's over the front of every single bloody newspaper!'

It was unfair. He shouldn't be taking it out on a duty clerk. But it was proving to be one of the most vexed mornings of the Prime Minister's life.

Usher should have been the one to tell the world about the missile. But the AAIB had sent the scrap of aluminium they thought was a missile to a specialist forensic laboratory for testing. They needed to be sure. Yet it was Christmas. The government's own forensic service had been shut down a couple of years before. And this private laboratory would be closed for another two days. So the *Telegraph* got there first and the others rushed in behind it.

Usher had badgered duty officers, press officers, Secretaries of State, even a couple of friendly editors, but only after several hours did he manage to track down the Chief Inspector of the AAIB at his holiday hotel on the Isle of Wight. He had just come back from a bracing walk when the receptionist thrust the telephone at him.

'Have you ... read the news?' the Prime Minister demanded, his exasperation causing him to stutter.

'I've read a deal of speculation,' the CI, Simon Galliani, answered defensively.

'Let's cut through the crap, Mr Galliani. Is it true?'

'Is what true, precisely, Prime Minister?' the other man

answered, lowering his voice and trying to cover the mouthpiece as he looked cautiously around the hotel reception area for potential eavesdroppers.

'Was it a missile?'

Galliani cleared his throat. 'Probably.'

'Probably? What the hell do you mean "probably"? We don't pay you to sit on the bloody fence.'

Galliani braced his back and found himself staring into the eyes of a stuffed moose with a threadbare nose. It's why he liked this place. The old dust. It didn't smell in the least like a laboratory. 'Prime Minister, I am a forensic engineer. It's not a matter of sitting on the fence but of gathering evidence. We are currently waiting on the results of technical analysis.'

'Waiting? *Waiting?*'

Galliani hesitated. This was, after all, the Prime Minister. But he was an engineer, not a moose. He had no intention of being stuffed and mounted. Anyway, he was only a couple of years away from retirement, they couldn't touch him. It was time to kick back. 'Sir, our workload this past financial year rose twelve-point-eight per cent. Yet you cut our budget by more than twenty per cent. Apart from that, it's Christmas. It's also Sunday. Which makes tomorrow a Bank Holiday. When the laboratory opens on Tuesday, and as soon as they are able to confirm any information, I give you my solemn undertaking that you will be the first to know.'

'But the whole world knows!' the Prime Minister all but

shouted. 'Didn't it ever strike you that you should have let someone know?'

'Someone? You mean someone like the Transport Secretary? We phoned and e-mailed her office on Thursday, but – well, I suppose it's Christmas, even in Westminster.'

At the other end of the phone, Usher began to realize he might have mishandled this conversation. He tried to back off. 'Look, I know you understand how important this is. Couldn't you ... just get the laboratory to open, even over the holiday? Get this thing resolved?'

'I'd be more than happy to do that,' Galliani replied, 'if only you would let me.'

'Me?'

'It's a matter of Health & Safety, you see. A wreck is a dangerous environment, carbon-fibre ash, chemical pollution, and always the possibility of blood-borne pathogens. We're required to have adequate staffing levels. Not just a couple of mere lab technicians but there's fire officers, of course, medical support staff, supervisors ...'

'Winston would have wept.'

'Mr Churchill didn't have to deal with EU Working Place directives, working-time limitations, budget restrictions, statutory employment practices.' Galliani found he was rather enjoying himself; above his head, he thought he saw the moose's glass eye wink. 'And if I ordered my staff to return to work I expect we'd be in line for all sorts of claims.'

'Claims?'

'For breaching their human rights.'

'Didn't those little children have human rights, too?'

'I entirely agree, Prime Minister. Perhaps that might have been a point to consider before you let all those EU directives through.'

'But I hate bloody Brussels,' Usher whispered beneath his breath.

'And, of course, if we short-circuited our set procedures, it's probable that as a result any evidence we obtained would be inadmissible in court. Is that what you want?'

'What I want? What *I* want?' He rolled the words around; they left a bitter taste. 'That doesn't seem to matter much any more,' the Prime Minister said softly, replacing the phone.

CHAPTER FOUR

Parliament was recalled. It was the middle of the recess; the elves and goblins weren't supposed to be back from their Christmas break until the second week of January, but this was too important to wait. It caught the system by surprise; there was still scaffolding on one corner of the Commons' Chamber where one of the ancient leaded windows was being refurbished, and no amount of huffing and puffing could persuade the mortar to set more quickly. There was huffing and puffing in every corner, for recesses are rare jewels in the battered crowns of most MPs, and now it had been snatched away. No one could remember anything like it since the House had sat on a Saturday in 1982 during the Falklands War.

But it was necessary. The media speculation had continued to grow, the headlines becoming ever more lurid. Accusations like *'Muslim Missile'* and *'Muslim Murder Squad'* thundered across the front page. Theories were hurled back and forth, often blindly, in the hope that if they kept it up long enough they'd eventually hit a target. But no one doubted it was an Arab plot, because the

Telegraph had said so, and that paper at least seemed to know what it was talking about. On the day of the recall it published further details. The terrorist who led the cell was Abdul Mohammed, his family name was Ghazi; it meant warrior or champion. He had been a conscript during the 1967 Arab–Israeli War, captured by the Israelis and turned fanatical by his appalling treatment, so it was said. Later he had been responsible for any number of indiscriminate atrocities, which ended only when Mubarak's men had dragged him onto their torture tables. The *Telegraph* reported he had lost an eye and, allegedly, a testicle during this time. The tabloid psychoanalysts had a field day with that. His survival was said to be a miracle, his release the result of the revolution of the Arab Spring, and he was now an agent of the Muslim Brotherhood who had come to rule in that blighted country.

The story was all supposition and speculation, there was no firm information to go on, the wonks at MI6 couldn't corroborate it, but neither would they disown it, since no ambitious spy can afford to admit he or she simply doesn't know. Ignorance doesn't read well on the annual assessment. Anyway, McDeath was known to have excellent sources and was considerably more reliable than the mistyped university thesis the British government had downloaded from the Internet and used as a pretext for war in Iraq. So the British government decided to act.

On the morning that Parliament was recalled, the British Foreign Secretary summoned the Egyptian ambassador to

King Charles Street, which runs parallel to Downing Street. As his car slowed to pull into the rear entrance to the building off Horse Guards Road, it was met by a posse of journalists and photographers who shouted questions through the closed car window and snatched photographs, a couple even kicking a side panel under cover of the scrum to see if they could get a snarl or look of alarm. The ambassador, however, remained impassive.

The Ambassadors Door, the discreet entrance into the Foreign & Commonwealth Office used by visiting diplomats, is tucked away at the back of Downing Street where it faces the park. As the Egyptian's car stopped he was met not by the Minister for the Middle East as protocol normally required but by an official, who conducted him to a small lift. The ambassador had a degree in comparative economics from the LSE where in his twenties he had gained a reputation as an irrepressible womanizer, yet the joys of life seemed to have been drained from his face, and despite his proficiency at English he had still brought with him an embassy official to act as an interpreter. They all knew this wasn't going to be fun and he wanted a witness. The lift to the ministerial floor was intensely claustrophobic.

Only once he stepped out of the lift did the Minister appear and offer a formal handshake. Their heels clicked along the mosaic tile of the hallway as they took the brief walk to the office of the Minister's boss, the Secretary of State, which was vast, constructed by Victorians to impress the natives. Gilded frames, heavy oils, cascading red

73

drapes and marble fireplaces, everything else clad in ornately carved dark wood that had been ripped from the forests of Africa. Somewhere near at hand the ambassador could hear the insistent ticking of a clock, even though this was a place that time seemed to have passed by.

'Darius!'

The Foreign Secretary, Andrew Judd, stood in the middle of his office, beaming welcome, but not moving, forcing the ambassador to come to him, even though the Arab was old enough to be his father. 'How are you? And how's that son of yours? Following proudly in his father's footsteps at the LSE, so I'm told.' And so that the Egyptian remembered they were keeping a watch on his son, too.

'As-salamu alaykum,' the Egyptian replied. Arabic. He wasn't going to make this easy.

'May peace be with us both, Darius.' The Englishman's greeting was cautious as he showed his guest to one of the pair of deep leather chairs by the fireplace. The Arab paused as he passed an old globe adorned with names like Siam and Persia and the Gold Coast, and so much of it splashed in red. His finger came to rest on his own country, also in imperial red. He muttered something; his eyes came up to meet those of the Foreign Secretary, and he stared. They were remorseless eyes, drenched in accusation.

And privately, inside, the Foreign Secretary flogged himself; this was his meeting, yet already he'd lost control of it.

The ambassador muttered something in his low, guttural voice: 'The world has moved on,' the interpreter translated.

Then the ambassador took his chair, while Judd took the other, its back to the window. It meant that he would be in silhouette, his face hard to read, while the visitor's face was laid bare to the weak winter sun, a game as old as empire that would show up every smile, inflexion, grimace or nervous tic. But the Arab was an old hand, he offered not a flicker.

Then the démarche began, any pretence of friendship pushed to one side and no tea.

'Your Excellency,' the Foreign Secretary began, 'I wish to read a statement that Her Majesty's government intends to publish later today, and I would be grateful for any comments you might have on it.'

A secretary handed him a single sheet; the ambassador's interpreter drew close to hover behind him.

The Foreign Secretary cleared his throat and began to read out loud. 'Following the tragic loss of Speedbird 235 and the lives of all the one hundred and fifteen passengers and crew on board, it has become clear that this was not an accident. In these circumstances it is the clear purpose of Her Majesty's government to establish the full facts of this murderous act. It will then be our duty to identify its perpetrators, and to see them,' – he raised an eyebrow – 'and all who have given them succour, suitably punished.'

He paused as the interpreter gabbled softly in the ambassador's ear; the ambassador continued to stare fixedly at his accuser, he didn't even blink.

'In light of widely circulating reports that the

perpetrators have links to Egypt, we call on the Egyptian government...' The language was formal and stuffy, but as he continued its meaning rang out simple and clear. The Egyptians had to hand over the suspects immediately or face massive retribution that might include but would not necessarily be limited to the slaughter of all Egyptian first-born. When the Foreign Secretary had finished he handed the sheet back to his assistant, who handed it to the ambassador. Still the eyes didn't flicker; he took the sheet and slowly, defiantly, throttled it in his fist.

The Foreign Secretary's tongue ran around the inside of his cheeks, as though to make sure no other unpleasantries were lurking there. 'May I ask, have you any comments?'

Only now did the Arab's face betray emotion. '*Zeft!*' he spat.

Behind him, the translator cleared his throat nervously. 'The ambassador says that these charges and insinuations are...' He hesitated. He couldn't possibly repeat what the ambassador had said. So he reinterpreted, heavily. 'He says they are rubbish.'

Everyone knew the language had been far more colourful and crude, but even during a démarche there are some niceties to be observed.

The ambassador waved the sheet of paper, now a crumpled mass in his right hand. Only now did he use English. 'These are lies. May you choke on them.'

With that he rose and left. The confrontation had lasted less than two minutes.

—∾—

When, barely an hour later, the Prime Minister arrived at the Dispatch Box in the House of Commons, the chamber was packed. MPs squeezed shoulder to shoulder on the green leather benches, others were squatting on the floor of the gangways, with an overflow of members left standing at either end. Many still bore the blush of the ski slope or beach from which they had been dragged, but almost all had come. It was an election year, there was only one story in town, and they needed to be part of it.

The Speaker, seated in his chair, cast around as he tried to get the measure of them. This place had a mood of its own, its currents swirling and unpredictable, and this moment was unique. 'Order! Order!' The familiar cry rang out. 'The Prime Minister.' The words cut through the hubbub and the House fell to silence as Usher rose to his feet. The silence that enveloped him was not a silence of subservience but more one of suspicion; they sensed he was no longer in control, demanded that he reassert his authority, bring the circus back to order, before the tigers ran loose.

He opened the folder in front of him, clutched the sides of the Dispatch Box, prayed that the dark tie and sombre brow betrayed none of the anxieties inside. He had spent the previous night and the entire morning working on the speech he was about to make, refining its words, testing their meaning, all the time growing ever more aware just how thin it was. The humiliation that had been showered upon him during his conversation with the stroppy sod from AAIB had at least been a private affair. Now he was standing on the most public stage of all. He had often wondered why the leather of the Dispatch Box became so worn; now, and to his surprise, he found his hands sliding back and forth, back and forth, like a mountaineer searching for a grip.

'Mr Speaker,' he began, 'the loss of Speedbird 235 was a national catastrophe. My first duty is to convey to the families of the victims who died on board the profound sympathies of this House. Rarely has a Prime Minister had to answer for a disaster so widespread and of such profound consequence . . .' And he was off. The sympathy was easy, and entirely sincere. Then he took a deep breath.

'Mr Speaker, this was no accident. On the basis of evidence that has now been confirmed by the Air Accident Investigation Branch only a few hours ago, I can tell the House that Speedbird 235 was shot from the skies by a missile.'

A low growl of anger ran through the ranks. It was the first time matters had moved from speculation to confirmation. Even those who had bent their backs in order to listen through the speakers embedded in the leather benches now sat upright.

'The preliminary indications are that the missile was a Russian-made surface to air weapon, an SA-24 more commonly known as a Grinch. These weapons are available on the black market and there is nothing to suggest that Russia is in any way involved in this act of terrorism.'

He looked up from his script, his eyes roving around the House, meeting their challenge. 'However, we have not been able to eliminate the suggestion of Egyptian involvement. This morning, the Egyptian ambassador was summoned to the Foreign Office ...' And with that, the emotions, like the first clouds of the monsoon, began to gather and the skies to darken. There was nothing new in any of it, they'd read it all in the *Telegraph* and seen it on SKY, and Usher had to struggle against their impatience, at times raising his voice. Beneath the jacket, his shirt was soaked in sweat, it restricted him, distracted him, kept him from his best. He felt a deep sense of emptiness as at last he worked his way towards his conclusion, and the words that had seemed so fine and heartfelt last night in draft, began to ring in his ears like the oldest clichés. 'Mr Speaker, I understand the intense anger ... I share the feelings ... We will not tolerate ... And as I said when this tragedy first struck, we will discover what happened, and who was responsible. We will not rest, we shall not tire, until justice is done. Whoever was responsible dare not sleep soundly in their beds tonight, or any night, for we are on their trail. We will catch them. And in the name of justice, they will suffer the consequences of their evil.'

At last he let go of the Dispatch Box and sank back in his seat. The moment was over. It wasn't bad but neither had it been great. His fate now lay in the hands of others. Dave Murray, the Leader of the Opposition, was young, new in post and relatively callow, a man not renowned for his skill with the rapier, but he didn't need it. He'd been handed a battleaxe. No matter how loosely he swung it, he couldn't fail to find the target. He knew he mustn't turn this into a party political battle, that wasn't appropriate, not yet, with tragedy still so fresh in the air. But, as the Prime Minister had said, it was never too early to point the finger of blame and identify those who were responsible.

So he thanked the Prime Minister for recalling Parliament, joined with the Prime Minister in expressing sympathy, was as one with him in denouncing the outrage. 'I have only one difficulty with the Prime Minister's position,' he declared, 'which is this. He is the Prime Minister, yet he always seems to be the last to know.' Murray held up his hand to stifle the indignation he knew his words would unleash. 'Was it the fault of the Prime Minister that he couldn't be at his desk to deal with this atrocity when it first occurred? No. But surely, in the days since then, he was duty bound to handle it with competence and clarity. The families of the victims deserve nothing less. We deserve nothing less.'

Usher's supporters began to howl, their jeers blown back by the Opposition benches. Murray threw up both hands, waved them, calmed them, bringing them back to order. He was turning out to be something of an actor. 'The other day,' he continued, 'the Prime Minister declared that there was no bomb. He got his press spokesman to denounce the suggestion. Yet today he tells us it was a bomb – a flying bomb, a missile. At last it seems the Prime Minister has got round to reading the newspapers, too.'

It was outrageous stuff, considering the gravity of the cause, but an election was looming and good taste had never stuffed a ballot box. The noise on all sides was deafening, and this time he didn't try to stem it. His cheeks were flushed, he was nodding his head like a rabbi at his Wailing Wall, until at last the House fell silent again. That took some time, but they all wanted to hear, wondering how far he dare go.

'The Prime Minister says that he doesn't yet know who is responsible, but that he will not rest until they have been identified. That they dare not sleep soundly in their beds tonight. Has the Prime Minister, even once, even for the briefest moment, considered his own responsibility? Will he be able to sleep soundly in *his* bed tonight?'

And that was it. He had done his job; Usher's humiliation was complete and made public. The Prime Minister didn't join in the floodtide of objection that burst around him. He sat in his seat, his face fixed, pretending not to mind. As he gazed around the chamber, his eye settled on the crests that ran along the wall, each one marking a Member of the House who had given his life on active duty. He found himself a little envious. None of them had been slowly strangled to death.

From above, Patricia Vaine looked down upon the Prime Minister's sea of troubles and discovered something new within herself. She was seated in the private gallery to which, as a senior official of the European Union, she had a right of access, a privilege recently granted throughout all the Parliaments of the EU. She found the atmosphere intoxicating. Information was a weapon, and she controlled it. The sensation was almost sexual, and perhaps even better than that, for the victim was a man she loathed. Usher was a typical English xenophobe, a Wogs-begin-at-Calais sort, a man with his arse stuck in the eighteenth century.

She had begun a game of unexpected consequences, one of which had proved to be Usher's discomfort. It was right that he should suffer. And, as she sat watching Order Papers being waved like the sails of capsizing boats, she thought it was right that he should suffer a little more.

In fact, he should go, be removed from the scene, like a car that had crashed and was obstructing the middle of a motorway. And she could do that, make sure it happened. She thought about it. She had the power to move history forward. It made her tremble from deep inside, like only a woman can.

—⁓—

'How was Christmas?'

'Fine,' Jemma lied. She'd wanted to be with Harry, was angry he hadn't made it possible.

'I missed you,' he said, and with such conviction that in a breath he blew away all her irritation. She didn't know how he had spent Christmas, didn't want to give him the impression that she cared enough to ask but, with those three words from him, her decision to give him a hard time was abandoned. She threw herself on him, and didn't release him until they were both sweating, naked and spent. Then she fell asleep.

When she woke she found Harry staring into the distance with that other-world look on his face. 'Where are you, darling?' It was the first time she had called him that; he didn't flinch, didn't even seem to notice.

'The Prime Minister had a terrible time this afternoon.'

She nestled back into his arm. 'Did he deserve it?'

'Probably not.'

'So how much trouble is he in?'

'If the election were four days away he'd be dead. But it's four months.' A hesitation. 'He'll be fine.'

'And you?'

'There's always the cock-up theory, it's one of the most violent forces known to nature, but I have the good fortune to represent the sixty-fourth safest seat in the country. Losing that would be as likely as ...' He stretched for a simile.

'Losing your innocence?'

He chuckled. 'Ah, my innocence. Is that why you like me?'

'I don't like you, Harry, I love you.'

It had slipped out. And Harry wasn't laughing any more.

'Shit, I didn't mean to say that,' she muttered hurriedly, biting her knuckle.

His fingers had been lying distractedly on her breast. Now he took her hand and squeezed it gently. 'Jemma, the next four months are going to be frantic. Election campaigns – they're like sitting in a bathtub of leeches, wondering where the bastards are going to go for you next.'

'I see.'

'Personal life on hold, everything on short notice, liable to cancellation.'

'Understood,' she whispered.

'So . . .'

'So.'

'Why not move a few things in. You know, clothes and stuff. In case I have to leave you stranded for a while.'

Shit, he hadn't meant to say that . . .

There was, of course, still much that needed to be sorted. A relationship couldn't hang on little more than a couple of coat hangers. So the following morning it was Jemma who sneaked out of bed first and began making coffee in the kitchen. She thought she might surprise him until the newspapers fell with a thump on the doormat. He was barely awake when she came back into the bedroom, bearing a tray piled high with coffee and pancakes, and the newspapers slipping from beneath her arm. He didn't make a grab for them, but she knew his restraint was only out of politeness. He was a political animal, she mustn't get in his way, yet she knew she couldn't allow herself to be left behind, either. Her eyes ran across the front pages as they fluttered onto the duvet. Almost all of them featured the Egyptian connection, and set about trying to inflame it. As she shuffled through them, each headline seemed more provocative than the last.

She chewed at her knuckle once again. 'I know you'll only call me a stupid woman, but – tell me, Harry, why would the Egyptians want to shoot down a planeload of kids?'

He stirred, rolled towards her, thumbed his eye to rub the night from it, thumped a pillow into shape. 'Well, it's because ...' Then he stopped. The reason was so glib, so simple. So blind. The Muslim Brotherhood resented the Americans for any number of reasons – because of their cultural arrogance, their constant interference, for cutting off the aid programmes, banning sporting visits, for their links with Israel. But was any of that, even all of that, enough to get them into the business of mass murder? They were angry, sure, but insane? He sat up in bed with a jerk that spilled the coffee into the tray. Despite all the angry words, and no matter which way he twisted and turned things over in his mind, he couldn't see it. Suddenly it made no more sense to him than it did to Jemma.

CHAPTER FIVE

Few things are as certain in life as the fact that Christmas is followed by New Year, and that bugger all happens in-between. The Junior Sergeant of the local militia who had made the initial inspection of the burnt-out huts north of Makhachkala had been instructed by his captain to take another look. There had been some confusing nonsense about a request from the Environment Commission in Brussels. It didn't seem to be that urgent or important, and anyway Anatoly, the Junior Sergeant, had precious little idea who or where Brussels was, or why anyone should be bothering about a mess of scorched paper and melted plastic, so he took his time. Anyway, it was snowing.

When at last he decided he could delay no longer, he drove north along the P215 road, turning off after a few miles short of the village of Sulak along a frost-filled track that threatened to shake the fillings from his teeth. The heater wasn't working, a problem that might have been connected to the three rusty bullet holes that decorated the bonnet of the Lada, and he had difficulty steering with one hand as he tried to keep the windscreen clear with his other. He followed the track to the point where it petered out just short of the shore, still fifty metres short of the flattened carcasses of the huts. He lit a foul-smelling cigarette, scratched himself, took his time. When at last he wandered over through the fresh fall of snow, he found even less than on his first visit. The bitter winds of winter had scattered much of the cinders and ash, and what little paperwork had survived the original fire would by now be floating somewhere in the Caspian. And, so it seemed to Anatoly, what remained of the wreckage had been systematically ransacked so that nothing remained. Hyenas, he guessed. Human hyenas. But there were plenty of those in these parts.

He stopped to urinate in the fresh snow, but it was too cold even for that. He lit another cigarette, climbed back into the Lada and wearily pointed it back down the track.

—⌇—

COBRA. In a land ruled by acronyms, this was one of the oldest. The Cabinet Office Briefing Room, an underground haven beneath Whitehall where the country's leaders went to sort out shit. At least, that was the theory, but it wasn't working.

The Prime Minister knew how badly he'd been beaten up at the Dispatch Box on the previous day, and it was time to reassert his authority. Or so he had planned. He gazed around the briefing table with its computer screens and microphones, the seats filled with senior ministers, defence chiefs and intelligence officers, two very senior policemen, yet not a single eye was engaging him, except for the Justice Secretary who was alleged to keep a notoriously irreverent diary that painted wicked caricatures, every indiscretion, every infidelity, including his own. 'Who screwed who. And how,' as he had once explained to an attractive female journalist. Rumour was that he planned to publish it as soon as he left the Cabinet, which was perhaps the only reason he'd been left to hang on in there so long.

'Well, can you help us hobble through this one?' Usher asked, glowering through his glasses at the Transport Secretary as he called the meeting to order. She'd returned from Verbier, on sticks, with her ankle in a surgical boot. She didn't rise to his bait but instead bent over her briefing folder, hiding the resentment in her eyes.

'Prime Minister, my officials at AAIB are still conducting their investigations, but I have their preliminary report.'

It was a mistake, thought Usher, for her to claim close personal ownership of characters who had sat on their arses all over Christmas and done little but quote EU directives at him.

'I can confirm that Speedbird 235 was struck by a surface-to-air missile of Russian manufacture, designated . . .'

Even as she read out the words, Usher began to tap the table in impatience. How long would he have to wait until he heard something he hadn't already read in the bloody

Telegraph? Now she was droning on about the missile's operational ceiling, something else he'd seen in the newspapers.

'... which means it was operating close to its maximum range. This might explain why it failed to explode. It struck the port engine, which immediately disintegrated, throwing parts of both the engine and the missile into the section of the plane containing the hydraulic system ...'

She tapped the computer screen. Diagram followed photograph as they relived the aircraft's last moments.

'Tracking back from the point at which the missile hit and they lost the engine, and using the angle of impact, we can pinpoint with a fair degree of precision the location from where the attack was launched ...'

Now this was something new. A map of the North Sea appeared on the screen, with British and continental coasts clearly marked.

'Approximately – there.' She placed a finger on the screen and a red dot appeared in the vast stretches of water. 'A ship or boat, of course. Or submarine, I suppose that's a possibility, but most likely a surface vessel. Probably something as simple as a small fishing boat.'

Usher glowered at the red dot. It was some thirty miles east of the tip of Kent, and not much further from the coasts of France, Belgium and Holland. 'So it could have come from ...'

'Almost anywhere.'

'But surely we can do better than that. We track every

ship or boat on the planet – or at least through the Channel.'

'We track every *transponder*,' the Transport Secretary emphasized. 'They probably didn't have one. Or switched it off.'

'But, but ...' He was beginning to splutter with exasperation. 'Next to the American President's bathtub the Channel is the most heavily monitored stretch of water in the world.'

'Yes, that's true. Up to a point.'

'Which point?'

She touched the screen again, and a line appeared that stretched from the eastern tip of Kent to France. The red dot hovered tantalizingly – several miles beyond its northern limit.

'You're kidding me,' Usher whispered, incredulous.

No one came to his rescue.

'You're trying to tell me that no one noticed a missile strike on a passenger aircraft that killed one hundred and fifteen people!' His fist pounded the table in frustration. 'Surely the coastguard—'

'As you will be aware, Prime Minister, we reorganized the coastguard service three years ago ...'

Cuts. Bloody cuts. And he was bleeding to death. He looked around the table, caught the eye of the Chief of the Defence Staff, was about to insist that some military radar must have seen something, but didn't. They'd cut the military to ribbons, too, aircraft carriers that had no aircraft, soldiers who had no boots. Around the room there was silence, except for the scratching of the Home Secretary's pen.

—w—

'You'd better come along,' Harry said to Jemma a couple of days after the New Year.

'Where?'

'Man with the shaggy dog.'

She didn't enquire further. If he was willing to include her, she was happy to scrub up or strip off as appropriate. It wasn't every day that a primary school teacher from Notting Hill got the millionaire treatment. Yet she couldn't pretend to be anything other than under-whelmed when they arrived at their destination, the Two Chairmen pub in Westminster's Old Queen Street. It was entirely presentable but scarcely the Ritz. And they stood outside.

They had come to meet Hamish Hague – McDeath. He and Harry had bumped into each other over the years but didn't know each other well, and the journalist was on his way back to Brussels, short of time, which was why he had suggested this watering hole midway between the Parliament building and the *Telegraph* office in Victoria Street. And they chose to stand outside because there were too many ears within, wrapping themselves against an erratic breeze as they rested their drinks on a polished brass windowsill.

'Thanks for sparing the time,' Harry said. 'I know how busy you must be.'

'Pillar to post, and all the way back again,' the newspaperman said, although his tone remained unhurried. He was not a man to rush.

'To your Pulitzer,' Harry continued, taking the head off his beer.

Hamish nodded in gratitude. 'I don't expect prizes, but perhaps my expenses won't be questioned with quite such anal intensity, for a while, at least.' He sipped at his whisky. 'But if that's the reason why you've asked me here, Harry, I'm afraid you'll be disappointed. I can't tell you any more than what I've been telling the Metropolitan Police and the security services.'

'Which is?'

'I have to protect my sources. You know that.' He gazed across the top of his glass with enquiring eyes. 'Anyway, what's your interest in all this?'

'A hundred and fifteen people died, Hamish.'

'And there's not a moment when I can forget it. I'm a grandfather myself and, dear God, I feel for those parents. But if I embarrass my sources I'll get nothing more, and then the rest of you will get nothing more, either.'

'So we can expect more,' Jemma suddenly intervened. Both men turned to stare at her. 'Oops, sorry. I'm supposed to be the wallflower or something, aren't I?' She looked awkward and tried to retreat from the cold breeze inside her overcoat.

The journalist shrugged, not offended but non-committal. 'Who can tell? We're dealing in some pretty dark places.'

It was Harry's turn. 'Then just one question, if I may, Hamish.'

'Asking is free.'

'Abdul Mohammed.'

'Ah, the one-eyed, one-balled bastard.'

'You're sure it's him?'

'Otherwise I wouldn't have printed it.'

'And his connection with the Egyptian government.'

'Now that's a bit beyond my pay grade.'

'But the press has been full of it. They've even suggested—'

The journalist cut him off with a scowl. 'I'm not responsible for what appears in the tabloids.'

'Is anyone?'

'Hasn't stopped your lot straining at the leash.'

'My lot?'

'The government. The Foreign Office. All this talk of sanctions and embargoes.'

It was Harry's turn to frown. 'That's what's got me puzzled, too. The connection between our Abdul and the Egyptian government.'

The Scotsman sipped cautiously. 'Is there a connection? I've never said so.'

'But what do you think?'

'I don't know, Harry,' he said doggedly.

'They can't just be making it up.'

Hamish smirked and Harry felt just a little foolish. Governments made things up all the time.

'Maybe they know more than I do,' the Scot added. 'Or maybe they're just terrified of being left behind. Anyway, one dead Arab is as good as another, isn't that the way it goes?'

Harry wanted to deny it, to reject the cynicism, but when had cynicism ever let him down? He'd fought in the First Gulf War, with scars and medals to show for it, but had been in Parliament by the time of the second, thank goodness, because he would have had problems obeying orders to go in for that one. They'd invaded Iraq, with all the horrors that were to follow, because some other Arab had flown airplanes into the Twin Towers. That, and because it had oil. Then they'd picked on Libya to invade, because that had oil, too. As Harry had said in the debate, much to the displeasure of his political masters, if only the West had loved oil a little less and understood the Arab a little more, the world might have turned a little more slowly.

So was it all happening again? The Arab, any Arab, as the whipping boy? He needed to think this through. 'Let me get you another,' he suggested.

The Scot glanced at his watch. 'If you insist. I can manage a quick one.'

Harry, with a troubled expression, disappeared inside, leaving Jemma and the journalist on their own. For a moment she was awkward, feeling out of her depth in this murky world. She smiled coyly and allowed her coat to fall open. Teeth and tits, rarely failed, and she could see he'd noticed. 'Doesn't your wife get tired of you running all over the world, Mr Hague?'

He laughed. 'She'll be tired enough of me when I retire. Only a couple of years.' His old eyes smiled kindly. 'You two been going out long?'

'No, just a very little while.'

'He likes you.'

'Really?'

'Trust me. A lot.'

She blushed in thanks. 'Did you ... I mean, I don't know, shouldn't ask, but ...' She trailed off, unable to complete the question.

He came to her rescue. 'Did I know either of his wives?'

Her blush deepened, but he shook his head. 'I don't know Harry that well.'

'I suppose with all your charging around ...'

'Me? No' me, lassie. London to Brussels, Brussels to London. That's been my life these last fifteen years, and not even enough time to spend the air miles.'

'But ... your nickname. They call you McDeath. I rather imagined you in all sorts of dark places up to your derring-do.'

The overtones of Edinburgh were growing stronger in her voice, and his face creased into a conspiratorial smile. 'Aye, that might be what I tell my grandchildren, but you don't get this' – he patted his extended stomach –'climbing anything much higher than a Brussels bar stool.'

'Oh, dear,' she sighed in disappointment. 'And there was me with this image of you riding camels past the pyramids or battling your way up the Nile fighting off crocodiles.'

'I've never been, probably never will. Only sand trap I ever want to find myself in is on a golf course.'

They laughed, two Scots playing away from home, as a motorcycle courier approached and roared past them, its throaty exhaust echoing back from the dark bricks of the Queen Anne terrace. As the noise receded, Harry re-emerged clutching fresh drinks. Hamish took his whisky, stared at his watch yet again, and drank hurriedly. 'I feel I've taken your hospitality under false pretences, Harry,' he apologized. 'I really must be rushing. Forgive me.' He finished the last drop of whisky and smiled at Jemma. 'It's been a pleasure meeting you, young lady.'

'Say hello to Mrs Hague, if ever you get off your plane,' Jemma said.

'I'll be sure to.' And he was gone.

They watched as the shambling figure of the Scot in a flapping raincoat retreated down the street.

'Sorry,' Harry said, 'rather a waste of time.'

'Was it?'

'Total.'

'I'm not so sure.' Her voice was soft, tantalizing. 'I think I can help you.'

'Really?'

Her chin came up in defiance. 'Oh, don't you go

dismissing me as just a silly girl, Jones. That was his mistake.'

'What do you mean?'

'Look at him,' she demanded, just as the rotund journalist finally disappeared from sight. 'Not the leanest of hunters, is he? Not exactly Woodward or Bernstein.'

'So?'

'He's only giving out what he's being fed.'

'I agree.'

'Which means that it's his source who is important.'

'And he's no more likely to give us that than to sell his grandchildren.'

'Then again . . .' She smiled coquettishly. 'What's in it for me?'

'What's your price?'

'Venice,' she replied immediately.

'This had better be worth my while.'

'Take me to Venice, Harry, and I guarantee to make it worth your while.'

'Great, but I can't wait till Venice.'

'That's your trouble, Harry, always in a hurry. Just like last night.'

'Jemma, dammit, I'll—'

'Brussels.'

'What?'

'Whoever he's getting it from, it has to be in Brussels.'

'How do you know?'

'He doesn't go anywhere else.'

'But . . .'

'Brussels,' she whispered. 'Trust me.' She took him by the arm and began leading him down the street. 'You know, if you stopped rushing things, Harry, there's no telling how far you might get.'

—⟋⟍—

The hedgerows were hung with berries covered in hoar frost that sparkled exquisitely in the sunlight like precious stones. Underfoot the snow was covered with a thick crust of ice, and at every step their boots hesitated before breaking through to the firmer ground beneath. Felix Wilton followed behind his wife, along the track through the fields, treading in her footsteps. It would be their last outing before Patricia returned to Brussels, and she was lost in thought, her head bowed, heedless of the endless views across Wiltshire on such a crystal-crisp day. There was no sound, except for their footfall. In a few weeks, when the thaw had arrived, the hedgerows would fill with life once more, but for now Felix and his wife were wrapped in a world of white silence.

They walked for several miles, in tandem, no words, the shadows lengthening, before they came to a farmer's metal gate in a field above their cottage. Only then did he draw alongside her to open it. 'Will you want rice or potatoes with your salmon?' he asked, thinking ahead, his words emerging in clouds of frost.

She said nothing, walked through the gate he held open.

'Rice, then,' he muttered.

'Sorry?' She looked up, puzzled.

'Nothing.' She was in another world, and he had learned not to be jealous. She'd been distracted these last few days, withdrawn, sombre, but he hadn't complained, knew both her job and her ambition were reaching more difficult ground.

'Sorry,' she repeated, this time meaning it. 'It's simply ... I have this problem.'

'Does this problem have a name?'

'Harry Jones.'

'Ah, the politician.'

She'd been worrying about it ever since Hamish had told her of the drink, and the digging. 'He's asking questions.'

'And that is a problem?'

'It's a bit like someone continuously opening the oven door to find out how the soufflé is doing.'

'Aggravating.'

'Intensely. Could ruin things.'

The gate was complaining as it swung to on frozen hinges.

'What do you think I should do, Felix?' she asked, grasping the gate, needing to make up her mind before they moved on. His hand came and covered hers. While they never slept with each other they would still touch, share moments of intimacy, like this.

'I know what I would do if it were my kitchen, Patricia,' he said.

'Tell me. I need to know. It's important.'

'I'd slam his bloody fingers in the oven door.'

With a jerk he forced the metal gate back into its place. The lock snapped shut, raising a clatter of complaint that rang in their ears. They said nothing more, walking back in silence to their door.

—〰—

At the moment Felix Wilton was scurrying around his kitchen to prepare toasted tea cake and coffee for his wife, Harry was settling back in the warm embrace of his bath. He stretched his legs, easing the creases of an afternoon spent bent over his desk.

'You keep your toes to yourself,' Jemma instructed from the other end of the bath.

Instead of heeding the warning he tickled her, and what had been a gentle moment cascaded into squeals of outrage and much splashing.

'What am I going to do with you?' he asked carelessly when at last a measure of order had been restored in the bathtub.

'I was rather hoping you might let me help you with your election campaign,' she said. His entire afternoon had been taken up with constituency correspondence and he hadn't even started the process of culling the hundreds of e-mails that had accumulated since he'd last opened his parliamentary account a few days previously.

'No secret I could do with more help,' he muttered.

'Since the air crash the atmosphere's turned, gone sour, our people are sitting on their hands. It was all looking so comfortable just a couple of weeks ago.' He would be fine, of course, with his thumping majority, but suddenly the polls – and his nose – were telling him that the government could be in for one hell of a fight. Still, plenty of time to go.

'I'd love to help, Harry, if you'd let me. Weekends, and then there's the Easter holidays.'

'You'd give that up for me?'

'Yes.'

It would change things. Jemma would be introduced to his constituents, be seen at his side, the two of them a public item. It had been a long time since there had been anyone to join him on the campaign trail. Perhaps it was too early.

'Elections are bloody hard work,' he said.

'Try teaching a classroom of five-year-olds.'

'You offering to iron my shirts?'

'I'm offering to pick them up from the laundry.'

'It would mean very little sleep.'

'What, more rushed sex?'

'A million sandwiches to make.'

'So long as you let me make you breakfast first.'

Damn, but she was good at this game. 'Then I accept your offer, Miss Laing. Frankly, at the moment, I need all the help I can get.'

'I'm all yours,' she whispered, her eyes suddenly serious.

They stopped the banter, beyond it now. He turned the tap for more hot water, wanting to prolong the moment, and the suds, suddenly refreshed, clung gently around her breasts. He stared, provocatively, but when he raised his eyes he found her thoughts elsewhere, a shadow across her face. 'Already going off the idea?' he asked.

'What?'

'Come back to me, Jem.'

'Sorry, I was thinking ... you know, those kids. And the more I think about them, the less I understand it all.'

'Me, too.'

'What would be the point of blowing them out of the sky? No one's claimed responsibility – isn't that what usually happens, try to humiliate the enemy, announce that it's all been done in retaliation for some other massacre of innocents? But there's been nothing. Except for a finger pointed at the Egyptians, and it's been a pretty wobbly finger, to my mind. Maybe I've got it all wrong.'

Harry sank back into the bath, allowing his muscles to relax and his thoughts to float free as the water rippled across his face, until suddenly he grabbed the taps and hauled himself back up with an urgency that sent waves of suds lapping over the sides. 'Maybe we all got it wrong, Jem. Maybe we've been climbing up a slope that leads nowhere. We keep talking about the kids. But what if it was nothing to do with them?'

'Then, why – who?'

'Somebody else on board, perhaps.'

'Who else was on board?'

'I've absolutely no idea. But I think I know someone who might.' He stretched out from the bath to retrieve his phone from beside the basin and began fumbling with it. He punched a number and, when it had been answered, asked for the Police Casualty Bureau. 'Shelagh – that you? Harry here,' he began. 'No, I'm not in a sewer, I'm in my bath.'

There was a silence as he listened to the voice at the other end; Jemma thought his jaw stiffened, trying to give nothing away – which meant there probably was something, so far as Shelagh was concerned.

'That would be great, I'd love to catch up, it's been too long, but in the meantime I need one small favour. Yes, OK, another small favour. The Speedbird crash. Can you let me have a full passenger list? No, not the one you've published, I need names, dates of birth, sex, addresses, nationalities, whatever you've got. Why? Because you know I'm curious about all sorts of things.' The voice had dropped and the jaw twitched. 'Yes. You, too. And thanks.'

When the call had finished he spent a few moments lost in thought, gazing at the phone.

'You take that bloody thing everywhere,' she said, feeling an unexpected flush of jealousy. It often rang at some extraordinarily inconvenient moments, could play hell with a girl's concentration.

'It has everything in here,' he said, waving it, 'my entire life.'

'Your entire *past* life. Sometimes I wish you'd drop it in the water.'

'Oh, I don't know, Jem, it has its uses.' He turned the phone to show her the screen. He'd taken a photograph of her in the bath. 'You know, if I stuck that on my election literature, I reckon I'd be home in a landslide.'

CHAPTER SIX

Patricia Vaine looked out of the window of the Eurostar at the flat, dreary countryside of northern France, a desolate landscape to which no one had ever paid the slightest attention, except when there had been a war. Nothing to inspire, nothing to write about, except for what it no longer was – a battlefield. And that was the point, wasn't it? The guns had been silenced, the slaughter brought to an end. One community built from so many dissident, fractious parts. If the wars that had been fought across these fields had been worth so much sacrifice, surely the peace that had replaced them was worth just a little, too? The growing pains of the great European adventure, Felix had said, and her thoughts turned to Harry Jones. A growing pain. Bloody man. She switched off the vanity light and closed her eyes, listening to the thrumming of the wheels on the rails, hoping it would soothe her troubled thoughts. She could no longer ignore him. He was becoming a pest. First Hamish Hague, now his request for the passenger manifest. That was the crucial moment, the point of no return. She didn't think he would be able to piece together the fragments, but she was no longer sure, and she couldn't take the risk.

Intelligence agencies can never be mere observers. While they watch events, they inevitably get drawn into shaping them, too, which made it inevitable that once Vaine had begun rocking Usher's boat, she wouldn't be able to stop. Once the poison had begun circulating around the system, it would carry on, until the end. But now there was Harry Jones, too. He was a different problem. Dealing with Usher was akin to bombarding a castle, you couldn't miss if you had the right weapons, but with Jones it was more like targeting a single soldier within the walls. Her aim needed to be more precise, more clinical, and she hadn't the experience. It was experience she would have to get.

She was still tussling with the problem when she arrived back at her house in Rue Faider, a narrow, four-storey town house that she had bought in dilapidated state for a song and had refurbished into an elegant and exceptional home – her home. She shared it with no one, not even Felix, although his expertise in the antiques world had been responsible for loading the high walls with a kaleidoscope of gilded mirrors, oils, portraits and tapestries that would have done grace to any minor museum. The windows were large, the light gentle, the furniture mostly French, the atmosphere heavy, and in the summer she could catch the scent of sweet honeysuckle that crept in from the small garden. She was preparing herself a lean and lonely dinner when there was a knock at the door. She was startled when she opened it to find a chauffeur at the door, standing in the rain. Behind him, in the back seat of a black Mercedes limousine, sat the Energy Commissioner, a German, Albrecht Genscher. When they had first met he had tried to hit on her, but he was round and fleshy, not her type, and she rarely sold her favours for simple pleasure any more. There were plenty of opportunities, of course, particularly in this capital of exiles, where men took her natural coolness for English allure, and didn't call her Pat or Patsy but by her full name, Patricia, which sounded all the more elegant for their drawn-out vowels. It was here and for the first time in her life that she had learned to use her sex, to dangle it as bait, although rarely to surrender it. She had slept with only three men since her arrival, on each occasion for professional purposes, men who could help her up the ladder as easily as they had slipped her out of her Max Mara dresses. In any event, the crease of concern across Genscher's florid forehead suggested he had other things on his mind.

'Patricia' – he pronounced it Patreezia – 'may I?' he asked through the open car window.

Soon they were sitting in her study, before the ornate marble fireplace with its nineteenth-century clock on the mantel, with substantial glasses of wine and smoke from their cigarettes trailing up to the high ceiling.

'Patreezia, I am sorry to intrude but I have a problem,' the German began.

'Then *we* have a problem, Albrecht,' she said softly, crossing her ankles, and making sure he noticed.

He nodded in gratitude. 'It is the pipeline.'

He didn't need to be specific. The Babylon pipeline was the project on which he had staked his reputation, a pipeline that once it was built would guarantee for a generation supplies of gas to Europe from the new republics of central Asia and put to flight those doom mongers who predicted that within five years much of Europe would freeze. Its potential was fabulous, and so was its cost.

'The contracts are prepared, everything is ready, everyone wants to sign. It will transform our future. But ...' He sighed. 'We have encountered a little local difficulty.'

'Of course, Albrecht. Otherwise you wouldn't be here.'

'The final piece of the jigsaw are the environmental approvals. You know what it's like. We have to certify that construction of the pipeline will not do damage.'

'"It is our duty to set the standards, not just for the continent of Europe but in all the corners of the world",' she declaimed with only a hint of mockery, reciting a phrase that their Finnish colleague Illka Lappi, the Environment Commissioner, was fond of preaching.

Genscher smiled, and nodded, but there was no humour in it. 'Yes. Of course. Standards.' He took a mouthful of wine. 'But there has been an accident.'

'What sort of accident?'

'The task force we sent to the Caspian to conduct the environmental and seismic studies has had their offices burned down. Everything has been destroyed.'

'I see.'

'A formality, of course, but ...' He waved his fleshy hand.

'So you have no report.'

'I am very confident that the report would have been favourable,' he said quickly.

'But of course.' Her eyes strayed to the photograph in a silver frame that sat on the side table. It was of her in a private audience with the Pope. She was bowing, her head covered in respect, as he blessed her, but her faith didn't blind her to the realities. Genscher was a thug, and she knew full well that the report would be favourable because he would have ensured the outcome from the very start. Fixed the casino. Something had gone badly wrong.

'No backups?' she asked, arching an eyebrow.

'Sadly, no,' the German said uneasily. 'The research facility was very isolated, all the records were kept on site, the computer backups, too. Now – gone. Everything.' He dived once again into his glass of wine. She poured him some more.

'So what do you need from me?' she asked quietly.

'There is no time to repeat the studies,' he said. 'If we delay any longer, governments in the countries through which the pipeline passes will change, get greedy, make impossible demands. Not to speak of all those fanatical environmentalists. It has taken us years of negotiating to get to this point, now it is all about to fall apart.'

'And we will be forced to live in windmills,' she said.

'We must have that pipeline! Otherwise Europe will

enter another Ice Age,' he said, agitated, banging the arm of his chair.

'I thought you said it was a little *local* difficulty.'

'Illka. It is in his hands. He can still approve the pipeline even without the environmental report. Override the system on the grounds of the security of the Union.'

'I assume he is being stubborn.'

'You know Illka, he is a bloody idealist. If we could burn his speeches we'd have an unlimited supply of energy, but he'd rather sit in the snow and beat himself with birch twigs.'

'You want me to change his mind.'

'Could you? Of course you could. You are a remarkable woman, Patreezia. What I mean is – would you? That's what I'm asking. A huge favour.' One that would require repaying at some point. 'You know what this means to me.'

Genscher was not simply a political thug, he was a most effective Commissioner. There was even talk he would in his turn become President of the Commission, the top man, which would make him a friend in a very high place. But not if his favourite project collapsed around his ears. As he drank, he failed to notice that she hadn't touched her own glass. The atmosphere had grown intense, almost claus-trophobic. The walls were painted in a deep, rich red, and covered in heavy gilt frames that created an almost Renaissance intensity amidst the haze of blue smoke, as they sat like cardinals in some papal palace, conspiring.

She made him wait. Then she dialled the EATA duty

office. She drummed her fingers in impatience as she waited for it to be answered – thirty seconds, unforgivable even on a Sunday night, something she would sort out in the morning. 'There is a third-floor apartment on Rue de la Croix,' she said, when at last her call was answered. She gave the street number. 'It will have a landline. I want its number. And we'll treat this as an initiative test, Fabiano. Let's see if you're quicker at digging out information than you are at picking up the phone.'

From the chair opposite Genscher was waving his mobile, mouthing that he had Illka's number, but she shook her head dismissively. It had to be the landline. Illka had to know that she knew precisely where he was.

It took some time for Illka to answer the phone, when at last she rang, and when he did he didn't announce himself, merely uttered a curt 'Yes?'

'Illka, it's Patricia. I hope I'm not disturbing you.'

Disturbing him? Of course she was disturbing him, pushing him to the brink of mindless panic, that was the point. He was standing naked but for his socks in the living room of a small apartment that no one was supposed to know about, but for his tarts. He was a pillar of family values and also of the Evangelical Lutheran church, a man whose ambitions were as broad as his wife was narrow-minded and unforgiving. He wanted to become President of Finland one day, not dragged down by lurid media revelations about his appetite for underage sex.

'Delighted to find you here on a Sunday evening,' she

continued. He still hadn't said a word, hadn't dared draw breath.

He wasn't the only one, of course. Ridiculous men. When they arrived in Brussels on a Sunday evening in preparation for their working week, they were faced with a choice – a lonely evening with a takeaway, or some more exotic form of distraction, what she called a Sunday Night Special. During a visit to Chicago she had been shown a collection of Saturday Night Specials, small, cheap handguns used by petty criminals, and although the Sunday Night versions referred to casual women they could prove to be just as deadly in the wrong hands. Particularly in her hands.

Still he hadn't spoken. She knew he was debating whether to put the phone down, deny it all, but she knew he wouldn't, not in the end. There was no point. She knew.

'How can I help you, Patricia?'

'A quick point, but really rather important, Illka. The Babylon pipeline. It requires either an environmental impact report or your waiver, in the interests of the Union's security. So I'm calling to set your mind at rest by assuring you that the pipeline, and your approval for it, are most certainly in the interests of our security.'

'I see,' he muttered dully.

'Look, Illka, I know about your deep-seated principles in all sorts of areas, but life is complicated. Sometimes you have to shout out loud about things, other times it's better just to keep quiet and avoid a fuss. You understand what I mean?'

He was about to ask her how the hell she'd found this apartment, tucked away so anonymously in the tourist district that even he had difficulty in finding it in the dark, but he knew it was pointless. Secrets were her business.

'Is there any point in a discussion?'

'No.'

'You strike a hard bargain,' he complained, his tone bitter.

'It seems to me a very fair one.'

Another silence, before: 'This week. I'll make the arrangements.'

The phone went dead in his ear as she cut the connection. From across the room Genscher shook his head in both disbelief and admiration. 'I owe you, Patreezia.'

'Oh, my dear Albrecht,' she whispered, coyly recrossing her ankles, 'you most certainly do.'

—ᴍ—

When Harry was eight his mother had turned up at the apartment his father used for business and found her husband in bed with another woman. The other woman had a similar coloured dress to his mother, although she hadn't been wearing it at the time. 'What a coincidence,' his mother had exclaimed. It had kicked Harry's belief in coincidence to death. So when he received an invitation to meet with the director of Europe House, the EU's headquarters in London, he accepted with a degree of suspicion. Brussels had begun to occupy too big a chunk of his life for comfort.

With a delicious sense of irony the EU had even set up its London base in a building in Westminster's Smith Square that had once been the headquarters of Margaret Thatcher, the most Eurosceptic of Prime Ministers, until her party had run out of money to keep fixing it. Now it had been refurbished, extensively and expensively, and the EU flag flew alongside the Union Jack above its door.

Security in the reception area was tight, with scanners, CCTV and guards. They even asked him to hand over his mobile phone, something he'd not been requested to do since he'd last visited Downing Street. Still, Jemma would approve. He passed it across the counter with reluctance; in return, they handed him a receipt.

As he passed through the foyer he found posters announcing the shortlist for The European Parliament Film Prize, which dealt with 'integration and youngsters, economic crisis and solidarity, the rules under which we live and the rules that drive our hearts'. God, there were rules for that, too? The films 'examine European issues with originality and sensitivity'. Last night Jemma had thrown a pillow and called him the most insensitive bastard she'd ever met, so he guessed this might be one prize he'd never claim, but there was little need for him to worry, there was a mass of others: youth prizes, journalism prizes, community prizes, even a viral video prize. In the new Europe, it seemed that everyone was a winner.

The director's office was large, designer decorated, overlooking the square and the deconsecrated church of St John through the bare branches of a London plane tree. She was named Mary-Anne, was in her fifties, hadn't been in post long, she explained, and hadn't got to know many MPs, so she was taking the opportunity to put right that omission – although Harry hadn't heard of any other politician getting this hands-on treatment. There was tea, the offer of biscuits, and did Harry have any special interests with which Europe House might help? It was all desperately nondescript stuff. It seemed only as an afterthought that they bumped into the subject of the crashed airplane. Such a tragedy, she said. And there she left it, waiting for Harry. What was Brussels' involvement, he asked, nonplussed. We are doing everything we can, she said, to support the British government in their efforts to get to the bottom of the matter. We stand ready to tighten sanctions against the Egyptian regime, if the Foreign & Commonwealth Office requests it, details to be agreed, of course.

And that was it. A young aide entered the office, nodded, with regret the next appointment was waiting, and Harry was ushered out of the room. He hadn't known what to expect, or what was expected of him, and as he walked around Smith Square, dodging taxis and scattering pigeons, he was still none the wiser. Perhaps it had been intended simply to dispel the myth of extravagance that surrounded the EU, washing it away with a simple cup of tea.

He had no way of knowing that while he was sipping his tea, his phone had been cloned and all the information on it, the contacts, calendars, notes, e-mails, even the photo of Jemma in the bath – everything – had been copied. The phone was protected, of course, with a four-figure parliamentary pin code, but even an amateur could break that. And it gave access to all his other security-coded accounts – banks, credit cards, investments, even his medical records. What was more his SIM card had now been replaced by a 'smart SIM'. It contained all the information of the old SIM and looked identical, but with one or two additional hidden tweaks. It had an embedded GPS, which meant they would know his whereabouts every moment of the day. And every call would be redirected through a proxy point where it would be monitored. 'Tapped', in the language of old. They would be able to listen to every call he made. Harry's life was now theirs.

Or, at least, hers.

—∞—

The life of a politician has many parts that are dreary beyond belief. These men and women come to Westminster fully intending to slay dragons, yet discover they are spending most of their time picking up other people's rubbish. The headlines would have them as power brokers, surrounded by an expansive group of aides with fingers in every pie; the reality is that often they are Don Quixotes who end up making their own tea. Of course it's different if you are Prime Minister: you'll get your tea made, but rarely get time to drink it. Downing Street is littered with half-finished mugs. In fact, there were times when Ben Usher thought that might be an appropriate title for his memoirs. A Half-Finished Mug.

An election year that had held such exciting prospects was turning into a time of torment. An abominable crime had been committed in the heart of the capital and people demanded two things. Answers. And revenge. He could give them neither. It was all very well blaming Abdul Mohammed Ghazi but the evidence for his guilt was painfully threadbare, little more than the fact that he was a man of known violence who'd been chasing around the right part of the world at pretty much the right time. It was entirely circumstantial. The Dutch even found the vessel that had been used – yes, a bloody fishing boat without a transponder – but although the owner had been interrogated and probably beaten, he could tell them little other than that it had been hired by three men, one or two of whom might have had dusky faces. They talked English, but with an accent – didn't everybody? There were no adequate forensics; any useful evidence that might have been left had long since been washed away in seawater. And most predictably, Usher had learned of this first from the *Telegraph* rather than the Dutch authorities. European cooperation was all very well, but paying a few backhanders worked a hell of a lot quicker.

And still there was the tantalizing question: Why? Where was the motive? There were two schools of thought on this, the first that the Muslim Brotherhood in Egypt had a longstanding record of anti-Western behaviour and felt duly aggrieved by any number of slights, real and imagined. Anyway, so the argument went, they were Arabs. Motive enough. And the more Britain and aggrieved America demanded evidence from them, the more the Egyptians grew stubborn, silent, refused to cooperate, couldn't find Ghazi, accused the West of intimidation, racism, militarism, Zionism, using threats of violence. Which only served to raise more lurid accusations. The truth no longer mattered any more, dragged down within a whirlpool of accusation and mutual loathing. It was like Iraq and Libya all over again.

There was another school of thought, there always was. This suggested that all the evidence against Ghazi was circumstantial, and in any event there was no clear connection between him and the Egyptian government, apart from the fact that he had been born there. One or two bold souls in MI6 even suggested that perhaps they had jumped to hasty conclusions, that perhaps they should be looking elsewhere, but 'perhaps' was quickly overwhelmed by the collective certainties of group-think and the demand for black-and-white answers that could be easily rendered into headlines. Both 'Ghazi' and 'Egypt' fitted headlines very well, so they were both guilty.

There was proof, of sorts, and at least enough to satisfy the Americans, who were offering fifteen million dollars as a bounty on Ghazi's head. While Egypt itself had never been supplied with Grinch missiles, they had been sold to

Gadaffi in Libya, and after his overthrow so much had gone missing. It was easy to suppose that some had ended up on the back of a truck and carted over the border to Egypt. So there it was. Even if the motive was a little hazy, the weaponry was very solid, and diagrams and updates on it so easy to download.

In an election year and prodded on by the Americans, there could be no pause for doubt, so the rhetoric was ramped up, the moral outrage stoked to overload. Civil servants scuttled throughout Whitehall finding draconian new initiatives for the purposes of their political masters. An arms embargo was slapped on, then ramped up, ambassadors were withdrawn, trade agreements broken. The British and US authorities were now talking of imposing travel bans on a number of named leaders in the Egyptian Brotherhood, the next step would be to freeze their foreign bank accounts. It was becoming very personal, and for no one more than Ben Usher. As the mood had hardened and events moved beyond his control, he had become accustomed to making a grab for the *Telegraph* even before he had risen from his bed. One morning he found the front page dominated by a cartoon that depicted him gazing out forlornly from a window of Downing Street. Behind him, on the wall above his desk, was an election poster with a simple message. 'Get Elected. Get Ghazi.'

None of this made life any easier for government candidates like Harry. There was no way his seat could be considered marginal, in danger, but even so he found that his constituents were no longer giving their usual tens or occasional hundreds of pounds for his fighting fund, and neither were they giving much of their time. Wars require foot soldiers, there were envelopes to be stuffed, leaflets to be delivered, doors to be knocked on, websites to be updated, yet instead of shouldering arms the troops were sitting in their fox holes reading the bloody newspapers. The government was in danger of losing this war.

Late one evening Harry was walking home after a long and wearing day at the Commons, his head down, lost in thought over such things when he found a woman, a stranger, wrapped in Burberry and on his doorstep.

'Mr Jones, I hope you don't mind, but I want to volunteer.'

She was late twenties, presentable, as if she'd just stepped out of a John Lewis makeover session, everything suggesting a young professional.

'Emily Keane,' she said, holding out a hand.

'And so you are,' he said, taking it.

Yet he wasn't used to being picked up on his doorstep. The new school term had started and Jemma was back in her own flat, and for once in his life sexual discretion got the better of Harry. Better not to take her inside. 'How about a drink at the pub?' he suggested.

'Yes, of course,' she blushed, 'but ...' She began hopping from one foot to the other. 'I've been standing here for ages. Do you think I could use your loo first, please?'

So Harry changed his mind. 'Come on in,' he said, reaching for his keys.

By the time she had sorted herself out Harry had already taken off his coat, so he offered her a drink, which she declined, her raincoat still firmly buttoned, so he suggested they move to the sitting room. He found that Jemma had left a scarf draped over the back of a chair; for some ridiculous reason, he hastily removed it.

'You could have written, made an appointment,' he observed as they sat down.

'Sorry, yes, but you must get a million letters,' she blurted, 'and I didn't want to end up at the bottom of a pile. Anyway, I'm trained to be proactive.'

'Trained?'

'PR, Mr Jones. I'm a senior account director. Getting on fine, but I've come to something of a crossroads.' She was perched on the edge of the sofa, her knees clenched coyly together. 'I've been with my company five years, it's time to move on, get more experience. I've always been interested in public affairs, politics – my dad was a local councillor in Devon – so I've been thinking about the election, seeing politics from the sharp end. Wondering if I could help you.' She was gushing, a little nervous.

'You live in my constituency?'

'No. But I'm sure I could find somewhere to stay. Bed and breakfast, perhaps a spare room with one of your supporters. I'm very flexible. I'd work something out.'

'So if you're not local, why me?'

She laughed as if it was the most ridiculous question in the world. 'But you're Harry Jones.'

Well, he had been Harry Jones. War hero, rising political star, a man who seemed to have an uncanny capacity for attracting challenges that would test him to the limit, and which had left scars both inside and out as evidence. It had also left bodies along the route. But it all seemed a long time ago.

'What could you do?' he asked.

She relaxed, sat back, the initial nervousness gone; she unbuttoned her coat, revealing a fine waist as she talked about her background.

'Could you handle the press?' he asked.

She laughed once more, bounced up and down on her cushion.

'Stupid question,' he apologized, 'but I couldn't pay you. Against election law.'

'I've done enough research to know that, but it's not a problem, Mr Jones, I've got plenty of accumulated holiday.'

'OK, let's try next weekend. See if you like the place.' See if the retired matrons who usually staffed his election headquarters with the passion of disgruntled dragons liked her. 'And call me Harry.'

'Thank you – Harry.'

She rose. In an earlier life Harry might have encouraged her to stay a little longer, but he was discovering that Jemma had changed many things in his life. He felt silly about the scarf.

'It seems I have a new press officer,' he said, leading her to the door. 'There's a chance I might hold on to my seat after all.'

Her face lit up as she stood on the doorstep in the lamplight. 'I've never yet been on the losing side.'

Although it was late, well past eleven, she declined the offer of a taxi. A truly focused, self-reliant young woman, he thought, ideal for the task. He didn't spot the man in the shadow of a doorway down the street taking photographs of her as she left.

CHAPTER SEVEN

It had been the darkest time of Sloppy's life. He and his wife were taking a bit of a break from each other, breathing space to recharge their separate batteries, as he explained it to his colleagues in the City. It meant he had spent Christmas alone with nothing but his demons for company.

The New Year gave him no respite. Quarterly statements were due to his clients, and no matter how much he shuffled the cards and the accounts he couldn't find a combination that would beat the bank. A temporary situation, of course, soon be through it, but for the moment he was so deep in fresh compost he'd do better opening up a mushroom farm. There was nothing but darkness. Pain. And more painkillers.

When he stood in front of the mirror, gazing into his own eyes, examining the lines, the marks of age, and pain, he didn't quite recognize himself. The world had changed, he had changed – but not as much as the rest of them. His clients demanded more, more, and ever more, yet gave nothing in return. They didn't deserve him. That was why it wasn't simply justifiable but entirely proper that he should give them a bit of their own medicine, taking back a little of what he had given them over the years. While they had sat around their Christmas tables exchanging useless presents and offering up empty wishes, he had been left on his own. No one cared, gave a damn, so let them all be damned, they deserved what they were getting. Payback time.

Except that, with a bit of time and good fortune, and a little accounting alchemy, they would never know.

He sat in Brokers wine bar in Leadenhall Market, at the table farthest from the entrance, avoiding others, waiting. It was a favourite haunt, from where he could stare out at the Victorian splendours of the ancient market and wash down the pills with a decent glass of something French. Always French. He was a man of tradition, old values and old wine. He'd received a phone call, a prospective client, referred to him by Angus, an existing client who couldn't introduce them personally since he was away in the Far East. At least, that's what the man had said. But how else would he have known that Angus was one of his clients? Or away in the Far East? Frankly, who cared? Sloppy didn't normally take on clients who walked in off the street, but the man had money. It was enough to drown a few doubts.

When Felix Wilton walked in, he was all but unrecognizable, even to close friends, and that almost included Patricia who had prepared him for this part. He had shaved his goatee beard, dyed his hair, changed his parting, replaced his usual rimless spectacles with a pair of heavy frames. And if he was supposed to leave behind his usually cautious character in favour of a flamboyance that touched on the camp, that was no great challenge.

'Mr Sopwith-Dane,' he greeted, extending a moisturized palm and flashing an acre of crisp shirt cuff. 'A pleasure.'

'All mine, Mr Anderson, all mine,' Sloppy replied. He could still rise to the challenge. He might be screaming inside, but he knew he had to smile.

They exchanged a few conventional pleasantries and ordered drinks before Wilton got down to business, leaning forward, lowering his voice. 'I have a situation, an interesting situation, with which I am seeking some assistance. It needs the utmost discretion, and I'm told you are discreet.'

Sloppy nodded, said nothing, not sure where this was going, and drank.

'I'm a private investor, I keep my ear close to the ground, so to speak,' Wilton continued, twisting an elaborate cufflink. 'I've done rather well for myself over the years. As they say, nothing ventured, nothing gained, eh?' he continued, piling up the clichés. He'd never make a playwright, but right now he thought he was acting out of his silk socks. 'There's a fund I've been watching for some while – Shengtzu Investments. Always thought there would be a time to strike. Very big into China and the rare metals market, that sort of thing. You understand?'

Again Sloppy nodded. Terbium, dysprosium, yttrium, thulium, cerium, all rare commodities without which the modern world simply wouldn't work. Phones wouldn't ring, light bulbs would flicker and fade, computers would crash and missiles refuse to fly. China was building up its strategic stores with the ferocity that the Tudors had built castles, while the rest of the world scrabbled to keep pace.

'My sense is that the fund is about to go big. Very big,' Wilton continued.

'Your *sense*?' Sloppy intervened for the first time, finding the expression very loose.

The other man pursed his lips, studied his glass, rolled it between his clammy palms. 'As I said, I've been making a close study.' He paused, the eyes came up. 'And, entirely by coincidence, I also have a close friend who works for it.'

'I see.'

'It's because of that coincidence that any direct investment by me into the fund would look . . .' – he stretched for an appropriate expression – 'a little clumsy.'

Criminal, you mean, Sloppy thought. This was insider trading. The other man hurried on.

'So I would like to make a substantial investment in the most discreet manner. No names, no pack drill. Which is why I have come to you.'

'Because I'm discreet.'

'Precisely.'

Discreet. And, of course, desperate. Patricia had scarcely

believed her luck when Harry's phone and a few additional illicit enquiries had revealed such a tempting target as Sopwith-Dane. Anyway, he deserved what was coming to him; a businessman should take more care of his computer records.

And she had judged her target well. There was a time when Sloppy would have thrown the bastard out without a further word, but not now. His mind was whirling. He was about to send out the quarterly statements, face disaster, and now this Fairy Godmother was offering him – what, exactly?

'How much are we talking here, Mr Anderson?'

From down the other end of the bar a group of young City workers burst into laughter; Wilton let the commotion subside before reaching inside his jacket and producing a stark white envelope. He laid it on the polished tabletop between them, keeping his fingers on it. 'This contains a cheque. Drawn on a reputable bank in the Caymans. For a quarter of a million pounds.' He watched Sloppy's bottom lip hesitate, just as his own had wobbled when Patricia had handed it to him across the kitchen table. 'Dare I ask, my dear, where this small fortune comes from?' he had enquired.

'You mean, is it ours?'

'I must be frank and say that was the question that popped into my mind.'

She had laughed. 'Oh, no, Felix, I would never do that to you. These are Agency funds.'

'Just like that? No questions?'

'Secrets, Felix. Remember, I deal in secrets.'

'Very large ones, it seems,' he had concluded, in awe, realizing perhaps for the first time just how powerful she had become.

Now Sloppy couldn't take his eyes off it. The size of the cheque was by no means unusual in his business, but the timing was exceptional.

'Three per cent,' Wilton said softly – double the usual commission. 'And I expect the investment itself to double inside three months, possibly even better than that. Well, in for a penny, in for a pound.' He withdrew his hand from the envelope; his crested pinky ring sparkled. 'You might even like to invest some of your own money, Mr Sopwith-Dane.'

His own money? He had damn-all left, but he might be able to switch some of the remaining funds around, scrape together enough to make a difference. Find his way out of the sewer. But doing that would nail him firmly to the deal and all its dirtiness, he'd no longer be able to claim he was simply following instructions. Sloppy had been pretty scrupulous about such things, up to now, but up to now he'd also been sane and solvent. Damn them, but he'd followed other people's rules all his life, and where had that got him?

'I'd need to know much more about the investment – if I'm to advise you properly.'

In response, Wilton took another, thicker, buff envelope

from his pocket and placed it on top of the first. 'The fund's own report,' he said quietly.

So, it was insider trading. Theft. If Sloppy touched the envelopes he would either have to run straight to the Financial Services Authority to reveal all, which would leave him wading even deeper through his own shit, or he would become part of a criminal conspiracy. He glanced at the group of young people further down the bar, made sure no one was watching, then he made a grab for the envelopes.

—〰—

Elections being periods of concentrated mania, it was some time before Harry was able to sit down with Jemma to examine the passenger list from the Police Casualty Bureau. They perched beside each other on the sofa, staring at the laptop, and a list that seemed almost endless, a hundred and fifteen names, with addresses and considerable additional detail.

'You owe Shelagh for this,' Jemma said.

'I already paid,' he said, distractedly, and more than a little clumsily, as he concentrated on the details.

'I'll make a cup of tea,' she said, as she often did when the only decent alternative was to kick the crap out of him.

She returned with two steaming mugs of muddy water to find him bent over the screen in concentration. 'What have you found?' she asked.

'Nothing,' he replied.

130

'What are you looking for?'

'A motive for mass murder.'

'Well, let's think about it logically.'

He looked up in surprise.

'I teach maths to five-year-olds,' she replied tartly. 'I suspect I can teach even you a little logic.'

'OK.'

'One hundred and fifteen on board. Seven crew members. And we think the target wasn't the thirty-seven kids. That narrows it down to seventy-one. So get rid of the rest of the kids on board, everyone below the age of twenty.'

'Seems reasonable.' He scrolled through the list, deleting another seventeen. 'What next?'

'Married couples.'

'Because?'

'They would have been in Brussels for a pre-Christmas jolly. Shoppers. Not the sort of people you need to take out with a missile.'

'That's very feminine.'

'You noticed.'

For some reason she was pissed off with him, but he didn't dare enquire why, he simply deleted another dozen names. They were down to forty-one.

'Were there any Egyptians on board?'

'No.'

'That would have been too easy. But look, there were a couple of Asian names.' She pointed at the screen.

'There are Asian names on almost every flight in the

country. Anyway, they were from Manchester,' he muttered. 'Being a United supporter's not enough to condemn them, not this season, at least.'

'Or give them an alibi,' she said.

He left their names on the list.

'You ruined football when you let all those foreign tycoons and oligarchs take over the clubs.'

'Me?'

'You English. Wouldn't happen to a Scottish club. We'd never sell out.'

'Those green eyes of envy are really sexy on you.'

'What colour are Shelagh's eyes?' Bugger, she'd let it slip.

But even as she bit her own tongue, she was reprieved. He didn't seem to have heard. His face was creased in concentration. 'You know, Jem, you may have a point. It's all about power and money, isn't it?'

'What is?'

'Everything. Football. Life. Politics. Mass murder. Something like that's got to be behind the attack.'

'So where do we look?'

'I dunno. Business class?'

Their heads almost clashed as they bent over the screen. Business class had been almost full, but not quite. A couple of seats spare. Eighteen names in the remainder.

'These are the people who we should be concentrating on, Jem, their jobs, their personal circumstances, that sort of thing.'

'How do we do that?'

'I could try Shelagh.'

'Let's start with the Internet,' she said firmly. 'All the victims will have got some sort of mention in the media – obituaries, local news reports, company press releases, something that will get us started.'

'Could take time.'

'I might do it.'

'You would?'

'I could be persuaded.'

'How?'

She placed the laptop to one side. It was some considerable time before either of them spoke again.

'By the way,' he panted, lying back, a bead of sweat trickling from his forehead onto a sofa cushion, 'they're brown.'

'What are?'

'Shelagh's eyes. Since you asked. And there was nothing like this between us.'

'Ah, just a friend. I see. And if I remember right, that was the year they discovered a cure for the common cold and Auchtermuchty Athletic became European Champions . . .'

—⁓—

Patricia Vaine's office was uncompromisingly functional, except for a solitary framed photograph on her desk. It was of her cat, Freya. Other senior figures in Brussels were surrounded by frippery and unnecessary aggrandizement, in offices spread out like tennis courts or dashing around on private jets, but in her view, the less people saw of her, the better.

A knock at her door disturbed her concentration, rapping out Morse code for 'B'. Bukowski's little joke.

'You might want to watch this,' he said, scuttling in and making for the bank of four screens that were mounted opposite the sofa. He played with the channels until he had found what he was looking for. It was a Russian news channel, no translation, and with a mediocre picture full of stray pixels and stiff movements betraying an inadequate feed to the satellite, but what it showed more than made up for the poor technical quality. It was broadcasting the scene from the outskirts of a shabby town with all the drabness and decay that marked it as part of the old Soviet Union. The road was rough, the buildings soulless and dust-smeared. The sky threatened rain, everything appeared as grey, except for the fire that was raging from the roof of a three-storey house in the centre of the screen. As she watched, angry trails of dark smoke twisted into the air, and there was the sound of explosions. She struggled to recognize any snatch of the commentary that was being poured out in breathless style by the commentator, then she saw a flash of a fresh explosion on the second floor of the house. A mortar round. That was when she heard the only words she understood. Abdul Mohammed Ghazi.

'It seems they've tracked him down,' Bukowski said.

'Who? Where?'

'The Russians.'

'This is Russia?'

'No, it's some little shithole in Azerbaijan, about ten miles from the Russian border. It seems the Russians decided not to bother with the border formalities, just went in after him.'

Azerbaijan was a nominally independent republic that hadn't been part of the Russian empire since the Berlin Wall came down, but old habits die hard, especially in troublesome frontier areas populated by militant Muslims. The Russians had never showed much patience with ragheads.

Patricia tucked her legs beneath her on the sofa as though ready to pounce, while Bukowski stood, offering sporadic translation, but words were scarcely necessary to understand what was going on. The house was substantial and set back from the road, protected by a robust wall of stone, and the Russian fire was being returned from within the building with some pretty formidable hardware. The assault seemed shambolic, accompanied by much screaming and uncoordinated firing of weapons – these troops were border guards, not the best the Kremlin had to offer, which suggested the assault had been mounted in a hurry. Those inside were giving a good account of themselves, and several bodies clad in the green uniform of the border guard service could be seen lying in the roadway by the wall. Yet the defenders were surrounded, with nowhere to go, and the roof was burning down upon them. There was so much smoke that neither side could get a clear view of their targets, so the Russians contented themselves with pounding the house to pieces with mortars. It didn't stop retaliation. The camera, in wide shot, showed a truck being blown on its side and erupting in a fireball before the scene hurriedly moved back to concentrate on the inferno of the building.

Slowly a story emerged from the commentary that Ghazi had been betrayed, his hideout uncovered, and surrounded, and now the Russians were going for him as if every man in the assault party expected to receive a sizeable chunk of the fifteen-million-dollar reward.

'Not a very exotic place for a super-terrorist to hide,' Bukowski muttered.

'Or to die.'

The end was inevitable, but took nearly fifty minutes to reach its climax. Slowly, as the walls, windows, ceilings and staircases of the building were reduced to rubble, the returning fire from within began to fade. Resistance became sporadic. Then it ceased. Shouts were coming from within the building, cries of submission, then a man stumbled out, blood pouring from a head wound and into his eyes, matting his long hair across his forehead. He stood still, raised his hands.

'It's not Ghazi,' Patricia whispered, as both the cameras and Russian troops closed in. 'Too tall.'

More shouting. The fighter lay down in the dust and debris of the front yard. Almost immediately two other men followed, emerging from what had once been a front door but was now no more than a jagged, gaping hole, dragging a wounded colleague between them. Slowly, reluctantly, they knelt, and lay in the dirt. Yet still there was a sense that the moment was unfinished.

'Will he give himself up, or take his own life?' Bukowski wondered out loud.

'He's a commercial killer, what do you think?'

And there, emerging from the hell that was behind him, a figure appeared.

'That's him!' Patricia whispered in a tone that sounded strained and urgent, as if she were no longer a spectator but was a player on this bloody field.

He was dressed in a simple smock of the local fashion with billowing cotton trousers that had a dark-red stain growing down the right leg. An arm of the smock seemed badly scorched. The face was pale, almost Western, despite the smears of smoke, and the beard and hair short, kempt, in a manner that would raise no alarm on the streets of Europe. He stood still, defiant, looking around him, and at what lay ahead, his arms at his side, silhouetted by the flames that seemed to be reaching for him and almost disappearing in the swirling wisps of smoke. The scene was almost biblical. For a moment, the only sound that could be heard was the crackling of the fire that was consuming the building behind him. At last, he took a step forward, limping. Then, another. And another.

A shout of command rang out, sharp, like an officer on a

parade ground. Suddenly a hand appeared in front of the camera lens, its fingers splayed, covering the view. The screen went blank, pixels dancing in desperation, trying to work out what they were missing. Sounds of some muffled explosion. Then the transmission went dead.

CHAPTER EIGHT

The stately pile of oriel windows and Tudor brick called Chequers is the country retreat of Prime Ministers. Put another way, it's where they go to cry. Yet, all politics being imagery, they have to put on a brave face, which was exactly the position in which Ben Usher found himself. He had gathered his backbenchers for a Sunday 'strategy session', where he and other ministers would tell the flock how high and in which direction they were to jump in the run-up to the election. 'This is war!' he shouted, banging the podium at the end of the Long Gallery, which was heated almost to excess by the crush of bodies sitting in rows of seats laid out before him. There wasn't much that was original in his conclusion; Clausewitz had long ago defined war as being a continuation of politics by other means, except modern elections didn't really deserve to be dignified by such high-minded analysis. For Usher, elections came straight out of a spaghetti Western, with several gunmen confronting each other, eyes darting, buttocks clenched, knowing that for whoever lost, there would be no tomorrow. Not that defeated Prime Ministers were shot, of course, that would have been an act of almost too much kindness. No, instead they were dragged from the scene, unwillingly, sometimes in tears, and left in an afterworld of reminiscence and regret. Few avoided that fate. Perhaps it had been different for John Major. He, at least, had his cricket. There were rumours that the Long Gallery had been used as an indoor wicket at some point in the past. But Usher hated cricket, so he banged the podium even harder, put on a brave face, and pretended absolute confidence in victory. Only twelve weeks to go, he reminded them. Twelve weeks until that first Thursday in May. He followed that up with some traditional bollocks about summoning up the spirit, facing the enemy and marching to the sound of gunfire. Why did his job always seem to reduce itself to grotesque cliché?

Then, as he faced the sea of upturned faces, many of which were glowing, and a few sweating, a thought struck him. May. Hay fever season, during which he suffered excruciatingly. Coughs, embarrassing splutters, headaches that felt like an exploring corkscrew, a nose turned hydrant and a throat that rasped itself raw. Bloody rape seed, but he couldn't complain, it would only have lost him the farmers' vote. But what confounded idiot had decreed that elections should be held in May? With the Easter holiday to screw things up just as the campaign was getting into its stride? Clint Eastwood never had to fight his battles with a soggy handkerchief stuffed up his sleeve.

He was glad when he had finished hectoring his troops.

He was too much of a professional not to have done it well, but he wanted to escape, get some fresh air, strip off the veneer of exhaustion that seemed constantly to cling to him, and as the party chairman took his place at the podium the Prime Minister gestured to Harry Jones to join him. Harry didn't need encouragement, and wasn't the type to show false enthusiasm. Always played the game by his own rules. Aggravating bloody man. Thank God they weren't all like him, but then, thank Heaven, a few of them were. Usher opened a door that was hidden in a dummy bookcase and disappeared into the Cromwell corridor. Harry followed.

'What's up, Ben?' Harry enquired as they passed by portraits and a mask of the great regicide.

'Oh, nothing. I'm just not used to being on my own any more.'

They continued in silence until they had made their way outside, into the rose garden.

'I guess you've heard enough of those rallying calls from beaten-up generals,' Usher said, popping an aspirin into his mouth as he squinted into a lowering sun.

'Actually, not too many,' Harry replied.

'No, that's right. I looked in your file once. You didn't do many regular wars, did you? Yours were largely unofficial, in strange places the British Army wasn't supposed to be.'

'The sort of thing my bosses could deny absolutely if things got screwed up.'

'So no rousing speeches.'

'Usually just a gentle whisper in the ear and a quick check to make sure I'd updated my will.'

'You were a useful man to have around.'

'I think the word was expendable. Anyway, what were you doing with my file?'

'Was thinking of offering you a job, a big one, but then I saw you'd already turned it down under my predecessor. There was a note somewhere, in his own handwriting, said you were an awkward sod. So many medals, so much insubordination. Quite a few bodies left along the track, too, I seem to remember.'

'Wars have this nasty habit of requiring casualties, Ben. Don't forget that, if ever you feel tempted.'

The Prime Minister paused, a little solemn, still staring into the setting sun. 'They say I've lost the plot, Harry.'

'That's not true, Ben.'

'No, but I have lost the initiative. And the electorate. Bit like losing your virginity. Once it's gone . . .'

Harry didn't argue.

'If only we'd been able to find that bastard Ghazi before the Russians, drag him down Whitehall. Beat the truth out of him . . .'

'You having doubts? About what the truth is?'

'Politics and truth. Now there's an interesting proposition in election year.' He paused, lips working, as though he had a sour taste in his mouth. 'They shot him, you know, Ghazi. In cold blood. They said he was wearing an explosive belt, that it killed him and everyone he was with, but that's bollocks. They shot every one of them, wanted them out of the way. Embarrassment at the fact it was one of their missiles, I suppose. Or sheer bloody stupidity. So we've lost the chance to interrogate them. We're back where we started.'

'You sure it was the Egyptians?'

Usher filled his lungs with cold, grey air, then sighed as he let it slowly escape. 'Everybody says it was the Egyptians, Harry. And I don't know enough to disagree with them.'

'I think they may be wrong.'

'And you may be right. There might be a time when we have to reconsider all this. But not before the election. *"For if the trumpets give an uncertain sound, who shall prepare himself to the battle?"'* The Prime Minister stood in thought, gazing into the distance to where beech trees stood gaunt and frostbitten against the skyline, ripped bare, rather like his soul. For a while he seemed lost, then suddenly, he was back. He laid a hand on Harry's shoulder and they began walking slowly along the paved path that marked the sides of the rose garden. 'They tell me there's a new lady in your life. That's good, Harry. It's been a long time for you. I wish you much happiness.'

The sentiment was perhaps premature, Harry thought, but this wasn't the time to argue the point.

'And, tell me, how is it out there, on the front line?' Usher waved a paw at some distant world that might lie beyond the boundaries of the estate.

'A little tougher than I would like, but fine. I have a new press officer, young woman, walked in off the street, literally. Doing rather well.'

'Then I may have to pull rank and confiscate her! Could do with a little help in whipping the jackal pack into shape. Or simply distracting them. She a looker, your press girl?'

'I haven't noticed,' Harry lied, and laughed.

'Best keep it that way. You know, I remember one press officer, when I was a junior minister at the Treasury all those years ago . . .' But once again he trailed off, standing still, staring at the ground, lost in his own world. And sadness, Harry thought.

'I fear you're offering too much information for a humble backbencher,' Harry prompted.

'What?' said Usher, startled.

'That press officer.'

'No, no,' Usher protested wistfully, 'it's just – these roses. They're beautiful in the summer. I was wondering if I'll ever get to see them again.'

—∞—

Patricia Vaine sat at an outside table on the Galerie de la Reine Koninginne, a covered arcade that ran a little back from the Grande Place in Brussels. The arcade was long and luxurious with a high glazed roof, and up there, amongst the metal rafters, she could see a tangle of children's balloons, the survivors of some New Year celebration. It seemed such a long time ago, but most things did. She never looked back; it was one of her firmest rules.

She was outside one of her favourite coffee shops. The Belgians could be hopelessly dull but they made excellent chocolate cake, and she had allowed herself a small slice along with her coffee, a deep, rich cup of the darkest liquid that was mostly Colombian with a hint of Brazil and had the kick of a mule. She was fussy about her coffee, had a nose for it, just as she had a nose for the weakness of men, and in particular a man like Ben Usher, whose poll ratings were chaotic and who had shown himself to be deliciously vulnerable, like a great actor who could no longer remember his lines. It was time for her to lead the cat calls – but how?

She spotted a middle-aged woman approaching, comfortable walking shoes, tourist map clutched firmly in hand and a look of determination stretched implacably across her face. She had two complaining teenagers in tow. As they drew nearer, Patricia could hear they were English, presumably on a half-term break, judging by the nature of the boys' complaints. Their hotel breakfast seemed to lack a certain Britishness; the cereal was stale, the fruit juice had too many bits in it, the butter too hard. They passed by, squabbling all the way. The English abroad were not an attractive sight, Patricia thought, so stuck in their ways that it was a mystery how they had once had the imagination to govern half the world.

Then it struck her. The absurdity of the English. That's

when she began to laugh, almost uncontrollably until tears gathered in her eyes. And in that moment she knew what she would do next. It was so simple, yet it would cause uproar. She enjoyed the idea so much that she decided to write it down on her paper napkin. It sat there, staring back at her, and she laughed all the more. Just one word.

Marmite.

—⟡—

The suggestion, splashed across the front pages of three tabloids, that Brussels was about to ban Marmite caused a storm that was impossible to understand, unless you were British. The little pot of dark goo had divided opinion in the country for more than a hundred years. Made originally from the discarded malt scrapings of brewers' vats, it had always been laden with salt, additives and controversy. Even its marketing campaign captured the schizophrenia of the product – 'Love It, or Hate It.' And many did.

But it was a uniquely British love-hate relationship, and when the rumour began that it was about to be removed from the shelves as part of some European crackdown on additives, the press went wild. They called parliamentarians and commissioners in Brussels demanding answers, but got nothing except confusion and contradiction – which was scarcely surprising, since the rumour was entirely false. Yet it was entirely credible. For wasn't this a European oligarchy which had once banned the selling of

British goods by British people to British customers in British weights – pounds and ounces? In 2001 a vegetable seller in Sunderland had been seized by two police officers at his market stall and charged with the heinous offence of selling bananas by the pound – an imperial rather than a metric measure. He was charged, convicted, and given a criminal record. Other metric martyrs followed in his footsteps, dragged to the dock and made criminals for giving their customers what they wanted. The pronouncement of the European Commission some years later that it had never intended to make selling bananas a criminal act only proved the extraordinary arrogance of those silly burghers in Brussels, and did nothing to wipe away the public resentment or diminish the imagination of headline writers who strained like hounds in the slips, ever ready to be released. Matters had been measured in pounds ever since Shylock's time, and the call had gone out throughout the land to fight his latter-day counterparts, on the landing grounds and the beaches, in the streets and the hills.

Other stories followed to stoke the ire. Bananas were supposed to be straight. Pints were going to be poured in litres. Eggs could no longer be sold by the dozen. So when the suggestion was made that the little yellow-topped jars were to be outlawed by people who ate horses and fricasseed frogs, the nation leaped to its feet, demanding action.

The problem for a Prime Minister already under pressure was that there was no action he could take. When he stood at the Dispatch Box, feeling as if it were every inch a dock, there had been no time to establish the truth of the story. His answers seemed evasive, unprepared, and wholly un-British. And when a few days later the story was finally and flatly denied, the press and the Leader of the Opposition claimed glorious credit for forcing Brussels to change its mind. No matter how hard the Prime Minister protested, his words were drowned out by the baying of the crowd. Usher was humiliated.

Politics and truth. Strange bedfellows, indeed.

—◊—

Nobody understands politicians. A ridiculous comment, but sadly too often true. People treat their elected representatives as though they are constructed from rubber – impervious, unfeeling and, of course, eminently flexible. They have no inkling of the physical and emotional pain that so often goes with the job. An elder statesman had once suggested that all political careers end in failure, but he forgot to mention that before their end a politician's days were filled with exhaustion and exasperation, too. That's what had made Usher's hay fever so much worse these past years, why Gordon Brown had hurled telephones at the wall, why Churchill had drunk and Macmillan turned in a lonely bed while his wife was off sleeping with one of his closest colleagues. It was also why Harry had trouble making his relationships work.

Jemma was waiting for him – she had half a cupboard of coat hangers now, and her own set of keys. It was well past eleven when she heard the front door bang. His nights were getting longer, the government rushing to get its business through, and there would be no respite until the other side of the election that was still nearly three months away. As he clambered up the stairs, a pile of mail in his hands, she was sitting at the desk in his study, in front of his laptop and printer, with sheets of paper spilling from the top of the desk and over a considerable portion of the floor.

He kissed the back of her head, a casual, tired gesture. 'How's it going in business class?'

'Slowly,' she said. 'What I'm getting off the Internet isn't enough. Most of the victims were very private people, some of them seem to have no web records at all.'

He threw the envelopes to one side and slumped into an armchair, the spring gone from his legs.

'If we want the information—' she began.

'We do,' he interrupted, almost fiercely.

'Then I'm going to have to visit. Call on them. Every one.'

'Can't you use the phone?'

'Harry, these are people who have lost loved ones in the most terrible circumstances. They're not going to be happy about a stranger who telephones out of the blue to interrogate them. They need a face. And I've only got nights, I can't call on them during the day.'

'Weekends?' he suggested.

'I was hoping to be with you. In the constituency.'

He sat, disconsolate. 'We need this, Jem. And you're the only one who can do it.'

She didn't know what to say, or was it that she had too much to say? She'd wanted to be at his side throughout the campaign, caring for him, claiming him. So she said nothing, lowered her head to hide her disappointment, went back to tapping at the keys.

Harry sighed, knew he'd hurt her, hadn't meant to. He pulled himself from his chair. 'Leave it now, Jem. Come to bed.'

'I'll be there in a few minutes,' she said, stubborn, not looking up, hiding the tear that was trying to force its way through.

He disappeared. And by the time she crept into the bedroom considerably more than a few minutes later, he was fast asleep.

—❦—

There is a tipping point in matters, more decisive than a turning point, which marks the place of no return. Sloppy had reached it. The strange Mr Anderson had presented him with a challenge in the form of the Shengtzu Investment Fund, and Sloppy had risen to the occasion. He had spent many hours studying the contents of the envelopes. Both seemed genuine, and the additional hours he spent on the telephone and interrogating the web had confirmed every bit of the story.

Yet still he hesitated. To make a quick-turn profit he

needed short-term money, and he could conceive of only one answer. Harry. To Sloppy's mind the papers he had deceived Harry into signing were entirely balanced – he had no deliberate intention of cheating his friend. If Sloppy had decided he needed to access Harry's funds, it was only because his friend didn't need them. And, being a fair man, Sloppy had balanced this little bit of larceny by giving Harry a share of the business. He had made Harry a partner. And, with the security of these letters, Sloppy was able to access funds that he then placed in the hands of the Shengtzu Investment Fund, along with the quarter of a million from his new and serendipitous client. Before anyone knew it the profits would be reaped, the money would be returned and the worst that could happen would be a few awkward questions, but Sloppy could handle that. And if this all seemed a little too good to be true, it was balanced by the fact that most things in Sloppy's life seemed entirely too bad. He deserved a break, and Harry deserved to give it to him. So in the end it was simple. Any remaining doubts were washed away with the whisky and painkillers.

Alas, it wasn't the entire story. The documents relating to the Shengtzu Investment Fund were genuine, but not complete; Patricia had seen to that. The papers had been taken from a much thicker dossier that had been handed to EATA by the authorities in Beijing, who were in the middle of an anti-corruption drive. Corruption was endemic and they would never eliminate the problem, but it was politically convenient for them to parade a few scalps in order to encourage others to behave a little more cautiously. The Shengtzu Investment Fund was a vehicle that had careened out of control and was about to be brought to a halt, taken to pieces, its director-drivers dragged to the side of the road where they would be lucky to escape without a bullet in the back of the head.

Sloppy was heading for disaster, and where he went, Harry was bound to follow. He was, after all, a partner, there were documents to prove it and his ignorance wouldn't save him. What would be his excuse, that he had trusted his best friend? Yet busy men often are forced to trust those around them, and in Sloppy's case Harry did that without reservation. Anyway, he had an election to fight, and a new woman in his life, they were distraction enough. He couldn't do everything, not by himself, couldn't even read all his mail, so when in the middle of the latest pile that cascaded onto his doormat he found an envelope from Sloppy, marked with its corporate logo, he tossed it to one side, unopened, for later. Much later. After all, he knew what was in it. The quarterly statement. Another in a long line of quarterly statements. They had never given any trouble before, and he expected none now, otherwise Sloppy would have called. He trusted Sloppy, with his life.

CHAPTER NINE

Harry's main opponent in the upcoming election was Zafira Bagshot, a young and energetic campaigner who had recently returned from several years as an aid worker in the Sudan and was now intent on campaigning on every corner. She had publicly accused Harry of being an absentee landlord, a man who took his constituents for granted while he strutted the stage at Westminster. He didn't take it personally, he rather admired her, but it gave the campaign an added edge. On the last Saturday afternoon in February he was walking through the market square, shaking hands, chatting to shoppers and greeting stallholders while on all sides his helpers handed out leaflets. Two journalists from the local radio station and newspaper were in tow, while Emily Keane hovered in the background, ever present but none too conspicuous.

'Oh, you must be the new lady in Harry's life,' one elderly volunteer gushed in her ear.

'Just his press helper,' Emily replied, and smiled.

The old lady offered a conspiratorial smile in return in the manner of all experienced gossips.

'No, really,' Emily persisted, but the old woman went off chuckling.

As they made their way through the afternoon Harry spoke to many of his voters – people were rarely unkind to his face, but he sensed an air not so much of disaffection as of disappointment, which when he pressed them for details tended to focus on Ben Usher. One trader who specialized in selling British produce even had an entire corner of his stall devoted to a display of jars of Marmite, and they were selling well. Harry even bought one himself, quietly suspecting that he'd end up with an entire cupboard full by the end of the campaign.

It was late, just as dusk was finally taking hold and the chill winter air beginning to bite, when Harry all but stumbled across a figure sheltering in a doorway. At first he had thought it was nothing more than a pile of rubbish waiting to be collected, sheets of cardboard and old clothes, but from its midst he saw someone staring at him. A girl, one of the homeless.

'Stupid sod!' she shouted, kicking out at him. 'Watch who you're treading on.'

'Sorry, didn't see you there.'

'You blind or what? What the hell you want, anyway?' she demanded, pulling a tattered duvet more closely round her.

And already the journalists were circling, crowding in.

He could have moved on, using her aggression as an excuse, but Harry didn't often pass by the other side, not without a close look first. He asked the journalists to give them a little privacy, and Emily ushered them to a safe distance.

'You OK?' he asked when at last he and the girl had been left on their own.

'Fucking brilliant,' she snapped, scraping the hair from her eyes. They were large, attractive, and she was not much more than twenty.

'Bit too cold for fucking brilliant in my opinion,' he replied softly, squatting so that he could make good eye contact. Her cheeks were red, flushed, not sallow like so many on the street, and her teeth still white. He guessed she was a newcomer. 'You been doing this long?'

'Piss off.'

'I'd like to help.'

'You gonna give me money?'

'What would you use it for?'

She glared, defiant. 'I'd probably book a holiday in the Seychelles.'

'You want something to eat? I can get you that.'

'Money!' she bit back.

He looked deeper into her eyes, saw the glazed, furtive look, and knew what she would use the money for.

'I'd really like to help.'

'You'd really like to bang me, you mean. That's all your type ever want.'

'What are you on?'

'On? What am I *on*? I'm on my own, wanker!'

This wasn't getting anywhere. It was time to leave. He stood up.

'You wanna help, then give me some money,' she said, more urgent, realizing she was losing an opportunity. 'I'll fuck you if you want.'

'What?'

'Twenty quid.'

He began to move away.

'Aren't you gonna give me some money?'

'No,' he said. 'Food. Not money.'

It had been a waste of time. Such encounters usually were. Yet there had been occasions when it had worked out. Usually ex-servicemen who had found the adjustment to civilian life too difficult. They came back from a war with their heads screwed, from a world that was black and white to one where everything was compromise and ill-discipline. Jobs that didn't work out, marriages that failed, homes that were lost. An alarming number of former soldiers ended up on the street, and he wouldn't turn away from them, knowing what they had gone through, and were still going through. In a few cases, a precious few, he had been able to help. And for those precious few, it was worth putting up with the usual crap and abuse.

When he cast a final look over his shoulder he saw the journalists, notebooks and recorders in hand, talking to the girl. One was handing across money. She was standing now, wrapped in cast-offs, eyes filled with pain and rage, pointing after him, and shouting. Something about him not being willing to help, refusing to give her money, only being interested in sex.

Harry hurried on, putting as much distance between him and the embarrassment as possible. Emily rushed to his side.

'Not my best bit of canvassing,' he muttered. 'I didn't even ask her if she was registered to vote. Still, I doubt whether I could have counted on her support.'

'Don't worry,' Emily said, 'they'll never use what she says.'

'But they'll report what she is. A young woman sleeping rough on my streets.'

'And that you tried to help.'

'They are journalists. They will report that I didn't help. Which is good news for the young lady, because doubtless my opponent will be here in the morning handing out hot tea and buns and offering to let her sleep in her spare room.'

'I'll put that down to cynicism, Harry.'

'And I'll put it down to experience.'

He walked on, thinking he had left the matter behind him.

—∞—

Felix Wilton had been in awe of his wife ever since she had taken the remarkable decision not to throw him out and had instead come to a more dignified arrangement. He had watched her build her secret life, just as he had built his own, and if it wasn't exactly a matching of souls it was much more than muddling through. It was an accommodation, a meeting of interests, protected from the distractions of sex that usually fouled things up. Yet the latest step along their way had left him almost overwhelmed. A quarter of a million pounds couldn't be seen as a lightweight gesture even in EU circles where accounting had always had a remarkably flexible reputation. Wilton knew his history, understood that such matters had always been a feature of the European dream, ever since the very early days when after the war the United States had sprinkled slush funds like stardust over Jean Monnet and the others to help kick-start the process. Funny money had been a bit of a problem ever since, and an entire European Commission under Jacques Santer had been forced to resign *en masse*, blown away by repeated allegations of corruption. But there was so much less need for that nowadays, when everything was up front, and the President of the European Parliament paid nearly a million dollars for his trouble, more than twice that of the US President and more than four times the salary of the British Prime Minister. Dreams don't come cheap. So perhaps a few hundred thousand didn't really matter that much.

Yet Wilton found himself worrying about it all, for her sake. He cared – not just for their arrangement, but for her, Patricia. He worried about her in the morning when he unlocked the door to his antiques shop, and found himself still worrying about her when he came to lock up at 5 p.m. prompt, so he did what he always did in such circumstances. He returned home and fixed himself a large drink, cooked himself a solitary meal (Dover sole, grilled, with a few greens, on this occasion) and waited until it had gone nine. Then he walked to Hyde Park, sat on a bench and pretended to read a newspaper – his eyes should be that sharp! – and made sure he wasn't being followed. He carried on down the Bayswater Road, past the bustle of Notting Hill Gate and into Holland Park Avenue.

It was 10.25 by the time he turned into Holland Walk, the path that ran alongside the park. He knew what to expect for it was one of the longest established pick-up points in central London. Gay turf. Except the turf was frozen and at this time of year pick-ups were the sexual equivalent of extreme sports. There were only hardy souls hanging around, leaning on the railings where the frost had turned the cobwebs into works of art that caught the intermittent lamplight and shivered like distant galaxies. There were enquiring eyes cast at him from the shadows but he ignored them, walking on, and when he stopped and looked back, it wasn't to change his mind, only to check yet again that he wasn't being followed. As he did so, from the opposite end of the Walk that ran off Kensington High Street, another man began to walk towards him, slowly, in no hurry. When at last they met, on a part of the path that was less well lit than others, they greeted each other like old friends, embraced, kissed, moved into a deeper part of the shadow behind a tree. They were there for some time in a monochrome world that was largely silent, until a shrill cry of alarm came from the park – a peacock, disturbed by some marauding fox. But the two remained locked, so close and buried in the darkness that any Peeping Tom would have been seen far sooner than he could have spotted what they were up to.

Then they were done. A final embrace. They parted. Wilton continued on to the High Street, where he took a taxi to the Chelsea Arts Club. The other man continued walking, in a long circuitous route through the streets of Holland Park that eventually took him back to his place of work. The Russian Embassy.

—m—

A young woman living on her own was – well, on her own. And vulnerable. Jemma made no bones about the fact that sleeping with Harry in Mayfair had attractions that far outstripped the appeal of returning to her modest top-floor apartment in a Battersea apartment block. Every time she returned the carpets somehow seemed to be more faded than she had remembered, and the paintwork a little more chipped. She recognized what was happening, of course. As much as she took pride in her sense of independence, she didn't really want to come back at all.

Yet here she was, again. She kicked her shoes off the moment she walked in, dropped her bag, punched the button to listen to her messages as she passed, and headed straight for the kitchen. She hadn't eaten, but discovered she had nothing but yoghurt in the fridge. Too much time with Harry – and too many evenings on the road. She had a job to do in finding out more about the crash victims that was not only important, it was for Harry. And the quicker she got it finished, the more time she could spend at Harry's side. She wanted to fight the election with him, and for him. But there were times when she thought that chasing after the bereaved to ask them questions about those they had lost was not only painful but utterly point-less. She didn't know what she was looking for, couldn't see why any of their loved ones might have become targets so vital that it justified blowing a plane out of the sky. She'd just come back from visiting a middle-aged woman who had lost not only her husband but also her elderly mother – he had flown to Brussels to bring his mother-in-law back as a Christmas surprise. What the hell was there that would justify mass slaughter?

She devoured two tubs of yoghurt and threw them in the bin. She looked around her. Her home seemed sad, strange. The plates that had stood neglected on the drain-ing board for a week and a half stared at her, accusing her of betrayal. This wasn't her any more. 'Time to move on, girl,' she whispered.

She cast off her clothes one by one as she headed for the shower, wanting to wash away the weariness, but it didn't work. The shower curtain clung to her in complaint – damn it, Harry had a wet room! – trying to wrap itself around her and demand attention. She turned the shower off.

It was as she was dripping, naked, struggling to make sense of the plastic curtain, that a knife slashed it through with a single stroke. Before she could reach for a scream it had been ripped to one side, and when at last she tried to scream she found her lungs paralysed. Standing in front of her were two men. Hoods. One had her carving knife in his hand.

'Make noise and you will never make noise again,' the knife man said in accented English.

A thousand thoughts flashed through her mind, and then a thousand more. She had no doubt she could end up dead. How she reacted was crucial to whether in ten minutes' time she would still be alive, but that told her nothing. What should she do? Scream? Be compliant? Fall on her knees and sob? But she was totally vulnerable, naked, her body shaking as she tried to take in her situation. Would they rape, or were they here simply to steal? But she was just a hard-up primary school teacher, for God's sake, she had nothing worth stealing. So she knew they would rape her.

Submit? Struggle? Get it over with, or try to show them that she was better than them? Someone had once told her that letting her bowels loose would put off an attack, but she couldn't control a muscle. She was astonished at what thoughts sped through her mind.

'What ... do ... you want,' she uttered eventually, shaking.

They said nothing, but took an arm each, dragged her

from the bath and threw her onto the bed. She lay there, didn't protest, her legs spread apart, didn't bother trying to close them. This wasn't a time for gestures, she had to concentrate on what might make a difference. They used a silk scarf and the cord for her dressing gown to tie her hands to the white metal bedhead. She tried to study their eyes, their weights, body shapes, their smell, hoping she might recognize them again.

Once she was secured, Knife Man leaned over her, his blade flashing in front of her eyes. He put it to her forehead, she could feel its cold bite. 'You want knife here – or here?' He dragged it, very slowly, down her body, the blade hesitating at her most vulnerable points, her eyes, lips, breasts, until it was resting between her legs. He used it to shave her.

Then, for the first time, the other man spoke. 'Jemma, let the dead rest in peace.'

That was when she knew they were going to kill her. Yet neither of them moved.

'You understand?' he continued.

The other man shaved her a little more, and more roughly.

'They do not need you knocking on their doors.'

Suddenly she knew. They were warning her off. The plane crash.

'I ... understand.' She couldn't manage more than one word at a time.

'Excellent.'

They stood back. Knife Man was admiring his handiwork. She had never felt more naked in her entire life.

'If you mention this to the police, we will come back and hurt you,' the other man said. There was no emotion in it, all a matter of everyday fact, as if they did this every night of the week and were almost a little bored.

She was shaking now, her body trembling on the bed. They weren't going to rape her after all?

'A warning. You understand?'

She nodded her head.

'Good. Friends.' He nodded to Knife Man, who sliced through the silk scarf, leaving her secured only by the heavily knotted cord.

And they left. They didn't even bother closing the front door. She could hear them laughing as they went down the stairs.

When eventually she managed to unravel the knot, she lay on the bed and cried as she hadn't done since the day her brother had died.

—⁂—

Harry rushed to her, a man pursued by demons he thought had gone from his life but that had been resurrected by her phone call. He threw a twenty at the taxi driver, didn't wait for the change, and took the stairs three at a time. Her door was still open. Experience told him to pause before he burst in, to look for signs, in case they were still there, but there was nothing. Then he saw Jemma sitting on the end of her bed. Her head was bowed, her dressing gown wrapped roughly around her, its cord on the floor. He threw himself down on his knees in front of her, tried to embrace her; she sat stiff, rigid, as though hewn of rock. Her voice, when it emerged from its hiding place, was no more than a whisper.

'They told me to keep away from the crash.'

The words hit him like a sledgehammer. 'Did they hurt you? Jemma! What did they do?'

Slowly, mechanically, she drew back the folds of her dressing gown to reveal the mess they had made of her most intimate parts, then she let the gown fall back again.

'Jem, Jem, I'm so sorry . . .'

But she wouldn't say any more. No tears, not yet, no further words, everything locked away deep inside.

He said he was going to call the police but suddenly she snatched at him, held his arm with ferocious strength, and shook her head.

'Why not?' he asked, but he already knew. She was terrified they would come back. It was reckoned that the vast majority of sexual assaults on women go unreported in the London Metropolitan Police area. This would be another. She fell back on the bed and began to shake uncontrollably.

He went to the kitchen, found a tub of hot chocolate, made a mug and loaded it with extra sugar, then sat with her as she sipped it.

'Would you recognize them again?' he ventured,

knowing he had to ask, not wanting to make her relive the nightmare.

'I tried, Harry,' she began, revived by the chocolate, 'to see if there was anything about them that was different.' She shook her head, it seemed too much, but then: 'One had blue eyes. Both were young. And fit, very strong.' They had left raw marks on her wrist where they had dragged her to the bed. 'And they were foreign. Accents.'

'Try to remember precisely what they said.'

'One of them – the one with the knife. Awful grammar. Kept dropping the definite article. "The" or "a" or whatever he should have said.' She was still trembling, and struggling, fighting to recapture every word before they became scrambled in her mind, while Harry tried to smooth encouragement into her hands with his thumbs. 'They laughed as they went down the stairs. Joking. About my body. My breasts. I could hear them. "*Dermo*, we should have *tranoot* her," that's what the one with the knife said. Words I didn't understand, but I can guess what they meant.' Suddenly, she drew back from him. 'Hey, you're hurting me!'

His thumbs had dug themselves deep into the palm of her hands. 'You sure? Are you sure that's what they said? Jem, this is very important.'

'Of course,' she said, resentful, pulling her hands away. 'I spend every hour of my working day trying to figure out what five- and six-year-olds are saying. You get an ear for it. Of course I'm sure.'

He pulled himself from the floor and came to sit on the bed beside her. 'Damn them,' he muttered.

'Damn who, Harry?'

'Dropping the definite article. And those words. *"Trahnouti"*. Means "fucked". It's Russian.'

'But I don't understand.'

'Neither do I.'

'But what are you saying – Ghazi, Russians, Brussels? What the hell does it all mean?'

He shook his head. He hadn't a clue. Jemma had been assaulted and terrified – but for what?

Now she started to cry, releasing the anger and humiliation through her tears that fell onto Harry's shoulder and stained his jacket. He sat beside her, holding her, trying to give her comfort, finding none for himself. This was his fault. And, as he looked into her eyes, he could see that she thought so too.

—◊◊◊—

To destroy a good man, it is only necessary to take his reputation. And that is what Patricia Vaine had decided to do. Her attack on Harry had started as a means of defence, of protecting herself, but she had begun to enjoy the aroma of power and it had caused her to cross a line without her realizing she had done so. It was some time before she would accept that pursuing Harry had become a professional pleasure. That pursuit was made all the easier because Harry had no idea that he was even a target, not until he discovered that his credit card had stopped working.

In its rush to clear up as much business as possible before the election, Parliament was sitting ball-breaking hours, beside which there were a thousand other distractions, with demands from his constituency, when most of all he wanted to be with Jemma. It didn't help that Jemma showed a marked reluctance to spend much time with him, saying she wanted time on her own, to heal, to reflect. That only made his sense of guilt worse. Torn in three directions. Even Harry Jones wasn't up to that.

And in the game of battleships and broadsides that make up every constituency campaign, Zafira Bagshot had landed a direct hit. Harry was woken up early one Thursday morning by a call from the chairman of his constituency party, Oscar Colville.

'Who pulled your chain, Oscar?' Harry grumbled, scrabbling for his wristwatch. Six-thirty. And he hadn't got to bed before two.

'Sorry, Harry. I truly am. I take full responsibility. It's my fault.'

'What is?'

'The screw-up over St Mary's.'

Harry groaned, struggling to recollect an early philosophy lesson that had suggested the world was imagination and might cease to exist if you kept your eyes closed. He tried it; didn't work. 'School or hospital?'

'Both.'

There had been a point where St Mary's had boasted both a school and a hospital, but both had fallen casualty to the campaign of cuts. Inevitable. No easy solution. Inherited problem. All the usual clichés had been marched before the public and put on parade, but very few had saluted. Even statistics that showed you had a considerably better chance of surviving any number of medical emergencies in the new, larger but more distant hospital hadn't won the day; the hospital and school had served the community for generations, and if they had been good enough for fathers and grandfathers, they should be there for grandsons, too. So Harry had made the argument, ducked, and moved on. The adjacent sites had now been cleared and made ready for the construction of a new business park, the sorry matter forgotten – or so he had hoped.

Yet, according to an uncharacteristically subdued and hesitant Oscar, the front page of the local newspaper that was about to flood the streets of the constituency was dominated by a photograph of Ms Bagshot, standing in the middle of the building site, her arms outstretched in the preacher position, beneath a headline that screamed: 'Harry's Howler.'

'It was the press pack, you see.'

'No, I don't,' Harry replied bluntly.

'We put together a press pack for the campaign. Usual stuff, to brief any visiting journalist about the wonders of the constituency. Look, Harry, I truly am sorry . . .'

'Oscar, wait. Slow down. What the bloody hell are you talking about?'

'Emily, she did the draft. Very well, we all thought. Updating the one we put out at the last election.'

'When we still had St Mary's,' Harry sighed, coming to enlightenment.

'I proofread it, but ... Harry, you know how many distractions there are, particularly with the Prime Minister getting his tail in such a tangle.'

'You're telling me that the press pack went out—'

'Proclaiming the virtues of the community hospital and school.'

A hospital and school that had been bulldozed two years ago only after picket lines had been pushed aside by the local constabulary.

'She's being very unfair, your opponent,' Oscar continued, blustering, not even wanting to use her name. 'She's said you are not only an absentee landlord but in danger of sounding like the village idiot.'

It was a mixed metaphor, but Harry could see where she was coming from.

'What's to be done?' Oscar pleaded. 'I'll resign, if it helps. Blame me.'

'No, Oscar, thanks but ... I'll put out an apology.' He sighed, stretched, ached. 'And we'll just have to work twice as hard.'

Which was precisely what he proceeded to do when he travelled to his constituency the next day, Friday. Tramping the streets with his band of volunteers, knocking on doors, handing out leaflets, getting fingers squashed in letter-boxes like bear traps, listening, explaining, trying to assess the state of play. It was gone seven and darkness had fallen before they stopped. Harry invited them all for a pub supper, fifteen in all, and while they were eating he toured the bars, chatting to old friends, hoping to make some that were new, and braving the inevitable ribbing about 'Harry's Howler'.

The bill came to nearly three hundred pounds. His card didn't work. The reader refused to accept it. The landlord tried a second time. Same result.

'You drowned it in cheap red wine or something?' Harry asked.

'Been working fine all day,' the landlord replied, per-plexed.

Harry tried a different card, and two others. They were all declined.

'Some screw-up,' Harry muttered, his mouth growing dry with embarrassment. He looked into his wallet, but he didn't have that much cash. 'I'll go to a machine, be back in a few minutes.'

'No worries, Harry, next time you're in,' the landlord said. 'Pity's sake, after all these years, I know you're good for it.'

But when eventually he shoved his cards into an ATM, once more every one of them was rejected. Insufficient funds. And when he tried yet again, the machine retained the card and instructed him to refer to his bank. But how could he? It was Friday evening. Late. Miserable. And dark. He wouldn't be able to scream at anyone until Monday morning. He intended to do exactly that, but in the meantime, as an interim measure, he pounded the console in frustration. Useless bloody thing. The machine was telling him he was broke.

CHAPTER TEN

If he hadn't had enough cash in his wallet to pay for petrol, Harry wasn't sure how he would have made it back home on Sunday evening. He felt lonely and lifeless as he kicked across the stack of mail that had accumulated inside his front door. He swept it up, intending to sort it into piles of varying urgency, when he was silly enough to switch on his laptop. There were more than a hundred and fifty new e-mail messages waiting for him, quite apart from the backlog. He cursed, switched it off and threw the post into a pile in the corner. He wished Jemma had been waiting for him, but she was spending the weekend with her parents. So instead he picked up the whisky bottle. It had been a bloody awful week. He had never expected a life in politics to be an easy touch, but right now he'd have swapped it to be back under fire from Saddam's Revolutionary Guard on the outskirts of Baghdad. That had left him with a bullet hole through his shoulder and, right now, that seemed like a better choice from a safer world.

He slept badly, rose early, impatient, but no one at the

bank was going to answer before ten o'clock. He made sure his was the first call.

'Tom? This is Harry Jones.'

'I was wondering when you'd contact us,' the private client manager said.

'So you've spotted the screw-up in my accounts, too, have you? What the bloody hell's going on?'

There was a silence before the other man spoke, and when he did, his voice was measured, almost over-controlled, as if he was trying to calm a wild cat. 'Harry, I can't talk to you. You know I can't.'

'What on earth do you mean?'

'The letters we've sent.'

'What letters?' Harry said, eyeing the pile in the corner. He hadn't opened a bank statement in months, as was the privilege of the super-wealthy, particularly when they were spectacularly busy.

'We've sent you e-mails' – the laptop glowered at Harry from near at hand – 'I've even left messages asking you to call.'

'Those? Tom, I thought you were phoning to arrange lunch.'

A silence of confusion filled the space between them.

'Tom, I've been banking with you for how many years? I haven't got a squashed gnat's idea what the bloody hell you're talking about.'

When he spoke again, the bank man's voice was more contrite. 'Harry, your account has been handed up the line to head office. Recoveries Department. I can't touch it or help you any more. Look, you know what it's been like since the Crash, everything is run by machines and mindless codes of conduct. I hate it, truly I do.'

But Harry knew Tom wasn't going to pack it in, and why should he, at the age of forty-seven with three kids and a subsidized mortgage?

'If only you'd been in touch earlier I might have been able to help you with your problem,' the bank man continued.

'Problem? I have a problem?'

'You really don't know?'

Harry had never taken money for granted; you didn't, not when you'd pushed yourself through uni on a diet of stale burger buns. Yet since his father had died, fortune had flowed upon Harry like snow in Santa's grotto. He had enough, more than enough. He could take a hit. 'Tell me I'm down to my last couple of million.'

The bank man sounded wretched. 'Harry, you're bust.'

'I can't be. Don't be preposterous.'

'I'm so very sorry, Harry.'

He was left speechless, scrabbling to understand. 'This is asinine, some ludicrous practical joke.'

Silence.

'A mistake. Has to be. For pity's sake, Tom, what the hell are you trying to tell me – that I'm in the shit?'

'Harry, you are in it so deep you disappeared several weeks ago.'

—ɷ—

It might have been handled better, and perhaps would have been, but for the Crash. It had left the banks owing so many billions that they could have filled every crater on the moon, and as far as most people knew, that's precisely where all the money had gone. It had destroyed the banks' reputation, and along with it their patience, despite the fact that it was taxpayers' money that had saved them. You can drag the bankers out of the shit, but as for dragging the shit out of the bankers, that was one miracle that had yet to be performed.

The Shengtzu Investment Fund had gone down, taking Sloppy with it. And, in turn, Sloppy had taken Harry with him. One of the letters Harry had signed over alcohol gave Sloppy access to his accounts, but that was only half of it – even the better half. One of the other letters made Harry a partner in the business, and in law that made him liable for all its losses. And the losses of the Shengtzu Investment Fund were enormous. The banks were going to retrieve their money from wherever they could. Grab first, ask questions later. Much later.

It was fraud, of course. But that was a matter between Harry and Sloppy. So far as the banks were concerned, they had Harry's legitimate signature and until some court told them otherwise they regarded his money as their own. They had tried to inform him of this fact, and it wasn't their fault that he hadn't opened his wretched letters or responded. Harry had gone down for millions, all of them.

And, inevitably, Sloppy wasn't answering his phone.

—∿—

'Order! ORDER!' The Speaker's voice rose, but his task was impossible. The chamber of the House of Commons was packed to oppression, even the Prime Minister had stumbled over outstretched legs as he had tried to negotiate his way to his seat by the Dispatch Box. It was the last Prime Minister's Question Time before Parliament was sent packing for the election. By the end of the week these men and women would legally cease to be MPs, and judging by the rising slipperiness of the electoral slope, a large number of them wouldn't be making it back.

'Order!' the Speaker shouted once more, jumping to his feet, a sign that all others must sit and desist, which they did but grudgingly. The Minister for Justice was proving a particular mouthy pain, making the Speaker wonder whether he'd already started upon his end-of-term party despite the fact that it wasn't yet lunchtime. The Speaker, who was old school, groaned in despair. 'The Right Honourable Gentleman must restrain himself,' he insisted – preferably by the neck, he thought, as he received another outburst in reply. When he had first been elected Speaker he had, in the traditional manner, been dragged to his chair while feigning reluctance. There was no pretence now, the lack of enthusiasm entirely genuine. Thank God this was the final week. The South of France beckoned, where only waiters and taxi drivers would shout at him.

'Mr David Murray,' the Speaker nodded, indicating that

the Leader of the Opposition should resume his efforts to be heard.

'Thank you, Mr Speaker.' Murray looked around the oak-and-leather chamber, keeping them waiting. He had deliberately started the row, now he intended to finish it. Speedbird 235. It was still a criminal investigation, of course, many aspects of it *sub judice* or simply secret, but none of that constrained his democratic duty to give the government a deeply unpleasant kicking. 'Mr Speaker, I would like to help the Prime Minister.' He smiled across the Dispatch Box, his eyes suggesting that it would be about as helpful as positioning a rectal thermometer with a hammer. 'Help him realize the magnitude of his failure so that he might consider it in his retirement, which I hope will be happy. And soon.' The troops behind him loved that, and so did the sketch writers scribbling away in the gallery above his head. He held up his arms, like a conductor demanding the attention of his orchestra, and the crowd fell silent once more.

'Question! Ask a question!' one of the more dogmatic members behind the Prime Minister demanded through the hole in the noise.

'Is it ...' – the question was coming – 'is it not incredible, inexcusable, inconceivable' – each thought was spat out with ever greater emphasis as he glowered at the man sitting only feet away – 'that in this day and age an airplane full of people could be shot down thirty miles from our coast without anyone seeing, hearing, plotting, tracking, recording, mapping or in any way marking what was happening?' Every word was a hammer blow, nailing Usher to his cross. 'In such circumstances, who can be surprised that those responsible weren't intercepted before they had committed their foul act? And who can be surprised that it was left to the Russians to catch them?'

That got them going again. The Justice Minister was puce. Once again Murray waited for his opportunity.

'We know from all the evidence of these past long years that the Prime Minister doesn't understand the meaning of humility. But would he, even at this late stage in his career, take a moment to look up the meaning of humiliation?'

That's what it had come to. Using dead children as political weapons. It was a day when the reputation of the House drowned in venom, but the reputation of the Prime Minister suffered still more.

Harry sat two rows behind Usher, squashed between the shoulders of colleagues on the packed benches. The shock of what Sloppy had done was so overwhelming that it had rendered him numb, like a man who had been given such a beating that for the moment his body had blocked out the pain. He had left the matter in the hands of his lawyer and accountant, while he tried to function as usual. He'd known men who had carried on fighting even with both legs blown away, so he just kept his head down and carried on, even when he hurt. So, like the Leader of the Opposition, he had also raised questions that day about the crash, but not here, not in this pit of vipers. Despite the many distractions he'd continued to struggle with the question Jemma had put so succinctly – Ghazi. Russians. Brussels. What connected them? What had brought such stray ends together? For brief moments he thought of giving Shelagh another call, but quickly squashed the idea. Even in his present state he wasn't that much of an emotional Neanderthal. So instead he had tabled a question for Written Answer to the Secretary of State for Transport, asking if she would identify which of the passengers on Speedbird 235 had connected with it from other flights, and where those flights had come from. In other words, let the government do the donkey work.

It was an entirely innocuous question. The Table Office hadn't raised any difficulties, the answer should be published in a few days. Straightforward. At least, that's how it seemed to Harry. But Patricia Vaine held a sharply different view. She was sitting in her red-and-gilt-clad dining room on Rue Faider later that evening; spring had come early in Brussels and the tall windows were open, the cigarette smoke drifting up to the ceiling before being sucked out into the garden. The food was done, the wine still flowing, the conversation lively and appropriately injudicious. McDeath was there, at the distant end of the table, and in-between she had assembled a collection of staffers from the European Parliament and senior Commission officials, men and women who saw the papers, heard the whispers, understood the rumours, and were responsible for making most of the decisions that their masters would later claim as their own. One of them, Callas, was responsible amongst many other things for the enormous fleet of S-class Mercedes that filled the basement beneath the Parliament building. He was also admirably drunk. The table rocked with laughter as he recounted the official version of the duties supposedly performed by the new executive assistant to the Maritime Affairs Commissioner, then contrasted that with the more analytical and anatomical version that was doing the rounds of the drivers' pool. Drivers knew everything. It was good to keep in touch.

She was making a mental note of the matter when she heard the alert tone pinging from her iPad. She excused herself and withdrew with her coffee to another room, then, after she read the message, sat motionless, staring sightless into an empty grate, her coffee stone cold. It was some while before she stirred. 'Oh, Harry Jones,' she whispered, almost in sorrow, 'do you never know when to stop pushing?'

She sucked her thumb. Part of her didn't want to do this. Then she reached for her phone. 'Emily? This is Patricia Vaine. We need to talk.'

—☊—

Harry's phone flashed into life.

'Can we talk, Harry?'

'Sure, Emily.' She sounded upset.

'It's private. Can I come to yours?'

Bugger. More bad news. Throw it on the pile with all the

181

rest of it. He was a little punch drunk with all the blows that had landed on him, made worse by the fact that he had spent the afternoon trying to track down Sloppy, but for some reason the bastard had gone missing. Office locked, no one had seen him for days, even at the club. Harry had ventured out to Sloppy's apartment in a warehouse overlooking St Katherine's Dock, so close to where the Speedbird had come down, and begun kicking the door so hard that the concierge had threatened to call the police, until he had recognized Harry. He'd explained that Mr Sopwith-Dane hadn't been there for days, and frankly wasn't expected back. Some sort of problem with the lease ...

Harry had slunk back home and taken it out on a bottle instead. Now more trouble. Emily. It was late, he was exhausted, but he hadn't been sleeping, so what difference did the time make? 'Twenty minutes,' he suggested.

It took her less than fifteen. It was only the second occasion she had been inside his home. This time she took her coat off. She looked good in clinging cashmere, no wonder the press men liked her. But her eyes were raw. He poured her a drink and sat her on the sofa, while he refilled his own glass and propped himself against the fireplace.

'Harry, I haven't had the opportunity before.' She sounded mournful.

'For what?'

'To say sorry. About the screw-up with St Mary's.'

He almost burst into laughter. 'Emily, it doesn't matter. Honestly, I haven't thought about that for days.'

'But I feel ashamed. I've let you down.'

'You think *you've* let me down?' He shook his head. There were others far ahead of her in the queue.

Yet she was not to be deflected. 'I came to work for you because I admire you, wanted to help. And I've failed miserably.' He shook his head but her eyes began to well up. 'I think you're wonderful,' she whispered.

'It's mutual.'

'Is it? Oh, Harry!' she cried out, burst into tears. Then she jumped from her place and, before he knew it, had flung herself into his arms, burying her head into his chest. He was startled, his drink spilled down her sweater, but she seemed not to notice. She was pressed up against him, wanting comfort, and when her eyes came up, he could see she wanted more than a warming hug. It didn't help his focus that the cashmere was low cut. She stretched up to kiss him.

He didn't push her away immediately – how many men would? Their bodies met, feeling for each other. She took his hand and slowly raised it to her breast, where she clasped it to her with such intensity that he thought it must be hurting her. Only then did he decide he had to back off.

'Emily, no ...' he moaned, pushing her gently away. 'There's Jemma.'

She looked at him with a mixture of incomprehension and despair that suggested he had slapped her. The tears returned, trickling down her face. Then she ran from the room, not even bothering to collect her coat. Seconds later the front door slammed. He knew he wouldn't see her again. He swore, very profoundly. How much worse could his life get? He replaced his spilt drink and downed it quickly, then poured another and put on some music. Meatloaf. Full volume, as it should be, hoping it would drown out his miseries.

It was less than an hour later when he heard a pounding at the door. Neighbours, he assumed. Music too loud. The assault on his door was repeated before he could get there. 'OK! OK!' he shouted through it, 'no need to kick it down.'

When he opened it, he found a uniformed police officer standing on his doorstep, an inspector. Two other policemen were standing behind him in the darkness. Bugger, he must really have hacked off the neighbours.

'Sorry, sorry,' he said, waving his glass in apology, 'I'll turn it down. Even better, I'll turn it off and go to bed.'

'Mr Jones? Mr Harry Jones?' the inspector asked, unsmiling. The porch light above gave his face a grim, awkward appearance, like a mask.

'Yes, of course.'

'Would you mind coming to the station with us, sir?'

'A bit excessive for playing Meatloaf, isn't it? What the bloody hell would you do if I'd put on a bit of Manilow, for goodness sake? Look, I apologize, all right? Won't happen again. Goodnight to you.' He stepped back, assuming that would be the end of the matter.

'Mr Harry Jones, I am arresting you on suspicion of a serious sexual assault. You do not have to say anything, but it may harm your defence if you do not mention when questioned something which you later rely on in court. Anything you say may be given in evidence ...'

The rest of it was lost on Harry; he couldn't take it in. 'No, no, you bloody idiot,' he muttered in disbelief, and took a further step back into the sanctuary of his hallway. That was when they handcuffed him, on his own doorstep, led him away to their car, which now had its blue light flashing in his face. That, combined with the alcohol and the shock, meant that he never saw the photographer sheltering in a nearby doorway, gleefully taking shots of the entire event. Even before he'd arrived at the police station, it was already getting calls asking for confirmation that Harry Jones had been taken into custody.

CHAPTER ELEVEN

Emily had fled from Harry's home in hysterics, wailing as she ran past the extravagantly decorated shop windows of New Bond Street, and she didn't stop until she had reached the bronze statues of Franklin D. Roosevelt and Winston Churchill perched on their bench outside Watches of Switzerland. The bench was a landmark, and now it became her refuge as she squeezed herself between them, sobbing, coatless. Passers-by hovered, trying to offer comfort, but could get little sense from her until someone called the police. Savile Row police station was nothing more than a rabbit hop away and a squad car arrived within minutes. Still no one could make sense of her through the weeping. Only when she had reached Savile Row and had the support of a female officer and a mug of sweet tea did her story come blurting out. That Harry had summoned her to her home. Was drunk. Had berated her for the foul-up over St Mary's. Then assaulted her. And only his drunken clumsiness had allowed her to escape.

They allowed her to pour out her misery without interruption or questions, as a red-eyed digital recorder captured every word. She wasn't accusing Harry of rape; even so, they wouldn't rule that out. The Met had adopted what it called a victim-centric approach to all sexual crimes, and it was a matter of considerable importance that political figures shouldn't be given preferential treatment – that would be unfair, particularly after a committee of those expense-scamming election monkeys had competed with each other to find ways of publicly humiliating the Police Commissioner. Politicians should think twice before bending over to pick up the sword of justice.

'We're going to have to ask you to undergo some tests, Emily. Is that OK? Take your clothes, and some swabs. You understand?'

She sucked the ends of her hair, then nodded. The inquisition of Harry Jones had begun.

—m—

Reputations are like airplanes. Once they start falling apart, things happen very quickly, and the results can be devastating.

Harry wasn't taken to Savile Row for fear of contamination by or with his accuser, so instead he was taken to Charing Cross station, a buttermilk stucco building in Agar Street, just back from the bustle of Trafalgar Square. He was taken to the custody suite; only then were his handcuffs removed. He was made to stand in line behind a couple of drunks before the inspector gave the custody officer reasons for the arrest, and the officer gave formal consent to Harry being held. He was taken to an inspection room where his clothes were removed and bagged – all of them, including his underwear. In their place he was given a shapeless white zip-up jump suit that felt as if it had been made from recycled paper. They took swabs – mouth, hands, genitalia. They had to get the permission of a superintendent as well as Harry himself before they started on that.

'What, no photos or fingerprinting?' Harry asked, when at last they had finished the humiliation.

'No, Mr Jones. We know who you are. And where you live.' It sounded like a threat.

They locked Harry in a cell. Bare walls, bright light, plastic mattress. 'Sleep it off, Mr Jones. We'll interview you in the morning.'

Sleep it off? They had to be joking. Then the door had slammed.

Harry had known many forms of incarceration. He'd been trained for it during his time in the SAS camp at Hereford, where the instructors had devised many ways of inflicting physical and mental punishment on their charges, pushing them to their limits, and sometimes beyond. It was one of the ways they sorted those who would die for their country from those who might just live. He'd been banged up on other occasions since then, sometimes in the most desperate circumstances. But never had he felt more lost.

They told him he could have two telephone calls, one to

his solicitor and another to a friend or family. But it was 2.30 a.m., too early for his solicitor, and even if their long relationship gave him the moral authority to drag him from his bed, Harry suddenly realized that he was no longer sure he had the financial authority to do so. And Jemma had enough on her plate, it wasn't how he wanted her to find out. So, at six, he called Oscar Colville.

'Getting your own back, Harry?' a weary voice enquired.

If only. Harry gave a brief explanation, and instructed him to call several people, starting with the Chief Whip. 'You can get him through the Downing Street switchboard. He will need to know.'

'Will he be able to help?'

'Help? No. He'll probably run a thirty-second mile in the other direction. An enormous amount of sewage is being poured over me, Oscar, and it's going to splash anyone who is standing too close.'

A haunting silence played down the line before his constituency chairman spoke again.

'Harry, you didn't do this. Did you?'

'I wish you hadn't felt the need to ask that, Oscar,' Harry replied, slamming down the phone. Suddenly he realized he wasn't going to be walking out of this place a free man.

It was almost nine before Theo van Buren, his solicitor, arrived, and only then was Harry allowed to put forward his version of events in a formal interview with a Detective Sergeant Arkwright and his colleague, Detective Constable Finch. No theatrics from them, no grandstanding, just a double-deck tape recorder and unaggressive questions about the events of the previous night. How much he'd had to drink. Whether he had kissed her. How much damage he thought the St Mary's story had done. Why he hadn't been married for such a long time. And particularly whether he had put his hand on her breast. Harry wanted to scream, to shout out his innocence, denounce it all as a fraud, but a warning eye from van Buren insisted he restrain himself. The lawyer had an expressive face and an equally expressive manner. A bit of a rough diamond for the high-powered legal world, a man who had got on not because of his accent or background, both of which were London-rough, but because of his ability. He had to work even harder than most to make it up through the glass-encased floors of his firm, and he did.

Nothing seemed to make much difference to the police, they plodded on with their questions, didn't seem even to listen to the answers, otherwise why was Harry still here. He felt cheated when it finished.

'Wait here, Harry,' van Buren instructed when at last it was over. He disappeared for ten minutes. When he returned, his expression was dark.

'What the hell am I doing here, Theo?' Harry demanded wearily.

'They're going to release you on police bail in a little while.'

'What does that mean? Exactly?'

'They think there's a case to answer but they can't make

it stick, not yet. So they're biding their time. Not prone to rushing to conclusions, are the constabulary, unless they're in a bar. Waiting for the results of the forensics.'

Harry sprang to his feet and began pacing, unable to contain his frustration. 'This is horseshit, Theo. Can't you see that?'

'Me? Of course. Sure I do. But our friend the Detective Sergeant can't, not at the moment. Your word against hers. And ...' A slight hesitation while he ran his tongue across his lips. 'Well, you had been drinking.'

'Since when has that been a crime in your own home?'

'Murky water, Harry. Very murky water.'

Harry snapped, turned on his friend. 'It was a neat malt, if you must know. Eighteen years old. From Islay. I'll take you to the distillery one day.'

The lawyer's eyebrows waggled in warning; this wasn't a great time for sarcasm, but Harry ignored it.

'For Chrissake, what sort of justice is this?' he demanded, voice raised, gesticulating wildly. 'I am a totally innocent man. Innocent, you hear me? She's the one who's lying, perverting the course of justice. Yet I get locked up in this urinal while she's out there with her feet up having her nails painted, for all we know. My word against hers, you say. So why isn't she here?'

'You know why, Harry. 'Cos sometimes life's a puddle of poo. Talking of which, they're suggesting you've been under pressure, with the election and everything.'

Pressure from the election? They're going to make a

mess of their trousers when they find out about the money, Harry thought.

'And you were alone with her. Very late last night.'

Harry stopped pacing. 'Whose side you on, Theo?'

'Yours, of course. Just showing you what the enemy's got.'

A cold hand seemed to settle around Harry's throat.

'You ought to be aware there's chaos out there. Underwear wrapped in knots. They don't know how to handle it, Harry, you put fire up their bums. The Assistant Commissioner got the Commissioner out of bed for this one, and I suspect he probably then went and spoiled the Prime Minister's breakfast. No one's going to crawl away quietly from this. There's a very large picture of you on the front page of the *Standard*. You're in handcuffs, being arrested. And did I tell you there's a media mob waiting outside?'

Harry slumped back into his chair, eyes fixed on the door. Any moment he expected Franz Kafka to walk in, pen and notepad at the ready.

'They'll release you soon, once they've had their tea and signed fifty different bits of paper.'

Harry stared at his lawyer with disbelieving eyes. 'Release me?' he whispered. 'They're throwing me to the wolves.'

And the wolves were waiting, an entire howling pack of them, spreading out across Agar Street, blocking pavements, interfering with the traffic. Harry had sent back to his home for more clothes; he couldn't appear in the white overall with the hopelessly wrinkled collar, as if he'd just jumped over the wall of an asylum. Yet still he was unshaven and unkempt as he stood on the front steps of the station, van Buren at his side, his eyes so raw the television lights blinded him. He couldn't see how many had gathered, but he could hear them, smell them. He told them he had a brief statement to make, then waited for them to stop screaming and snarling at him before he took a deep breath.

'I have been arrested on a charge of serious sexual assault made against me by my press officer, Emily Keane. There is not a single shred of truth in those allegations. They are, quite simply, lies, and time will prove them to be lies. But the law requires a full and proper investigation. I will help the police in every way I can. In the meantime, I remind you all, that I am an innocent man.' He stared around him for a few moments, chin up, knowing he had to exude confidence and calm, then made his way through the scrum to the taxi that was waiting for him. Questions were hurled at him from all sides, but he ignored them, even the retard who asked him if he was going to sack Emily Keane.

There was another mob outside his home. He had to battle his way through elbows and camera equipment onto his own doorstep, in the melee he thought someone might have punched him. Even after he had slammed the door they kept banging on it. The telephone was ringing, a hundred messages demanded his attention; in blind fury he ripped the phone cord from its socket and threw his keys down beside the other set on the hall table. He noticed someone had been inside the house, forensics presumably; it was, after all, allegedly a crime scene. The sofa cushions had been moved, the whisky glasses gone, as was the coat she had left behind. He hauled himself upstairs, had to use the banister rail, surprised at how exhausted he was, then threw himself on his bed. He closed his eyes, hoping the world might cease to exist.

He felt close to despair. He was alone, wanted to have Jemma by his side; he sat up, intending to call her, until he realized she must already know. He was juggling words in his mind, struggling how best to tell her about what had happened, when he noticed a wardrobe door was slightly ajar. Dammit, had forensics been everywhere? He rose, intending to close it, then opened it instead. An entire half rack was empty. Her half rack. Jemma's clothes were gone, every one of them, and the same with her toiletries in the bathroom.

He charged downstairs to his front hall, ignoring the hubbub that was still coming from the other side of the door. There, on the table, was his set of keys. And beside them, hers, lying on top of a neat turquoise file of the interviews she had completed into the Speedbird crash. There was no note.

—ɯ—

'A beautiful day, my love.'

'Isn't it just, Felix? Simply perfect.'

They were walking along the South Bank in the shadow of the London Eye whose great wheel was moving magisterially through a freshly washed blue sky. It was the Easter holiday, the weather warm, the spring sun generous. Couples and young families were spreading across the grass, turning their backs on winter.

'It's good to have you home for a while, Patricia.'

'Just for a few days.' Before she returned to her other home.

'You've been so busy these past months.'

'Let's just say, Felix, that the time has been profitably invested.'

'Mr Jones?'

'Is no longer a problem.'

'He's not yet been charged.'

'But disgraced. That's enough.'

They walked on in silence beneath Westminster Bridge, sharing their thoughts, until they were opposite the Houses of Parliament. There was little sign of life. The Palace was closed, except for tourists, the river terraces empty but for the striped canvas awnings that were used as hospitality marquees.

'Hideous,' Felix muttered. 'Look at it, an extraordinary Victorian Gothic palace, a most wondrous gingerbread confection that was once the envy of the world, and now look at it. Despoiled with those hideous tents.'

She looked at where his finger was pointing. The tents – pavilions, as they were pretentiously described – seemed hideously out of place, and shabby. 'They have no idea how ridiculous they look from the outside,' she said.

'The tents?'

'The entire place.'

'You know, if this were France, or Berlin or Rome or Madrid, those awnings would have been ripped out and replaced with something significant, something truly cultural. But instead they make it look like a village fête.'

'Don't upset yourself, Felix. It simply doesn't matter any more. Best leave the place as it is. A tourist attraction.'

They watched as a boat filled with tourists leaning on rails, their cameras clicking, turned at the end of its run up from Greenwich, negotiating the current, churning up the heavy silt waters.

'By the way,' he mentioned as an afterthought, 'I put you down for a postal vote. Wasn't quite sure where you'd be.'

'Thank you, but . . .'

'Did I do wrong?'

'No, it's simply that I don't think I'll bother to vote. What's the point? It doesn't make much difference who parks their car in Downing Street. We've gone beyond that. The rules aren't made here in Westminster any more.'

'You intrigue me,' he said, turning to face her, staring inquisitively, 'if it doesn't make any difference, then why . . .'

'Why have I been so unkind to poor Mr Usher?' She

threw her head back, the sun catching the highlights in her hair and sparkling from her eyes. Then she started laughing, as if he couldn't have invented a more preposterous question. The sound was so intense it almost seemed masculine, and continued for many moments, almost uncontrollably. Then she looped her arm through his and began walking him on. 'For fun, Felix. I do it for fun.'

—⚭—

Spring. But the blows continued to fall on Harry with the determination of a winter gale. He had neither cash nor credit, so he sold his Audi S5, for notes, in a hurry, and inevitably well below the market price. The buyer screwed him. As Harry was discovering, it's what happens when your luck runs out.

His team of campaign volunteers, so dedicated and willing, was suddenly struck down by plagues of a biblical proportion. There was an outbreak of unseasonal colds, others were kept at home by minor domestic crises, or had distant relatives in need of their immediate attendance. If his constituents passed him on his side of the street, they averted their eyes, or if on the other, they stared. Kids made idle by the school holiday followed him down the street, dancing in his wake, taunting him.

The Prime Minister refused to take his call. When Harry telephoned Downing Street, the switchboard put him through instead to Usher's parliamentary aide, Archie Dodgson, an old friend of Harry's.

'He's preparing for the final leaders' debate,' Dodgson explained. 'Sorry, Harry, you know how it is. Try not to take it personally.'

'OK, suggest some other way I can take it, Archie.'

'He's got too much on his plate,' Dodgson responded abrasively, then softened. This was Harry he was talking to. 'Look, you know what the polls are showing. Our private polls are even worse. The voters have never particularly liked Ben, you know that. But now they don't respect him either. The tide's turned.' There was a dullness in his voice that spoke of more than late nights and exhaustion. He had lost hope.

Every ray of sunshine seemed to start a forest fire in his soul. He had friends, even former lovers, who stood by him, offered him support, but there were many who didn't know what to say or were keen to move on, so said nothing. It was the silence that hurt, wormed its way inside his confidence and dragged him down, those who should have called, but didn't.

Then, precisely a week after his arrest, Harry was called back to Charing Cross for a further interview. He dressed carefully, polished his shoes in the old military style, wasn't going to sit there in prison garb again. Van Buren had phoned ahead and asked permission to use a more private, rear entrance. It was denied. Another posse of inquisitors and photographers was camped out in Agar Street, waiting for them. 'Don't worry,' the lawyer had said as the taxi approached, 'they're just the foreplay.'

They read him his rights all over again, put him through the nightmare once more. But it was a different interview room, bigger, smelling of old dust and disinfectant, no windows but a dark glass panel in one wall that Harry assumed allowed others to see him unobserved. They were kept hanging around for nearly half an hour. Harry kept glancing at his watch. 'Can't you complain?' he demanded.

'Course I could. But it wouldn't make a bloody bit of difference.'

So they sat, and stifled.

Eventually the door opened and the two investigating officers, Arkwright and Finch, entered. No smiles, no handshakes, no apology, all formality. Detective Constable Finch was carrying a number of clear plastic evidence bags. Despite the presence of his lawyer, Harry felt outnumbered.

The Detective Sergeant trotted him through his version of events once more, checking for inconsistencies, wondering if he would trip himself, save them the bother, before they moved on to the meat of it all.

'Forensics, Mr Jones,' Arkwright said. 'Usually tell the whole story in this sort of thing. And very clear in our little case.' He pushed an evidence bag across the table. 'For the purposes of the tape, I'm showing Mr Jones Exhibit KAA1. It's Miss Keane's sweater.'

Harry stared, but didn't touch.

'You see the stain there, on the left shoulder? That's a drink stain. Your drink, Mr Jones.'

'I don't deny it. It spilled when she rushed me.'

'Fibres from this sweater were found in considerable quantity on the shirt you were wearing that night, consistent with there having been considerable contact between the two of you. You know, as if she had been held very tight.'

'Or thrown herself at me. Can forensics tell the difference?'

Arkwright didn't reply, sat staring, wondering if Harry might say more, change his story. Then he moved on.

'I am now showing Mr Jones Exhibit KAA2. Is this your shirt, Mr Jones?' Another evidence bag was pushed across the table.

'You know it is.'

'You see these marks? They are Miss Keane's lipstick. There are also clear traces of her saliva and tears. Consistent once again with her being held very firmly by you, against her will.'

'Look, you know they'll be equally consistent with her pushing herself on me. She's lying. Set me up. Why can't you see this?'

Van Buren's hand came out to touch Harry's sleeve and stem the anger that was beginning to bubble to the surface and could so readily betray a client, but Harry was not to be so easily deflected.

'And let me make this simple for you, Sergeant,' Harry snapped, his voice rising, 'you'll also show me some forensics report which will have my saliva on her face, because we kissed. She was most insistent on that. Very persistent and passionate, she was, which is one of the reasons I pushed her away. Maybe there were marks on her shoulders – like that.' He made a sharp shoving gesture.

'Seems like you were angry with her,' Finch intervened. 'About the press guide.'

'And you've only got her word for that, too, haven't you? For pity's sake, I know you have to take these matters seriously, but lying to the police and perverting the course of justice are also pretty damned serious offences, aren't they? That's what you should be investigating here.'

'Why would Miss Keane do such a thing?' Arkwright pressed.

In a manner that surprised even him, Harry's tirade came to an abrupt halt. 'I – I really don't know. She's a fantasist, I suppose, can't take rejection,' he muttered, subdued.

Arkwright had gained a small victory, the accused had been thrown off course. His lips creased into a thin smile. 'You were in the habit of taking Miss Keane back to your place late at night.'

'No.'

'You sure about that?'

'Absolutely positive.'

'Not to drink? To maybe offer her a good time in the bedroom?'

'Never.'

The smile was hovering once more. 'That's strange. How

do you explain this, then?' The policeman produced a document from his file. It was a photograph, of Emily leaving late at night with him waving to her from the doorstep. It was date marked. Harry felt his heart rate rise, and his skin turn clammy.

'That was the first time we ever met. She turned up on my doorstep.'

'You invited her in. Showed her around.'

'That's not how it happened.'

'Even into your bedroom.'

'That's a lie!' Harry protested through clenched teeth.

The Sergeant remained determinedly calm. 'Strange, then, how she's been able to give us a pretty accurate description of your bedroom, right down to the design of your duvet, which apparently you invited her to sit on.'

'No!' Harry slapped the table with the palm of his hand. 'Look, I found her on the doorstep. She invited herself in. Asked to use the toilet. If she sneaked into the bedroom, it was entirely on her own.' He glared across the table. 'She's saying that I came on to her that first time, yet she came back for more?'

'She's saying you didn't attack her. Not that first time.'

'Not ever!'

'And yet, Mr Jones, the forensics show without a shadow of a doubt that your hand was very firmly on the lady's breast. How do you explain that?'

'Take my word for it, she is no lady.'

'But there was bruising on the lady's breast. It precisely

matches the hand pattern on the sweater. Your hand, Mr Jones. I have a doctor's report here' – another piece of paper was produced – 'and photographs of the injury.'

'I suspect very strongly that the evidence shows those injuries were slight.'

'A charge of sexual assault doesn't depend upon the severity of the attack, only on the fact that it took place,' Finch intervened.

'They were self-inflicted. With her squeezing my hand. Just as I told you before. That's why they were slight.'

'You see, what's got me puzzled here,' Arkwright continued, 'is why Miss Keane would construct such an elaborate charade when your motive seems – well, so very much stronger than hers, wouldn't you say? You were drunk—'

'There is no evidence my client was drunk,' van Buren interjected.

'You had been drinking,' Arkwright corrected himself. 'You were under considerable pressure. You are a man with a reputation for having – what's the right way of putting this? – a considerable sexual appetite—'

'My client is a single man,' van Buren said.

'Precisely. That's my point. He's not married. Free to . . . indulge himself. All over the shop.'

'I'm in a relationship,' Harry snapped.

The Sergeant raised an eyebrow, as if for the first time he had learned something new. 'Ah, I see. And the lady's name?'

Arkwright prepared to scribble a note, but Harry shook his head. 'I don't want to involve her.'

'Why not?'

'It's not material.'

'I think I'd better be the judge of that.'

Harry's mind swirled. He might just have lied. Was he in a relationship still? Jemma wasn't answering any of his messages. And, in truth, their relationship had been sailing choppy waters ever since the visit from the Russians. Hell, the last time they'd had sex was ... on that bloody sofa, just where Emily had been sitting. Bringing Jemma into it wasn't going to help her, and most certainly wouldn't help him, either. He turned to van Buren. 'Do I have to answer that?'

'No, you don't,' van Buren replied.

Harry turned back to the Sergeant. 'I'm telling the truth.'

'But not all the truth, it seems,' Arkwright replied softly.

And for the first time Harry was no longer helping the police with their enquiries.

The Sergeant stared, hoping to dislodge something more, waiting. Arkwright's eyes flickered, seemed to dart for a moment in the direction of the glass panel, as though he thought he should be taking instruction. 'That will be enough,' he said eventually. 'For the moment.'

—◊—

They sat in the back of the taxi on the way back to van Buren's office, not speaking, lost in the gloom of their private thoughts. The traffic was heavy, ground to a halt with horns blaring, until Harry could take no more of it. He jumped from the cab. 'Come on, Theo, the walk will do you good.'

'Will it?'

'It'll cost you less. I'll have to ask you to pay. If you don't mind.'

'I'm a very expensive lawyer for a man who's got no money,' van Buren said, pulling out his wallet and paying the fare. Then, on the pavement, he turned to Harry. 'I know you've been worrying about that minor little point. But don't. I owe you, Harry, and I'm a man who pays my debts. When I joined the firm and first walked into the office, most of the bastards started reaching for their barge poles. Hadn't been to the right school, had I? Had too much of a chin. So first they expected me to learn how to bow and kiss butts.'

'Instead you wore jeans and introduced them to the delights of a Walkman.'

'It was bloody hairy until you came along. You were Harry Jones. If I was good enough for him, they thought, I could at least be trusted to sit in a client meeting without breaking wind. You got me started.'

'I wonder what they think about Harry Jones as a client now.'

'One of them asked me that this morning.'

'And you said?'

'I said that either I'll win a victory so famous they'll write plays about me.'

'Or?'

'I'll make a mint as a speaker on the after-dinner circuit.'
Harry chuckled drily. 'I'm glad to be of service.'

'And me to you, Harry, old mate,' the lawyer said softly,
the bravado gone.

They began walking on. They were on the Strand,
approaching the grey stone towers that were the Royal
Courts of Justice. A television news crew was loitering outside, already set up, waiting; Harry and van Buren crossed
the street to avoid it.

'But I need to sort this money thing, Theo,' Harry began
again, returning to his troubles. 'I can't do that without
finding Sloppy.'

'You tell the police about him and you'll be cutting your
throat. They'll use it as evidence you were under extraordinary pressure. Acting out of character. They'll have both
opportunity and motive, and enough circumstantial to
screw you.'

'But I'm screwed if I don't,' he protested, kicking a waste
bin in frustration. 'That bloody woman seems to be making
sure of that. Give me five minutes with her and I'll find out
what's going on.'

Suddenly the lawyer grabbed Harry's arms and spun
him round. 'Give you five seconds with her and I'll rip
your balls off myself. Harry, listen, you go anywhere near
her and you're dead. They'll have you for threatening a
witness, interfering with a police investigation, criminal
conspiracy. You'd go down for sure, and there'd be nobody
to wave you goodbye.'

'Great. What's the good news, Theo?'

'Good news? I'm such a rotten lawyer you'd be wasting your money on me anyway. If you had any.'

'The tragic thing is, that really is the best news I've had all day.'

'So let me buy you a sandwich and we'll celebrate.'

CHAPTER TWELVE

At every election the churches and other houses of faith in Harry's constituency gathered together and invited the candidates to a public debate that they entitled 'In Faith and Hope'. It was to be held this evening.

Harry was driving his new-old Volvo up from London for the event; he hadn't been spending enough time in the constituency since his arrest, but Oscar tried to reassure him, insisting that it didn't make much difference that he hadn't been there. Harry was not reassured.

As he turned north off the slow-moving M25 onto the road that would eventually take him to the chapel of Haileybury School, he was struggling to think of what he should say, and how he would phrase it. This might yet prove to be the most important part of the campaign; if he found the right tone, everything might be resolved, and if not ... The strains of a Billy Joel song came over the radio, something about being an innocent man, taunting him. He switched to a classical station. Yet no matter what he tried, his thoughts kept coming back to Emily.

So what was the woman's game? He'd suggested to

Arkwright that she was one of life's rejects, but he didn't believe that himself. Emily Keane was in all other respects focused, competent, entirely professional, enjoyed a drink, had plenty of previous, so far as men were concerned. She even had a sense of humour. Not a woman who spent her life swimming in a sea of fantasy.

He decided to take the scenic route, through the woods of Wormley West End, taking his time, trying to find inspiration in the signs of the new spring that flaunted themselves on all sides, letting his mind wander. It was as he was driving up the hill in the direction of the golf course that he realized Emily had made a mistake, one that was perhaps profound. As professional as she was, she hadn't been professional enough, had relied too much on coincidence, pushed it too far. That a photographer was present on the occasion of one of her visits was just about acceptable, but to have a photographer at both was about as likely as the BBC finding God or the Greeks regaining their marbles. Such things just didn't happen. He pulled over. This was no hysterical woman flying at him, she was a professional. Being paid. Someone – someone else – was setting him up.

He wasn't yet sure what it meant, but it was a start. He pounded the wheel in excitement. The fight-back had started. He turned the key, restarted the car, it spluttered a couple of yards, then died. He tried it again, and again, but the engine spun and spluttered most eloquently; it was going nowhere. He looked at the dash, the gauge said he still had sixty miles left in the tank, but something was telling him it lied. He glanced at the clock, it was getting late. His euphoria began leaking like air from an inflatable doll.

He climbed from the car, gave the door a bloody good kicking, then with relief saw a car pulling up the hill towards him. He stepped into the middle of the road, waving, and it slowed. A middle-aged woman rolled down her window.

'I'm so sorry,' Harry said as she stared, 'but I've broken down. And I've got this hugely important meeting in twenty minutes at Haileybury. Is there any chance you might be kind enough to give me a lift?'

'To you? To Harry Jones? You've got to be bloody kidding,' she said, slamming the car into gear and leaving him showered in road grit and gravel.

Harry never made it that night. They left an empty chair in his place. Zafira Bagshot made an impromptu sign to hang on it. Rough, handwritten, but entirely legible. 'Absentee Landlord', it said. No one had the wit to instruct her to remove it. And there was scarcely a moment throughout the entire evening when she wasn't seen smiling.

—ɯ—

Five-thirty in the morning. Polling day.

Harry's eyes were already open, even before the alarm began to vibrate. A disturbed night, vivid, unhelpful dreams, and when he'd got up in the middle of the night to get a glass of water he'd forgotten he was in his cottage in the constituency and had smashed the bedside lamp. He'd left it where it fell. Now a vicar on the local radio was in the process of delivering an uplifting homily, a verse taken from St Matthew about the many being called but few being chosen. Harry seemed to recall a snatch of the previous verse, about some poor sod being bound hand and foot and cast into outer darkness. About as uplifting as a stair hoist. He reached out and cut the vicar off. If these last few months had been a reflection of his boss's mercy, he'd run the risk of Him not being on side today.

Harry rolled out of bed, showered, found himself in the kitchen. He was in a hurry, didn't leave long enough for his tea to brew; it was weak, tasteless, he poured it down the sink. It was always like this, before the start of battle, the nerves, and the crap tea. Kill or be killed. Welcome to election day.

But the world didn't stop spinning simply because politicians had decided to wage war between themselves. Even as he pinned his rosette to his lapel, his phone rattled. A new e-mail. From his accountant. Who told Harry he had taken advice from two different legal sources, which inevitably made the message more grammatically mind numbing than usual. But it was easy enough to translate. Since Harry didn't deny he had signed the documents Sloppy had used to raid his accounts, the claim that they were signed in confusion or under duress was irrelevant so far as the bank was concerned. They had paid out his money in good faith. The fact that he had no money left wasn't their fault. And, for the same reason, since he had signed the partnership agreement, Sloppy's creditors were entitled to pursue him for all Sloppy's debts. Which, because of Shengtzu, were huge. Absolutely astronomic. So bloody high they hadn't even finished counting. Financially, Harry was space debris, burning up on re-entry.

The accountant suggested Harry had three alternative courses of action. He could make a claim against Sloppy himself. This was the simplest thing to do, but there was one big drawback. Sloppy had gone AWOL, wasn't answering letters, no one knew where the bastard was hiding. Or Harry could make a formal complaint to the police and ask for it to be treated as a criminal matter. In those circumstances, perhaps, there might be some hope of wriggling out from beneath the creditors, although that would inevitably take time. 'Yet you have directed me,' the accountant wrote cautiously and a touch pompously, 'that this is not an option you care to pursue.' So in the circumstances, his accountant concluded, his third and most obvious option was 'to retain an insolvency practitioner who might seek to come to an Individual Voluntary Arrangement with your creditors'. Pay them pence in the pound. It might just work, if all the creditors agreed to cooperate. Worth a go.

'Otherwise, I fear we must consider the probability that

one or more creditors will move against you and initiate proceedings to declare you bankrupt.'

A bankrupt.

A sensation he recognized as fear sent a shiver down his back. It was the first time Harry had allowed himself to think about it, to bring together the word with his name. Then he burst into laughter. Bankruptcy. It was one of the few reasons that could get a sitting MP thrown out – that, and mental disorder or a serious criminal conviction. His eyes were watering, his foot stamping. Lunatics, criminals – and Harry Jones! At this rate the election was going to be a complete waste of time.

Then the gallows humour was gone. He sat on a stool in his kitchen, staring into nothing, into the future. He was profoundly lost in what he found there until a persistent knocking on the door brought him back. It was Oscar's wife. She had come to drive him round the constituency. The future wasn't going to wait.

—ɷ—

Sloppy didn't turn out to vote. He could scarcely walk. It's difficult to rise above much more than a stumble on a diet of painkillers and alcohol. He was now also downing anti-depressants, on prescription, signed for by his doctor as an antidote to what the overqualified idiot had diagnosed as stress. Sloppy was sure it was these wretched new pills that had given him the sense that an ice pick was being driven up through his sinuses and into his frontal lobe, and it was this, of course, that had caused him to stumble and fall headlong against what was laughingly called his kitchen. The kitchen in this one-room short-term let was no larger than a park bench, and it was Sloppy's typical luck that he had fallen against something hard and spiteful instead of onto the bed. He thought he might have cracked a rib. So more painkillers. And more alcohol, even though the doctor had warned him not to drink with the anti-depressants, but then the doctor was, of course, an overqualified bloody idiot.

The single room was in one of the narrow alleyways that ran off Fleet Street, the *pied-à-terre* of a photographer who was spending six months on assignment, and it was here that Sloppy spent election day, spreadeagled on the bed, not struggling up until he had finished the bottle of vodka and was forced to head out in search of another.

So Sloppy didn't vote. And neither did Patricia Vaine, or several thousand voters who had previously turned out for Harry.

—⚏—

Oscar's wife spent the morning driving Harry round the polling stations, while Oscar himself took the afternoon shift. Harry thanked the staff, encouraged the waiting voters, smiled, lied with his eyes. In mid-afternoon he sat down in his constituency offices with six others, while they called up those who had been canvassed and identified themselves as supporters, encouraging them, making sure they came out to vote.

'Hello, Mrs Gordon?' Harry said, reading from a canvassing card. 'This is Harry Jones. I'm just calling about the election and wanting to thank you for—' For what, Mrs Gordon never found out. She had put the phone down. She wasn't the only one.

It was the women he was losing, most of all. As his old agent, Ted, had told him when Harry had first stood, that where women lead, the men will always end up following. It was as much a political as it was anatomical certainty. Ted had been a good man, and a wise one, and had died in harness. Harry missed him, but was glad he hadn't been around to witness this.

Then the time had come. Ten p.m. The polling stations closed their doors. It was done. Harry, Oscar and his wife made their way to the town hall where the votes were to be counted. They were met by a group of supporters, not as many as at previous elections, but tribal loyalties continue even when life itself is extinct.

'You going to win, Mr Jones?' a young reporter from the local press asked as he made his way up the steps.

'Of course we're going to win!' Oscar's wife answered for him, and fiercely, carried along by the long day of adrenalin and builder's tea.

'But people are saying it could be tight, Mr Jones,' the reporter persisted.

'Young man, when you have a little more experience you will realize that this is *our* constituency,' Oscar's wife responded. 'Always has been. We've never lost here!'

He pushed his way inside. There was a stage at one end of the hall from where the Returning Officer would announce the result, dressed in a careful selection of flowers of so many colours that no one might accuse the plants of showing political favouritism. The body of the hall had been cleared, long tables laid out, waiting for the ballot boxes to arrive and throw up their contents. Overhead, in the balcony, three television crews were setting up, their lights blazing into life, then off again, waiting for the moment. This count had been marked as one to watch.

Harry sought out Zafira Bagshot, shook her hand, wished her luck, she nodded in acknowledgement, offered nothing in return, except a smile. She couldn't stop smiling, dancing from foot to foot, and she quickly turned away to be amongst her own supporters.

From the door, a ripple of excitement. The ballot boxes arriving from the polling stations, lifted onto the tables, emptied. The scrutineers huddled round. And it began.

It wasn't the only count that night, of course. Results were already coming in from other constituencies that had raced for the obscure honour of being the first to declare. Some constituencies had reduced the weight of the ballot papers to make them lighter and quicker to carry, had given strict instructions to voters how to fold them (only once, North to South), employed schoolchildren to hurry the ballot boxes down the line. Sunderland won, again, but others weren't far behind and Oscar, standing to one side of the hall, was consulting his iPad, checking how things were going elsewhere. From across the room, Harry raised an eyebrow. Oscar stared, then went back to his screen.

As the ballot papers were counted and confirmed, they were wrapped in bundles of a hundred and stacked in lines on one table. As the minutes passed the lines for each candidate grew, but at different paces, like trenches stretching across a battlefield. In previous elections they'd scarcely needed to do more than weigh Harry's vote, the count itself little more than a legal formality, but elections aren't decided on tradition. Bagshot had already stretched into a lead.

'Don't worry, Harry,' Oscar's wife whispered, 'these are her wards. Ours are coming in now.' But the fire she had shown on the steps had dwindled.

The size of the Bagshot lead waxed and waned, but never completely disappeared. The final boxes from the five most distant polling stations arrived. This was when they would know. 'Our boys and girls,' Oscar's wife whispered in encouragement from behind Harry's shoulder as the lids were hauled off and a tsunami of paper flooded across the tables.

He turned, wanting distraction, saw Oscar, was about to ask how the results were going elsewhere, but Oscar had switched off his screen. The hall was filling with the rustle of barely restrained excitement as activists from all parties crowded around the last counting tables. The atmosphere was growing heated, uncomfortably sticky, when Harry realized he hadn't thought of a thing to say. Whatever the result there would be a need for words, yet at this moment his mind was an empty canvas, devoid of colour. He retreated from the hall, found the washroom, splashed water over his face, trying to revive his brain, staring into the mirror, and it seemed like a stranger who was staring back at him. Perhaps it was the crappy lighting, but the face seemed a thousand years old, full of creases and shadows.

When he returned to the hall he saw Zafira Bagshot almost lost in the middle of a huddle of her supporters, their heads down, conferring. Suddenly she was jumping up and down for joy.

Oscar rushed to his side. 'I think it's over,' he said ambiguously. 'The Returning Officer wants you.' And, as one, the television lights on the balcony kicked into life. Bagshot's supporters broke into song. 'Another One Bites the Dust!' they chanted. In a corner, Oscar's wife was weeping.

One of the most searing memories of Harry's political life had come as a kid, in 1979, too young to know much about anything, but he remembered a face from election night – that of Jeremy Thorpe, who had been leader of the Liberal Party. He was a huge figure of his day, and after a previous election he had been offered the post of Home Secretary, yet five years later, caught up in lurid allegations of an attempt to murder his homosexual lover, he had been driven to the brink. He stood there on election day, and the voters pushed him off.

Harry had been watching television with his mother that night when Thorpe appeared from his count. Except it wasn't Thorpe. The face was a mask, the eyes were dead, the lips barely able to part, the voice a monotone of fear. As near a ghost as Harry had seen. The youthful Harry had understood very little about politics and nothing at all about buggery, but even at that age he had known there was a better way to die. There had to be.

The Returning Officer was beckoning. Harry found a smile, pinned it on and strode forward.

CHAPTER THIRTEEN

Sleep was impossible. Too many thoughts, too much hurt. Harry rose from his bed long before the sun and began writing letters of thanks. It was like the times he had been required to write to the wives and parents of men in his command who hadn't made it back. Then telephone calls, with plenty of incoming. He avoided those from the media, had said all he was going to say the previous night, after the count, when for a little while he had been besieged. But it had quickly passed. Yesterday's news.

He didn't turn on the radio or television. Usher had lost, the government had fallen, Harry's wasn't the only seat lost that night. He didn't have the heart to count casualties.

There would be compensation, of sorts. A pension, around £25,000 a year for his length of service. He wondered whether he would see any of it, or whether it would all go to his creditors. One of his supporters was a local estate agent. He picked up the phone.

'Kishor? Harry. No easy way to deal with this except to say thank you. You and Ruth have been brilliant. I couldn't have asked for more, but there is one more favour, if you would. Will you sell the cottage for me, discreetly, not too much of a fuss? Any reasonable offer. Furniture, too, if they want. Just send on my personal stuff. No, I won't be standing again. I'm not coming back . . .'

He had nearly completed his list, the names ticked off, when the phone rang. A blocked number. He thought it might be media and almost put it through to his voicemail, but answered it anyway. 'Yes?'

A female voice. 'I have Mr Usher for you.' Not the Prime Minister any longer, just plain old Ben Usher.

'Hello, Harry.'

'You sound like I feel.'

'I'm just waiting to go to the Palace,' Usher said. 'Twiddling my thumbs. Got a flat full of removal men upstairs and a room full of secretaries downstairs in tears. Never did know how to handle tearful women, particularly by the dozen. It's simply . . .' A deep sigh of exhaustion rattled through his ribs. 'I wanted to say I'm sorry.'

'There's nothing you could have done to save me, Ben.'

'No, perhaps not. But I could have taken your call. I feel wretched about that, a little cowardly, to be frank. I believe in you, Harry, you tell me you're innocent and I'm one hundred per cent behind you.'

'A very long way behind me, it seemed.'

'Yeah. You know what elections are like, people telling me I mustn't get dragged into your difficulties. I don't feel proud of that. I hope you'll be able to forgive me. I'm trying to make amends. I'd be happy to appear as a character witness.'

'A character witness?'

'You know, in court.' Bugger, he hadn't expressed that very elegantly, but the night after rarely shows itself to be a time for subtlety. 'Sorry, Harry, I'll have to dash. My tumbrel awaits.'

Harry knew a news helicopter would already be hovering, waiting to accompany Usher on the short drive from Downing Street to the Palace for his final conversation with the Queen. It would still be there an hour later when Dave Murray did the journey in the other direction. The battle was over, the hour had come for the dead to be removed from the field. Except Harry would be a long time dying. With a charge of sexual assault hanging over him, the media would take it in turns to come down from the hills to bayonet him on a regular basis, and there would be plenty who would help to give the blade a twist. Politics. Taken from the Greek. 'Poly', meaning many. 'Ticks' denoting tiny blood-sucking insects ...

Then it hit him, so hard that he gasped in pain. He had lost everything. He had lost. Everything. And so quickly that he still had no firm grasp on what had happened. He was physically exhausted, financially ruined, publicly humiliated, emotionally disembowelled. He had been hurled into a pit of despair and there was still no sign of him hitting the bottom. He was falling, tumbling, utterly helpless.

The screen on his phone came to life once more. A message. From Jemma. 'So very sorry. J.' He erased it.

He stood up from his chair, straightened. Do this like a man. He took one last look around, like a refugee, leaving everything behind. Then he walked out of the door. He didn't look back.

—⁘—

It took him two hours to reach London. He drove in silence, no radio, his phone switched off. He found a parking meter in Berkeley Square, dumped the car, didn't pay the fee, what was the point? They'd stick him with an eighty-pound ticket which would grow with every passing deadline, but by the time they sent heavies knocking on his door it would be too late, he'd be a bankrupt. Probably wouldn't even be his door any longer. So to hell with them. Every single one of them.

The old man with the kindly, downcast eyes who ran the gallery further along his street waved as Harry walked past. Harry ignored him. He stood on his doorstep, produced his keys, registering only vaguely that he hadn't double-locked the Chubb, slammed the door shut, dropped his bag, ignored the messages, stood in the middle of his sitting room, too drained and numb to register what was around him. When at last he saw, he stared, and the room stared back, insistent. The final insult. He had been burgled. He stepped back in pain, and disgust, hit a wall, slumped to the floor, and there he remained for many hours.

It was dark by the time Harry stirred once more. He now knew what he wanted to do, to walk away, close the door, as he had already done that morning, leave no trail. And he knew he could do it. What was there to hang around for any longer? He felt sick, angry, ashamed, humiliated. He had faced many enemies, but never one as virulent as this. Everything that had happened to him these past months – Emily, the money, even the assault on Jemma – had cut away at his sense of self-worth. Now he'd been turned away by those who were supposed to know him best, his constituents. Harry Jones, unfit for duty. That had never happened before, he didn't know how to deal with it. Silly, he knew, but he felt grubby and dishonoured. So move on, Jones, find some other life, another place. But before he left he resolved that he was going to get blindingly, chokingly drunk, so comprehensively obliterated that he hoped it wouldn't hurt any more.

It took him three days to finish off all the booze in the house. By the time the last empty bottle had toppled onto the floor, he was in desperate need of fresh air and a change of company, so he staggered out in search of rein-forcements. His recollections of the next few days were so obscure and filled with fog he half expected Sherlock Holmes to come sauntering out of it, and he had no memory whatsoever of staggering back to his front door and being intercepted. The next moment of cognition was when he woke an untold number of hours later, on his bed, naked, with his face being swabbed by a cold flannel. As his eyes regained focus, he saw someone staring down at him.

'Have I died?' he murmured. Then he stared. It was Jemma. Her face was drenched in fury. 'And if I died, did I go up or down?' He laughed feebly at his own joke before finding that even that paltry effort made him feel profoundly sick. He staggered into the bathroom and vomited. Afterwards, as he washed his face, he stared into the mirror. A total stranger stared back. It had worked. He was no longer Harry Jones. His new life had started.

'You total bloody fool!' Jemma snapped as he found his way back into the bedroom.

'What the hell are you doing here?' he snarled.

'Apart from letting you in your own front door which you were too pissed to open yourself, you mean?' She threw a bathrobe at him. 'A friend of mine told me he'd bumped into you. Quite literally. You were flat out on the grass near the Serpentine. Makes me wonder why you didn't get yourself arrested. Again.'

'Cuts.'

'What?'

'The cuts. Never enough policemen around when you need them.' With a savage tug of anger Harry tightened the belt of his robe; it made him want to throw up once more. 'So what are you doing here, Jem? Come to gloat?'

She was about to retaliate with her own bucket of abuse when she bit her tongue. It would serve no purpose. She lowered her voice, and with it her temper. 'I came, Harry, because people were telling me they'd stumbled over my boyfriend in the park. Does wonders for a girl's reputation.'

'Boyfriend?'

'Ex.'

'But the stench still lingers.'

'Dammit, Harry!' And suddenly she was fighting back tears. 'Let's get some food into you.' She disappeared in the direction of the kitchen.

When she reappeared a little later with a tray of coffee and toast, she found him sitting in the living room, staring at the chaos. Chairs pulled over, shelves pulled down, books scattered, cushions thrown, pictures smashed, and everything covered in a million pieces of paper.

'I was going to clean up,' she whispered, 'but I felt it would be intruding.'

'Some bastard's already done that,' he muttered, no longer wanting to fight. He gazed around him, and the mists of despair closed in once again, allowing no escape. His house had been violated. But it wasn't simply his, this was Julia's house, too. They'd chosen it together, decorated much of it themselves, often late into the night, sleeping in their paint-spattered T-shirts, even though they'd been able to afford a dozen decorators, and Julia's presence here had survived everything that the years had thrown at him since then, even Mel. There had always been a part of this place that was Julia. Her father's brass shell casing in the hallway for umbrellas, his own ridiculous cooking apron that she'd found at some hunting store in the Adirondacks, the pair of hideous, funky champagne glasses that made him cringe and always made her laugh. And her desk. He bought it for her, that last Christmas, before they'd gone off skiing. Now it was lying on its side, where they'd left it, the drawers spilled out, its contents scattered. He pulled it upright, replaced the drawers, knelt down, sorting through the mess. He found her passport. The date said it had expired, it didn't seem that way to him.

'Julia's?' Jemma asked. They'd got far enough in their relationship for her to know.

He nodded.

Well, no point in a jealous twitch, it didn't matter any more to her, did it? 'I'll help you clear up – if you want?'

He nodded again.

Jemma began scouting round the room. 'What did the police say?'

He seemed startled. 'Police? Never called them. Too many police around this place recently. Too late now, anyway.'

'Looks like they got in through the back window,' she said, pointing. 'You must have left it open.'

'Better see what's missing.'

Slowly, methodically, they began sorting through the mess, Jemma righting the displaced furniture, making orderly piles of the displaced books, cleaning up the broken picture glass, while in the manner of a robot Harry gathered all the pages of paper that had been strewn about and dumped them on the dining table. And as they began to re-impose a sense of order, it became clear to him that little physical damage had been done. She was fixing the shade back onto a side lamp when she noticed he had sunk to the floor once more.

'Harry, you OK?'

'I didn't leave the bloody window open.'

'You might have done—'

'No, Jem,' he insisted. 'And the front door wasn't properly locked, not the way I always do it.'

'What are you saying?'

'Buggered if I know for sure. That ... maybe ...' He shook his head trying to clear the swarm of fireflies that had found their way inside. 'They came in the front door, left the window open as a distraction.'

'Who has keys?'

'No one. Not since you.'

'So how does a burglar get through a locked front door?'

'I don't think it was a burglar,' he insisted impatiently.

'What?'

'There's nothing missing. Nothing I can find, at least.'

'They got disturbed.'

'No, I don't think they came here to run off with the candlesticks. This was about something else.' Like the thugs who had broken into her place, he thought, but he didn't say so, there was no point in making her go through that again. Now someone was trying to get at him, too, and he didn't very much care any more about who or why.

228

He felt like a wounded animal that wanted nothing more than to crawl back into his cave and shut the rest of the world out. Yet he couldn't. Over the next few days there were too many things dragging him back out into the open. The need to clear out his office, say goodbye to his secretary, accept the commiserations of colleagues before they hurried on their way, leaving him staring at their backs. Because a man in public life is raised higher, so his ultimate fall is deeper and more difficult to control. Harry knew politicians who had suffered nervous breakdowns, seen their marriages collapse, become ill. One close friend had committed suicide. Being a Member of Parliament wasn't merely a job, it was a passion for a certain way of life, and once that life support system had been switched off, things had a habit of breaking apart into razor-sharp shards, reminders of things that once were, and every attempt to pick them up only made you bleed all the more. The hundreds of letters Harry received and tried to read did nothing to help, only ground in the sense of failure still further.

He wanted to lean on Jemma, and more, but she made it clear that her help was available only on the basis of friendship.

'Don't you believe me when I tell you I didn't assault that bloody woman?' Harry asked, petulant, a little aggressive.

'Yes, but ... Harry, she was with you late at night, you were drinking. Kissing.'

'It wasn't my fault.'

'Nor mine, either. Anyway, I'm seeing someone else.'

'Seeing?' He made the word sound as if it was an activity that ought to end in a charge at the European Court of Human Rights.

'Not serious, not the love of my life, Harry, but ...'

'But?'

'But grow up about it.'

He was hurt, didn't want to play the man. So Harry spent his evenings alone, climbing the walls of his home – a home that his accountant told him he was in all probability going to lose. He was there one evening when his phone rang. It was the steward who ran the bar at the Special Forces Club. 'Mr Jones, you asked me to let you know if ...'

He never got to finish the sentence. Harry was already running. It was little more than a mile. Harry flew, blind to the traffic or the shouts of startled pedestrians, his heart pounding, lungs screaming, and he made it in less than ten minutes. He was still running when he hit the stairs and raised eyebrows when he burst into the bar. The man was still there, sitting at the bar, back to the door, but his figure was unmistakable.

'Hello, Sloppy,' Harry declared, placing a firm hand on his shoulder. 'I think you owe me a drink.'

CHAPTER FOURTEEN

Sloppy had scrubbed up remarkably well, considering his circumstances. Immaculate St James's shoes, creases in all the correct places; the old customs of a regiment refuse to die. It was the eyes that told the story, with their glaze of defiance and rims raw from being washed in drink. He was too far gone even now to show much surprise as Harry sat down next to him at the bar, offering little more than a flash of confusion. Yet behind the glower, in layers that peeled away, Harry could see pain, humiliation, and fear. It reminded Harry of a face he'd got to know recently, staring back at him from his mirror. He'd wondered how he would react when he finally got to Sloppy – smash a bottle over his head, break an elbow or an arm? Find some way of releasing his anger through gratuitous and excessive violence. Yet now he came to it, he didn't see the point. Or, perhaps more accurately, that wasn't the major point.

'Seems a long time ago, doesn't it, Sloppy?'

'What?'

'Christmas.'

'Yeah, we've both had some bloody awful luck since then.'

The steward intervened: 'Is that to be your usual, then, Mr Jones? On Mr Sopwith-Dane's bill?'

'Of course my bill,' Sloppy interjected. 'Let's make it a bottle – Krug, not the cheap muck.'

The steward offered a cautious eye before disappearing in search of his prey.

'Krug, Sloppy? Are we celebrating?' Harry asked.

'Doesn't make any bloody difference,' he muttered. 'Can't pay for a pint of piss. Might as well go down in a blaze of glory.'

'Now why didn't I think of that?' Harry replied coldly. 'What the hell happened, Sloppy?'

Mean, red eyes shot at Harry. 'What happened? We went belly up, that's what happened.'

'Talk me through it. For old times' sake.'

Sloppy chewed his lips, his expression full of contempt. 'You remember Belize? Jungle training? Hot as hell and ants all up your arse? There's a liana that grows there, one of those huge bloody tropical vines, thick as a man's waist. Wrapped itself around a tree and just grew and grew like Topsy. Covered the tree, smothered it. Until it got just so greedy that it sucked the life out of the tree and the whole thing collapsed. Dead tree. Dead vine. That's what you lot are like.'

'You lot?'

'You were all over me in the good times, when the

money was easy for you, but at the first bit of bad luck ...'
He swallowed the rest of the drink as the steward came
back with the Krug in a bucket of ice and poured two
glasses.

'It isn't bad luck conning me into signing false documents.'

Sloppy's lip curled into a snarl. 'At least you've still got
your fucking leg.' He turned back to his glass.

'I want to know what happened, for God's sake. I have a
right. I'm told it all went into an investment fund.
Shengtzu. Why?'

'You think you're the only one who got hammered? Lost
everything they'd ever worked for? I didn't inherit, I
earned. And I lost everything!'

Yet Harry refused to get dragged into recrimination.
Instead he gathered himself, fought back against his desire
to throttle the bastard, knew he would have to tease rather
than tear what he wanted out of him.

'Shengtzu, Sloppy. Why Shengtzu?'

And, between flashes of defiance and fresh drink,
Sloppy's story emerged. Of Mr Anderson and his moist
palms, his cufflinks and camp lips, and a ream of confi-
dential papers about a fund that even to this day Sloppy
believed were genuine. The truth, but only half the truth.
And the wrong half, at that.

'So this stranger walks in and spins you some line, and
you bet the entire factory on it?' Harry said, incredulous,
knowing there must be more.

'It wasn't as simple as that, of course it wasn't!' Sloppy bit back, raising his voice, pouring himself another glass. The steward raised an eyebrow, but Harry's eyes warned him to back off.

'How "not simple" was it?'

'Money, money, money, it's all you bastards care about.'

'That was your job. All of it.'

'He had a quarter of a million in his pocket. Money where his mouth was. And you'd have taken it, too.'

'He just gave it to you? Handed it across?'

'Just like that. In a beautiful white envelope.'

'Which you invested for him.'

'In Shengtzu.'

'And which he subsequently lost.'

'Every single brightly polished farthing.'

'That's one hell of a lot of farthings.'

'Oh, don't worry, I'll pay him back. Pay you all back. In farthings.'

Sloppy made some noise, a snort or a snigger, and drowned it in his glass, leaving Harry lost in confusion.

'So has this Mr Anderson been on your tail, too, chasing you for his money back?'

'No point. Don't have any money. Diddly-squat broke, like you. I went down with my ship.' He drank. 'But Mr Anderson couldn't complain. He doesn't exist. Oh, I checked him out, of course I did. Seemed entirely genuine. Until the ship went down. Then he sort of vanished. I did some digging, not sure whether I should be apologizing or strangling the bastard, but it turns out he was never there. All the contact details he gave me were false or entirely temporary. Service addresses and pay-as-you-go phones, and all the rest buried somewhere so deep in the Caymans it'd take an earthquake to get at it.' Suddenly his shoulders slumped, his face melting in misery. 'Should have dug a little deeper, maybe, but we needed a bit of luck, Harry, you and me. Thought Mr Anderson was it.' He was growing maudlin, the alcohol taking him prisoner. Nothing he said made much sense any more. The portrait of the Princess Royal gazed down in disapproval.

Harry knew it was time to call his accountant, his bank, the police. Get the wretched man run in. Salvage something. But he couldn't. Wouldn't save himself by sacrificing Sloppy, that wasn't the way they had ever worked. It had been Sloppy who bailed him out with his CO when Harry failed to follow the orders he'd been given – Harry had found a better way of doing it, and done that instead. It was also Sloppy who'd got him out of the mess in Armagh, when Harry had been out on surveillance of a farmhouse stuffed with very bad men and been rumbled. In the ensuing firefight, Harry had been almost out of time and ammunition before Sloppy and his troop turned up to drag him out. That's when he'd taken the bullet in the knee, one that would otherwise have finished up in Harry. He owed Sloppy. The sort of debts that don't expire.

Now he shook his old colleague's arm, trying to rouse

him from his stupor. 'Sloppy, I need to know. Where are you staying? Where can I find you?'

'Sending round the heavies?'

'No, that's not going to happen. You know that. Too much previous. But I need to know how to get hold of you.'

'Me?' He shook his head. 'I'm the Scarlet Pimpernel.'

'Where, Sloppy?'

Sloppy got out his wallet, inspected the cash in it. Less than a hundred pounds. 'While this lasts, at the Cheshire Cheese. After that, who the hell knows? Or cares?' He picked up the bottle, but it was empty. He let it fall back into the ice bucket and soak the counter. Harry pushed his own glass over to him; it hadn't been touched. Then, with a nod of gratitude to the steward, he got up and left.

—∞—

Harry had called saying he was stuck on a bench with a bottle. Jemma found him in sunshine by the Serpentine, with nothing more than a bottle of water.

'You bastard,' she scolded, but smiled.

'I wondered what would get you here quicker, telling you that I cared, or that I was drunk.'

'What are you doing here, Harry?'

'Measuring the bench up for size. For when I sleep on it.'

She might have told him not to be so ridiculous, that things would be fine, something would turn up, but she knew it would be nothing more than bromide, and Harry would know it, too.

'This is also my office,' he declared, moving up. 'Please, come in.' He patted the wooden slats beside him.

'I can't stay long,' she said, taking the seat. 'I've got an evening function.'

'Is that what they call it nowadays?' he asked, his voice mean. Hurt.

'What do you want, Harry?'

'I'm celebrating. This morning I got a call from a TV producer asking me if I'd consider starring in a television series.'

'Sounds fascinating.'

'He said I would be perfect, it could rehabilitate my reputation, but I declined.'

'Why?'

He smiled, a tight, bitter expression. 'It was for *Big Brother*.'

She wanted to cry out. Hadn't he been humiliated enough?

'And I've found Sloppy,' he added.

'And?' she said, brightening.

He gave her an outline, but as she listened she started stubbornly shaking her head.

'No investor hands over a quarter of a million pounds, watches it being poured into an abyss, then quietly disappears into the night.'

'The man wasn't Mr Anderson, and neither was he an investor. He set Sloppy up.'

'Harry, I don't—'

'Don't you sense a pattern, a rotten smell? Just like you can smell a muck spreader even with the windows closed.' He held her hand, squeezed it between both of his. 'Mr Anderson was a set-up. Emily was a set-up. You were beaten up, too, Jem.'

'But what's the connection?'

'Me,' he said softly.

'Why, Harry?'

'Not sure. My past, I suppose, catching up with me. I've made a good number of enemies in my time, Jem ...' Destroyed men. Killed more than a few. She didn't need the details, not now. 'Someone is targeting me. Trying to obliterate me.'

'And doing a damned good job of it, too.'

'But that's the point, they're doing almost too good a job. This isn't casual or amateur. Someone very powerful is behind all this. Which got me thinking – what's the first thing you do to worm your way inside someone's life?'

'If you're a journalist, or a private detective, say?'

He nodded. She twitched her nose in concentration.

'I'd ...' She blinked. 'Hack your phone.'

He reached into his pocket and extracted his own. 'These things can tell you almost everything you want to know about its owner, if you're clever enough to get inside them. Know Sloppy handled my money. Know about you. Know everything that was necessary to skin me alive.'

She looked uncomfortable. 'Can you tell, for sure?'

'No, but I know a man who can. Old friend. Think it's

about time I had a drink with him. Can I borrow your phone?'

She handed it across. He made a call, arranged to meet at a bar in an hour.

'Thanks, Jem,' he said, handing the phone back to her. 'Should be fun. Think about it this way – the fight-back begins!' A brief, taunting smile wriggled across his face, the first she'd seen in a while. 'Oh, but I'm sorry, you can't stay, can you? Your "evening function".'

Her nose wrinkled again, this time in disgust. 'God, but you can be such a smug bastard, Jones.' She sighed, shaking her head in defeat, already thumbing the text buttons on her phone. 'How do you spell "pathetic excuse"?'

—w—

Glen Crossing was a man whose waist had seen leaner days. Much leaner. He liked to lay the blame on his kids and the diet of crap they shared with him, but since leaving the Army he had pursued a lifestyle that befitted a senior corporate executive, and both salary and belt size had increased substantially. Twenty years earlier he'd been the best squash player and telecommunications wonk in the regiment. He was still the best telecommunications wonk.

As Harry walked into the hotel foyer, Crossing waved at his old friend from his post at the bar, rising to greet him, buttoning his jacket as he saw Jemma in tow and trying to hide the midriff. Stuffy hotel bars weren't the preferred habitat for either of them, but the early summer weather had taken hold and most of the usual drinking joints were packed and noisy, and Crossing had assumed that whatever Harry wanted to see him about so bloody urgently was unlikely to be the sort of thing he'd want to have to shout across a crowded bar. 'Harry, my old mucker, so very good to see you. And ...?'

Harry introduced Jemma.

'A new lady in your life,' Crossing declared.

'We're just friends,' Jemma said.

'Then he's a damned fool,' Crossing replied.

'Thank you,' she smiled, accepting the compliment.

'Let me buy you both a drink,' he announced.

'Er, no thanks, Glenny. I'm afraid I can't let you do that.'

'And why the bloody hell not?'

'Wouldn't be able to return the favour. I went down with Sloppy.'

'Well, bugger my boots,' Crossing sighed, his exuberance deflating rapidly. 'Only one thing for it. I'll have to buy the whole bottle.' He busied himself ordering drinks. 'I'd heard whispers about Sloppy, of course, but I had no idea he'd taken you with him. Life's rather left you hanging on the old barbed wire, hasn't it, my friend? Goes without saying, if there's anything I can do ...'

'One thing.'

'It's yours.'

Harry produced his phone and laid it on the bar. 'I think

someone might have tampered with it, Glenny. Copied the information. Might even be listening to phone calls.'

'How wonderful. You handed it over any time recently?'

'Every time I've been to the gym, through a scanner, been laid out cold in a bar. You know how it is.'

'It's possible to set these things up as remote microphones, listen to conversations, even when the phone appears to be switched off. Israelis are brilliant at that. Trouble is, it really buggers up the battery life.' He put on a pair of heavy-framed reading glasses and began peering at it, his face puckered in concentration. 'So you want to know whether there's mischief afoot.'

'Can you do that? How long will it take?'

The eyes came up from examining the phone to give Harry the most withering of looks. 'About ten seconds, if you stop prattling on.' He produced a paper clip, bent it, and used it as a tool to prise out the SIM card. 'You know what your UICCID serial number is, Harry?'

'My what?'

'No, most people haven't the foggiest. Nerd stuff. It's like knowing the chassis number of your car. Who ever bothers with it? Unless you're good, very good, like me.' He looked up through his glasses. 'Yep. You've won yourself a major prize.'

'Meaning?'

'Someone's had a go at this. Or should I say, more likely *is* having a go at this. The serial number on your card isn't one of the regular ones your phone should have.'

241

'I still don't understand,' Jemma intervened, trying to peer over his shoulder at the small chip.

'This card isn't the original,' he said, holding it for her inspection between his finger and thumb. 'Looks identical, except for the dodgy serial number.'

'Which means?'

'Well, only reason for doing something like that is to nobble you. My guess is that your calls are on permanent divert to another number where they are almost certainly being intercepted. All your SMS stuff, and data, too. Inbound and outbound. Pretty much everything. You wouldn't notice, the increased delay in connection is barely a nanosecond. Standard practice in the City nowadays, they have to do it by law.' He fiddled some more, head bent, muttering technical stuff that was gibberish to Jemma, until he raised his eyes in triumph. 'Yup. They've definitely screwed around with your IMSI. This one belongs to one of the small specialist mobile operators.'

'Can you find out who's doing it?' Harry asked.

'Now that might take a little longer. About a minute or so.' He produced a notebook from his bag and began clattering with the keys. 'Just checking your account, Harry ... Gotcha! Your inbound calls are being routed to this number.'

'Which is?'

Cross peered closely at his screen. 'Registered to a company that I very strongly suspect is a dummy.'

'I get the feeling that if we followed the trail it would

take us somewhere exotic and untouchable like the Caymans,' Harry said.

'Which is about as useful as sticking your head in quicksand.'

'Is there no way of tracking it down?' Jemma said, struggling to keep the disappointment from her voice.

'Oh, yes. If we involved the security services and they got a warrant. But otherwise . . .' Crossing shook his head, and Jemma sighed. But Harry's brow remained rapt in concentration.

'Then we will have to find out for ourselves,' he said, very quietly, but with an edge that made her feel she was in the presence of something dangerous, as if she had walked into a darkened room and found the eyes of an untamed animal peering at her.

'How do you plan to do that, Harry?'

'By rattling their cage a bit. In fact, by rattling it so hard their teeth fall out. Preferably through their bloody ears.' Then he paused. 'Trouble is, I suspect a few of my own teeth are going to have to come out first.'

—⋙—

A cloud passed across Jemma's face. She knew he wasn't joking. She excused herself, headed for the ladies. The two men watched her retreat.

'You want to make secure calls, Harry, get yourself another mobile. One of the cheap throwaway jobbies,' Crossing said, his eyes still on Jemma.

'Thanks, Glenny. I owe you.'

'Be happy to take that young lady of yours in compensation.'

'You know something,' Harry sighed, 'so would I.' He sat inspecting his phone. Even while he was staring at it, the thing began to vibrate. A blocked number. He tapped the screen to answer it.

'This is Detective Sergeant Arkwright, Mr Jones.'

Harry froze, had difficulty locating his wits. 'What can I do for you, Sergeant Arkwright?'

'*Detective* Sergeant Arkwright,' the policeman corrected him. 'Your case file, it's been sent to the Crown Prosecution Service for review.'

Harry felt as though a hundred horses were stampeding across his stomach.

'As a result of that review, we have decided not to take your case any further, Mr Jones. We're closing the investigation.'

'Could you say that again? Very slowly?'

'It's closed down.'

At last Harry found himself able to take a deep breath. 'But why? Tell me why?'

'The witness, Miss Keane, has withdrawn her allegations. So, until such time as any further evidence might come to light—'

'It won't. I'm innocent!'

'—we will not be taking the matter any further.'

'What you mean is that I needn't have lost my seat.'

'I will be informing Mr van Buren of this, too.'

'And will you be prosecuting Emily Keane for making false charges and wasting police time?'

The detective hesitated before replying, his voice a little less officious. 'Take my advice, Mr Jones, forget all this. Put it behind you. Get on with your life.'

'And how, Detective Sergeant Arkwright, do you expect me to do that?' Harry spat.

There was a brief silence, then the phone went dead.

Harry sat staring at the phone, for how long he couldn't afterwards tell. He was still sore from the thundering hooves. Yet, as indescribable as was his relief, the anger within him was unfathomable.

Forget? Forget Emily Keane? He'd play roulette with the Devil before he'd do that.

—⋙—

First Sloppy, then Emily. It made sense to Harry. Keep digging. But he had one significant problem. He had no idea where Emily was. And it was clear that she was hiding, and had gone to considerable lengths to cover her tracks. Her mobile number was no longer operational, she'd moved out of her apartment, and he didn't need to call her old place of employment to know she'd left there, too. So he asked Jemma to do it. A woman's voice was so much less threatening.

'Hello, is it possible to speak with Emily Keane, please?'

'Who's calling?'

'Oh, my name's Sally. We met a couple of months ago, said we'd meet up for a girls' night out. But I've been working up in Scotland, only just got back.'

'I'm sorry, Emily no longer works here.'

'Oh, that's a pity. She said she liked her job.'

'And we liked her, but she got headhunted. A very nice offer, so she said.'

'Can you tell me where she's gone?'

'I'm sorry, we're not allowed to give out those details. She had a little trouble, you know.'

'Yes, wasn't that just dreadful? I understand. I was just wondering if we could get together this evening, that's all.'

The receptionist laughed. 'I'm afraid that won't be possible. She's gone abroad, you see.'

'Abroad? You know, she mentioned she might do something like that. No, don't tell me, I think I can guess where. It's Brussels, isn't it? Any chance you could, you know, let me have an address where I can write to her?'

Emily Keane had been in Brussels since a fortnight after the attack. Move on, move away, protect her from trouble, that had been part of the deal. It had never been intended that she would go through with the charges against Harry, even if the CPS had believed they might stick. Distract him, disgrace him, then destroy him. There was no need to take matters further, so Patricia Vaine had said. They could forget about Harry Jones.

It was a rare and catastrophic lapse of judgement.

CHAPTER FIFTEEN

Place du Luxembourg – or Luxemburgplein, as more than half the population in that bitterly divided nation would have it – is a modest square of pavement bars and eating places in the part of Brussels that is known as the European Quarter. The quarter is said to be the heart of Europe; locals jest that it has yet to find its head. Place du Luxembourg is of no particular architectural merit, indeed it is something of a stylistic mess with its mixture of ancient and modern. Its significance derives entirely from its position, for it squats on the doorstep of the European Parliament, which looms behind it like the spaceship of some alien life form that has landed from a distant world. At the centre of the square, protected by an expanse of grass, is the statue of John Cockerill, a hugely inventive Anglo-Belgian industrialist of the Victorian era. He was noted for his integrity and stands on a plinth engraved with his motto: 'Work and Intelligence'. For some reason, he has his back turned towards the Parliament. But that may not be the case for long, for there are plans to wipe out Place du Luxembourg, to flatten it and use the space to construct a triumphal avenue or boulevard that will reach out from central Brussels to the place of the Parliament, yet in the meantime, while the planners plot and the construction companies sharpen their shovels, the good burghers get on with their lives, dodging between the Mercedes limousines that clog the cobbled square during rush hour, finding ways of making their own buck from the growing bureaucracy.

Emily was sitting at one of the restaurants that line the broad pavements of the square, drinking an afternoon coffee. She had plenty of time to finish it, because she had found little pressure on her since arriving in Brussels. The job that had been arranged by Patricia Vaine had a fine title and pleasingly substantial salary, along with all the usual perks, but as yet it had few duties. She rather thought that the job had been created by Patricia in something of a hurry, with the details to be worked out at leisure after the long summer. So Emily sat in the afternoon sun, content with her new life, browsing through a lifestyle brochure. She needed new furniture – the rents here were so accommodating compared with London that she had far more space to fill than in Clapham, and she was wondering whether a new sleigh bed might fit in with the rest of her bedroom pieces when she glanced up and found instant terror. There, no more than a handful of yards in front of her, map in hand, gazing around him like any innocent tourist, was Harry.

She wanted to cry out, to flee, but did neither. She sat frozen in fear and bewilderment, praying that he wouldn't turn, look her way, recognize her. And when, after what seemed like the passing of several lifetimes, he moved slowly on, disappearing in the direction of the train station, she found herself trembling, still holding her cup of coffee, which had spilled over the tablecloth and was spreading into a dark and embarrassing stain. The waiter was quick to see her predicament and provide consolation in the form of a new tablecloth and fresh coffee, while Emily reached for her phone.

The call was hurried, whispered. As soon as it was finished she jumped up from her table, leaving her fresh coffee untouched, and ran towards the taxi stand at the side of the square. She was agitated, didn't see another woman approaching on a path that would intercept her, and almost beat her to the door of the taxi.

'*Oh, pardon,*' the other woman said as they both bent for the driver's ear.

Emily was flustered, and evidently in a hurry. 'I'm sorry,' she panted, 'but I think I was—'

'*Mais pas de probleme,*' the other woman said. 'There are many others,' she added in accented English. '*S'il vous plaît, après vous.*'

Emily nodded in thanks. 'The Avenue de Cortenbergh. You know it?'

'But of course, *mademoiselle,*' the driver said as Emily jumped into the back seat. She didn't look up as they drove away across the cobbles, her eyes fixed in concentration.

As she watched Emily disappear into the distance,

Jemma took off the sunglasses and hat that she had been wearing, and looked forward to wiping off the heavy make-up that was caked across her face. During the election she'd been upset about being able to spend so little time in the constituency, jealous of all the others who had a slice of Harry, but now she gave thanks. It meant that a distracted Emily had little chance of recognizing her, and none at all in her disguise. What was more, she'd discovered where Emily was heading. Harry's plan had worked well.

He had decided not to confront her, try to rip the truth from her. He knew he was unlikely to succeed where the Metropolitan Police had spectacularly failed, and even trying might leave him stuck in even more accusatory mud. Instead he had been more subtle. Had scared her. Encouraged her to reach out for reassurance to someone who would understand, someone who knew – someone who had conspired with her. It was a fair assumption that she was headed for that person right now. Someone in the Avenue de Cortenbergh.

They were getting closer. And they got closer still when, later that evening, he and Jemma took a stroll down the avenue. It was a broad street that led from one of Brussels' main railway stations to the Schuman roundabout at the very heart of the European Quarter. It was lined with a clutter of commercial offices and several embassies, along with a very strong presence of EU Commission buildings. One of them was the headquarters of EATA. Discreet, nondescript, modest. But with very tight security.

'This is it,' he whispered to Jemma, almost in awe.

'But why?' she asked.

He took her arm and hurried her on in case the CCTV picked them up dawdling and took a closer look, knowing that their every step was taking them further away from the answer.

—⁓—

Patricia Vaine knew she had underestimated Harry. It was a weakness she would never indulge again.

When Emily turned up in a state of panic, burbling about having seen him, they came to a rapid conclusion. Coincidence. It could be nothing more. Nothing surprising in such a thing, for Brussels was getting to be like the streets of Westminster. They even suspected that Harry might be searching for a job, pastures new, in a place where his reputation hadn't yet been ruined. It was a supposition that would be confirmed in their minds when Patricia later ascertained that Harry had arrived, and left, on a cheap day ticket on Eurostar booked with an offer in the *Daily Telegraph*. It was precisely what Harry had hoped they would think.

Yet Patricia didn't have the luxury of dealing with a world of certainties, there were always doubts, suspicions, and she wasn't a woman to take things for granted. Harry Jones had been stupid enough to stumble onto her turf. Her vengeance was swift and utterly remorseless.

Less than a week after Harry's return from Brussels, his accountant asked him to visit her offices in Holborn. He took the bus. She was waiting for him at the reception area and took him straight through to a conference room, where she closed the door and sat him down. She seemed distracted, no offer of tea or coffee.

'There's no easy way of telling you this, Harry,' she said, two crimson discs of distress standing high on her cheeks. 'You know we'd been hopeful of coming to an understanding with your creditors – an Individual Voluntary Arrangement, in the language of the debt business.'

He nodded.

'I'm sorry, but that's not going to happen. If it's to work, we need most of your creditors to agree – and one of them seems to have changed his mind. It was all on track, making progress, but suddenly he's pulled out. One rotten apple that's turned the rest of the barrel sour. So frustrating, I'm sorry, particularly as he's one of the smaller creditors. Just a few thousand.'

He found it difficult to find words, his mouth run dry. 'Who is it, Jilly?'

'The printers you use, Maundy's. Says he won't accept pence when he's owed pounds.' She looked at him sharply. 'Suddenly changed his mind. Yet you told me you'd been doing business with them for years.'

'I have.'

'It's such a surprise, out of the blue.'

'Nothing surprises me much any more.'

'We can't move forward without him, and he simply won't budge.'

'So what do we do now, Jilly?'

The red spots on her cheek flared still more brightly. 'There's nothing we can do. He says he's going to bring a bankruptcy petition against you.'

'I see.' His voice sounded dull, as if it came from a distance, from another mouth. 'If I'm declared bankrupt I seem to remember that the court will take almost everything – my house, pension, piano. Even the plasma telly.'

'You can keep the tools of your trade.'

'But I don't have a trade any longer, Jilly. Perhaps they will let me keep the back copies of *Hansard*.'

'I'm so very sorry, Harry.'

'I assume this will be a very public spectacle.'

'I'm afraid so.'

Harry's humiliation was about to be complete.

—⚒—

The premises of George Maundy & Sons, Designers & Printers, was located in the Hertfordshire countryside at the end of a long gravel drive, which wound through laurel bushes and at its end was guarded by a five-bar gate. On the other side of the gate was an elegant Georgian farmhouse surrounded by a substantial swathe of carefully mown lawn, while Maundy's business was housed in a converted red-brick dairy. A new BMW with alloy wheels and a personalized number plate was parked at the side. This was Home Counties commercialism at its most elegant. As Harry walked up the drive, his shoes crunching on the gravel, a small terrier darted out from the door of the small office and scurried around before disappearing back inside, but Harry didn't follow. He knew from his previous visits that the office would be manned by the elder Maundy's daughter-in-law, while the father and son would be busy in the back, from where Harry could hear the humming of machinery. He found the son bent over a drawing board, studying the proof of his latest commission. The printer looked up, startled to see Harry at his elbow.

'Mr Jones, I wasn't expecting you.'

'I hope you don't mind, George.'

'You should have called.'

'Is your father around?'

'Retired. Not before time. I reckon it's me you want to see.' He stood up to face Harry in a manner that suggested he expected something of a confrontation. He was in his late thirties, receding hair, straining belt – a considerable way up his own arse, Harry reckoned, judging by the flash machine outside.

'Very well, George. You must know what difficulties you've put me in. I was hoping I could appeal to you, man to man.'

'These things are always awkward, Mr Jones,' the printer said, folding his arms across his stomach. He didn't suggest they move elsewhere, somewhere quieter. He didn't seem as if he expected the conversation to last long.

'I've been a good customer of you and your father's over the years. You know me. Now I'm in a spot of trouble.'

'Not our problem. Not our fault, either.'

Harry's lips were working, trying to find the right words to get past the man's mulishness. 'I owe you less than eight thousand pounds. I can't understand why you want to force me into bankruptcy rather than accept a deal.'

'Company policy.'

'Not your father's policy.'

'He's not here.'

Harry gazed around the workshop, with its machines whirring away, the boxes of product piling up, the eight men and women who made up the workforce all busily occupied. It was clearly a thriving concern. 'The eight thousand will ruin me, George, but it seems like it wouldn't get in your way very much at all.'

The printer ran his tongue around his mouth as if he were searching for lost breakfast. 'It's a matter of ethics, Mr Jones. The sort of thing you liked to preach when you were in Parliament. Promises made, promises kept. That's how this country runs, or used to.'

'And a bit of give and take, too, George.'

'Sure, until you politicians opened the floodgates and left us hard-working folk doing the giving while every Tom, Dick and Sanjay did all the taking.'

Ah, one of those. Closed mind, clenched fist.

'If you make me bankrupt you'll probably end up getting less than by coming to a voluntary agreement.'

'As I said, a matter of ethics. You come here accusing me of putting you in difficulties. Well, I didn't. You made your mess, not me. Up to you to clear it up. Now, if you'll excuse me, I'm busy.'

Harry was wasting his time, the printer pointing towards the door. A large white van had drawn up outside and two of Maundy's workmen were loading pallets of finished product into it. A second van was hovering in the background, waiting its turn. As Maundy escorted Harry out, making sure he left, they passed a cliff face of the boxes waiting to be loaded. Samples of the content were stuck to the outside. Harry stopped, ran his finger across a carton. They contained promotional leaflets for the European Union. The man had been bought. He stared at Maundy. 'Ethics?' he said softly.

The printer's eyes betrayed only a flicker of shame before he threw Harry out.

—ᚾ—

Harry walked away from the printers, down the hill towards the bus stop that would ferry him to the local train station, now aware that they were intent on destroying him completely. Soon he wouldn't even be able to afford the price of his bus ticket. It had always been the likely out-come, but still he hesitated before making his next phone call. He didn't even know who 'they' were, only that they wouldn't stop. But he was Harry Jones, the idiot who didn't know when to stop, either.

'Hi, Jem.'

'How did it go, Harry?'

'It didn't. They wouldn't budge. They've bought the bastard off with a shedload of printing orders.'

A sharp intake of breath. 'I'm so sorry.'

'Yeah. Me, too.'

'So . . .'

'We do what we discussed.'

'Are you sure?' She sounded reluctant.

'I need you on this one, Jem,' he said firmly. 'This crap is coming straight out of EATA in Brussels. Now I've got some press cuttings and other bits about it – pretty meagre stuff, they don't give interviews or hand out press releases. Like trying to spot a rat in a sewer when someone's switched off all the lights. But I need your help in going through it all. You up for that?'

'I suppose so,' she replied hesitantly.

'Good, can we meet up tonight?'

'No, I'm busy.'

'Tomorrow then. Saturday. Got to get going with this. Five o'clock in the pub OK?'

'All right.'

'Thanks, Jem, I'll see you then.'

He cut the connection. He gazed at his cloned iPhone, almost as though it were a loaded weapon, before he put it back in his pocket.

—ɯ—

He knew it would be hours rather than days. After all, he'd given them a deadline. He waited at home, and filled his time by sorting through his belongings, packing boxes, deciding what was truly important to him. Not the expensive acquisitions and antiques, which in any case he was likely to lose, but the memories. The books from his primary school, with the inscriptions inside. A copy of *Moby Dick*, its cover a little torn, its paper beginning to go yellow: 'Awarded to Harry Jones. First in Class. July 1978. E. L. Vale, Headmaster'. It was one of several. Clever little sod. And there were the photos, of his father, and mother. So few of them together. And, of course, of Julia.

His memories of Julia weren't of this house but of Julia herself; they would go with him wherever he went. He'd witnessed so many others who had lost everything, their communities destroyed by Saddam Hussein, the villages burned out by Colombian drugs gangs, the bombs that had gutted places like Belfast and Armagh. He'd been there, seen these things happen, knew that others somehow found the means to survive. Yes, all of that, but even so. This was his life, more than forty years of putting his neck on the line for others, Queen, country, constituents, and what had he got to show for it? A private life that resembled an Indian train crash and – this. Now he was losing it all, and along with it all, his reputation. Mr E. L. Vale would not have approved. Harry threw the book across the room into a distant corner.

It was lunchtime. Saturday. Harry was finishing off his

second drink of the day along with the reheated remains of last night's noodles when he was distracted by a knocking at the door. He found two well-dressed gentlemen on his doorstep, one late twenties, the other a little older.

'Mr Jones? I am so very sorry to bother you,' the elder of the two said with only the merest brush of a foreign accent, 'but I am in London only for a couple of days with my brother. Forgive me, I am looking for a home in this area for my family, and one of your neighbours' – he waved a vague hand in the direction of the other end of the street – 'said you might soon be considering selling. It is most rude of me, but I am a cash buyer and I wondered . . .'

It wasn't the best cover story, but Harry knew what was coming. They wouldn't take no for an answer, would kick their way through the door if necessary, but it wasn't. He let them in.

They tripped him from behind as soon as the door was closed, and pushed him to the floor. He could have put up a better fight before he succumbed, but that would only have served to make them more vicious. They left his face alone, no marks, and concentrated on his body. After the first of the blows he brought up the takeaway, noodles and nausea all over their shoes, which he hoped might discourage them, but they were professionals. While he was on his knees, retching over his carpet, they found a towel and wiped themselves down. Then they started over again, knees as well as fists; Harry knew at least one of his ribs had gone. Soon he was losing consciousness.

When they had finished on him they made a brief search of the house, kicking over the piles of books he had been sorting through. They found what they wanted in his study – his laptop, a few files. They threw them in a small holdall, along with his camera for good measure. Harry was no longer moving. They left him lying amidst his own bodily mess.

—⚶—

After they walked out of Harry's house, his attackers sauntered down the street, their casual pace designed to attract no attention. They had no reason to suspect they might be followed, and as a result they didn't spot Jemma. She was making a mess of the job, darting forward, drawing too close for fear of losing them, then stopping dead, because of her still greater fear that they would see her. She sensed from their build that they were the same men who had assaulted her, left her naked and terrified.

She tracked them around Berkeley Square, grateful for the crowds that gave her cover, then on into the crawling traffic of Curzon Street. It was there she lost them, as her eyes were on the approaching cars, waiting to cross the road, and when she looked up once more they had gone. She panicked, heedless of the vehicles now, dashing across the street to the spot where she had last seen them, and discovered an alley that led her into a backwater, an unhurried square filled with small, pavement eating places and boutique shops. And there, sitting at an outside table, were her two men, talking to a third. She slipped behind a table some yards down the broad pavement, reached into her bag, produced a map that she spread out in front of her and placed a camera on top of it, as might any tourist. She ordered a drink from the waiter, making sure she paid for it as soon as it arrived, and began inspecting her camera, as though checking the results of her morning's work. That was how she took photographs, of all three of them. She had to work quickly, because the two men soon got up and went on their way, leaving the holdall behind. The third man, who was older, and in no hurry, opened the bag and rifled through its contents, before smiling quietly to himself and zipping it closed once more. He paid for his tea and left. Once again Jemma followed, keeping her map to hand, ready to bury herself in it if he looked in her direction, but he didn't, pacing on steadily, as if he had found a new purpose.

As, indeed, he had. The man did what he always did after a moment of tension or triumph had passed. He strode purposefully along a route he had taken many times before, which sometimes led to a different destination but always took him in the same direction.

Jemma followed him, feeling sick not just from her inner tension but also the thoughts of Harry. She knew his two assailants were dangerous men, and there was a small part of her that hoped they had left him tied up, unmarked, as they had done her, but there was a much more insistent part of her that doubted this was possible. No way he would have handed over the contents of the holdall quietly, he would have put up a fight, bloody Harry always did. And the thought of what they might have done to him soon overcame all her other fears.

They had neared Marble Arch. She watched as he disappeared inside a pub, then followed him to the doorstep. That was when she saw the sign and knew she could go no further. 'This is a majority gay and lesbian pub', it proclaimed. It was a step too far for her, she would give herself away, ruin everything. She turned and ran all the way back to Harry.

—⁓—

She found him where they had left him, amongst the overturned piles of his books, in his vomit. She couldn't help noticing there was blood in it, but he was breathing, heavily, his lungs rasping. 'Harry, you bloody fool,' she sobbed, kneeling by his side.

He opened an eye. 'If this is what a man has to do to get you back, I think I'll try Internet dating instead.' He tried a sardonic smile, his face wrinkled in agony.

She helped him to the sofa, trying to make him comfortable, cleaning him up, crying quietly. She gasped when she took off his filthy shirt. She found more bruising and weals than there was skin. She bathed him, tenderly, in warm water, trying not to cause him too much pain, when suddenly he grabbed her arm, so tightly it was her turn to hurt. 'What did you see? Tell me, Jem.'

As he listened to her, his body seemed to relax. His breathing became less frantic, he stopped sweating, the colour returned to his face. 'Did you follow him in?' he demanded when at last she told him about the pub.

'I couldn't, Harry. I'd have stuck out like a . . .' She struggled to find a metaphor, but decided none was necessary. 'I got photographs.' She pulled out her camera and held it up for him to inspect. Many of the images were fumbled, out of focus, betraying how much her hands had been trembling, but amongst them were several excellent images. And they needed only one.

'Good girl,' he whispered, falling back on his cushion. 'Were you scared?'

'No.'

'Liar.'

His eyes closed and he fell deeply asleep.

When he woke again, he found he was lying beneath a duvet. His books had been set into neat piles once more, and she had washed the carpet of all trace of the attack. He still felt like shit, every breath cost him dear, but he found he was able to smile, and he did. Only one or two cracked ribs, and he hadn't even lost any teeth. In the world of Harry Jones, this wasn't exactly a famous victory, but at least he was still in the fight.

CHAPTER SIXTEEN

A cry came from the tennis court. 'I think that was out.'

A second voice warbled from the other end of the net. 'Was it? Then point to you.'

'No, let's play a let.'

'You sure?'

'Thirty-forty,' the first player insisted, and prepared to serve again.

Doubles, of course. Singles would have been far too limiting for the annual tennis tournament of a small village like Upper Marlsford, ruling out most players over fifty. That didn't prevent the matches being fought with considerable intensity, even while being wrapped in a blanket of neighbourly politeness.

This was the final. Felix and Patricia played hosts, handing round the squash and sandwiches he'd made. A good number of the villagers of Upper Marlsford had gathered to watch, dressed in their bleached straw hats, cotton dresses and open collars, sitting around the court on freshly mown grass or standing in the shade of the crab apple tree. Others had gone for a stroll through the gardens, constructed for the low maintenance that a weekend couple required yet nevertheless nurtured with enormous fondness by Felix.

'It's comforting to be able to do our bit,' Patricia remarked as their paths crossed by the ancient sundial, a birthday present to him from her that was slowly being claimed by the lichen.

'Love this time of year,' he replied, his voice larded with nostalgia for his childhood. He was in starched shirt-sleeves, which protruded from a multi-hued silk waistcoat that seemed to catch every colour of the garden. 'Few weeks' time we'll be picking the early plums and apples. You know, Patricia, next year I'd like to try keeping some bees. What do you think?'

But she appeared not to have heard. 'The English at play,' she remarked, without much apparent approval, as a further cry came from the tennis court and at last the game was lost.

'Next year you should enter,' he encouraged, 'you used to enjoy a game.'

'You forget, Felix. I don't like losing.'

'Then let's put in a swimming pool. Good exercise, and we could use one of those ground-source heat pump thin-gies. Ingenious bits of kit, so I'm told, very green and environmental. I suspect we could get some sort of grant.'

'We don't need a grant. We could do it on my expenses.'

'Your expenses would cover a swimming pool?' he said in surprise.

'Felix, my expenses would fill a swimming pool. We'd open it once a year to the village, of course. Put it down as entertainment.'

She smiled contentedly, but he didn't join with her. Instead he stroked his renewing beard, still not much more than stubble, not yet at its best. His brow said he had something on his mind. 'I sold two picture frames this week. Broke my heart.'

'To sell them?'

'No, for what it said. You see, one was entirely authentic, wonderful rich patina, original gilding. Oh, a little battered here and there but only what you'd expect from something that was probably Georgian. The story of centuries told in every little chip and layer of dust. A one-off. It only needed a little restoration and retouching to be perfect once again. And the other ... Well, that was no more than thirty years old, all pretence and brashness. I got twice as much for it. Yet in another thirty it will probably have fallen apart.'

'The world moves on, Felix,' she said distractedly, adjusting the sundial a fraction.

'Yes, of course, my dear. But sometimes it pays not to push the future too fast. Let it get there in its own time.'

Ah, one of his homilies. An eyebrow arched halfway to her scalp. 'Do I sense the brush of criticism?'

'Of you? Never. But ... sometimes, my dear, I wonder if you don't require the world to be a little too precise. Orderly. All its ends tied together rather too neatly.' He pulled a pocket watch from his waistcoat and examined it carefully. Then he moved the sundial back to its original position.

'You know I don't do untidy, Felix,' she scolded. 'After all, I'm a bureaucrat, remember. Everything in its little box.'

And everyone, too, he thought, but didn't say. She moved away, not wanting a trial of strength over a wretched sundial.

'This Jones business,' he said, pursuing her, 'you've made him entirely irrelevant.'

'With your help.'

'Precisely, which is why I make bold enough to wonder.'

She stopped suddenly and turned. '*What* do you wonder?'

'Is it really necessary to humiliate him completely? Make him bankrupt? It seems ...'

'A step too far?'

'Unnecessary.'

'That's the difference between the antiques trade and my business, Felix. I don't live in the past, or even move with the times. I make the times. One can't keep going back, letting things gather dust.'

From the court came a cry of despair, a point lost, and with it the match. Polite applause rippled through the onlookers, the vicar jumped to his feet, brushing crumbs from his chest, scrubbing his brow with a vast handkerchief as he prepared to present the winners' cup.

'Come on, Felix, we have more work to do.' She struck out once again, leaving their conversation behind.

'Yes, dear,' he sighed, and dutifully followed.

—⁓—

Ye Olde Cheshire Cheese might easily have given itself over to tourist tat, seeing that it had stood on its site near Fleet Street for more than four centuries since the Great Fire had burned down its predecessor, yet it had resisted the temptation. Its mishmash of corridors and staircases and wood-panelled rooms conjured up traces of earlier times, and that is precisely what Sloppy wanted. To go back. Forget about now. That was why he drank. When Harry arrived, soon after the doors had opened, he found his old colleague sitting alone in a booth down in the stone-clad vaults, cradling a glass. Harry had brought Jemma with him, suspecting that Sloppy might find the presence of a woman less threatening, quite apart from reducing Harry's temptation to grab the man by the hair and beat the crap out of him. Not that his ribs left him in much of a condition to mete out physical punishment, but in Sloppy's case, he'd be happy to make an exception.

Sloppy raised two bleary eyes as they approached. 'You're in luck,' he muttered. 'Money will be gone by this evening. So will I.' He swallowed some of his wine, not tasting. 'Who's the new tart?' he said, eyeing Jemma.

'I'm just a friend.'

'Sure,' Sloppy muttered, 'always lots of friends, has

Harry.' A smile, cold and hard, cut across his face. 'Friday nights, when they let us out of Sandhurst and we bombed down to town. You remember? That very first club on the Kings Road, what was its name?' He shook his head, trying to clear the mists, and turned once more to Jemma. 'Don't worry, it was only completely meaningless sex. They didn't give us time for anything else. Spent too many months and too much money on our training, so they didn't want romance getting in the way.' A wistful tone crept into his voice. 'There was that little blonde we used to argue about, I always thought she'd be better off with me instead of you. From Latvia or Lithuania or wherever. What was her name?'

It was Finland, her name had been Kaarina, but this wasn't the time.

'Sloppy, for pity's sake. Concentrate! This is important, for both of us.'

'Yes, she was.'

The bastard. Sloppy was enjoying making his old friend squirm. Harry produced a large manila envelope, and from it he took three photographs. He moved Sloppy's drink in order to lay them out on the table. 'Take a look, Sloppy. Is this our man?'

Sloppy seemed to be struggling. The alcohol was waging war with his eyesight and some bastard had moved his drink. Yet there was something in these photographs that was insisting on his attention. He lowered his head for a closer look, sticking his finger on the central photo as though to pin it down, in case it tried to escape. He shook his head. 'Different hair, different glasses. Didn't have that ridiculous bloody beard.' He slumped back in his seat. 'But they're the same bloodsucking eyes. Like a lizard. That's the piece of slime. I can feel his clammy hand even now.' Sloppy closed his eyes. When they returned something had changed, as though he were no longer completely lost in a storm of alcohol but had been washed up on some beach, a place where he could find a little firm ground once more. 'Who is he, Harry? Who the hell is he?

'Dunno, Sloppy. But I know where the pisshead drinks.'

—⁂—

In fables, the fight against evil is pursued without quarter or hesitation; in the world of Harry Jones, there were always distractions. One of the most pressing was a letter he received by Special Delivery, for which he had to sign. It was a Statutory Demand. He scanned it, trying to take it all in. Insolvency Act ... Debt for Liquidated Sum Payable Immediately ... 21 days after its service on you, you could be made bankrupt ...

It had started.

He spent the afternoon with more sorting, sifting, knowing it must be done and determined not to run from it. Jemma was assisting, taking pity, since Harry's ribs still hurt like hell. She was helping him fillet the endless yards of filing he had accumulated during his parliamentary career and that, now his office in the House of Commons had been closed down, had been dumped across his dining room. Campaigns he had pursued, speeches he had made, and letters. As she read through them she grew aware for the first time how much of his work had been low-key, but vital for the constituents concerned. Over the years Harry had helped keep many families and homes together, even though he couldn't keep his own.

The radio was on, a news report that the new Prime Minister, Dave Murray, had made a speech on a visit to the White House promising to repair the damage to relations caused between the two countries by recent misunderstandings. Privately, and on a few occasions publicly, the Americans had been suggesting that the Speedbird crash had been handled even more incompetently than Lockerbie. The Americans wanted justice, retribution, some means of restoring their national pride, and all they had was a grainy bit of footage from somewhere in Russia. They hadn't even had the pleasure of watching that ball-less bastard Ghazi die. Yet Harry chose not to listen. Politics just brought back the pain, so he took himself off for a shower while Jemma ploughed through more of the filing.

He came back into the room, wrapped in his bathrobe, towelling his hair with clumsy care as he still found it difficult to raise his arms above his head. She waved a file at him.

'What did you do with this in the end, Harry?'

'With what?'

'The Speedbird file. The one with all the interviews I conducted.'

The crash. It had been so long since he'd even thought about it. Too many distractions. He coughed apologetically. 'I was going to read through it, but . . .'

'You mean you didn't?'

'Never got round to opening it. Sorry.'

'Well, someone has.'

'How can you tell?'

She flicked through the papers with her thumb. 'The papers are in exactly the opposite order I left them.'

'You sure?'

'As sure as I am that you're not wearing underwear.'

He hurriedly readjusted the bathrobe.

'It's as if someone has taken them all out, gone through them meticulously . . .'

'Copied them, even?'

'Then replaced them. Except back to front.'

'But who?'

'The men who beat you up, maybe?'

'Then why?'

'To find out what we know.'

'Sod all!'

'Perhaps more than we realize, Harry.'

He looked at her. 'You are beautiful,' he said, putting emphasis on every word.

'If that's why you had a shower, Jones, forget it!'

He came and sat down beside her on the floor, put an

arm around her, wincing with the effort, and not in any way that was predatory. It seemed more a gesture of protection.

'What's wrong, Harry?'

'My life. The disaster it's become. It's all happened since the crash.'

'And ...'

'Because of the crash.'

'I don't understand, what's your connection?'

'What's *our* connection, Jem. You've been on the receiving end, too, remember?'

She shivered. 'But all we've done is ask a few questions.'

'Precisely.'

'And it's not over, is it?' She rested her head on his shoulder and could feel the tension inside. 'You scared, Harry?'

'Not for myself. What the hell can they do to me they haven't already done? But I'm scared for you, Jem. I never had any intention of getting you involved.'

'All this – for a few wee questions?'

He was silent for a few moments. 'It's my fault. I'm so sorry.'

She looked up, a new fire burning in her eyes. 'They did all that to us – just for asking?'

'Forgive me?'

'Harry, you know I'm Church of Scotland, prayers with the little ones and butter wouldn't melt in Miss Laing's mouth. But I am so *incredibly fucking furious!*'

'Please, tell me what I should do, Jem.'

'Why, you idiot, ask a few bloody more.'

—ᴍ—

Shaking a tree to discover who is hiding in it is a dangerous undertaking. You have no idea who or what might fall upon you. But Harry was determined. The Speedbird crash seemed to mark the start of it all, so he turned to the man who had become the acknowledged source of authority about it. McDeath. Harry tracked him down to his office in Brussels.

'Harry, you're a fortunate man. Just clearing my desk for the summer. Away for a couple of months. Grandchildren. A little sailing. Putting greens.'

'Sounds arduous.'

'Nothing more to keep me here once all the birds have flown.'

'It's early July, Hamish.'

'Few days' time, this place'll be like the Sahara. Watering holes closed, nothing left but bait for the buzzards. We're all exhausted – why, sometimes we have to work a four-day week.' He chuckled. It had been a good year for him, no point in denying it.

'Hamish, I was wondering if you could give me a bit of a steer,' Harry said. 'On Speedbird.'

Harry had hoped it might prompt some spontaneous revelation; he got nothing but silence.

'I've heard mutterings that the case isn't dead and

buried, that's it's not going to end with Ghazi. Still a few ghosts to exorcize,' he continued.

'Is that so? I've heard nothing. Where did you hear that from?'

'Oh, in dark, dusty corners. Even heard a whisper that there could be a Russian connection.'

'Russian? Connection? With what?'

'I was hoping you could tell me.'

'I can't imagine what you're talking about.'

'Pity. You might like to ask around a bit, Hamish. Check the story out. If there's anything in it, I hope I'll be the first to know.'

'You know I've done a deal with the Devil, Harry, in the form of my editor. He owns not only my soul but every scrap of story.'

'Of course. But you know my interest in this, and if you find anything that's new, particularly about any Russian interest, I hope you'll remember where you first heard it ...'

—⁂—

Harry had been hoping for some reaction, some fresh and unexplained disaster in his life that might peel off another layer of the mystery, but when it arrived it seemed so inconsequential as to be no more than a gnat bite. A couple of days after his conversation with McDeath, he discovered his car had been broken into. It was out in the street, residents' parking bay, beneath a lamp, but that hadn't saved him. A rear window had been smashed, lots of broken glass, but with no other damage, nothing of any value ripped off or ripped out, apart from an old T-shirt that had been lying on the back seat. The car had been parked there for several days – Harry wasn't doing much driving, petrol was too expensive for his budget – and he couldn't even be sure when the break-in had taken place. The damage was superficial, the loss of a T-shirt scarcely worth reporting to the police, and it seemed so obvious that it was vandals, although a clapped-out Volvo was so much less interesting than almost any other vehicle on the street, and they hadn't even bothered opening the glove compartment to see if there was a satnav or some other item of value in there. Truly tedious stuff. He decided to repair the damage himself rather than paying the ridiculous excess that his insurance company would charge him, and he spent an afternoon sweeping out the glass and replacing it with a window bought from a car knacker's yard.

Meanwhile, Jemma was spending what little spare time she had in the frantic days leading up to the end of the school summer term in her local library consulting back copies of newspapers and current affairs magazines. Everything from October last. She could have done some of it at home, on the Internet, but since her attack she felt safer in public places like the library. She didn't know what she was looking for, apart from something major to do with Brussels, or any link with Russia. It was a bit like firing a catapult at shooting stars. Apparently Russia and Brussels had reached agreement on the protection of peat bogs, but she didn't think that was it. Progress was slow, at times seeming non-existent.

Harry concentrated on his own enquiries. It was mid-week and mid-afternoon when he walked into the Montreal, the gay pub where Jemma hadn't made it past the door. It wasn't particularly crowded, or particularly plush, a rather run-down Victorian drinking joint like so many others dotted around the capital. Yet as he stood at the bar and looked around, he began to notice the telltale signs of its interests that stretched rather wider than simply offering a choice of drink. The chalkboard advertising the quiz night later in the week also promoted a drag night at the coming weekend. The framed photos on the wall weren't of old Victorian street scenes but entirely contemporary and artistic shots of men's bodies, in close up, very muscular and eminently over-oiled. At the rear of the main room was a small stage, presumably for the weekend cabaret, with a multicoloured gay pride flag standing to attention in the corner. Two Japanese couples came in, sat at a table, dropped their bags, and looked around. Then, after a brief discussion and much nodding, they picked up their bags and left. It wasn't their environment, they'd only wanted a drink.

'Haven't seen you here before,' the barman said to Harry, smiling.

'Haven't been here before.'

'What are you looking for?'

'A drink. A bottle of beer. Preferably something British without a slice of lime stuffed down its throat.'

'You look like a Dog's Bollocks man to me.'

'Too hoppy. I prefer a Silent Slasher.'

The barman raised his eyebrows provocatively, recognizing he was likely to be beaten in any game of find-the-firkin. 'Well, we don't have either. Heineken do?'

'Fine.'

'You looking for anything else?'

'No.'

'Right. One straight Heineken coming up.'

The barman scuttled around at the back of a refrigerator behind the bar. Above his head a screen was playing a recording of some Californian chat show, no sound, all teeth and tans.

'You will let me know if there's anything else, won't you?' the barman said, sliding Harry's beer across to him.

'There is something, actually.'

'There often is.'

Harry pulled from his pocket one of the photos he'd shown to Sloppy. 'Recognize this man?'

The barman's smile faded like the light through a drawn curtain. 'Of course not.'

'You haven't even looked at it.'

'And I'm not going to. What sort of creature do you think I am?'

'Would this help?' Harry produced a twenty-pound note and laid it on top of the photo.

The eyes flashed angrily, the theatricality cast aside. 'I suggest you enjoy your drink, sir, then leave. There's nothing for you here, least of all a loose tongue.'

'I'll take your word for it.'

The barman turned his back. Harry rather admired him. He wouldn't have expected such discretion in most other pubs in London. He sat at the bar, examining the fading head on his beer, wondering what to do next as the scattering of other drinkers cast curious eyes in his direction, only for the barman to warn them off with a firm shake of the head.

Harry was getting near the end of his drink, his inspiration already gone, when he heard a voice from behind his shoulder.

'Hello, Boss. Bit of a surprise to find you here.'

Harry glanced into the mirror behind the bar and saw the reflection of a familiar face. 'Well, I'll be . . .'

'No, I doubt that very much. Not Harry Jones.'

'Troop Sergeant Barry Baldwin,' Harry smiled in greeting.

The other man slipped into the seat beside him. 'Let me buy you another? For old times' sake.'

'If the barman will serve me.'

'Suzie, same again,' Baldwin instructed. The barman complied, but with a scowl of suspicion instead of a smile.

'Long time, Boss.'

'A lot of water.'

'And a few bodies.'

Baldwin had been the Sergeant in Harry's sixteen-man troop in Northern Ireland. Good friend, exemplary soldier, until he'd got into an argument with some low form of swamp life from the Welsh Guards who somehow knew, and had made explicit jokes about Baldwin's sexuality. Not good publicity in an Armagh bar. Baldwin resigned immediately.

'I'm sorry to have let you down, Captain Jones,' he had said.

'You never did, Sergeant. Not once.'

Even the rest of the troop weren't having it. 'But we always knew you were an old queen, right from the moment you joined,' they'd protested. But it had done no good. Baldwin had gone. Until now. Not that he appeared to have changed so much. Still the same short cropped hair, all muscle and moustache.

'So what brings you to our little citadel of sin?' he asked.

'This man.' Harry produced the photograph once more; Baldwin's brow clouded.

'It's not because he's gay or anything like that,' Harry reassured him.

'Don't tell me, you just want a chat.'

'Truth is, Barry, I want to break his bloody neck. He's ruined Sloppy, cheated him out of everything. And because of that he's done the same to me. I think he's a very dangerous man.'

'What, Wendy?'

'You know him?' Harry couldn't keep the urgency from his voice.

The other man pushed aside his beer, troubled, struggling with conflicting loyalties. 'I'd rather not get involved.'

'Barry, since when in your life did you not get involved?'

Baldwin's head sank, his eyes closed. When eventually he spoke, his voice was low, reluctant. 'It's Wendy Wilton.'

'His real name?'

'I don't know. We just know him as Wendy.'

'Any friends here?'

'None in particular.'

'So where does he live?'

'Live? I don't know. But not too far, I'd guess. Seems to me he usually walks here – you know, coat, brolly when it's raining.'

Harry pressed his old friend, but got nothing more. 'I don't know anything else, Harry. And I don't want you coming back here and turning this place upside down.'

'I wouldn't.'

'You always used to. Everywhere you went.'

'With you covering my tail against the bad guys.'

The other man smiled once more, mischievously. 'When I was covering your tail, I was the bad guy.'

—✦—

There were others apart from Harry who were intent on causing chaos. Emily Keane was back from Brussels. Her shadow job had little enough to detain her there during the summer, so she was back amongst her old haunts and staying with friends. She was walking back alone past Battersea Park late one night – nothing too threatening, even after dark, and nothing she hadn't done before. There were usually plenty of people around, and Emily was young and immortal. Yet there were also stretches of the way that were less well lit, full of trees, shadows.

She never saw who attacked her. They came from behind, grabbed her, flashed a blade. She had no chance of defending herself. She had time for nothing but a single piercing scream before it was cut short by a savage blow to the head and she fell to the ground.

CHAPTER SEVENTEEN

Harry's screwdriver was missing. He needed it to fix a loose shelf he'd discovered while sorting through the books, but couldn't find it anywhere. Then he remembered. The broken car window. It was parked a little way down the street. He sauntered past the sculpture gallery; from within his lair the proprietor waved, but to Harry's mind the greeting was not as it once was. But nothing in his life was. Perhaps it was merely his imagination, and his depression, but small slights had begun to take on a painful significance. He knew that Oscar, his chairman and longtime friend, would be celebrating his sixtieth soon, and yet he hadn't received an invitation. Would he ever now? And the invitation that had gone out from party headquarters to all former MPs following the last election – what was called the 'End up a Peer Show' – had definitely passed him by, as one verminous gossip columnist had taken protracted delight in pointing out. The world was turning its back on him. Scarcely surprising that Jemma wouldn't let him into her bed. He felt like a leper, and despite his best efforts to do otherwise, he blamed her a little for that, too, a mood not helped when he found yet another ticket taped to his windscreen. He ripped it off and dropped it in the gutter.

Yet his screwdriver, at least, was reliable. There it was, staring at him from the front seat. He climbed in and retrieved it, and was checking the glove compartment to see if he had left anything else behind when there was a sharp rap on the window. He groaned. It was Arkwright, along with three other officers. He wound down the window.

No foreplay.

'Henry Marmaduke Maltravers-Jones, I am arresting you—'

'What, for a sodding parking ticket?'

'—on suspicion of a serious assault . . .'

'Dear God,' he whispered to himself in bewilderment, 'not again . . .'

—ɯ—

The Interview Room. The tapes winding their slow way towards his entrapment.

'Where were you last night between midnight and two a.m.?'

'At home.'

'Can anyone corroborate that?'

'No.'

Another evidence bag. 'Is this your T-shirt, Mr Jones?'

Oh, damn. 'Yes.'

'It was found at the scene of a serious assault last night on Emily Keane. Can you explain that?'

'It was stolen from my car a couple of nights ago. Someone broke into it.'

The tape would catch every drop of disbelief. 'They broke into your car – to steal a T-shirt.'

'My client isn't required to speculate,' van Buren interrupted.

'Very well, did you report the break-in to the police?'

'No.'

The tape recorded the rustling noise of van Buren shifting in discomfort.

'Where was your car broken into?'

'Outside my home.'

'In Mayfair.'

'Yes.'

'Interesting. Fascinating, in fact. Because we found fragments of window glass at the scene of the assault in Battersea. We'll want to compare them to the broken window in your car.'

'You can't. I replaced it.'

'Which body shop?'

'I did it myself.'

'Yourself?' The recorder noted a sharp rise in intonation as incredulity bounced back and forth between Arkwright and his colleague. More uncomfortable rustling from van Buren. 'I think this time, Mr Jones, that even a novice nun would have trouble believing you. Miss Keane won't be

285

able to withdraw the charges this time, you know. They're too serious. A knife slash across the back of her hand, down to the bone. We're talking grievous bodily harm here, with intent. Do you know what that means?'

'No, but I'm sure you're going to tell me, Detective Sergeant.'

'Anything up to life.'

'Don't threaten my client, Detective Sergeant,' van Buren snapped.

'Threaten? But I'm doing my best to help him, Mr van Buren. To understand just how deep he's landed himself in it this time.'

'I'm being set up.'

'By who?'

'I don't know.'

'Then why?'

'I don't know that, either.'

'Let's not waste any more time, shall we? You clearly had motive for this attack. And opportunity. Your DNA has been found at the scene. You don't even have an alibi. How much worse do you think it can get, Mr Jones?'

The tape recorded a silence, where there was no reply.

Arkwright smiled, thinly, no humour in it. 'I think that wraps it up. Rather neatly, in fact.'

The tape couldn't record the look that Harry gave to van Buren, or the shake of the head that the lawyer offered in return.

—⚹—

'I'm sorry, Miss, you can't bring coffee in here,' the librarian said, bouncing on the toes of her polished shoes.

'Then I'm the one who should be sorry,' Jemma replied, putting the plastic cup carefully to one side. She'd been at it for hours, interrogating the Internet and rifling through back copies of newspapers and periodicals. She needed the caffeine. It had been like a game of blind man's buff, trusting to fortune that she would not only bump into something, but recognize it when she did. The thirty-something librarian was still standing guard, officious, no ring, when Jemma's phone jumped into life.

'Jem, it's me.'

She knew by Harry's tone that something awful had happened.

'I've been arrested. Emily again.'

The librarian was bouncing up and down once more, looking formidable and very cross; Jemma fled from her presence and into the corridor.

'Where are you?' she asked.

'At Charing Cross. Should move in here when they take my home away,' he quipped, but it fell flat even before he'd delivered it. 'You're one of my two phone calls, Jem.'

'What, to tell me you'll be a little late for that dinner you promised to cook?'

'I don't think I'll be making dinner, Jem. Emily was attacked last night. Something pretty nasty. They think it was me.'

Only a moment of supreme self-restraint prevented Jemma from asking if they were right.

'I've been charged. I'm up before the magistrate shortly. They want to remand me in custody.'

'Oh, Harry . . .'

'But can't you see? This proves we're right.'

'About what exactly?'

'How important this game is.'

'I think we ought to stop, Harry.'

'Why?'

'Because they're so obviously bloody winning!'

She could hear another voice in the background, interrupting.

'Jem, I've got to go. You're right . . .' He faded in a rustle of confusion before his voice came back. 'Be careful, Jem. I'm sorry to have got you into this.'

Then her phone went dead. She didn't know whether to smash it against the wall or on the floor. Instead, she walked back in to the reference room. The librarian was waiting to intercept her, a look of thunder on her face. Jemma decided to get in there first.

'Sorry,' she said, waving a finger at the phone. 'My ex-boyfriend. Total loser.'

The librarian relaxed, nodding in understanding, and returned to her post behind the desk while Jemma went back to her labours.

—◊—

Harry didn't like cells. Had a deep aversion to them. It had started with his training at Hereford, where his SAS mentors had inflicted many kinds of indignities upon him, in preparation for what was to follow, but, of course, it could never do that. He'd once even found himself inside a condemned cell in central Asia, listening to other prisoners being executed, waiting his turn. It had put him off being locked up.

When they came to unlock his cell at Charing Cross, it was only for the stuffy pleasures of a white Securicor prison van, where he had his own tiny cell along with five other prisoners. And when, after a short journey, he was in turn released from the van, it was only into the arms of further security officers who escorted him down to the cells beneath the court complex in Marylebone Road.

'Never expected to see you here, Mr Jones,' one of the security officers muttered, leading him down. 'I'm bloody sorry.'

Harry assumed the man was a former soldier. It made him feel worse.

Harry waited his turn, the sliding of doors like the clattering wheels of the tumbrel, the voices from beyond the cheering of the crowd. The prisoner before him returned to his cell in tears. 'You bastard!' he sobbed, raging eyes fastening on Harry, but Harry assumed it was a condemnation intended for the entire world, he didn't take it personally. He was almost relieved when at last the door to his cell was opened and he was led up the short set of steps to the dock.

The courtroom was new, laminated, none of the rich dark oak of traditional justice. It had replaced the old court complex at Horseferry Road, the site now sold off for luxury flats. Cuts. Already the discolouration on the bar in front of him betrayed the presence of an army of sweaty palms. Van Buren was sitting in the seat beneath him, the Crown prosecutor a little farther away, the district judge presiding over all beneath the royal coat of arms with its lion rampant. And it began.

Harry was asked to confirm his name and address. 'Yes, sir,' Harry replied, standing to attention, on parade. Then he was ordered to sit, and played no further part in proceedings. He'd been told by van Buren that this would be the case, yet it did nothing to stifle his despair. As he sat down, his defiance seemed to leak away like a deflating balloon. He had wanted to deny the charges, protest his innocence, but van Buren had said that wouldn't be possible, not at this stage. Don't cause a fuss, Harry. In any event, as Harry sat, he found he couldn't breathe. He'd often imagined such a scene, not with himself but with his father, who had sailed so very close to the wind that it had seemed merely a matter of time before he capsized. Only his early death had saved him, a heart attack brought about by overambitious fornication. Harry could hear his ghost mocking – 'The way to go, Harry, not like this . . .'

The Crown prosecutor was setting out the case. Section 18, Offences Against the Person Act. The Act dated from 1861, one part of the British legal system that appeared to have withstood the test of time. Grievous bodily harm, with intent. Trial by indictment. Seek permission for the case to be admitted to Crown Court. That was inevitable, given that the maximum punishment was so severe – life in prison, as Arkwright had warned him. The Detective Sergeant was sitting in the court even now. He was looking confident.

The prosecutor asked that Harry be remanded in custody, objecting to bail. It was a most serious offence, he said, the evidence the prosecution intended to present would make a custodial sentence almost inevitable, it was not the only allegation made against the defendant by the witness, there was the all too serious possibility that the defendant might try to interfere yet again with the prime witness. And more.

Then it was van Buren's turn. He did his best. Argued that Harry was a man of previous unblemished character, a man who had given immense service over many years to his country, had medals, was far too well known to hide. This was, the lawyer declared, a man of substance, not likely to run off with his life packed into a suitcase. Yet, after a night in the cells, Harry was looking dishevelled, as if he were already on the run.

The system of hearings before a district judge has been frequently criticized. Unlike magistrates, they sit on their own, and can come to highly individual and patently idiosyncratic decisions. The district judge in Harry's case had never met him but had, of course, heard of the accused, even knew of the allegations of sexual harassment made against him by Emily – well, who hadn't? But the judge also knew how casually and unfairly such allegations were thrown around by young women; after all, some years beforehand a close colleague on the bench had been accused of similar conduct. Hushed up and brushed over, the woman clearly hysterical, but judges rely on their own experience as well as that of legal precedent to reach their conclusions. The judge had a brother only recently retired from the military, while he himself had once considered a political career, all of which gave him an inclination to trust Harry. They had never met, but there were ties that bound men like them. What was more, the judge held a patholog-ical loathing for journalists. Now he looked across his courtroom, at those press men present, all poised, ready to pounce, wanting to devour this man on their front pages. They gave him every excuse he needed. Anyway, the pris-ons were overflowing like blocked drains. Cuts!

So Harry wasn't remanded in custody, as Arkwright and the prosecutor sought, but released. Wasn't even given a tag or put under curfew or required to pay a surety, merely ordered on pain of extraordinary punishment not to approach any witness and to report once a week to Charing Cross police station. Van Buren blanched, scarcely able to believe his client's good fortune. On another day, before another judge, Harry would be chasing cockroaches around the Scrubs.

Instead, Harry was released, into the clutches of a mob

of journalists who were determined to get their victim, one way or the other.

—〜〜—

Harry suggested they meet up in St James's Park. He couldn't go home, which was under siege, and he was feeling desperately claustrophobic, in need of fresh air, wanting to breathe again. He sat in a deckchair, his face shaded by a sunhat even though the sun had gone, peering out at the pelicans squabbling on their perch in the lake and listening to the evening serenade provided by the musicians from the Wellington Barracks who were crowded onto the bandstand. Harry had walked through this park for years, from the Parliament buildings to the clubs and restaurants of St James's, but usually with his head down, his mind elsewhere. How long had it been since he'd slowed down enough to soak up its gentle atmosphere, smell the fresh-mown grass, admire the reflections of Buckingham Palace in the lake and the chimes of the light-throated clock echoing from Horseguards? When had he last eaten an ice cream? Now, for a couple of hours, he'd done all of that. While he sat here, it seemed he had all the time in the world.

'I was always worried I'd be bored when I left the Commons,' he declared, as Jemma appeared through the trees and came to sit beside him, 'but I could get used to this.'

They both knew he was lying.

'I'm afraid I can't cook you that dinner,' he said, 'the place is swarming with vermin. You wouldn't like it anyway. It was only going to be pasta.'

Again, they both knew he was lying. He'd been trained how to live off the land, deep in jungle or on the Arctic ice, but he had never taken to it and was an accomplished cook.

'Pasta at my place, then,' she said.

'I can't go back to the house, Jem, not tonight. They'll rip me apart.'

'Pasta – and a pillow. On the sofa. I'll cook.'

The look he threw at her suggested he wasn't sure which prospect he found least appealing. Even she acknowledged that her skills in the kitchen might provide clinical evidence of why the Scots were burdened with one of the highest rates of coronary disease in Europe. She threw a file of papers into his lap. 'And here's a little appetizer.'

He sat up and began to open it. The file contained photocopies of press reports and Internet printouts.

'We don't know what we're looking for but we know it has to be big. Huge, in fact. But I couldn't find it. I was so desperate, I even began imagining that it might have something to do with the recent deal between Russia and Brussels for the exploitation of ancient bogs, with some fanatical environmentalist wreaking vengeance on them.'

'Mind you, they can be ferocious. When I was at uni I spent part of a summer vacation in a protest camp,' Harry muttered, sifting the papers.

'Getting to know the enemy?'

'Were they the enemy? I'm not sure even now.'

'So why did you go?'

He looked up sharply, a look of incredulity on his face. 'For the same reason you probably took a gap year and didn't want your parents to visit your college digs too often.'

The animated twitching of her nose suggested he had found his target. 'Leaving aside your dubious environmental credentials,' she said, 'I came across this.' She directed his attention to a particular press clipping from the file. 'The Babylon pipeline. It will bring gas from central Asia to Western Europe and save us all from igloos. It's huge. Original construction costs eight billion, currently estimated at fourteen, so you can guess there won't be much change from twenty.'

'Dollars?'

'Pounds.'

'That's big enough to move a few mountains.'

'Precisely. It's a huge piece of engineering. But there's more. The real money comes from the supply of gas itself. Babylon is going to provide fifteen to twenty per cent of the EU's gas needs. Year after year. Can you imagine how much power that gives those involved?'

'So who is involved?'

'The central Asian republics themselves. The gas companies that do the drilling. But there's someone else. The countries through which the pipeline runs.'

'From central Asia? There must be a number of different routes a pipeline could take.'

'Exactly!' It was as though her dullest pupil had suddenly discovered the theory of relativity.

He was studying one of the maps in the folder, his finger following the track. 'From central Asia, to Western Europe, via ... *Russia*.'

'It doesn't own the gas, only controls it – so long as the pipeline goes through Russia.'

'You remember a few years ago? Russia got into a bust-up with the Ukraine. Some bollocks about unpaid bills, supposedly, but it's never that simple, not with the Russians. It was all about muscle. Making sure the Ukraine remembered who the bosses were. So when the guys in Kiev got a bit uppity, the guys in Moscow simply turned off the gas tap and left them to freeze. A gentle reminder of what the power game is really all about, and how to play it. Two weeks later, the Ukrainian government bends its knee and, like a miracle, the heating comes back on, with Stalin applauding from the celestial grandstand.'

'The Babylon pipeline has always had to cut across the Caspian, but it had a choice of two basic routes. One that crossed into Russia ...'

'Ah, and one that didn't!'

'Russia already controls a huge amount of the gas supply to Western Europe. If Babylon had gone through the alternative route, Azerbaijan and Georgia, or some of their own frontier republics like Chechnya which they barely control, their stranglehold would have been broken.'

'Moscow stuffed.'

'End of empire.'

'And I can imagine the Russians getting very upset about that. Very upset indeed.' Suddenly his exhilaration had vanished. He turned to her, the file and its papers tumbling to the ground, but he didn't seem to care. 'Jem, that would explain a lot of what's happened. Not the details, but the viciousness of it all.'

She waved forlornly at the fallen papers. 'These are reports, downloads from energy analysts, telling how the Russians offered all sorts of concessions, new licences, Siberian prospecting rights, in order to get Babylon approved ...'

Her voice faded away when she saw he wasn't listening. He was looking at her, pain in his eyes, squeezing her hand. 'But there's one thing that makes no sense at all. The Russians have got the pipeline. So why all this aggravation?'

'The press cuttings don't tell me that.'

'Jem, you've got to stop. This is dangerous.'

'Of course it is. I've watched them destroying you, Harry.'

'They'll do the same to you if they think you're getting too close.'

'I think I am getting close, don't you?'

'Yes.'

They spent some time staring quietly into each other's eyes.

'Are you going to stop, Harry?'

'You know I can't.'

'Why not?'

'It's what I do, what I am.'

'Then I'm with you.'

'I won't let you get hurt, Jem.'

'Not your choice. I'm a big girl.'

'Yeah. I'd noticed.'

'So you'd better take me back to my place. Just in case I need a little personal protection.'

He started to protest some more, but knew it was no use. In any case, he needed her, and wanted her. His shoulders sagged in submission. 'OK, but on one condition.'

She raised a sceptical eyebrow.

'Jem, please,' he said, his voice filled with earnest, 'let me cook the pasta.'

—⋙—

Harry wasn't the only one who had been showing an interest in Felix. Another man appeared at the Montreal, asked similar questions and got the same blunt answer from the barman. But this man had time, and plenty of it. He stayed and drank, and waited, night after night, so long that the regulars stopped taking any interest in this sad, lonely drunk.

It was three evenings later that Felix turned up. That was when the man quickly slipped away, before he was seen, but he didn't disappear completely. He lurked in the shadows outside, and waited a little more.

—⁓—

She cooked. She was stubborn like that, and Scottish, and seemed to be making most of the domestic decisions. They sat at her kitchen table, quietly chewing.

'So where the hell does the European Union come into this, Harry?'

'If it hadn't signed the contracts for the gas, the pipeline wouldn't be getting built.'

'Have I put enough ketchup in the pasta sauce?'

'More than enough, Jem.'

'And what has any of this to do with the plane crash?'

He shook his head.

'More pasta?' she asked tentatively.

'No, no thanks.'

She scraped the remnants of the dinner into the bin, then turned. 'I would stay out of this, Harry, but I can't. All those kids who died, and their families. They wouldn't want me to do that, would they?'

'Better sleep on it.'

'Yes.'

She closed the door of the dishwasher very gently. 'There's another problem.'

'What's that?'

'The sofa. No way it's big enough for two.'

—⁓—

The man followed Felix down the Bayswater Road, and beyond, into the growing gloom of the summer's night.

Felix was hurrying, then glanced at his watch and slowed; no point in getting there too soon. After they had passed beyond the bright lights and turbulence of Queensway, Felix's pursuer crossed to the other side of the road, lest he appear too obvious. They continued like that for more than half an hour, until it was gone ten, dark. Then Felix disappeared up the pathway beside Holland Park. The man followed.

Felix stopped halfway down the track, leaning against the railings, consulting his watch repeatedly, a little nervous; he was a few minutes early despite his efforts to slow. The man loitered further down the path, not attracting attention; there were several other men, singly, in twos, doing much the same.

Felix stirred. Another man was approaching from the other direction. They embraced, talked briefly, then disappeared into the darkness of the trees, but never completely out of the pursuer's sight. They were there but briefly, a few minutes, before they emerged and soon the other man was disappearing back along the track the way he had come. Felix, meanwhile, lit a cigarette, perhaps looking for another encounter.

He was lighting another cigarette when he looked up through the swirl of smoke to find a face staring at him.

'Hello, Mr Anderson. I'm Jimmy Sopwith-Dane. Remember me?'

CHAPTER EIGHTEEN

She woke up to find him staring at her, his nose less than an inch from hers, and a sheet wound round her ankle. The bed was a glorious mess.

'Your timing's rubbish, Jem. Taking up with me again when I'm just about to be locked away and fed on bromide.'

'On the other hand, Jones, your own timing is getting much better.' She kissed him. 'Thank you.'

She fell asleep once more. He made his own breakfast. Cereal. Toast. And Marmite.

'That's it, Jem!' he cried out, staring at his plate.

'What is?' she called sleepily from the bedroom.

'Don't you see? For the pipeline to be given the go-ahead by Brussels it would have to pass all sorts of quality controls. It's what they do with everything nowadays. Even bloody Marmite.'

'No! No, you're wrong, Harry.' She emerged from the bedroom shaking the new day into her head, stumbling over to her file. She began ransacking it, casting sheets to one side before grabbing a press cutting and holding it high. 'Babylon got an exemption.' She thrust the sheet at him. 'There's a provision, an exception, where such matters can be put to one side by—'

'"The overriding security considerations of the Union or its member parts",' Harry chimed in, reading aloud. 'And guess when? The Environment Commissioner announced it. Just after Christmas.'

'It still doesn't make any sense, Harry.'

'Oh, but it does! Security exemptions. It all leads back to—'

It was her turn to interrupt. 'EATA.'

She came and sat beside him. 'Even so, what could that possibly have to do with Speedbird? Why was I attacked simply for asking questions?'

'There has to be a connection,' he insisted.

'But I've gone through the files over and over again, all the notes I made. Everything I got from the relatives. I can't find a thing.'

'So if it's not what you got from them, Jem, it must be something you didn't get from them.'

'Like what?'

'Did you ask any of them about a bloody pipeline?'

—⁓—

Felix was not a physically courageous man. He talked before he died, and the drawn-out moments of interrogation left their marks.

His violent murder, the police concluded, had been committed by one or more men of considerable strength. The injuries on the face and the deliberately and separately broken fingers attested to that. The body had been dumped in the undergrowth just inside the park, with no attempt to conceal it, suggesting panic, so probably not premeditated. A queer bashing gone too far, that was the initial and lasting assumption. And probably two men because queer bashers didn't usually work on their own but in pairs, or even gangs, feeding off each other's intolerance. It might have been a mugging for the wallet was missing, but that didn't seem to explain the seemingly gratuitous infliction of pain. The police began scouring local CCTV footage. The path by Holland Park would be exceptionally quiet for many evenings to come.

Sloppy hadn't intended to be cruel, least of all to kill. He wanted little more than a few answers, and his life back, but he wasn't in a particularly good state to understand the whimperings that poured from the other man, particularly after the bridge on his front teeth broke away and blood from a split cheek began frothing through the gap. Sloppy himself was in excruciating pain, in some faraway place, had been for a long time, too long, and what with the drugs and alcohol that were dulling his senses, he simply went too far. He hadn't thought breaking a couple of fingers would kill him. He hadn't known about Felix's weak heart.

—⁂—

Sloppy appeared in the Cheshire Cheese almost as soon as it had opened the following morning. Change of clothes, unshaven, no sleep, confused, not knowing what to do, grappling to understand what he had done, wanting to be someone else. He ordered his drink, scrabbled for money in his pocket. As it appeared, in the palm of his hand, he remembered that it was Felix's.

The barman was seeing to Sloppy's order, waiting for the optic to refill, remarking how terrible his customer looked and wondering whether he should call time on him, throw him out before the first glass. More than simply a problem drinker; a man at war with alcohol, and losing. So why wait until that time came? Do the pub a favour, do this poor drunken idiot a favour, too. The barman didn't enjoy taking money from fools.

But when he turned, he discovered that his dilemma had resolved itself. The man had vanished. And scattered on the bar, at the place where he had been sitting, lay a fistful of crumpled, abandoned notes.

—⁂—

Much later that day and in a different part of London, Suzie, the barman from the Montreal, found himself outside his local police station. He was agitated, deeply distressed, didn't want to be there. He took a step in one direction, then in the other, hoping for some god of fortune to make up his mind for him. In his overheated hand he held a desperately crumpled copy of the *Evening Standard*, to which he kept referring, but the headline hadn't changed. It still screamed at him. Earlier, and uncertain what to do, he had gone home and dressed in his best formal suit, even polished his shoes with the buckles, anything to delay doing what he knew he must. As he'd told a friend at the pub, he had never blown a police constable's whistle without regretting it, but eventually he had taken his courage in his hands and walked here. And it was while he was twisting and turning on the steps leading to the station that the gods came to his aid and caused him almost to trip over a constable in his summer shirtsleeves.

The constable eyed this apparition up, then down, curious, both amused and a little suspicious of this moisturized young male with plucked eyebrows and glittering studs in his ears. 'Can I be of assistance, sir?'

In normal circumstances Suzie would be the first to pick up on any unintended entendre and exploit it, but the circumstance had dulled his wit. 'It's this, constable,' he cried, opening up his copy of the newspaper to reveal the headline – 'Murder in the Park'. It was accompanied by an inadequate image of Felix, dragged from the archives of an antiques trade magazine. 'I think I know him,' Suzie babbled breathlessly, jabbing his finger at the photo. 'And I think I know who did it.'

—⁂—

A pounding at his door. Insistent. Flashing lights from three patrol cars. His value seemed to be increasing, to the police force at least. Harry knew he was in desperate trouble, he didn't have any idea why, but he knew it was the sort van Buren couldn't fix. That's when he knew he couldn't answer the door, because he would end up wallowing at Her Majesty's pleasure, and with the odds already stacked against him, she was never going to let him out. He saw one of the policemen advancing with a sledgehammer; they were going to smash their way in. He was trapped – until he remembered the burglary, the rear window that had been left open, the way to the fire escape and the roofs beyond. He could hear the doorjamb splintering as he forced his way through.

—⟊—

He was clambering over a party wall, across the rooftop of the friendly gallery owner, when his phone began to ring. The noise would betray his whereabouts, so he reached into his pocket to silence it. Then he saw it was Sloppy.

'Not a great time,' Harry began to say, but his own words froze as he began to listen to his friend. 'I killed him, Harry,' he mumbled. 'Didn't mean to but . . .'

'Who?'

'Felix Wilton, that's his name, not bloody Anderson. Wouldn't tell me it at first so I . . .' Sloppy's voice faded, and Harry could hear a car engine in the background, making it difficult to catch everything. 'Didn't know what to do, been driving all night . . .'

'Where are you?' Harry demanded, but the other man wasn't listening. The words were slurred, with alcohol, with exhaustion, and something more. Despair.

Sloppy kept muttering that it was his fault; Harry stopped running and hid behind an old brick chimney breast to try to catch every word.

'Cost him his front teeth, it did, before I got the name. Didn't hurt him much. Nothing you and I haven't seen before, done before ... Remember that pub in Armagh? Lost some of mine there ...' He sobbed, might have been crying, in great pain. 'Jesus, I never meant to kill the bastard. Please believe me, Harry.' He sobbed some more and Harry lost the next few words. 'But not your fault, Harry, all this. I made it easy for them. Screwed up. Big time.'

Harry glanced along the rooftops. Nothing. Yet.

'Set me up, just so they could get to you, Harry.'

'Who did? Why?'

'That's what I asked him. Said you'd been asking too many questions. Too nosy. Not your business. You were in too deep, he said. Much too deep.'

'What, Sloppy? Concentrate, dammit! What wasn't my business?'

'Plane crash? Didn't understand, so I broke one of his fingers. Shouldn't have done that. He was crying, pissing himself. Mumbling. I just didn't understand ...'

Harry heard a clattering from the fire escape. They would soon be upon him. He could see a head poking above the roofing now. He rolled over another party wall, ducked behind a water tank.

'Sloppy, I've got to go. Where are you, Sloppy? I'll come and get you.'

'Can't come with me, not where I'm going.'

A policeman had climbed onto the roof and was searching around. Harry scampered still further away, but he was running out of roof.

'But who's behind it all? Who did this to us?'

'Broke another finger. That's when he started to tell me. Something about the Russians.'

'You sure? What about the Russians? This is important, Sloppy!'

'He said they didn't kill Ghazi straight away. Needed to know.'

'Need to know what?' Harry pleaded. From further down the roof he heard a shout; they had seen him.

'That's when he stopped talking, Harry. He just fucking died.' Sloppy moaned, a misery that came from deep within and was inconsolable. 'I hurt, Harry, God but I hurt. I'm so sorry ...'

He could hear them running on the roof now, their feet pounding on the felt, and getting louder. 'Sloppy, I'll call you back, I promise.'

But all he could hear down the phone was the revving of a car engine. He cut the link and started to run.

—⁊⁊⁊—

A desperate man has the upper hand in a fair race, because desperation, unlike health and safety regulations, doesn't require fire-escape ladders to be climbed one rung at a time. So Harry evaded the pursuit across the rooftops.

Desperation is also more imaginative, and Harry didn't use any of the fire escapes that the police spent their time swarming over, but instead used a drainpipe, and jumped the last twelve feet, landing in a sprawl on the cobbles of an alleyway behind Berkeley Square. The pain from his complaining rib caused him to pass out for a few moments; when he came round, he discovered he had gashed his arm. He staunched the flow of blood with a handkerchief. He lay back against a wheelie bin and groaned. How long could he outwit them, remain free? Long enough to go bankrupt? Not even that long, not walking round with a bloodied arm and torn shirt, not with Arkwright and every one of his friends looking for him. And some bloody Russians, too.

He spotted his phone on the cobbles, not his treacherous iPhone that he'd left behind but its cheap replacement. He reached out for it, trying to ignore the screaming from his ribs. The screen had been cracked by the fall but mercifully it flickered back into life. He called Sloppy, as he had promised. A message came onto the screen. 'Call Failed.' He tried again, several more times. And always with the same result.

—⁂—

He had nowhere else to go. He walked to Jemma's, didn't run, it would have excited too much attention for a man with a bloodied arm and a wild look in his eye. But when eventually he made it to her place he bounded up the stairs three at a time. When she opened her door, he saw she was shaking. The television was on in the background.

'You're all over the news, Harry,' she whispered, her voice hoarse with shock that was made no better by the sight of his arm. 'They want you for questioning, they say. In connection with a murder. Of ...' She could no longer fight the fear that was making her tremble. Her voice faded away, unwilling to complete the words and the terrible thoughts that accompanied them.

'It was Sloppy,' he said, trying to take her arms, but she backed away, shaking her head, unable, or unwilling, to take in what he said. 'Jem, you have to make up your mind,' he said, almost fiercely. 'You're with me, or you must wash your hands of me. And you have to make up your mind right now because there's no time. They could be knocking on your door any moment.'

'What do *you* want?' she said, hesitant.

'Clothes. Another place to stay. Somewhere or someone who has no connection to me.'

She took a deep gulp of breath, she had stopped shaking. 'I must be totally mad.'

'You don't believe me?'

'I must love you.'

Her words seemed to stop their world spinning for a moment, but not for long. The television was recounting how Harry Jones, the former MP who had lost his seat at the recent election, was already on bail having been arrested for two earlier vicious assaults against a woman.

Now a murder. The implication was clear. This was a dangerous man, in all probability a demented man. On no account was he to be approached if sighted, the news reader instructed; the police were to be contacted immediately.

'They will catch me eventually, Jem. But we need to buy time. Wilton talked to Sloppy before he died, we're getting closer.'

'And you look a mess. If you think I'm going to be seen with you looking like that . . .' She crossed to the wardrobe in her bedroom and opened a drawer. She brought out two new shirts, still in their wrapping. 'I meant to give you these for Christmas. But then you really pissed me off.'

'I'm glad I've made things so much simpler for you since then.'

She was also dangling a set of house keys. 'A friend nearby, Caitlin, another teacher at my school. She's on holiday. I'm watering the plants and taking care of the cat.'

'I promise I'll try to behave myself,' he said, ripping the cellophane off a shirt and scattering pins in every direction. Suddenly he stopped and turned.

'Thank you,' he said softly, the roughness of recent weeks gone from his voice.

'At least when they catch us, I'll be able to plead insanity. No question about it.' She began throwing clothes into a shoulder bag.

From the television came the sight of Suzie being interviewed by a young journalist outside the Montreal. He was explaining in breathless fashion how Mr Wilton had been a valued customer and that his death would devastate his many friends. 'He often told me that this was his favourite bar,' he said shamelessly, 'and we'll be holding a festival here all weekend to commemorate what a beautiful person he was. The best party of the year. To celebrate his life. He wouldn't want us to drown in misery, oh no, he wasn't that sort of person, was our Mr Wilton.' Suzie paused to smile at the camera.

'Do you know if he had any links to the former politician, Harry Jones?' the reporter interjected, trying to reclaim control of his interview.

Suzie rolled his eyes and bounced on his toes. 'Ah, the police have asked me to be especially discreet, as they expect me to be a key witness.' Then his expression grew very serious. 'But I can tell you this. He came looking for Mr Wilton. Searching him out. Even showed me a photograph. But I can't breathe another word about it.'

Harry groaned. No wonder Arkwright was so enthusiastic.

'Then do you think the murder could have anything to do with his sexuality?' the young interviewer pressed.

'But how could it?' Suzie replied. 'Everyone loved her.'

Harry switched off the television. He was feeling desperate enough without Suzie adding to his woes. Meanwhile Jemma finished her hurried packing, then stood taking a last look around her home. The African violets would die. Her parents would never understand.

Worst of all was her fear that she might never be allowed to teach her kids again. She was leaving everything behind. She faltered, struggling to find the courage.

Harry took her into his arms, kissed her. 'I'm so sorry,' he whispered.

She grabbed him fiercely, clinging to her belief. He winced and pulled away. 'I think I left some of the bloody pins in the shirt,' he gasped.

'Love can be a real pain,' she said, grabbing her bag.

—∞—

As they hurried away from the building where Jemma lived, they could hear the sound of approaching sirens. It could have been nothing more than the daily life of London, but their pace quickened. They passed the entrance to the Underground where fresh piles of the *Standard* were waiting to be grabbed by scurrying commuters – the late edition, with a new headline: 'Ex-MP Link to London Murder'. It seemed as though everyone in the crowded street was looking at them, every CCTV camera pointed at them, every television store flashing images of his face. Harry had been hunted before, many times, but never like this, not in his own country. His legs were beginning to ache in the heat, hinting they weren't as young as when he'd fled through the mountains of the Koh-i-Baba with Taliban on his trail, or pushed his troop on an insane trek through the Arctic wastes of northern Norway from Bardufoss to Bergen, beating the ferry carrying the rest of the regiment, earning him a cataclysmic bollocking from his CO and bragging rights for years. But, damn it, he was allowed to hurt, from his broken rib, his leap from the drainpipe, and that niggling voice from deep inside whispering that this was one battle Harry Jones wasn't going to win.

They were passing a bank. Harry grabbed Jemma's arm. 'Sorry to do this, but ...' He nodded towards the cash machine. 'Just in case.'

'How much?'

'Everything you can. Full daily limit. Bank accounts, credit cards—'

'Whoa. I'm a primary school teacher with an overdraft. How much do you think there'll be?'

Not enough, he feared, and he was right. A meagre £480. She split it in two and gave him half.

'What's that for?' he asked, examining his share.

'Just in case.'

Caitlin's apartment was on the top floor of a converted Victorian semi, the attic flat. Small, very stuffy in the heat, and smelt of cat litter. A coal-black Bombay stared at them from her perch on the back of the sofa.

'That's Sammi,' Jemma said, making the introduction as she threw open windows to let in some air.

'Hello, Sammi,' Harry said. The cat hissed and disappeared behind a curtain. 'Join the crowd,' he muttered.

The apartment was decorated in an idiosyncratic style that involved trying to recreate the feel of an Indian ashram; the colours were hideous and intensely claustrophobic. Both freezer and fridge were empty, the cupboards Spartanly bare, apart from cat food, but he was in no position to complain. There was a telephone, thank goodness.

'How long have we got?' he asked, mindful of Caitlin's return from holiday.

'How long will your Sergeant Arkwright give us?'

'Long enough to contact the relatives, I hope. That's the key, Sloppy said so.'

'Then I'd better get back to the chase,' she said, getting out her laptop and her phone.

'No. Landline only, Jem,' he said. 'Your mobile could lead them straight here.'

'Caitlin might just come to hate me,' she said, as she sat beside her friend's phone, which was pink and in the shape of a sleeping cat.

'We'll have to get you a throwaway like mine. And then only use them away from here.'

'That's twenty quid straight of our less than magnificent pot.'

'I'm almost out of credit, too. And there's one call I've got to make while I can.'

'But it's a risk going outside.'

'It's a risk staying in this place, too,' he said, looking around the apartment. 'I could go colour blind.'

—◊◊◊—

McDeath was preparing to chip out of the bunker on the seventeenth, twisting his feet, finding a secure place in the sand, knowing that if he got this one right the match was his, when his phone came to life. He ignored it. A substantial drinks tab back at the clubhouse hung on this one. He made a hash of it anyway. The ball rolled back down from the rim of the bunker and finished exactly where it had begun. He threw his wedge away in disgust and then reached for his phone. He didn't recognize the number of the missed call. 'Damn your heathen eyes,' he swore before retrieving his club and starting on his shot all over again.

It was the height of summer. McDeath was on leave. No one expected him to file anything at this time of year, so when he putted for the match on the eighteenth and missed, he was in no mood to respond to the caller who had cost him so much with anything other than oaths. But McDeath was a polite man as well as an enthusiastic golfer; he always returned calls, although in this case not until after he'd paid for his losses and washed away the pain with a tumbler or two of whisky. He stood on the verandah of the clubhouse, overlooking the final green, thinking of what might have been, and punched the button for his voicemail.

'Well, suck my old granny's toes,' he whispered in awe as he listened to the message. He pressed the return call button immediately, walking away to the practice green where he could be on his own. 'Hamish Hague,' he announced. 'Sorry to keep you waiting, Harry.'

'I was just about to call the *Mail* in despair.'

'Don't go cheap on me, Harry. How can I help you?'

'Got a small story for you.'

'Small? Why bother with small when you're the biggest story around? I walk into my clubhouse and you're all over the infernal television screen.'

'I want to do a deal with you, Hamish. A little help now, and in return I promise that whatever happens, you get the first interview with me, if you want it.'

Want it? His editor would expect him to boil bairns for it. Harry was currently the most notorious man in Britain. 'You're taking one hell of a risk, Harry. This call alone guarantees me the front page tomorrow.'

'But there's a much, much bigger one, if you're willing to be patient. Here's the deal, Hamish. I give you a story now, a little speculative. I can't give you proof, not yet.'

'Don't you read newspapers, Harry? At this time of year the press world is run by cretins who spend their time covering hamster-eating contests and claiming to have unearthed Osama bin Laden's private love diaries. It's why I prefer to play bad golf.'

'It's the Speedbird thing. You interested?'

'Daft question. But why me? You could feed the story to a dozen different hacks.'

'It's partly because I know you protect your sources, and I'm feeling in need of a little protection right now.'

'So this – whatever it is – doesn't come from you?'

'You don't mention me, this call, or this telephone number, to anyone.'

'And the exclusive?'

'From the scaffold, if necessary.'

A pause. 'That would make it a very attractive offer. I think I'm your man.'

So, for several minutes, the old journalist lit a pipe, looked into a setting sun, and listened without a breath of interruption.

'And two other things, Hamish,' Harry said when at last he had finished. 'I want you to know that I've not done those things they're accusing me of. I've been most expertly set up.'

The breeze changed, ruffled the Scotsman's hair, blew smoke into his eyes. 'If what you're suggesting is true, perhaps we both have.'

'You weren't given the full story, I'll bet my life on it. I might have to.'

'I suppose there's only one way to find out.'

'Thanks, Hamish. I owe you.'

'You most certainly do. Ruined my game of golf, so you did. Left me well and truly bunkered.'

'I know that feeling well.'

'But the second thing. You mentioned there was something else.'

'It's about being set up, Hamish. I don't want you to check this story out with your usual sources.'

'Why, pray?'

'I think they'll find some way of stitching the story up. Just like they've stitched me up. They are very powerful people.'

'But you haven't the faintest idea who my sources are,' the Scot protested.

'EATA.'

There was a long pause as Harry could hear nothing but the sighing of a gentle breeze across the links.

'Tell me I'm wrong, Hamish.'

But Hamish wouldn't say. He cut the call.

CHAPTER NINETEEN

'How's it going, Jem?' he asked when he returned from making his call.

She was sitting on the sofa, her legs drawn up beneath her, the cat phone at her side. 'Not great,' she said, downcast. 'You wouldn't believe how many of the relatives are away on holiday, have moved, are out shopping. I called one poor woman only to be told by her deeply distressed daughter that she had died just last week.'

'I'm sorry. You want to take a break?'

'I want to put some pins back in your shirt. But I suppose, like all good things in life, that'll have to wait for the moment. Meanwhile ...' She consulted the file on her laptop, straightened the multicoloured sofa throw that threatened to embrace her like an octopus, and picked up the phone. 'Good evening, could I speak to Mrs Gracie, please? Hello, Mrs Gracie, I hope you'll forgive the intrusion. This is Jemma Laing – remember me? You very kindly spoke to me a couple of weeks ago about your husband. I'm so sorry to trouble you again but we're still looking into some of the questions surrounding the crash. May I ask – I hope you don't mind – but did your husband ever have any connections either with Russia, or gas pipelines, or perhaps even environmental matters? I know this all sounds rather disconnected but—'

Jemma was listening intently to what the woman was insistent on saying, interjecting with an occasional 'I see' and 'I'm sorry'. Then, after another lengthy pause: 'Yes, that's right. My name is Jemma Laing. No, I'm not connected to the police or any newspaper. I'm not a spiritualist, either. I'm so sorry to have troubled you, Mrs Gracie.' She put the phone down before looking up at Harry, troubled. 'She said I was harassing her, suggested I was operating some sort of scam. She threatened to report me to the police, Harry.'

'Sorry you had to go through that, Jem.'

'If she did, they could trace us back here, couldn't they?'

'It's a possibility.'

'Should we go elsewhere?'

'Any ideas?'

'I don't know. Friends. Family. Do you have family, Harry?' she asked. She was surprised she didn't know the answer; there were still dark spaces in his past she knew nothing about.

'A son. He's still a teenager.'

She paused, shaken. That hadn't made it into his Wikipedia entry. 'You were married a third time?'

'No. It's a long story.'

'Oh, I see. One of *those* stories,' she said quietly. She

didn't pursue it, not for now. It would wait. 'Well, look on the bright side.'

'There is one?'

'Our Mrs Gracie. She said the late Mr Gracie had never been to Russia, had nothing to do with wretched pipelines and would never have bothered with any of that environmental nonsense. Her words. So I guess that's one we can cross off our list.'

—⚭—

Daily Telegraph. P. 6

FRESH QUESTIONS OVER GHAZI DEATH

A new line of enquiry emerged last night into the Speedbird 235 flight that was shot from the skies shortly before last Christmas, killing all 115 passengers and crew on board, and the fate of the terrorist held responsible for the atrocity, Abdul Mohammed Ghazi. Usually reliable sources have suggested that Ghazi was not killed immediately by Russian forces who discovered his hideout in Azerbaijan. Instead, allegedly he was captured, wounded but alive, and subjected to interrogation about the circumstances of the crash. It was after, or during, this interrogation that he died.

The sources suggested some disquiet in Brussels that Ghazi was not handed over for questioning by the proper international authorities. 'If this is true,' the source suggested, 'it raises questions about what the Russians were looking for – or trying to hide.'

The Russian authorities have been sensitive in recent months to any accusation of high handedness as they try to repair the economic and financial damage of the recent Great Crash, which hit their wealthy elite particularly hard. Moscow recently signed a multi-billion pound deal for the construction of the Babylon gas pipeline which is seen as being of huge economic and diplomatic importance to both Moscow and Brussels.

Last night the Russian Embassy denied there was any truth in the allegations, insisting they should be credited with apprehending Ghazi and his gang after all attempts by British and US forces had failed. 'We take great exception to these reports,' a spokesman said . . .

Harry rustled his copy of the paper with a sense of satisfaction. Small, but not insignificant. The Russians knew about it, and so would anyone else who mattered in this mess. Confusion to the complacent.

He was congratulating himself when his eye fell on another, still smaller story. About a man found dead in his Jaguar XK140 sports car, a hose connected to the exhaust. In a lane just off a Dorset coast road near Abbotsbury, where as a child he had lived. The man had experienced recent domestic and financial problems. No one else was being sought by the police in their enquiries. In other words, a suicide. Another sad, pathetic, loser of a man – the report didn't say that, of course, didn't need to. Neither did it say that this man was a man of honour, and of extraordinary courage, a man who had thrown his own body over an IRA grenade to save his colleagues, not aware that it had been badly stored, had rusted, was a dud. A man who had risked his life for others many times, and would have willingly given it, had the call come, and who had been able to live with anything other than shame. A soldier, a friend of many, a father of three beautiful girls, who had lived, loved, drunk, fought and fornicated with the best of them, who had guarded his monarch and fought for the good name of his country when its politicians and puppet leaders had led it astray. A man who believed, almost too much, in honour, and when he failed his own high standards blamed no one but himself. A leader, a brother, a soldier. A man so much better than his faults.

Not the words of the newspaper, but images and sorrows that filled Harry's mind, and tears shed for his friend, Jimmy Sopwith-Dane.

—ɷ—

They had been stuck in their psychedelic prison for almost a week, their meagre pot of money diminishing, along with their spirits. Jemma continued with the task of trying to contact the relatives, while Harry beat himself up. He had been the last person to talk to Sloppy, might have talked him out of it, but hung up on him instead. Not his fault, Jemma said. Then whose fault was it? The weekend *Mirror* carried two pages of invented bilge devoted entirely to him, under the headline of 'Hero to Zero', and they didn't even know about how he'd let down Sloppy. He hated himself, and hated those who were truly responsible all the more.

'Jem,' he said one evening, 'I have to go to the funeral.'

'You can't. It's too risky.'

'I know. But I have to.'

She was going to argue, but the pain in his eyes told her it was pointless.

'Where is it?'

'West Sussex. I'll need the fare.'

'We don't have much money left. They've stopped my cards, Harry. Just as you said.'

It meant that Arkwright was getting closer. She was at risk, too.

'I need the fare,' he insisted again, stubborn, a little fierce.

'You'll also need a jacket. A suit, even.'

'Oh, save me,' he sighed wearily, in misery.

'Don't worry. I'll take you to my favourite shop.'

When they found the dark suit at the local branch of Oxfam, it was clear why it had been left behind. It had lived several dry cleanings too far, but it fit, almost.

—✠—

They had expected few to attend. He was a suicide, a failure. A man's failures linger, long after his triumphs have been mislaid. Not even his mother-in-law would come. There was his wife, of course, and his daughters, mourning the man they had once known, then lost, angry that he had allowed them no chance to help bring him back from the darkness. Yet as the time of the funeral drew near in a Norman church of oak beams and stained glass, the pews began to fill. Men, in suits or dark blazers, old comrades with their regimental ties and memories, enough of them to fill the church all the way back to the old Tudor font. The family turned round, struggling to believe what they saw, but regaining pride.

The battle flags of the local regiment, long extinct, hung down from their masts along the nave, some so old they were little more than gauze. At the rear of the church the men of the Royal British Legion held their own flags, furled, in gauntleted hands.

Harry arrived shortly before the coffin. He had no tie and he hadn't shaved for a week, hoping that it would give him some measure of disguise, but every man there ecognized him. He tried to slip quietly into an end pew yet heads turned. Soon the entire congregation knew of his presence. A man on the run, still one of theirs. Briggsie, the Regimental Sergeant Major of an earlier era, walked slowly up to Harry, with all eyes upon him. He saluted, shook Harry's hand in welcome, before walking back to his place. Almost everyone there knew of what he had done in Iraq and Armagh, some had even heard the stories of Afghanistan and the Colombian drug trail that had become a legend. That all mattered more than any detective sergeant named Arkwright.

326

The coffin arrived, pushed by anonymous men in black on a wheeled frame. As they entered the church, they were stopped, a Union flag appeared from somewhere and was draped over the coffin. Then, as the cortege proceeded, the men of the Legion formed a guard of honour and lowered their flags, now unfurled, in sadness as he passed.

They sang traditional hymns, *Onward Christian Soldiers* and *I Vow to Thee My Country*, stirring stuff when sung with strong male voices, the morning sun shone through stained glass and filled the church with rich dappled colours, and the oration, delivered by an old regimental padre, told the girls of sacrifices their father had made for others that he would never have told them himself. Even old men were shedding silent tears. And the time had come for the coffin to be taken. The bearers appeared once more, but as they approached Harry stepped forward, laid a hand on the sleeve of the funeral director, and took a place. And in an instant there were others, beside the coffin, to lift their old friend and bear him on their shoulders to his final resting place in the graveyard, through the ranks of the men who had known him best.

And it was done. Sloppy was gone. They filed away solemnly, still bound by their sense of loss.

Harry was at the lychgate when he tugged a sleeve. 'Corporal Battersby.'

The man turned. 'Hello, Boss. How are you, sir?'

'I think you know. Daft bloody question.'

'Sorry about all the fuss, sir.'

'You used to be a canny sod at transport.'

'Thank you, sir. Still am. In the motor trade.'

'Wheels outside?'

'The Beamer parked outside the pub.'

'I wouldn't ask if it weren't important.'

'Of course you wouldn't.'

'There's another funeral in Salisbury. Two hours' time. Think we can make it?'

The corporal scratched his chin dubiously. 'Not if you stand there prattling, we won't.'

—∽—

Summer seemed endless that year. As they pulled up, a workman in shirtsleeves was mowing the deep grass verges beside the driveway and the heavy air held the scent of roses and lilac. An excellent day for an Englishman, and for a cremation.

They could see that the ceremony had already started. The hearse and another funeral car were parked in their bays outside the main entrance to the crematorium, but there was little sign of anyone else, five cars in the public parking area. The undertaker's staff waited patiently in the shade, stifling in their suits of black. As Harry walked towards the entrance he could hear desultory singing coming from within, the voices masked by the efforts of the organist. He checked the name on the card outside. Felix Bartholomew Wilton.

'You're late. It's almost over, sir,' one of the pallbearers said.

As Harry gazed into the brick-built funeral hall, he found a gathering of seventeen, which included the vicar, and Felix had already been dispatched, sent on his way to the burning place below, while the vicar was delivering his final blessing. Then he was done, the mourners raised their bent heads, the organist began upon his endeavours once again, pumping out a suitably anodyne tune, and the vicar walked out from behind his podium to the front row of the congregation where he grasped the hand of a woman clad in expensive mourning black and whispered condolences in her ear.

'Who is that?' Harry asked the pallbearer.

'The lady? That's the deceased's wife.'

It was as though he had been hit by a bullet. Something exploded inside him so unexpectedly that the body didn't know how to react, left him numb, his heart racing while it tried to find something it could recognize out of this sudden chaos. He heard his own voice as though it came from far away.

'He ... was married?'

'Why, yes, sir. Mrs Patricia Wilton. Although she doesn't go by her married name, of course.'

'She ... doesn't?'

'Calls herself Vaine. Patricia Vaine.'

The pallbearer scurried off to his duties, leaving Harry scrambling for his senses. He'd had no idea. Stupid of him, to have jumped to conclusions, that a man who prowled gay haunts wouldn't be married. After all, he could name at least two Cabinet ministers who ...

As Harry struggled with his surprise, he watched as the woman thanked the vicar, nodded to those around her, put on dark glasses and began to walk out. Then she stopped. Took off her glasses once more. She had seen him standing in the entrance. And he could tell from her expression that she recognized him, knew him, and not just from newspapers. The eyes were filled with more than recognition, there was also alarm and a little fear in them, too. She pulled her phone from an elegant bag and pressed a single button, began talking, without ever once taking her eyes off him. That she knew him, and wanted him out of her life, was confirmed some minutes later when two patrol cars, lights and sirens clearing their way, came hurtling down the approach road. And they, in turn, confirmed that Harry had found what he had come searching for. The next link.

The patrol cars set off in pursuit of the BMW that had been seen speeding away from the crematorium. It took them several miles before they caught up with Battersby and managed to persuade him to pull over, but by that time Harry was tucked away on the back seat of a bus travelling in entirely the opposite direction.

—m—

It was market day in Salisbury, the centre was milling with people. Excellent cover. Harry had a head start, but he knew it wouldn't last long. They would be searching for him, watching the train and bus stations, and he had less than fifty pounds in his pocket. He couldn't keep running for ever. There was also something else, other forces more powerful than Arkwright, which were hunting him. He still didn't know what, but now he had a name. Patricia Vaine. And this was her territory, her home patch. Still more danger but also, perhaps, opportunity.

He avoided the main streets, keeping an alert eye for those who wished him ill, and when he saw an approaching patrol car he slipped into the nearest shop. It was a computer repair place, one of those that ekes out a living on a side street, not trying to compete with the bully boys of the trading estate or the High Street. A bleary-eyed youth with tussled hair and John Lennon glasses stood behind the counter, idly flicking through a tattooing magazine. He looked up, rather like a shipwrecked sailor spotting a ship on the horizon, not expecting it to make land.

'Hi,' Harry said. The patrol car still hadn't passed by, was loitering, and Harry needed an excuse. It also gave him an idea; circumstance had perhaps played him a fair hand for a change. 'Do you have any laptops for sale?'

'New or second-hand?'

'Either.'

'We only do recons.'

'Something I can connect to the Internet with while I'm travelling.'

'They all do that.'

'Nothing too fancy. But I'd like to have a look at one with the operating system already set up. Don't have a lot of experience with this sort of stuff.'

The assistant at last peeled his eyes away from the magazine. 'Cash or credit card?'

'Which do you prefer?'

The young man gave Harry a look that suggested he might have landed from a planet located in the farthest reaches of the solar system, then led him through a clutter of computer bits to the end of the shop where several machines were lined up on a bench. He spent several minutes outlining the prowess of the most expensive before Harry cut across him.

'What's the deal on these?'

'Six months warranty, labour and parts. So long as you don't drop it in the bath. Take one with you now and I can do you a deal.'

'Try before I buy?'

'Take your pick.' For the first time the assistant looked curious. 'You from round here?'

'Moved in recently,' Harry muttered, bending over one of the laptops, trying to obscure his face.

The young man shrugged and retreated behind his counter as Harry began manoeuvring with the mouse and tapping at the keyboard.

—⁓—

Jemma had been waiting to hear from Harry, anxious about the progress of his day, reluctant to call him – funerals were rarely the right moment for phones to ring – but growing ever more anxious as the hours passed without any contact or message. To cover her unease she picked up the cat phone and set once more to her task. She was two-thirds of the way through her list, well into the economy class, had eliminated almost all of what she had seen as the more obvious possibilities and, although she hated herself for it, was beginning to lose heart. She was reduced to going through what remained of her list alphabetically, putting any form of judgement to one side, trusting to blind luck. As she made her next call, she wondered why she had overlooked Farrokh Maneckjee, not put him on her initial list of likely suspects. He was a little on the young side, had no identified occupation. She hoped it hadn't simply been because of his Indian background; she was better about that than her father, wasn't she? But why had Maneckjee been on the flight? There was only one way to find out.

When a woman answered the phone, Jemma slipped into her well-practised script, explaining carefully and slowly how saddened she was to make this call, apologizing for the intrusion, enquiring about Farrokh, yet the accent of the woman – his mother – was so lilting and deep that Jemma had considerable difficulty in understanding much of what was being said, a struggle made all the more difficult by the other's evident emotion. As she spoke about her son, the words came pouring out at incomprehensible speed. Jemma began to lose the flow of what was being said, until one word hit her that she couldn't possibly misunderstand.

'Russia'.

CHAPTER TWENTY

It was there, so eventually he found it. Hidden, elusive, yet nonetheless undeniable. It was almost impossible to hide in a world where the merest detail, real, imagined or simply manufactured, was captured and computerized. Run a search on Rupert Bunnyrabbit or Patsy Dipstick and something will turn up. The European External Action Service got more than fifty million hits, but searching out the European Anti-Terrorist Agency was like trying to find butterflies in a desert. Of the entries the search engines did find, many were some years out of date, others opaque and confusing, many more were from websites that saw conspiracy lurking in every corner and demanded open government. As for Patricia Vaine, there were practically none at all. There were any number of Vaughans and Vauns and Vanes, but Patricia Vaine found only three direct hits. The first two came from people search directories based in the US which, although they promised to be interrogating billions of public records, kept timing out and came up with nothing.

Yet the third was all he needed. A brief, formal employment notice, twenty months old, about a woman who was being employed as a senior liaison officer within the European External Action Service, the mothership of EATA.

He had found her.

—⚯—

Russia. The word kept ringing in her ears. Jemma began dancing around the room of many colours with the cat in her arms, knowing she had found what they had been searching for. The missing link. The cause of it all. Not the details of it, but enough to know that they were very close to discovering why Speedbird 235 had been ripped from the sky. Yet even as she danced and rejoiced, her happiness was about to be stripped from her, so savagely that it caused her to cry out in pain. For now her new, vibrant, joyful world had grown altogether too colourful. Lights of acid ice blue were burning through her window, overpowering even Caitlin's garish ideas of taste. Outside, on the road below, Jemma saw two patrol cars and many men. Mrs Gracie had done for her, after all. She knew there was no way out; the premises didn't have a fire escape and Jemma didn't do drainpipes. She was lost. She sat on the sofa, cradling Sammi in her lap, in tears, waiting for what was to come.

—⚯—

Harry's ear was bothering him. It had once been attacked – cut off, in fact – but the repair work had been superb and it no longer gave him pain. Ever since the surgery that had sewn it back, his new appendage had revealed an uncanny knack of warning him of approaching danger, growing hot, itching, responding perhaps to some innate inner sense that saw just that little bit further ahead. It hadn't bothered him in ages, yet now it was talking to him once more, tingling, warning him. He glanced over his shoulder at the shop assistant; he was standing at the counter, shuffling, pretending to be engrossed in his magazine, but his eyes kept darting to the door, and then to Harry. When he saw Harry returning his gaze, he blushed and tried to bury the guilt amongst the pages of tattoos.

Harry knew he had been betrayed. A phone call made while he'd been pursuing his prey across the Internet. He wondered how much time he had left, yet already the answer was screeching to a halt outside the door. Two police officers jumped out, a male and female, and made straight for the door. There was no time for Harry to run.

By the time they accosted him from behind, Harry was back, bent over his computer.

'Mr Jones? Mr Harry Jones?' they demanded, addressing the back of his head.

He hit the delete button and switched off the computer, his back still towards them. 'You mean Harry Jones, the one they want to question about a murder and violent assault on a woman in London? Yes, that's me.' He stood up. Only then did he turn to face them. His right hand was in his suit pocket. He was clutching a highlighter pen, stretching the cloth. Just as the barrel of a gun might.

'You're kidding!' the young male constable said.

'You're really willing to take that chance? After what I've done?'

Harry knew that if the constable laughed he was done for, but instead he was glancing sideways at his colleague.

'Ron?' the WPC asked, her voice wavering in uncertainty.

'There'll be another squad car here any second,' Ron insisted, but it seemed from the tic in his lips as though her doubts were becoming infectious.

'Any second, you say. But until then, there's just you and me.'

'Oh, bugger,' Ron's colleague cried. Ron was trying to stand tall, firm, but his hand hadn't moved any nearer the weaponry on his belt.

'Do you get paid enough for this?' Harry asked.

And Ron backed off.

'Back of the shop, no one gets hurt,' Harry instructed, waving them on with his hidden highlighter, wondering where he'd come up with such a dreadful line. Whatever life he had to live after this, it would never be as a Hollywood scriptwriter.

Yet they did as they were told, joining the assistant, whose eyes bulged behind his glasses in paralysing confusion. They squeezed themselves tightly into a corner behind the counter.

A traffic warden suddenly appeared outside the window, walking slowly past, inspecting the patrol car. It distracted Ron. And that was when Harry ran.

They weren't far behind him, once they had scrambled from behind the counter, but Harry needed little time. The hapless Ron had left the keys in the ignition, and Harry was away even as the wretched man was reaching for the door handle. As he glanced in the mirror Harry saw the policeman almost obliterated by a plume of burnt rubber, twisting in frustration, barking frantically into his radio. Harry dropped the highlighter onto the seat beside him.He might have laughed out loud like some vaudeville villain, if he hadn't been thinking of Jemma, and Sloppy, and of what was to come.

—◇◇—

There had been a time, some years before, when Jemma had lost her temper with her mother. Mrs Laing had found a lump on her breast, and done nothing about it for months apart from sitting at home and praying for it to go away. Now Jemma was doing the same. She could hear the policemen banging at the front door, so ferociously it was sure to bring the elderly lady from the rear flat to open it. Her own door would be broken down if she didn't let them in. Her time was almost out.

But it was not gone, not yet. She still had perhaps seconds, and a secret to share. Desperately she grabbed the phone once again.

Harry's mobile began burbling as he was speeding recklessly along a country road, watching for signs of the inevitable pursuit. 'I can't talk now!' he barked at her.

'We won't be able to talk later. I'm just about to be arrested. They're about to break down the door.'

He almost missed the corner. 'Jemma!'

'Shut up and listen! I think I've found it. Farrokh Maneckjee is the name, lived in Andover. Worked in Russia. Can you take down his mother's details?'

'I'm driving at eighty trying to kill myself.'

'Then you'd better have a bloody good memory, Jones!'

She gave him the information he would need, while he offered a short prayer of thanks for the ability he'd developed for remembering numbers, like map references, when an error would have cost him his life. And as he listened, in the background he could hear muffled shouts and banging, like a door being smashed off its hinges.

'One more thing,' she shouted above the confusion and noise. 'Do you think there's any chance of us getting cells next to each other?' She was trying to laugh, be brave, but he couldn't mistake the tremble of fear in her voice.

'Jem, I don't think they're planning to let me get as far as a prison cell.'

Yet even as he spoke it was too late. From the other end of the phone came the sounds of scuffling, a cry of pain, and protest, and the wail of an angry cat.

—◊—

They would catch up with him, too, and very soon, he knew that. Even now there would be helicopters in the sky, every policeman in the county would be on alert. They would search for him and eventually get him. The police car was probably tagged and transmitting his location to within a mean yard. How long did he have?

He couldn't outrun them, but he might just outwit them for long enough to do what he had to. And in the middle of the silage that life had poured over him in unbelievable quantities, there was one fragment of good news. Andover, where Mrs Maneckjee lived, was close at hand, but first he would have to dump the car. This he did in the car park of the nearest train station, Grateley, deliberately blocking the access, causing an obstruction, making sure it wouldn't go unnoticed for long. Then with most of the money he had left he bought a single ticket to London. The watching eye of a CCTV camera caught it all. Another crumb of good fortune; the train arrived immediately, he even had to scamper across the bridge to catch it. Every minute would count.

As soon as he was on board he made a further point of seeking out the conductor, questioning him about the arrival time in London, looking at his watch, expressing muttered doubts about whether he would get there in time. Yet, at the next stop, which was Andover, he slipped quietly from the train, trying to avoid being seen by either conductor or station staff, walking out through the car park rather than going through the ticket barrier. It was a small ruse, an attempt to trick them into believing he was headed for London, but it might keep them off his back for a little while longer. Then he started walking.

It took him more than an hour before he reached Mrs Maneckjee's street. She lived in a small red-brick semi on a residential estate. As he walked up to the front door he noticed that unlike most of her neighbours' houses that were fronted by hard, utilitarian parking areas, her house still retained its front garden, carefully manicured, bursting with colour instead of oil stains. He rang the bell, and felt a surge of anxiety as he saw a figure looming behind the door. He knew this might be the end of it. The door was opened by a diminutive Indian woman dressed in a bright orange sari, with bangles on her wrist and greying hair tied neatly in a bun.

'Mrs Maneckjee, my name is Harry Jones. A friend of mine called you to ask about your son, Farrokh. Mrs Maneckjee, I've been looking at the crash that killed him and I think something very strange and extremely wicked has been going on. I don't believe your son was killed by accident, and I'm hoping you will help me find the truth.'

She studied him through careful, cautious eyes that had flecks of ochre and hazel. 'He was a good boy, my Farrokh,' she said in an accent as thick as treacle.

'He was important, too. Because of what he was doing in Russia.'

'That is true.' She nodded her head sadly.

'Mrs Maneckjee, there is absolutely no reason why you should trust me, but if you don't mind I'd like to come in and talk to you about Farrokh. You haven't been given the truth.'

She held his eye. 'I know that. And you are the first to

agree with me. So I don't mind at all if you come in, Mr Jones. You look hot. Would you like some tea?'

'Yes. Very much.'

'Then, please.' She stepped back and ushered him through. The house was bright and immaculately kept, in the Indian style. As she led Harry through to the sitting room at the rear, he saw a small shrine to Farrokh that had been placed beneath an old stone tree of life. The light from several small candles shone onto a portrait. His graduation photo.

'He graduated with first-class honours, you know, Mr Jones, in geographical sciences. From Bristol University.' Her head was shaking back and forth as she spoke, in the manner of the sub-continent, and a light had crept into her face, a mixture of pride and defiance, as if at last someone was ready to listen to her about her son. She seated him on the sofa with a view out to the rear garden, and with the tea served him tiny cakes of almond that she placed upon a small end table with legs carved in the form of elephant heads.

He looked around for other photographs of her family, but could find none. 'Farrokh – was he your only son?'

She nodded and gazed into her cup as though it were a sea of troubles.

'I am so sorry. And your husband?'

'Away on family business in India.'

'Forgive me, but you are very brave to allow me into your home, Mrs Maneckjee.'

'I am probably a foolish old woman to let someone like you into my home, Mr Jones – oh, indeed, I know what is being said about you. But you are the first person who has shown any interest in the truth about my son.'

He leaned forward. 'You will need to be very brave when you hear what I have to tell you.'

'It could not be any worse than what has already been told to me. That he died for nothing.'

'Tell me, what was Farrokh doing in Russia?'

And as he listened, all Harry's pain and weariness seemed to drift away from him, replaced by understanding and irresistible anger.

'My son was a trained hydrologist and environmental expert. Young but very accomplished, you understand?' Her head wobbled; he smiled in encouragement. 'He was leading a small team that had spent several months making observations in the Caspian Sea.'

'Why were they doing that, Mrs Maneckjee?'

'Oh, because of the pipeline.'

Harry put his tea aside, concerned it might fall from his fingers. 'What pipeline is that?'

'But you must have heard of it, Mr Jones,' she scolded gently, 'it is very large. It will carry huge amounts of gas to Europe. It is called Babylon.'

'Yes, I've heard of it.'

'Before the EU can sign contracts for such a thing, it has to undertake an environmental audit. That is its own law. And that's what Farrokh and his team were doing. Very important work, very secret. But you see, Mr Jones, there are bad people out there, very bad. As soon as Farrokh and his team began their work, he found his office was being broken into, his papers being stolen, his records copied. Then as they got closer to the end of their work they were threatened, several times, their vehicles and equipment sabotaged. Wicked men trying to stop them.'

'Who was doing that, who was trying to stop them?'

'Farrokh did not know, not for certain. He never saw them face to face, it was always in the shadows, in the dark, you know? But I think there is very much at stake with this pipeline, so my son and his team decided to expedite their work, to finish their report as quickly as possible. And even as they were trying to complete their task, their offices were once again ransacked and all their computer equipment stolen or destroyed.'

'So all the work was lost.'

'No,' she said firmly. 'My Farrokh was a clever boy, he knew there was such wickedness afoot. He made a copy, you see, of the most important pieces of the research. On his laptop. And he kept it with him so that whatever happened he would be able to complete his report. But he told me he was very worried, Mr Jones. I think a little afraid for his people. So he sent them home. None of them knew what was in the report, except for my Farrokh. And at the first opportunity he flew back to Brussels to present his findings.'

She poured fresh cups of tea; Harry was desperate to

urge her on, but he knew she must do this in her own way.

'Would you care for some more biscuits, Mr Jones? You seem to enjoy them.'

He glanced down at his plate; it was empty. He had eaten automatically, both his mind and his manners adrift two thousand miles away on the shores of the Caspian Sea. 'Forgive me. That was rude.'

'Not at all. I regard it as a considerable compliment to my poor cooking skills. But I suspect that most of all you would like me to finish my story.'

'Yes. Please.'

'When he arrived in Brussels he waited to present his report. And he waited, and he waited. He kept being told that his superiors on the Commission would see him the following day. Always the following day. It was Christmas, you see, and eventually he was told that everyone had left and he should come back after the New Year. Farrokh was very angry, but there was no one to whom he could protest. And he was more than a little frightened by this time. He thought he had – how do we say it? – covered his tracks on his journey from Russia, but one night he found his hotel room had been broken into, and his luggage was searched.'

'The laptop?'

'He had kept it with him. He was such a clever and careful boy, Mr Jones, everyone used to say so. He called me the morning before he left, saying he was coming back home.'

'On Speedbird 235.'

'Precisely. With his laptop.' Suddenly tears began to fall, making tiny dark spots on her sari; she fought to control them.

'But I don't understand, Mrs Maneckjee. Why did you not tell all this to the police?'

'But I did!' she protested, the tears wiped by a flash of anger. 'I called, they said they would come, but it was many, many days. They complained that they had so many relatives to see. And when I told them, they looked at each other, closed their notebooks, and said I must be mistaken. The plane had been shot down by the Egyptians, they said, because of the children, not because of my Farrokh. I insisted they make enquiries, they said they would, but nothing happened. I telephoned many people, wrote many letters, but you know how it is. They concluded I was simply a disturbed old lady, an immi-grant with a foreign accent, and it is the truth that nowadays unless you think in the accent of Essex, they believe you cannot think at all. No one took any notice, Mr Jones. Until you.' She smiled, even though it hurt, while he felt a little ashamed about his countrymen. 'So you see, Mr Jones, I don't have to be brave about what you came to tell me. I already know.'

'Then you are even braver than I thought.'

'No. It was Farrokh who was the brave one.' She got up and went to his shrine, picked up his photograph. Harry stood beside her as she showed it off with pride. 'Such a wonderful son,' she whispered, and kissed his image. She set about making tiny, entirely unnecessary adjustments to the immaculate shrine, wanting still to do something for her son, repositioning the candles, adjusting its garland of small white flowers. Then she turned to Harry. 'Is there anything else you would like to know, Mr Jones?'

Much, but he didn't think Mrs Maneckjee would be able to tell him. 'I don't think so. You have been very kind.'

'What will you do now?'

'I'm not sure. I wish I could promise that I was in a position to reveal all this and get you a little justice – but justice isn't being very kind to either of us right now.'

She nodded in acceptance. 'At least I have been able to share my feelings with someone who understands. Who believes. Not even my husband ... Thank you for coming. And for caring, Mr Jones.' She led him slowly towards the door. 'He was such an intelligent boy, wrote such clever things. But I think I have already said that several times. You must forgive a mother's pride.'

'Such a pity we couldn't read his last report.'

She stopped, her hand on the door latch. 'Oh, but you can. He emailed me a copy before he left from Brussels. In case they stole his laptop.'

'What was in that report?'

'I do not know. It is far too technical for me.'

'May I see it?'

'If you would like.' And once again Harry was invited

into her home. This time she took him to a small side room filled with books and files. A comfortable chair sat in one corner with sewing paraphernalia around it. In the other was a computer. 'Please make yourself comfortable. And I have some food prepared. Would you like a plate, while you read?'

'That isn't necessary, thank you.'

'Not necessary, perhaps, but my very great pleasure, Mr Jones.'

So he ate, while he read, and began to understand.

—⚬—

When he had finished, Harry sat quietly for many moments. The report had been technical and dense, as Mrs Maneckjee had suggested, but its conclusions rang out with a clarity that took his breath away and, for a while, scrambled his sense of everything that had happened. Only when he had grappled with its findings and forced them into some sort of submission did he reach for his phone and tap at its keys.

'Hello,' he said dully when it was answered. 'This is Harry Jones.'

A silence. 'How did you get this number?'

'You don't cover your tracks well enough.'

'Tell me.'

'Through the Internet. I got your village by searching the local press for its report of your husband's death, then your address from the electoral register. After that, your

349

phone number was easy. It was kid's play, once I realized you were Mrs Felix Wilton.'

'How despicable of you to turn up at his funeral service today,' she said, her voice controlled and unyielding.

'It was necessary. To discover who else turned up. You. I'm sure you understand.'

'You keep turning up in all the wrong places, Mr Jones.'

'Just as you seem to have been turning up under every stone I lift.'

She hesitated; he thought he could hear a cigarette being lit. Then: 'What do you want?'

'To meet.'

'What, meet a man with your violent reputation?'

'You know it's not true.'

She sucked in a lungful of nicotine. 'But why on earth do you want to meet? You know I'll have the entire police force of Wiltshire waiting for you, plus some very interested parties from London.'

'I don't think you would want me to talk to the police. Not about the pipeline. And the Russians.'

A much longer pause, one that seemed to stretch as long as a hangman's rope. 'Very well. Where?'

'I'm not so far away.'

'Then come to my home.'

'I don't think so, I'm sure it's bristling with security. Somewhere neutral.'

'Then the village church.'

'Very well.'

'The churchwarden opens it at ten every morning. Shall we say ...'

'Ten-thirty?'

'Tomorrow morning. It will be most interesting to meet you, Mr Jones.'

CHAPTER TWENTY-ONE

He had just finished the call when Mrs Maneckjee came in. 'I am sorry for the interruption when you seem so thoughtful, Mr Jones.' She had brought him a cup of tea.

'No, I should apologize. I have overstayed my welcome.'

'You have discovered what you are looking for?'

'I think so.'

'Then you should celebrate with tea.' She put the cup down beside him.

'Thank you.'

But there was no hint of celebration. His mood seemed resigned, focused, inexorably sad. It made her feel uneasy.

'I've stolen some of your writing paper and an envelope, ' he continued. 'I hope you don't mind. I'd like you to post it for me.' He sealed it and handed it across.

'To Mr Usher? The former Prime Minister?' she exclaimed in surprise.

'At his home address. I don't want to send it through official channels. Neither of us have any reason to trust such things, do we?'

'I think you are very wise.'

'But I'm afraid I don't have a stamp.'

'Do not worry, I shall take the most excellent care of it.'

'It's just some things I think he ought to know.'

She gazed deep into his eyes, saw trouble, resignation. 'In case you are not in a position to tell him personally,' she said softly.

'Something like that.'

'I think my Farrokh was not the only brave person in this matter, Mr Jones.'

He tried to muster a reassuring smile, it didn't convince. 'I'd better get going. I've got to be about thirty miles away by tomorrow morning and I doubt whether taking the bus or train would prove a very good idea for a man in my position.'

'So how will you manage?'

'I'll walk, Mrs Maneckjee,' he said, pointing to his feet. 'These things haven't let me down yet.'

She shook her head. 'Walking at night is not to be recommended, either. Come with me.'

She led him to the garage in the rear garden. Inside, amongst a collection of boxes and garden paraphernalia, was a motorbike, a Honda, 250cc, far from new but meticulously polished and cared for, with neat panniers on the back. 'Farrokh's,' she declared.

'That would be wonderful but . . .'

'I know. You cannot promise to return it.' She knew. 'I think my son would understand, and so will I. May your god travel with you, Mr Harry Jones.'

He drove through the evening, the light fading, the wind whipping through his hair – Farrokh's helmet had been too small to fit. He kept to the back roads, throwing the bike into the corners, slipping through the gears, filling his lungs with the heady, scented air of the hedgerows, bringing back memories of moments like this when he'd been in his twenties and thought he was immortal. It felt so long ago.

Harry didn't drive into the village but pulled over well short, not sure of what might lie ahead. He hid Farrokh's bike in a copse of scrub beech and took to the fields, using the hedgerows as cover. At this time of year there was always light in the sky and he made good progress, catching the laments of the countryside as owls, foxes, ferrets and feral cats lay about their business. Cows continued to tear at the grass as he passed, heedless of his presence, but at one point he stumbled upon a covey of resting partridge and they stormed low across the field, their wings beating like kettle drums in protest. Yet for the most part he heard nothing but the nocturnal rustles of the undergrowth and the sighing of trees in the breeze.

The village of Upper Marlsford lay in the fold of the valley along the course of the river that at this time of year flowed languidly through its midst. It was a community that time had treated gently; its walls were of flint, brick and chalk, its roofs mostly red tile or thatch, and from its size Harry reckoned that it was home to no more than five or six hundred souls. The church was easy enough to spot, even from a distance, its bell tower thrusting through the jumble of surrounding trees. He worked his way around those parts of the village that appeared most busy, like the pub and the manor house where lights still blazed, but for the most part Upper Marlsford was falling to sleep, and as he approached, cautiously, along the path that ran beside the riverbank, he disturbed nothing but the occasional drowsy dog. He avoided the road and came to the church through the graveyard, where he found a gardener's hut nestling beside a looming cypress tree. The rich smell of composting grass seeped from somewhere close at hand. The gardener was trusting, the lock even more so, and it came away easily. Harry slipped inside, and waited.

—⁂—

The sun rose early and Harry was soon fully alert, and aching from a night spent sitting propped against a slatted wall. He'd brought water with him, a large plastic bottle, and he used it to rinse his face. His hair was matted from the bike ride, his suit a fearful mess; the trouser leg had got itself ripped somewhere along the way. With his many days of stubble he looked more than unkempt, yet just a few months earlier he'd been one of the most eminent men in the country, a home in Mayfair, a life that glittered and had him showered with respect. Patricia Vaine had done her work well.

355

As the light grew, the village came to life; dogs wailed at newspaper boys, cockerels crowed across the lanes, farmers thundered through on their oversized machines. No buses, of course, not any longer. The hours moved slowly on leaden feet through the heavy midsummer air. As the temperature began to rise, an elderly man appeared in the graveyard, his legs bowed, leaning heavily on a stick, with a small bunch of flowers clutched doggedly in his free hand. He used them to replace stems that were wilting at the foot of a recent stone. He stayed several minutes, head bowed, back bent, talking quietly to whomever was beneath. He didn't look towards Harry's hiding place. It was some time later that the churchwarden arrived, just as the steeple clock was chiming. He stopped at the lychgate, replacing a notice on the board, then walked up the short path to the church's clay-tiled porch. Harry heard him opening the door, but he didn't stay long. The time was close at hand.

She was early, tracing the footsteps of the churchwarden, her tread slow, purposeful, crunching on the gravel, until she disappeared inside. Harry waited many minutes, checking to see whether she was being followed. He saw nothing. Eventually, warily, he slipped from his hiding place.

He tarried inside the porch, listening. Nothing. He lifted the old latch and let himself in. The church was ancient, constructed of flint, its walls thick. As he took a step inside the latch clattered back into place, the noise echoing around the interior, which was cool, dark, and smelled of polish. He looked around, expecting to find her, but he was alone. Then he saw a door at the far end of the church that gave access to the belfry. It was open. His instruction. He followed her through it. On the far side he found worn wooden steps that carried him up to the heavy wooden scaffold where the bells were hanging, but still there was no sign of her. He pressed on, upward. From somewhere near at hand came the slow, persistent ticking of the clock mechanism; everything smelled of damp and ancient dust. At the top of the tower a small, low door opened onto the roof. It was ajar. He had to duck as he clambered through, and as soon as he straightened he found himself blinded by the sudden brilliance of the day. He stood, blinking, shading his eyes. It was there, at last, he saw her, waiting for him.

'Mr Jones. I wish I could say it was a pleasure.'

She was dressed in a simple cotton blouse with floral skirt, open-toed shoes and a straw shoulder bag in a manner that would have passed for the vicar's wife, except for the Versace sunglasses, and the small aerosol she was pointing at him.

'A little insurance, Mr Jones. It's pepper spray.'

'I thought that stuff was illegal.'

'Oh, I have a *laissez-passer* for all sorts of things. So if you wouldn't mind ditching your jacket, turning around ...'

He did so. The jacket fluttered to the ground, clearly not

concealing a weapon, and he turned to show there was nothing in his belt.

'Well, just look at you, Mr Jones,' she said, her face flooded with contempt. 'What a mess.' She moved to the farthest part of the roof, putting her back against one of the weather-stained castellations that surrounded them on all sides. She dropped the spray into the top of her bag, ensuring it was still to hand.

Harry gazed around him. Beyond the rooftops and gracious old trees of Upper Marlsford he could see to the fields, a patchwork of greens and glorious summer golds. Beneath him, on the path that ran alongside the slow-moving river, two women had stopped to gossip while walking their dogs. Nearby a pair of swans raised their necks, alert, guarding signets.

He shook his head. 'Someone like you in a place like this. It's . . .'

'What?'

'Not what I expected.'

'I'm not what most people expect,' she said curtly. 'Why did you want to see me?'

'For much the same reason, I suspect, that you agreed to see me. To know it all. And to finish it.'

They were disturbed as a large number of rooks flew over, like dark rags caught on the updraught, calling to each other before settling into the branches of a family of Scots pine. She pulled a handkerchief from her bag and began dabbing at her nose.

'Hay fever,' she announced. 'You see, I am human, after all.' She managed to leave the impression of being annoyed by the fact.

'I'm sorry about your husband.'

'Sorry won't bring him back!' she snapped, her blue eyes suddenly igniting in anger.

'It was an accident, unintended.'

'He was a good man, despite his weaknesses. He didn't deserve what you did to him.'

He shook his head. 'Not me.'

'Oh, really,' she spat in disbelief.

'It was Jimmy Sopwith-Dane. He killed your husband. Didn't mean it, but . . . You drove him too far.'

She started in surprise, twisting her handkerchief around her finger as she considered the possibility. 'It doesn't make any difference to me which of you killed him. He didn't deserve to die,' she repeated emphatically.

'Neither did the children.'

'Of course they didn't! What do you take me for, some kind of monster?'

'Why, then, did you hide the truth?'

She shook her head with the air of a disappointed schoolmistress. 'Oh, Mr Jones, you've been around long enough to know how very harmful the truth can be.'

'I'm not sure Mrs Maneckjee would agree with you.'

'Maneckjee?'

'Mother of Farrokh. You remember him, don't you?'

And for the first time she seemed troubled, looking distractedly at her shoe, twisting it uneasily, as though trying to stub out a cigarette. 'Yes, that was most unfortunate.'

'And that's why the plane was shot down.'

'A terrible thing.'

'So terrible you decided to hide what had happened.'

She looked up sharply. 'In the wider interest.'

'In your interest, I think, and that of your friends.'

She seemed irritated by his words. 'Shall we get on with this? I have a game of tennis in a little while.'

'You like your games, don't you? Like the ones you played with Ben Usher. You ruined him.'

'I hadn't intended that, not at the start. But he was such a dinosaur, couldn't find his way out of Downing Street without a guide. Kept stumbling, getting in the way, and so ...' She flicked her hand, as though he had been no more than a gnat.

'And so ... Marmite.'

She threw her head back and laughed, the blonde wisps catching the summer light. 'You figured that out, did you? Well done, Mr Jones. He was done for anyway, but I thought it was an amusing touch. You know, when those Neanderthals at the CIA tried to get rid of Fidel Castro they used poisoned shoe polish and still managed to make a mess of it. I thought, why not show that we Europeans are better than that.'

'Are we?'

'Oh, I think so. Very much so. And the best still to come.

It's a dream, Mr Jones, and everything I've done has been about that dream.'

'It's people like you who drag it into the gutter.'

'It's the future, don't you see?' she said, her tone exasperated. 'But of course you probably don't. You've been fighting so long for Queen and country you can't understand that it's all been a ludicrous waste of time. Britain isn't the future, Europe is. And yet . . .' She gazed out over the sights of the English countryside, wistful. 'I do love it so. All this.' For a moment her face seemed to soften, but it was fleeting. 'It's not enough, is it? That American – Dulles? – he was right when he said we'd lost an empire and hadn't found anything else to do. But now we have.'

'As part of a new empire.'

'And why not?'

'But I had this quaint, ridiculously old-fashioned idea that the people were supposed to have a say in all this.'

'They've got comfortable sofas and reality television. It seems to be enough for them. In any event, democracy's vastly overrated. It's a little like cheese, only to be taken in moderation. Have too much of it and you end up like California, completely out of control.'

'It's a wonder you never thought of standing for election.'

'I leave elections for people like Mr Murray. A great victory, I thought. With perhaps just the gentlest push in the right direction from me,' she added smugly.

They were standing on opposite sides of the tower, like

boxers in a ring. The day was growing oppressive, the heat rising, bouncing back from the lead roof.

'It's all for the good of the country, you know, Mr Jones, every bit of it.'

'Some would call it treachery,' he replied softly.

'I beg your pardon?'

'You've betrayed your country.'

'Ridiculous,' she sighed, 'you simply don't understand. Anyway, it's Brussels, not Britain—'

'And you've been betrayed yourself.'

'Oh, indeed?' she said, with the shadow of a frown, suddenly interested.

'By your husband.' It was his turn to mock.

'By Felix?'

'He was double-dealing. You've been building up this great castle in the sky, but on the ground floor, even in the bedroom, the men from Moscow had already moved in. All that time, your husband was working for the Russians. He was an agent!'

She shook her head. 'No, not the bedroom,' she replied tartly, but said no more. She didn't startle, didn't fall to pieces with shock. Instead she took off her dark glasses and stared at him, her blue eyes intense, on fire, defiant. It was Harry who was left reeling.

'You knew?' he whispered, struggling to recapture his wits as suddenly he saw everything in a new and twisted light.

'If this were a game of tennis you'd be about forty-love

down by now.' Her tone was contemptuous. 'I take pride in having a good working relationship with the Russians, Mr Jones. Together we can achieve so much.'

'We?'

'EATA. The agency has come a long way since I took over. No one accuses us of being paper pushers or press cutters any more. But we live in turbulent times and I'd be the first to admit that we lack teeth. So the Russians occasionally – how can I put this? – help us out.'

'The messy bits.'

'Precisely. Russia isn't the enemy any more, and the Americans aren't particularly our friends. It's a new world out there.'

'So who is the enemy in this new world of yours? Just people like Ben Usher? Me?'

'Oh, but Harry, I have the highest respect for you, truly I do. Do you mind if I call you Harry? I feel as if I've got to know you so well these past few months.'

'So long as I don't have to call you Patricia.'

'You've been remarkably resourceful. If only I could find people like you, I wouldn't need the Russians.'

'You can find people like me everywhere. But I'm not sure they'd want to help.'

'The pay and rations are extremely generous.'

'Tell that to the Greeks.'

'Oh, Harry, stop being such a bad loser. We have to move on. It's a great adventure. But in any adventure it's inevitable that some will get left behind.'

'Like the kids in the plane.'

'I don't feel the need to apologize yet again.'

'If you apologized, I didn't hear it,' he spat, his voice soaked in disgust. Her hand went to her bag, for the pepper spray, just in case, but he swallowed his anger. There was still more to be done. He took a couple of slow paces to the corner of the tower, head bowed in thought; she matched the move, cautious, keeping her distance.

'So, Ghazi wasn't working for the Egyptians,' he said, facing her once more.

'No, of course not. That tale was no more than a convenience. It kept the Americans happy, you know how they love their Muslim fanatics. They swallow such nonsense so blithely, it's like feeding chocolate to children. And, of course, it left your Mr Usher chasing up his blind alley.'

'Which leaves the question, who was Ghazi working for?'

'And what do you think?'

'Not the Russians.'

'An interesting speculation,' she said, sniffing, dabbing at her nose once more.

'They caught Ghazi. Killed him.'

'To keep him quiet.'

'But they didn't kill him straight away.'

Her face came up from her handkerchief, her eyes swimming in curiosity. 'How do you know that?'

'Felix said so. Before he died.'

For the first time she looked disconcerted, as if a net cord on a vital point had dropped on her side of the court.

'They questioned Ghazi. We both know what a messy business that can be with your Russian friends. He wouldn't have died quietly, he would have sung like a nightingale – or, more accurately, like a man who was having his last remaining testicle crushed. They wanted something from him.'

'Like what?'

'I've been thinking about that, very hard, and there's only one conclusion that makes sense. They wanted to know who was paying him ...' Suddenly, Harry's head jerked as though an entirely new thought had hit him, hard enough to make him wince. 'You ... you didn't know, did you? You thought it *was* the Russians. All along you assumed it was your messy-handed friends who ordered the attack on the plane because of what they feared was in young Farrokh's report.' He laughed, mocking, clapped his hands. 'You were covering the whole bloody thing up, but there was no need.'

She was still smiling, but the eyes had turned to glass. 'Mr Maneckjee never completed his report.'

'He never presented his report because your chums in Brussels were too busy rushing off for Christmas. You never got to know what was in it. But he completed it all right.'

'Sadly, it seems all the copies were destroyed.'

'Except for one. The one he sent to his mother. The one I read yesterday afternoon.'

365

Her eyes had begun to melt and he thought he could see a bead of perspiration on her brow. It was as hot as hell, the heat from the lead roof burning through the soles of his shoes, but he was back in the game.

'It was full of technical gobbledygook, I couldn't understand it all, but the conclusions were as clear as fresh ice. It was OK for Babylon to go through Russia. There was never any need for them to blow that plane and the report out of the sky.'

'But they didn't—' She stopped herself abruptly, struggling to reclaim her composure. 'But if they didn't know that, it would have given them every motive.'

'Which, in turn, gave you your motive for concocting your cover-up.'

She shook her head, but a blush of confusion had erupted on her chest and was creeping up around her neck.

'Maneckjee's offices had been repeatedly raided. Someone knew all right, someone with a far bigger motive than the Russians could have had.'

Her lips twitched in bewilderment.

'The other guys, Mrs Vaine. The losers who were going to miss out on billions in transit rights. The countries along the alternative route for the pipeline who so hate the Russians.'

'The Georgians? Or Chechens?' she whispered, at last coming to understanding.

'Who knows? Well, the Russians know. They squeezed it out of Ghazi.'

'Then why haven't they said so?'

'Oh, they will, but only when it suits them. In the mean-time they have their pipeline, and their hands around some cringing neighbour's throat, ready to put the pressure on any time it suits. They're sitting pretty. Got everything they wanted and more than they could ever have expected.'

Her eyes darted out across the rooftops of the village as her thoughts and fears tumbled over each other, but she recovered remarkably quickly. When she turned back her voice was firm, stubborn. 'I didn't know for sure, you see. It's not the sort of thing you go to ask the Russians, is it? Oh, by the way, did you just blow one of our planes out of the sky? There was no time, I couldn't get hold of Felix, so ...'

'You covered up what you thought your friends had done.'

'Yes.'

'Then you had to cover up the cover-up.'

'It was in everyone's interest.'

'There you go again. But it was only ever in your interest.'

'I'm not that sort of person. I made a mistake, that was all.'

'And as part of that cover-up you tried to destroy me.'

'Tried?' Suddenly she was on the attack once more, mocking his crumpled clothes, his turbulent hair, the beard, the wild eyes. 'Succeeded, surely. But it was your fault. You pestered, kept getting in the way.'

'You seem to have made something of a habit of destroy-ing people. It's almost as though you enjoy it.'

'And there speaks Harry Jones, a man who's filled graveyards in every corner of the globe.'

'I was doing my duty.'

'As I have done mine.'

'It was more than that, wasn't it? Had to be.' He was still troubled, didn't have it all. 'You rushed – panicked – when the plane came down. There was no need for that unless . . .' His words died as his thoughts led him on to an entirely new destination.

'Oh, but you are good, Harry. You can spot a girl's weaknesses from a very long way away.' She smiled, coquettishly. 'I wonder, do you think at some other time that you and I might have . . .' She twisted her handkerchief around her finger once again, flirting with her eyes, then sighed as though in frustration. 'But no, I suppose we're too much alike for that.'

'By God, I hope not.'

'You see, I'd heard whispers about Ghazi and the missile. I had no idea what he was intending, believe me, but I didn't do anything with the information, didn't share it, I wanted to follow it, to see where it led.'

'And claim credit for it.'

'You know how these things work.'

'Instead you were left with a nightmare on your hands. You might have stopped it.'

'No, I don't think so. Please believe me on that. The information was too vague, I had no idea anything would happen so quickly. But if the media had found out they'd have made an appalling fuss, asked far too many questions, looked into all those dark corners – demanded my resignation, and there was no point in that.'

Harry was stunned. It took him some time to understand what it all implied. 'So all the Egyptian nonsense . . .'

'Had many benefits.'

'It was all to cover up your own mistake.'

'That's not how I would put it but . . .' She nodded in acceptance.

'Why are you telling me this?'

'We both came here to understand. I think we have.'

'And to finish it.'

'Yes, that, too. You've played superbly, stretched me almost to my limit, Harry.'

'But this isn't a game of tennis.'

'You've scored some excellent points, taken a couple of sets off me, perhaps, but despite it all I'm afraid the match is mine.'

He said nothing, waited.

'What were you expecting when you came here? A polite little chat? That I would withdraw quietly? An early retirement to my cottage in the countryside?'

That was when he knew for sure he was going to die. He had always known it was the most likely outcome, which was why he'd written to Usher, telling him so, knowing that his death would give his words more power. Now only the means of death was to be decided.

'Why, Harry?'

369

'I had to know the truth.'

'But I keep telling you that the truth is a hideously dangerous weapon. That's why it's entrusted to people like me.'

'To twist. To hide.'

'What isn't known can't hurt.'

'The gospel of the whore.'

'Only the really good ones.' She laughed, the gold bangles at her wrist jangling in applause.

'Didn't take you long to get bored with playing the grieving widow.'

His words brought her mockery to an abrupt halt. 'You know, Harry, you're truly a remarkable man, willing to die for a cause. I admire that. It's such a pity you've chosen the wrong one.'

She produced a pack of cigarettes from her bag and lit one. The smoke hung languidly in the heavy air. 'I told you, Harry, that the Russians sometimes help me deal with . . .'

'The messy bits.'

'Exactly. Right at this moment a rifle is trained on you, has been from the moment you stepped out onto this roof. A Dragunov SVD.'

He recognized it immediately as the standard Russian sniper rifle. Brilliant scope. Could take out a man at more than three-quarters of a mile, so long as it wasn't silenced, and what would be the point of that in these parts?

'Forgive my slight deception, but I fear that's become part of our relationship.'

He resisted the futile temptation to glance round, to try to fix the location, where the bullet would be coming from. Instead he stared at her. Now the sweat was unmistakable, beading on her brow.

'For the greater good, Harry.'

'Spare me the sermon, I've seen it done so much better.'

She took another deep lungful of tobacco, the tip of the cigarette glowing bright as it was consumed. 'Don't blame me for the children. Not my fault. It's what I want to stop, all this unnecessary dying, all your ridiculous wars. That's the dream, that's what we can achieve together. No more wars, Harry, no more battlefields, no more victims.'

'Except one.'

'The final casualty. That's not a bad epitaph, when you come to think of it.'

'I might drown in gratitude.'

She raised the cigarette, examined its glowing tip. 'As soon as I throw it away ...'

'You couldn't do it yourself, then.'

Her expression suggested she had never considered it.

'Your kind never can. All those ideals you're happy for others to die for, so long as don't get your hands mucky. That's why you won't win, not in the end, because one day you're going to run out of friends to do your dirty work for you.'

'It's a point of view, Harry. Who knows, maybe you're right? But I'm afraid you won't be around to see it.'

She held the cigarette out at arm's length. He watched, exhausted, the fight gone. He wasn't afraid. There was no pain in death. Yet suddenly he was in pain. He realized that his dying would make no difference to anyone, and that hurt. Hurt so much.

Her hand was trembling, unsteady, her breasts rose and fell rapidly beneath her crisp cotton blouse as she snatched for breath. She hesitated. 'Bye, Harry,' she whispered. Then she dropped the cigarette.

It took the 54mm round little more than a second to travel from the muzzle to its target. Harry sensed rather than heard the air about him being torn apart. The bullet casing for the Dragunov is made of thin steel with a small lump of lead at the rear, which is designed to thump forward as soon as it hits the target. The explosive effect can be terrible. Harry watched as a small, neat hole appeared on Patricia's forehead and a hideous mist erupted into the air around her. The world seemed to freeze, turn silent, solid. Was it his imagination, or did those eyes of blue ice sparkle in surprise, in that moment before she collapsed to the ground? She lay staring at him, her eyes still open. He was glad he couldn't see what little lay behind them.

Then the world returned. The rooks rose from their roost, squabbling as they fluttered into the haze-filled sky above Upper Marlsford, but otherwise the village remained untouched. Yet Harry couldn't move, overwhelmed in disbelief, struggling to comprehend. There was no point in throwing himself behind the parapet for protection, not any more; if they'd wanted them both dead he'd be there now, lying alongside Patricia. Someone, somewhere, had changed their mind. He had been spared.

CHAPTER TWENTY-TWO

The Athenaeum sweltered in the heat, as did all who entered. It was so unrelentingly hot that even the gilded statue of the virgin goddess after whom the club had been named seemed to shimmer in sweat. The doors had been thrown wide open in an attempt to catch stray zephyrs, but all they got was traffic fumes.

The three men lunched on the terrace beneath the shade of a sprawling umbrella, in a corner and in shirtsleeves, thanks to the relaxation of the strict dress code by the club secretary, with the neighbouring table left empty to give them a measure of privacy. Even in this club whose membership was made up of the most illustrious figures from the British Establishment and where all men (if not women) were held equal, these were individuals who made their own rules. Harry sat with Ben Usher and their host, a man in his fifties with a long aquiline nose, immaculate silver hair and a complexion like fresh blancmange. His name was Sir Rupert Mowbray. He was the head of MI6.

'Roop and I wanted to say thank you, Harry,' Usher was saying, as they began attacking a salad of salmon.

'Most assuredly,' the spymaster echoed in an accent that betrayed his Etonian and Scots Guards origins. He stretched for the bottle of Chablis; the wine steward had been discouraged from hovering. 'You've been most hugely helpful.'

'In all honesty I have difficulty trying to comprehend what you've been through,' Usher added, 'yet still you had the sense of public service to write me that letter, Harry. Forgive me, I know such things are entirely superfluous in your case, but that was the mark of a very special man.' The former Prime Minister raised his glass in salute.

'*Illegitimis non caborundum*,' Harry muttered, raising his own. He noticed the slightest wrinkle of doubt on Mowbray's face. 'Never let the bastards get you down,' he translated, very roughly. 'Oh, I know it doesn't scan or parse or whatever it is you classical scholars do, Rupert, but I always think in English. Especially when my balls are roasting.'

'Ours is such a convenient language,' the spymaster added. 'Why, almost everybody speaks it nowadays.' He nodded to the maître d', whose name tag identified him as Alonso, and the plates were cleared.

'You fully recovered from it yet, Harry?' Usher asked when they were alone once again.

'Batteries recharging. Slowly.'

'Take your time, as much as you need, but you know we want you back in Westminster. Not just in harness but right at the top.' Usher reached over and grasped Harry's sleeve, squeezing his arm. 'Now your name's been cleared, the world's your oyster.'

'Must be early stages, Ben. Just feels like a bit of grit.' His dreams were still filled with nightmares, and much of his days, too. He rolled his glass between the palms of his hands and studied it; even this *grand cru* tasted flat. 'You know, I don't understand why I'm here, why I wasn't the one shot. That was the plan, must've been. I'm still trying to piece it all together ...'

'I think,' Mowbray said, in the manner of a man who knew many secrets and enjoyed handing them out in a parsimonious fashion, 'you might owe much of your survival to the blessed Ms Vaine.'

'Then I'm filled with surprise and disgust.'

'Nothing totally clear in this murky world, but reading between the lines ...' Mowbray paused to make sure they couldn't be overheard. 'She rather jumped the gun, you see, put the Russians in a very awkward position. Imagine it. They'd been working for years to secure the pipeline contract, and suddenly they wake up one morning to discover they've got everything they want and even a little bit more, thanks to Ms Vaine's machinations. For a while they're willing to go along with her plan. They have the contract, the West is getting itself bogged down ranting about yet more mad Muslims, while the men in Moscow have entirely clean hands and are busy running their eyes over the specs for their next generation of super-yachts.' He paused to wipe a stray flake of salmon off his shirt cuff with the corner of his napkin, very fastidious. 'Christmas came early for them, and the New Year was all about sitting back and making money. You know, occasionally on a dull afternoon I get the impression they're tired of always being put on the naughty step, they think it's someone else's turn.'

'And we gave them their chance in the form of the Egyptians. Not our finest hour,' Usher said, making it sound as if it had been entirely someone else's fault while he buried the admission beneath a forkful of lettuce.

'It continued. Got better. Once they had hold of the unfortunate Mr Ghazi and presumably ripped the last crumb of truth out of him, the Russians had an additional prize, their boot on the testicles of some vile neighbouring despot who is now in the uncomfortable position of having to jump every time the Russians stamp their foot, or be exposed as an international mass murderer responsible for shooting babes and sucklings out of the sky. American sucklings, what's more, and you know how sensitive the Americans get, particularly in an election year.'

'But – who?' Harry asked.

Mowbray furrowed his brow, sipped his wine. 'That's what's been bothering us, too. Not sure yet. It'll come out eventually, of course, some defector selling his story, or perhaps we'll have to wait for Putin's memoirs. But for the moment you can take your pick. Georgia, Ingushetia, Dagestan, Chechnya. Some lowlife republic with an alternative interest in the pipeline or who hate the Russians so much they'd skin their own grannies to get back at them. My guess is the Chechens but of course the Russians aren't letting on, deny all knowledge of it. And why the devil should they let on when they can still squeeze more out of the situation? It's like money in the bank for them.' He shook his head in the manner of a schoolmaster confronted with a page of appalling maths. 'For a while all of this seemed wonderful, but Ms Vaine proved to be ... well, a bit of a wasp in the wine glass, and everything got out of hand. Moscow yearned for the quiet life, yet suddenly they were being asked to get involved in assaults on the streets of London, burglaries, beatings. They lost the unfortunate Felix.' He paused, his voice a little lower. 'Then they were asked to assassinate you, Harry, bodies littered around the countryside. I think that was probably when they fell out of love with her. I'm speculating here, but I suspect they remembered all that fuss a few years ago when they poisoned Alexander Litvinenko – you recall that, of course. Polonium in his teacup. Not a pleasant way to go. Not something they wanted to risk again.'

Harry nodded. The wretched Litvinenko, a former Russian security agent and outspoken opponent of Vladimir Putin, had been poisoned in a restaurant less than five minutes' walk from where they were sitting. It had taken him three weeks to die, in agony.

'It's my reading of it all that someone in Moscow concluded she was causing more trouble than she was worth. They sought a life of tranquillity and instead they got

378

Patricia Vaine. A woman out of control, which is not at all the Russian thing. She proved to be a little too enthusiastic even for their taste.'

'But she was *their* woman,' Harry said, yet to be convinced.

'No, never that. Her husband was their man, surely – presumably some embarrassment in his private life that they were able to exploit, but she was never truly theirs. A very inconstant lover, was Ms Vaine. And the men from Moscow would eventually have found themselves dragged into her little foibles. Then there was an article in the *Telegraph* about some Russian double-dealing, not coming clean on what they knew of the crash. You saw it, Harry?'

He nodded, very slowly.

'Pretty speculative stuff, frankly, but it came from the man whom the lady had clearly been spoon-feeding. That stirred the chamber pot, raised doubts, suggested she might even be playing some sort of double game, and so . . .'

'Her instead of you, Harry,' Usher said, completing the thought.

'But she was their line into EATA, everything right from the top. One hell of a prize to throw away.'

'Oh, don't suppose for a moment she was the only rotten Russian apple within that rather undistinguished barrel,' Mowbray continued with an air of disdain that had been nurtured over many years in Whitehall. 'They'll have more, rest assured, you know what those bloody Cossacks are like.'

Rest assured? When had he last done that? 'What the hell am I supposed to say at the inquest?' Harry asked.

Mowbray took his time before replying. He put aside his knife and fork in a deliberate manner that made the gesture seem significant. 'Glad you mentioned it,' he said, not meaning it. The words came slowly, as if they were being forced to clamber over some obstruction before they emerged. 'There's not going to be a public inquest, actually. Everything under wraps for this one, being handled *in camera*. Friendly coroner. National security grounds. Taken out of the hands of the police. You know how it is. A suicide after the tragic death of her husband.'

'Suicide?' Harry almost spat out a mouthful of salmon in surprise.

'Didn't you know? Apparently they found a shotgun up there on the tower.' The spy chief stared brutally at Harry, almost challenging him to contradict.

For a moment Harry was lost. There were so many lines that didn't join up. He'd been in shock for some time up on that tower, didn't know for how long. Her phone had rung, several times, went unanswered. Shortly after that people had started arriving – police, a medical examiner, an unmarked ambulance, but also men in well-cut suits who seemed to have some sort of authority over the others. Harry had been taken away, questioned but not interrogated by the police, with the men in suits in constant attendance.

The next thing he'd known he was being invited to lunch.

'It's a delicate matter, Harry,' Usher joined in. 'If this all came out right now, God knows where we'd be. The truth is . . .'

'A dangerous weapon,' Harry whispered, remembering her words.

'Well put. We'll sort it, of course we will,' Usher assured.

'Sort . . . *what* exactly?'

'Everything. You, for a start. Get you up and running again. The first safe by-election.'

'And forgive me if this seems a little like asking coal to come to Newcastle,' Mowbray weighed in, 'but I happen to know for a fact that the energy companies involved in the pipeline project would welcome someone with your experience being brought on board. Very *much* welcome.'

Harry sniffed the air, didn't much care for the smell of it. He was being bought off. 'The pipeline? But won't there have to be a rethink, at least a pause for consideration?'

'No one wants delay, Harry, it's too important, any more than we want the bloody thing running through bandit country,' Mowbray said.

Harry pushed his plate away, his appetite evaporating in the heat. 'Forgive me, but you've just told me the Russians are hiding a mass murderer.'

'Speculation – and a short-term situation, I'm sure,' Mowbray said.

'There's a limit to how much pressure we can put on them,' Usher joined in.

'After all, this pipeline is important to everyone,' Mowbray came back. 'We have to share the bathroom with some pretty unpleasant people; the view is that at least the Russians are learning to flush.'

'But the children . . .'

'I think you can expect total satisfaction on that front,' Mowbray said. 'In a few days' time there will be a joint announcement from Moscow and Brussels that the Speedbird sabotage wasn't the responsibility of the Egyptians after all, that Ghazi was acting to sabotage relations between East and West, which isn't far from the truth. As for the victims, we're going to set up an international fund to support the families and it'll be jolly generous, I can assure you. There'll have to be a little shading of the details for a while, no mention of any connection with the pipeline – which in any respect is entirely supposition. Washington will give the whole thing a warm welcome – after all, it rather lets them off the hook, along with us. Frankly we're not getting anywhere with all this Egyptian nonsense. There'll be vague words about an aid package for them, too. So, end result – everyone happy.' He smiled like the conjurer he was.

'How about it, Harry, old friend?' Usher pressed. 'Come back on board.'

But Harry shook his head wearily. 'I need time.'

'Of course, all the time you want,' Usher assured him.

'What's going to happen about EATA? What's to stop this happening all over again?'

'We're going to watch it like a bloody hawk, that's what!' Usher insisted, repeatedly banging the point of his finger into the table. 'Absolutely disgraceful. Never again! It's clearly gone way beyond its brief.'

'It doesn't really have a brief, does it?' Harry said, with conspicuously less enthusiasm. 'Not one that anyone's approved.'

'Well, you know how it is in Europe.'

'But it's been engaged in assaults, money laundering, fraud – for pity's sake, even murder.'

'It's *anti-terrorist*,' Mowbray joined in again. 'Gives the buggers cover for all sorts of mischief.'

'It's out of control. Infiltrated by the Russians. You said so yourself,' Harry protested, growing irritated.

Mowbray responded with an insouciant smile. 'The truth is, Harry, we're infiltrating it rather well ourselves. In order to keep an eye on it, you understand. So we can put it back into its box. Stop all this mission creep.'

'And we believe Ms Vaine was something of a one-off,' Usher added.

'And if not?'

'Look, we're going to make sure it's sorted, Harry, I promise you that.' Once again Usher's hand reached out to grasp his sleeve in reassurance. 'We can't rush these things, but have no fear, it will be done! It's not all over yet, Harry, not by a long chalk.'

'A long chalk, on an even longer pipeline,' Mowbray sniffed, returning to his fish.

The weather had turned. Some celestial hand had brushed across the landscape and washed new life into it. A few days of spectacular thunderstorms that had left midday skies as dark as night and sent children scurrying into the arms of their mothers had passed away into gentle breezes that brought softer air and lighter spirits. But not, it seemed, to Harry. He and Jemma lay amongst the sand dunes of Embleton Bay, listening to the rustling of marram grass and the breaking of waves along this spectacular stretch of Northumberland coast. It was their second day, they hadn't spoken much except for trivialities, she had known he wasn't ready, lost somewhere inside himself, hurting. Long, silent walks, fingers touching, but no more. She knew he hadn't slept.

'It must have been like this for those early explorers,' she said, as much in an attempt to fill the space rather than follow a line of thought. 'You know, gazing up at the clouds, watching them pass, wondering where they were headed.'

It was a little time before he replied, and his words came slowly. 'My mum and dad split up one summer like this. Don't remember too much, I was thirteen. Spent the summer lying in a corner of the school sports field, listening to the grass being cut, making pictures in the sky. Wishing the clouds would take me away with them. Perhaps that's what drove men like Shackleton and Columbus. Pain.'

'You'll be all right, Harry.'

He turned to look at her. 'I know I will. It just takes time, Jem. I'm so bloody angry inside, it's burning me up.'

It was time to ask. 'What's going to happen?'

'Happen?' He rolled onto his back once more, gazing into the sky. 'To EATA and what lies behind it? Very little. Probably nothing at all. Usher and Mowbray promised to do everything they could, short of actual help. The same endless crap.'

'I was thinking of you. Are they going to charge you with anything?'

He laughed for the first time in days. It lacked passion and died quickly, but it was better than the endless anger. 'You should have seen Arkwright's face, could have fired a thousand cannon. We were sitting in that same old interview room with him just about to start the next round when a WPC pops her head around the door and says he's got a phone call. He was just about to suggest something very rude to her when she tells him with one of those deeply theatrical whispers that it's the Commissioner's office. From the look on her face I suspect it might even have been the Commissioner himself. Anyway, he disappears for several minutes, and when he comes back he's a changed man. Absolutely livid, shaking with it. He's already told me that I had both opportunity and motive, not just for the attack on Emily but for Felix, too, and as for Patricia . . . In it up to my neck, he knows that, but he's had his feet nailed to the floor. Told not to pursue it. Another

Establishment stitch-up. The fact is he's a good copper and hates it.'

'As much as you.'

'They're not charging Emily, either,' he said bitterly, snatching at a blade of waving grass.

'But she was attacked,' Jemma said in mitigation.

'Then perhaps there is a God.'

'Harry!' she protested. 'Her hand was slashed.'

'And it'll heal. Compared with what she tried to do to me, I think she's got off lightly.'

The grass had disappeared inside a clenched fist; the pain was back. His breath was coming in short bursts of anger, the chin was set stubborn, the eyes burning and fixed. She had to draw it all out.

'What about Sloppy?' she asked. And even as she watched, she saw the anger dissolve and the eyes, still fixed on the clouds, turned to pools of sadness that threatened to overflow.

'Silly bugger,' he whispered, his voice tight with emotion. And he could say no more for a few moments. 'Apparently the autopsy found a brain tumour. I like to think that's what made him ... Anyway, they'll never be able to connect him with Felix's death, not now. And he wrote two letters before he died. One to his wife and the girls, and the other to his solicitor. About me. Admitting that he'd defrauded me, falsified the paperwork, stolen the money. Silly, *silly* bugger!'

'It was a little late for that.'

'Perhaps not. Gives me a fighting chance, Jem. The bankruptcy petition's been stayed – apparently old man Maundy came back from his extended holiday and gave his son hell. And since the money was taken from my accounts by fraud, my lawyer is arguing it should be the bank's responsibility, not mine.'

Yet he seemed to find no joy in it, and she thought she knew why.

'What about Sloppy's folks?'

His words came slowly. 'Jem, he was one of my dearest friends. Like a brother. Family. That also goes for his wife and kids. If I get through this, they will, too. I'll make sure of it.' It was as though he was swearing an oath. Then the passion was spent. He lay back in the sand, exhausted, the breeze soothing away the pain from his face as his attention wandered to a seagull that was hovering above them, inspecting their nest in the dunes.

'We could go see the puffins on Farne Island tomorrow, if you'd like,' she said, hesitant, not sure what was within him.

'Sure,' he replied as if he couldn't care one way or the other. 'You got any other plans for this summer?'

'A few. I thought I'd find myself a new job.'

'They fired you?' he said, turning his head sharply to look at her.

'I was harbouring a dangerous man, the police battered down my door and dragged me off to custody. Not the finest recommendation for a woman who's supposed to be in charge of the moral welfare of five-year-olds.'

'Damn. Will that be difficult, finding a new job?'

'No, I'm a very good teacher.'

'Jem, I'm sorry. My fault.'

It was her turn to show passion. 'Will you stop trying to pretend you dragged me into this against my will?' she snapped. 'The truth is I wouldn't have missed out on this for the world. I – I just haven't worked out how to explain it all to my parents yet.'

He smiled, thinly, no great joy. 'I've spent so long on my own that sometimes I forget to say thank you. You didn't just put your job on the line but your neck, too. Risked everything. I never meant for any of that to happen.'

'You can make it up to me.'

'How?'

'You can help me redecorate Caitlin's apartment.'

'Was there a lot of damage?'

'What, apart from the smashed door, ruined sofa and all the scratched paintwork, you mean?'

'She must have been bloody furious.'

'Not at all. She says she's over the ashram phase. Came back from her holiday with a new boyfriend, someone very cool and Swedish, lucky thing.' She tried to sound wistful, but failed. 'Anyway, she wants everything white and bare wood. You can sand a few floors.'

'I am your slave.'

'Get paint in your beard.'

'What do you think, Jem, should I shave it off?'

She stared at him, and her mood changed. 'No, not yet.'

The words were whispered, her voice pensive, no longer trying to shrug off what had happened to them. They had both been hurt. She stroked his chin lightly with the tips of her fingers. 'Right now, Harry, right this very second, I think your beard is the most attractive thing I've ever seen. Perhaps you'd like to take outrageous advantage of that fact before I come to my senses.'

'What, here? In the dunes?'

'Only seagulls watching.'

He levered himself up onto an elbow. 'I'll try not to hurry.'

'Why, what else do you have to do?'

'Our table's booked at the Ship in a couple of hours.'

'It's only a ten-minute walk.'

She kissed him, but he drew back.

'And I've got a phone call to make.'

'Jones!'

'To McDeath. I promised him an interview. I think between us we might just stir things up a little.'

'Then start here,' she insisted.

'But what about the interview?'

'Too bad,' she said, moving much closer. 'No signal. I checked. Anyway, you're going to be pretty breathless for the next couple of hours. I don't expect you to have any-thing coherent to say for some considerable time.'

ACKNOWLEDGEMENTS

I was on the point of writing a rather different book until one of my oldest friends, Andrei Vandoros, made some comment about the European Union. I was sitting on his sofa at the time, we were engaged in one of our endless debates, and something he said lit a fire in my mind. Patricia Vaine was the result. But, I hear you say, fireside chats are all very well, yet the book begs the question of whether an organization like EATA could ever exist. Well, it already does. Its name is SitCen – the Joint Situation Centre, to give it its full title. It is an EU intelligence body based in Brussels, in its relative infancy and staffed, so far as I can tell, by entirely charming and well-meaning people. But if it turns out to be like every other European institution, it will grow larger and more powerful than most of us ever imagined, while if it ends up like all other intelligence agencies, it will eventually find itself mired in controversy for acting beyond its authorized powers. It is the First Law of Bureaucracy: I am, therefore I grow.

So *A Sentimental Traitor* began to take shape. By the time you've reached these words I hope you will have enjoyed it, and perhaps even been stimulated enough either to recommend it to friends or even, exasperated beyond endurance, to throw it on the fire. The future of Europe, a dream for some, endless nightmare for others, should be a matter for passion. Yet whatever pleasure you've had from these pages is largely down to my many friends, old and new, who have helped me bring these ideas together. Apart from the ubiquitous Andrei, I would like to thank David Perry, Neil Sexton, David Miller, Martyn Morris and James Body who gave me invaluable help in various technical and aeronautical areas, while David Jolliffe, Jim Ryan and Robert Lefever advised me on medical aspects. For the legal and criminal side of things I turned once again to Sean Cunningham and Mark Pepper, along with my old university colleague Robert Sykes. Mian Zaheen, Kishor Sonigra and Steve Paramor helped out with the financial bits. Kevin Hughes lent me the atmosphere and inspiration of Brokers, his Leadenhall Market wine bar, and Eugenia Vandoros sustained me in magnificent fashion with food from her family kitchen. My old flatmate Farrokh Jhabvala was the inspiration for his namesake. Nirj Deva and his wife Indra were wonderful hosts during my researches in Brussels. Another former flatmate, Graham Wynn, who helped guide me through the treacherous landscape inevitably required by novelists. And I make no apology for squeezing the name of E.L. Vale into the script. Ernie was my primary school headmaster at St Clement's beside the brook in Turnford, and taught me not only to read and write but also so very much more.

Most of all, I have to thank Ian Patterson, a man of endless patience and courtesy, who understands Harry as well as I do.

From all of these good friends, I must ask forgiveness for anything I have misunderstood and also the occasional deliberate dramatic licence I have taken with their advice. My only excuse is that I am a politician, so I'm expected to take a flexible approach to the facts.

My wife and sons showed their usual endless tolerance during a year of many milestones for our family, and gave me distraction when it was sometimes desperately needed. None of this would happen without them, or have been half as much fun.

Michael Dobbs
Wylye, October 2011
www.michaeldobbs.com

This book belongs to

....

CLASSIC TREASURY

FIRST POEMS

Compiled by Tig Thomas

Miles Kelly

First published in 2014 by Miles Kelly Publishing Ltd
Harding's Barn, Bardfield End Green, Thaxted, Essex, CM6 3PX, UK

Copyright © Miles Kelly Publishing Ltd 2014

Some of this material was first published in 2010 by
Miles Kelly Publishing Ltd as part of *Poems for Young Children*

2 4 6 8 10 9 7 5 3 1

Publishing Director *Belinda Gallagher*
Creative Director *Jo Cowan*
Editorial Director *Rosie McGuire*
Senior Editor *Claire Philip*
Designers *Michelle Cannatella, Joe Jones, Jo Cowan, Venita Kidwai*
Production Manager *Elizabeth Collins*
Reprographics *Stephan Davis, Jennifer Cozens, Thom Allaway*

ISBN 978-1-78209-582-8

Printed in China

British Library Cataloguing-in-Publication Data
A catalogue record for this book is available from the British Library

ACKNOWLEDGEMENTS

The publishers would like to thank the following artists who have contributed to this book:
Cover:
Central image: Sharon Harmer at The Bright Agency
Other elements: Alice Brisland at The Bright Agency, LenLis/Shutterstock.com,
kusuriuri/Shutterstock.com, Lana L/Shutterstock.com, Markovka/Shutterstock.com
Inside pages:
Carly Gosnell, Frank Endersby, Kirsten Wilson
The Bright Agency: Mark Chambers, Richard Watson
Beehive Illustration: Rosie Brooks, Mike Phillips
All other artwork from the Miles Kelly Artwork Bank

The publishers would like to thank the following sources for the use of their photographs:
Fotolia.com 192 Dariusz Gudowicz **iStockphoto.com** 153 mcswin;
290 Stanislav Pobytov; 350 Andreas Kaspar; 372 Stanislav Pobytov
Shutterstock.com (paper background used throughout) Keattikorn; 154 & 155 Togataki

Made with paper from a sustainable forest

www.mileskelly.net
info@mileskelly.net